DAUGHTER OF REALMS

BOOK ONE OF THE FIRST WITCH SERIES

EMBER EAST

EMBER EAST

Cover Design by Muhammad Kaleem

To my husband— Thanks for being there every step of the way through this crazy process, and for buying me that chair that helps my back. Without you, I'd probably be dead.

To Lauren, Alex, Sam, Erin, and Skyler— Thanks for being my biggest cheerleaders and for reading my horrible rough drafts. You guys helped me realize I could actually do this, and do it well.

To the neurodivergents— Don't doubt yourself. We can do all the things too.

Contents

Chapter One

A mid the relentless cascade of raindrops, I crouched with near-feline grace on top of a weathered shipping container, cloaked in shadows. The rhythmic patter of rain on metal mingled with the distant sounds of overlapping waves, creating an eerie symphony that surrounded the docks.

My eyes scanned the surrounding forest through the heavy torrent of rain. My target tonight was a demon, a lower-level one that loved to feast on the intoxicated mortals who stumbled home every night. The demon had been seen hunting close by, and Wren, my closest and only friend had found it and chased it here in his wolven form. And so the hunter had become the hunted.

My thoughts danced on the edge of anticipation, every nerve alight with preternatural awareness as I threw my keen half-fae, half-demonic senses out in the night. I frequently thought about this reality: being half-demon, I couldn't help but notice the thin line that separated me from the very monster I was tracking tonight. Raindrops slid like liquid diamonds off my silver hair, and my body crackled with restrained energy.

For anyone else, the promise of their demonic bounty would have died in the downpour, but I was no ordinary hunter. I reached my hand up to my mouth, my finger resting on the point of an elongated canine, and bit down hard, blood welling to the surface. I quickly put the digit between my lips before the blood might be scented, and pulled deeply on the small wound.

A few precious drops of blood spilled down my throat like white-hot lightning as I felt my blood magic flow through me— a potent tool of my trade, sharpening my senses and heightening my perception.

Like a wave crashing against the shore, my senses surged to life. My amber eyes, aglow with a supernatural intensity, pierced the misty night, the darkness coming to life under the thin moonlight that managed to peak from the clouds. A chilling tingle traced its way along my spine, an intangible connection forming between Wren and me, who was drawing near. I drew a slow, steadying breath, the moisture-laden air filling my lungs with a heady mix of anticipation and determination. Through the cascading veil of rain, my gaze locked onto a shadow, darker than the night itself, writhing with malevolence. The demon, lurking at the edge of my awareness, had finally revealed itself.

As raindrops mingled with the magic that permeated the air, my heart quickened, ready to unleash the force that burned through my veins. I leapt from the storage container on silent feet, the vicious creature still unaware of my presence. I could feel Wren off in the darkness, getting closer now. He'd want me to wait for him, but the beast had begun pushing through the downpour towards the inky dark woods.

The scent of wet earth mingled with the acrid tang of a demonic presence, a noxious cocktail that pricked at my nose. I tightened my grip on the cold iron haft of my axe, my blood magic surging within me, a tempest of conflicting energies that promised both creation and destruction. Not wasting another moment I raced toward the creature.

The demon emerged from the shadows, turning towards me as I charged it. It was a grotesque fusion of flesh and nightmare. Its eyes glowed like smoldering embers and its snarling maw revealed rows of serrated teeth. A low growl rumbled in my throat as I met its gaze, determination clashing against the icy tendrils of fear. The rain-soaked ground squelched beneath my boots as I pressed on, the weight of my purpose driving me onward.

With a guttural roar, the demon lunged at me, all claws and baleful fury. I sidestepped the attack with a dancer's grace, the rain-slicked ground aiding my swift evasion. My axe whistled through the air, meeting the demon's hide with a resounding thud. The iron cleaved its flesh, electing a screech of pain that echoed through the stormy night.

But the monster was relentless. It retaliated with a savage strike of its own, raking its claws across my arm. Fire and ice coursed through my veins as I stumbled back, gritting my teeth against the searing agony. Blood mingled with rainwater, staining the ground in dark rivulets. The deep gnash would heal soon, thanks to my supernatural healing abilities.

Desperation fueled my next move, I reached into the folds of my jacket, fingers closing around the hilt of one of my throwing knives. With a flick of my wrist, the blade sailed through the rain, finding its mark in the demon's hide. It howled in anguish, its form writhing in torment. But still, it refused to yield.

Just as it turned to once again strike out, a primal snarl shattered the air. Wren, his russet fur glistening in the rain, burst onto the scene, muscles rippling beneath his drenched fur. His fangs gleamed in the dim light, and his green eyes locked onto the demon with predatory hunger.

Wren's arrival renewed my resolve, together we were a force to be reckoned with. As the demon lunged at me once more, Wren intercepted its attack, his powerful jaws clamping down on its arm. The demon thrashed and roared, its struggles futile against Wren's vice-like grip.

I seized the opportunity, my axe splitting open the demon's back with a sickening jerk. It writhed and spasmed, its dark black blood bubbling out past the hilt of my axe. Wren's jaws tightened, his fangs sinking deeper into the demon's flesh.

In a final, desperate bid for survival, the demon tore itself free from Wren's grasp leaving behind a trail of inky ichor. It staggered back, its breathing ragged and labored. With a primal snarl, it turned and fled into the darkness.

The demon's anguished cries still echoed in the air as Wren and I exchanged a determined glance. We had wounded it, driven it to the brink, and now we intended to finish what we had started. The thrill of the hunt surged through our veins, our senses sharpened by the scent of victory mingled with the lingering rain.

Without hesitation, we plunged into the night, following the fading trail of blood left by the wounded demon. Our footfalls were muffled by the wet underbrush, our breaths coming quick and heavy. Each step brought us deeper into the heart of the unknown, closer to a realm where even the bravest of souls might falter.

The landscape twisted and contorted around us, the very fabric of reality warping as we gave chase. Shadows danced at the corners of my vision, and the air grew thicker, suffused with oppressive malice. The rain ceased to fall, replaced by otherworldly mist that clung to our skin like a shroud.

And as we ran, a disorienting sensation gnawed at the edges of my consciousness. The ground beneath our feet shifted, and suddenly, we stumbled into a realm beyond mortal comprehension. The demon realm stretched out before us, a nightmarish landscape of jagged spires, churning mists, and ever-shifting shadows.

We skidded to a halt, breathless and bewildered, the gravity of our situation sinking in. Wren's growl rumbled through the air, a symphony of unease that mirrored my apprehension. We exchanged a tense glance, unspoken questions passing between us. How have we ended up here? And more importantly, how could we find our way back?

"We're in hell right now," I said as a loud, goofy panic bubbled to the surface as it always did when I was in an impossible situation. "Actual literal hell. Do you think they have welcoming centers?" Wren let out a chuffing sound, one I could only describe as a laugh.

But the demons' pained cries echoed once again, piercing through the eerie silence. Our determination, rekindled, pushed us forward, even in the face of uncertainty. The pursuit led us here, and now we had a task to complete.

"Let's finish this," I declared, my voice, firm and resolute, despite the tremors of doubt that danced within me.

Wren's green eyes gleamed with unwavering resolve, his lupine form tensed and ready. Together, we pushed forward into the heart of the demon realm, the very air crackling with dark energy. The land-scape twisted and shifted beneath our feet, an ever-changing labyrinth that seemed determined to confound and challenge. It was a mass of unnatural shapes and angles. One moment we stood in a forest of inorganic-looking trees, their limbs stretching toward the sky like sharpened spikes. The next moment it changed to a low flat plain, covered in jagged rocks and broken stone buildings.

The smell of smoke and rot clogged our noses and burned our lungs. The land before us was like a graveyard of dreams, each step we took inching us closer to the brink of damnation. A tainted air swirled around us, stifling out hope and leaving only despair in its wake. This cursed place held no mercy, only nightmares that would haunt us for eternity and death that stalked our every move.

Hours turned into an indistinct blur as we pressed on, our pursuit of the wounded demon growing more desperate with each passing moment. The demonic realm toyed with our senses, distorting time and space, but we refused to be deterred. The air grew cold around us, and I could feel my warm breath turn into mist; we were falling deeper and deeper into the realm.

Determined and resolute, we strode forward with every step. The chill shadows that danced at the edge of our vision seemed to shrink back in the face of our resolve. The eerie silence was shattered by the echoes of our footsteps and the creature's pained howls. We marched on toward the darkness as it drew closer

The wounded demon's cries grew louder, a cacophony of agony that urged us onward. The twisted spires and churning mists were now our battlegrounds, the very essence of the demon realm a testament to its dark and enigmatic nature.

As we pressed forward, our steps guided by an unshakeable purpose, I couldn't help but marvel at the strange beauty of this nightmarish landscape. It was a realm of contradictions, a place where danger and wonder intertwined, and where the limits of reality itself were tested.

The demon realm had become our crucible, a trial by fire that would push us to our limits and force us to confront the depths of our strength. With every breath, every stride, we embraced the challenge, ready to face whatever twisted reality the realm could throw at us.

In this nightmarish realm, our resolve burned like a beacon, cutting through the darkness and guiding us ever closer to our quarry. The demon's cries were a testament to its pain and vulnerability, and as we neared our goal, a fierce determination took root within me. The demon realm may have been a place of shadows and uncertainty, but we would emerge from its depths victorious, our spirits unbroken.

The air in the demon realm was thick and oppressive, a heavy blackness that seemed to sap the life from my very bones. We had been hunting our prey for hours it seemed, tracking its winding trail through these cursed lands, until finally, we had cornered it.

The wounded demon lay huddled in a shallow ravine, its once mighty form now a grotesque parody of itself. Its eyes were dull, its claws limp, and its defiance reduced to ragged gasps and feeble swipes.

Wren stepped forward, his fangs bared. With a primal snarl, he lunged, sinking his teeth deep into the demon's throat. The creature let out a shrill shriek of agony, and then I stepped forward, axe raised. I brought it down in a single, decisive blow, my blood magic still pounding in my ears. The creature's screams cut off abruptly as its life force slowly ebbed away.

With the demon's death, a palpable wave of energy spread through the realm like a ripple in a pond. Its essence dissipating into the mist, the oppressive atmosphere that had shrouded us before was now gone, replaced by an eerie stillness. Our victory was hard won—the toll of the battle etched exhaustion into our faces.

But as the echoes of battle subsided, a chilling realization settled over us—we were still trapped in the demon realm. With no way to escape, we were left with one option: to find a way back to our own world.

We had ventured deep into the abyss of the demon realm, our steps guided only by determination and the flickering hope of escape. The air was heavy with an otherworldly chill.

Wren shifted back into his human form, his dark skin slick with sweat. He looked around cautiously as if expecting something more sinister to rise out of the darkness at any moment. "Do you think we could find our way back to where we came in?" he asked warily.

There was no telling which way we had even come from, the landscape behind us was completely different from what we had left behind. But this was no time to despair. "That sounds like our best bet right now."

Wren and I moved in unison, our senses heightened. Every rustle of shadows and every distant whisper a potential threat.

As we forged ahead, our goal clear — to find the elusive portal back to the mortal realm— I felt a subtle shift in the energy around us. The oppressive darkness seemed to recede, replaced by an unsettling sensation that prickled at the edges of my awareness. Instinctively, I tightened my grip on the hilt of my axe, my muscles coiled like a spring, ready to strike.

A figure materialized before us as if emerging from the very fabric of the demon realm itself. His dark black hair skated like a waterfall, framing a face of sharp angles. He had an air of calculated elegance. Dark brown eyes, nearly black, locked onto mine, their intensity threatened to pull me in. He was eerily beautiful. His gaze captured mine with an intensity that shook me. My heart quickened my pulse, echoing in my ears as a surge of wariness coursed through me.

"Who are you?" I demanded, my voice steady, despite the uncertainty that churned within. I brandished my axe, ready to fight.

The stranger inclined his head, a hint of a smirk playing at the corner of his lips. His eyes were dark pools, deep and fathomless, and in them, I saw lifetimes of knowledge and secrets. A shiver ran down my spine, my breath catching in my throat. I knew that this demon was powerful, perhaps more powerful than anything I had ever encountered. And yet, there was something about him that intrigued me. "I am Kaelan," he replied, his voice soft yet commanding.

Wren's low growl reverberated through the air, a testament to his distrust. We shared a wary glance, the bond between us reinforcing our shared sentiment. Demons were cunning, their intentions often veiled in shadows and deception.

"What do you want, demon?" Wren pressed, his gaze unyielding.

A chuckle escaped him, a sound that seemed to reverberate through the very air itself. "I merely wish to offer my assistance." He stood tall in the shadows, his black jacket whipping around him in the chilling wind of the demon realm.

Wren's shoulders remained raised, his wolfish eyes narrowed with suspicion. "We don't need your help," Wren said. I could feel his skepticism mirroring my own, our instincts urging caution even as the stranger presented himself as an unexpected guide.

"Don't be so sure," the demon said, his tone tinged with amusement.

I met Kaelan's dark gaze, my expression defiant. "And why should we trust you? You're a demon, after all."

Kaelan smirked in the face of our doubt. "Do you not think," he said, cool and collected, "that my understanding of such realms makes me uniquely suited to brave them? Agreements of this kind can be fragile, but sometimes it is necessary to forge even unlikely partnerships."

"What's in it for you, demon?" I hissed, the accusation burning in my throat.

"I'm not looking for much, little half-breed. Just your name." He drawled, his lips curling into a wry smirk.

"My name? What could you possibly want with that?" I ask incredulously.

"Well, I've given you my name, it would be rude of you not to give me yours."

I stood there for a moment, crossing my arms. Wren gave me a knowing look as the demon continued to hold us in his gaze.

"Vale," I finally breathed out, immediately regretting my decision, the finality of it sinking it. What mischief could this demon possibly get up to with my name?

"Vale." The demon smirked, my name rolling off his tongue dripping with oil and honey.

"Lead us to the portal," I commanded, my voice unwavering. The urgency of our situation demanded action, and while Kaelan's motives remained shrouded in mystery, the promise of escape was too enticing to ignore.

Kaelan inclined his head, his dark eyes locking onto mine with an intensity that sent a shiver down my spine. "Very well, Vale. Follow me, and I'll lead you through the shadows."

Wren's gaze remained fixed on Kaelan, his wariness a tangible presence. I shared a silent exchange with him, the unspoken understanding between us a testament to our shared determination.

"Lead the way, then," I said, my voice laced with authority and caution. With each step, the path we had chosen grew more uncertain, and as we followed the mysterious demon into the heart of the demon realm, I couldn't shake the feeling that we were stepping into a web of intrigue that had been intricately woven long before our arrival.

With trepidation gnawing at our heels, we followed Kaelan. Each step carried us deeper into the demon realm, the twisted landscape shifting as if responding to his command. The shadows around us grew thicker, the crushing chill seeping into our bones. Kaelan led us through the labyrinth of the demon realm, his dark gaze fixed on the path ahead.

Time seemed to stretch and contract, the boundaries of reality blurring as we traversed the demon realm under Kaelan'sguidance. And my skepticism remained an ever-present undercurrent, but be-grudging respect began to take root. There was an undeniable mastery in his command of the realm, a power that was both captivating and unnerving.

The tension and unease were palpable, the weight of uncertainty bearing down on us. We had placed our fate in the hands of a demon, a being whose motives were unknown and who was undoubtedly dangerous. Yet, we were left with no choice but to rely on him if we wanted to survive.

Kaelan led us deeper and deeper into the twisted landscape, his steps sure and confident. "Do not stray from the path," he warned, his voice a low murmur.

The ground beneath our feet was now shifting, the shadows be-coming more insidious. The air around us grew colder, and I could feel a subtle shift in the atmosphere. The demon realm was a dangerous place, a land of endless possibilities, both wondrous and horrifying.

"Are you sure this is the right way?" Wren whispered. His gaze flickered around us, his body tense and alert.

"Yes, this is the way," Kaelan answered, his voice firm and confi-dent.

The shadows were closing in, and the air was filled with an unmis-takable sense of foreboding.

"I can't see a damn thing," Wren muttered, his words barely audible.

"Stay close," Kaelan ordered. "We're almost there."

We moved together, our steps in sync, each movement guided by the sound of Kaelan's voice. The darkness seemed to press in around us, its inky tendrils threatening to engulf us.

"How can you be sure we're even going in the right direction?" I questioned, the uncertainty creeping into my tone.

"Trust me," Kaelan responded. "I know these shadows better than anyone. We're getting closer to the portal, I can feel it."

Ahead, the darkness seemed to grow denser, a swirling vortex of shadow and chaos.

"There's something in the darkness," Wren murmured, his voice laced with curiosity.

"The portal is up ahead," Kaelan confirmed. "Be prepared, the shadows are thick here."

I could feel the anxiety rising within me, my heart pounding in my chest. The air was thick with an ancient power, a force that was both dangerous and exhilarating.

"Don't worry, half-breed," Kaelan murmured, his voice low and steady. "The portal is close, you can make it through."

Finally, as if emerging from a dark dream, we stood before the portal, our promised return to the mortal realm. The weight of our journey hung heavy in the air, we had ventured into the heart of darkness and emerged.

I turned to Kaelan, his gaze holding mine. "Thank you," I uttered, the words a reluctant admission of gratitude.

"It was my pleasure," he replied, his voice rich with promise, his dark eyes glinting with the hint of a secret. Without another word, we stepped through the portal, our journey coming full circle as we left behind the demon realm, and returned to the mortal world.

As I stood once again on familiar ground, rain-soaked and battle-worn, I couldn't help but wonder about the beautiful but mysterious demon who had guided us through the abyss. His motives remained a mystery, his secrets hidden in the shadows, but his aid had been a crucial turning point in our quest. As I took in the sight of the mortal realm, its mundane landscape a stark contrast to the twisted landscape of the demon realm, I was filled with an overwhelming sense of relief. We had survived the journey, and our path forward was clear.

The night was a cloak of darkness. Our bodies were still recovering from the rigors of the day, but our spirits were high. We had defeated the demon and made it back home, a victory hard-earned.

Chapter Two

S unlight filtered through the windows of my bookshop, located downstairs from the apartment I shared with Wren, casting a warm glow upon the wooden shelves that held an eclectic assortment of books. The old button factory had been transformed into a haven for literature lovers, its rustic charm inviting visitors to explore its treasures. The air carried the comforting scent of aged paper and a hint of earthiness, a reminder of the herbs we nurtured in the sunlit room at the back.

Juniper, the green-haired mortal we had hired to help run the shop, flitted about, her enthusiasm infectious as she rearranged the display of new arrivals near the entrance. She had a knack for making even the most mundane tasks feel like a joyful adventure, and I loved her for that. Her charm never failed to put me in a good mood.

After the events of last night Wren and I had returned home just long enough for him to change clothes and leave again, going to collect our bounty for the night's work then going to check in with his pack for patrol. We hadn't yet spoken about what had transpired.

"Vale, have you seen the latest shipment of fantasy novels?" Juniper called out, her smile crinkling her almond-shaped eyes.

I smiled and shook my head. "Not yet, June. But I'm sure they're going to be great."

As I straightened a stack of books on the counter, the bell above the entrance tinkled, announcing the arrival of a customer. I looked up to see Juniper greeting the newcomer with her usual warmth.

"Hello there! Feel free to browse, and if you need any help, just let me know." She chirped.

Turning my attention back to the counter, I began to organize a stack of receipts. The rhythmic clatter of the cash register punctuated the soothing hum of quiet activity in the shop.

"Juniper," I began, my voice carrying a note of curiosity, "do we have enough chamomile tea in stock? It seems to be quite popular these days."

She glanced up from her task, a thoughtful expression on her face. "I believe we might be running low. I'll make a note to restock it."

"Thank you," I replied with a smile.

As the afternoon sun bathed the shop in a warm embrace, Juniper and I continued our tasks in comfortable companionship. She recounted stories of her recent exploits in town, while I shared anecdotes from the shop's early days. The friendship we had formed over the years was a comfortable and easy one.

"Did you hear about Mr. Pendleton's excitement when he found that rare first edition?" Juniper laughed, her brown eyes dancing with mirth.

I chuckled in response, recalling the avid collector's enthusiastic exclamations. "Yes, it's always a pleasure to see –" My breath caught in my throat and stopped me in my tracks. A ripple of unease coursed through me, a sensation that tugged at the edges of my awareness like a distant warning, my senses prickling as if something had shifted in the very air around us. Juniper noticed my abrupt silence and cast me a concerned glance. "Vale, are you alright?" she asked.

I raised a hand, motioning for her to wait, my gaze fixed on the shop entrance. It did not take long before the bell above the door jingled, heralding the arrival of an unexpected visitor. Time seemed to slow as a figure stepped through the door, his presence a stark contrast to the cozy atmosphere of the bookshop.

Kaelan sauntered in, an air of confident nonchalance surrounding him. His dark hair seemed to absorb the ambient light, casting shadows that danced along his features. My heart clenched, wariness and recognition flooding my senses.

"Speak of the devil," Kaelan quipped, his voice a velvet-tinged drawl that grated against my defenses.

I bristled my guard immediately up. "Or should I say, the demon?"

Juniper's eyes darted between us, her confusion evident, "Vale, do you know this... gentleman?"

Kaelan's lips curled into a mischievous smile, his dark eyes locking onto mine, "Oh, we're well acquainted."

I crossed my arms, my stance defiant as I stared him down. "So you followed me here."

He chuckled, his tone dripping with amusement. "No need to follow you when it's far too easy to track you down."

Juniper glanced between us, clearly perplexed by the dynamic at play. "Are you two... friends?"

Kaelan winked at her, a gesture that only deepened my distrust. "Yes." he exclaimed just as I said, "Definitely not."

"You wound me, Vale." That wry smile never left his face.

I shot him a withering glare, my skepticism burning like a smoldering ember. "Let's not sugarcoat it, demon. You helped us escape the demon realm, but that doesn't erase the fact that you're still a creature of darkness."

Kaelan leaned against a bookshelf, his posture casual despite the tension in the air. "Ever the charmer, Vale. I see your opinion of me hasn't wavered."

"Since just last night? No, I'd say it hasn't" I replied.

Juniper's eyes darted between us, the curiosity in her gaze palpable. "Wait, you and Wren got trapped in Erebus?" She almost stumbled on the true name of the demon realm, her eyes widening, the shock there evident.

I hesitated, torn between revealing the truth and protecting Juniper from the complexities of last night. Despite being mortal she knew of Otherworlders and our world, but that didn't mean she knew just how dangerous it could be out there. Kaelan spoke before I could respond.

"Yes, indeed. Dear Vale here was in quite the predicament, and I simply couldn't resist coming to her aid," he drawled, his tone laced with smug satisfaction.

I clenched my jaw, my patience wearing thin. "Don't make it sound like some heroic act, Kaelan. I still don't trust you, and I certainly haven't forgotten which realm you call home."

Kaelan's smirk remained in place, his eyes glinting with a playful challenge. "You wound me once again with your skepticism. But I'm not here to win your trust. I simply wanted to see how you are faring in this charming little shop."

I narrowed my eyes, the tension between us thickening like a storm cloud. "Well, you've seen it. Now you can leave."

He chuckled, pushing himself away from the bookshelf. "Very well then. Until next time."

With a casual wave, Kaelan turned and started toward the exit, but his departure was halted by my voice, curiosity compelling me to continue the conversation. "Wait," I called out, "what really brings you here?"

He turned, his expression a blend of amusement and something more inscrutable. "I came here to give you a warning." My heart skipped a beat, a surge of trepidation coursing through me. Had he decided we were to be enemies then? He would be a deadly adversary.

"Juniper," I said, turning to her, "can you please go check on the Althea root? It should be ready for harvest soon." She gave us one last curious glance before turning and walking into the back of the shop. I turned back to Kaelan.

"Cut the theatrics, demon. What kind of warning are you talking about?"

He flashed me a wry smile, his dark eyes locking onto mine. "You caused quite a stir in Erebus last night. That blood magic you used," he paused to take in the shock in my eyes, "Yes, I know about it, and now so does every demon who was near us. I took out a few of them myself, but word has spread."

A chill spread through me at his words and his reference to my secret blood magic. "You know what I am, don't you?" I said softly. How could this be possible, all these years hiding my secret and my biggest fear was staring me in the face? Sweat broke out on the back of my neck.

Blood magic was dangerous and forbidden, Otherworlders who had control over it were put to death, their existence brought on by an unholy union of demon and fae. As far as I knew none like me had been born in hundreds of years, at least none that had not been killed upon their birth. I studied Kaelan's expression, my skepticism waning.

"I dare say I know quite a bit more about what you are than you do." His gaze held mine, his tone unexpectedly earnest. "Vale, I'm not here to expose you. I simply thought you should be aware of the ripples your actions might have caused."

I scoffed, my defiance a shield against the uncertainty that threatened to unravel my composure. "How noble of you. Concerned about my well-being, are you?" I had no idea why he would tell me all this, he owed me nothing.

He shrugged, a mask of indifference that seemed to be his trademark. "Just consider the warning a favor, one you might feel obligated to repay at some point in the future." Kaelan's smile took on a teasing quality.

My skepticism remained, tempered by a begrudging acceptance of the situation.

"Just know this— the consequences of blood magic can be far-reaching. I'd hate to see you caught in the crossfire."

I bristled, my anger flaring despite his seemingly genuine concern. "Don't presume to lecture me, demon. I know the risks all too well."

He held up his hands in a placating gesture, a glint of sincerity beneath his facade. "I'm not your lecturer, Vale. Just a messenger of sorts."

"Well, message received, thank you," I said, a clear dismissal in my words.

Kaelan nodded, his gaze lingering for a moment longer before he turned to leave once more. "I'm sure our paths will cross again, Vale. Until then, try not to get stuck in the demon realm again."

With his departure, the shop seemed to exhale, the weight of our conversation dissipating like smoke in the wind. Juniper, having heard the bell jingle, walked out from the back of the shop.

"Who was that, really?" she asked, her voice a whisper and curiosity shining in her eyes.

I let out a sigh, my thoughts a tangle of uncertainty and unease. "Someone neither of us should have anything to do with. Someone who's a little too well-acquainted with the shadows." Juniper gave a small shiver at my words.

As we resumed our tasks in the bookshop, I couldn't shake the feeling that Kaelan's words were a harbinger of things to come, a whisper of a storm on the horizon. The boundary between trust and suspicion had been further blurred, leaving me to grapple with the knowledge that the mysterious demon would continue to weave his influence into the fabric of our lives, whether I liked it or not.

☾☽

The old, abandoned main floor of the button factory had become a cherished refuge, a hidden sanctuary that provided solace from the daily grind of the bookshop. In this forgotten space, I could immerse myself in the rhythm of movement and steel. The air bore the weighty perfume of rust, a fragrance that whispered tales of time's relentless passage. The very atmosphere was steeped in the essence of neglected history, echoing the stories of bygone labor and industry that once thrived here. As I moved gracefully across the cavernous expanse, my knives, like loyal companions, felt like an extension of my own being. In this silent haven, I engaged in a wordless dance, a mesmerizing choreography where I was both performer and audience, locked in a graceful contest against phantom adversaries.

Kaelan's cryptic words lingered in the corners of my mind, a relentless echo that refused to be silenced. The memory of his presence, the weight of his knowledge, and the layers of intrigue he had woven around me all gnawed at my thoughts. Was he genuinely concerned about the ripples of my actions, or was there a hidden agenda beneath his enigmatic demeanor?

My blades sliced through the air, the sound of steel meeting with wood a sharp counterpoint to my racing thoughts as I lodged one knife into the training dummy. A small part of me couldn't help but wonder if Kaelan's warning held any merit. Had my actions inadvertently set in motion a chain of events that could disrupt the fragile peace we had established here since leaving the Academy?

I shuddered thinking of the Academy. A treacherous and unforgiving institution whose solemn duty is to police the Otherworld, presumably protecting it from the monsters that wriggled their way here from the other realms. It was there that I grew up. First in the orphanage, then among the ranks of the recruits. It was there that I was honed to a razor-sharp edge, tempered through unyielding miseries. It was there where I had first met Wren. And it was from there we had fled in the night at eighteen, the year we would have been spit out after graduation, sent out to do the Academy's dirty work. We had been in hiding for five years.

All through the torturous years spent there I had kept my lineage a secret, claiming to be a typical half-demon, knowing I'd be immediately put to death if anyone found out the truth. It was a secret I had only shared with Wren, the same night he had saved me from a group of older boys while running for my life through the woods during one of the Academy's nightmare tests.

I had only found out when I was 6 years old, living in the Academy's orphanage. One of the other kids had been beating me, and as I lay on the floor, their kicks aimed at my stomach, I felt the first surge of my magic and knew right then what it meant. It had meant that I would forever have a target on my back.

The door to the abandoned floor creaked open, interrupting my solitary musing. Wren's tall form appeared in the doorway, his wolfish gaze meeting mine with curiosity. He had returned from patrolling with his pack. He had found and joined the one that claimed the territory fairly quickly after we had made this town our home. His presence was a welcome interruption to my brooding.

"Hey there," he greeted, his voice carrying a soothing undertone that eased the tension within me.

I sheathed my knives and offered him a half-smile, grateful for the distraction. "Hey yourself. How was patrol?"

He shrugged, his movements fluid and relaxed. "Same as usual," he said, hesitating. "Until it wasn't."

I arched an eyebrow, curiosity piqued. "What do you mean?"

Wren's gaze held mine, a flicker of concern passing through his hazel eyes. "We encountered something... unusual. Six demons, all in one night. That's not something you see often."

My heart quickened at his words, a sense of foreboding settling over me. Demons were creatures of shadows and secrecy, their presence was usually carefully concealed or spread out over time to avoid drawing attention. The fact that six had been spotted in a single night was an unsettling departure from the norm.

"Six demons? That's...concerning," I murmured, my thoughts racing as I tried to piece together the implications, remembering Kaelan's warning.

Wren nodded, his expression serious. "Exactly, it's got the whole pack on edge. We're not sure what it means, but it can't be a coincidence."

I turned away, my gaze fixed on the worn wooden floor. "No, it can't"

Wren took a step closer, his presence a grounding force amidst the uncertainty. "Vale, are you alright? You seem… worried."

I took a deep breath, the weight of secrets pressing upon me. "Wren, there's something that happened earlier."

He regarded me with concern. "What?"

I recounted the encounter with Kaelan in the bookshop, the demon's words and revelations weaving a tapestry of intrigue and unease. Wren listened in silence, his expression growing more surprised with each word.

"He knew about your blood magic?" Wren asked, his voice tinged with disbelief.

I nodded, a sigh escaping me. "Yes, he said it had been sensed by higher demons."

Wren's mouth dropped open, I would have laughed at the sight if it were not for the gravity of my words. I could see him putting two and two together, coming to the same conclusion I had.

"You don't think that's why we saw those demons last night?" He asked and I nodded wearily.

The idea that my actions could have drawn the attention of demons, that I had inadvertently become a beacon in the darkness, was terrifying. "I never meant for any of this to happen," I whispered, my voice tinged with guilt and frustration.

Wren stepped closer, his hand finding mine in a comforting gesture. "I know, Vale, but you can't change what's been done. We'll simply deal with whatever happens."

I met his gaze, a determined fire igniting within me. "You're right, we need to be prepared."

Wren's grip on my hand tightened, his gaze steady. "And we will be. We'll face it together, just like we always have."

Wren's presence offered a sense of solace, his unwavering support a comforting anchor amidst the storm of the unknown. We remained standing there, our hands entwined, as the weight of the situation settled around us.

"So, what do you think about this demon guy?" Wren finally asked, breaking the silence.

I let out a sigh, my thoughts churning as I tried to make sense of the beautiful demon's motivations.

"It's hard to say, we know absolutely nothing about him. He could have been genuinely concerned, which I highly doubt or, more likely, he could have his own agenda."

Wren's brow furrowed, his gaze thoughtful. "He did help us escape the demon realm. That has to count for something, doesn't it?"

I nodded, conceding the point. "True, but demons are complex beings. Their actions are often driven by self-interest and hidden motives. We can't afford to take anything at face value."

Wren finally dropped my hand, his eyes searching mine. "And what about his knowledge of your heritage? How could he possibly know about your fae and demon blood? How could he have known about the blood magic?"

A shiver ran down my spine as I recalled the moment Kaelan revealed the unsettling truth. "He must have sensed it like the other demons. If he's old enough, he could have been around before blood magic was forbidden and can identify it when he comes across it. My main concern is what he might do with the information."

Wren's expression grew more concerned, his voice suffused with worry. "Could there be someone else who already knows?"

The thought sent a chill through me, the realization that my secrets might not be as hidden as I hoped. "It's a possibility I can't ignore."

Wren's gaze remained steady, his determination unwavering. "We'll find out, Vale. We'll uncover the truth behind all this, no matter how deep the shadows go."

A surge of determination coursed through me, bolstered by Wren's unfaltering support. As we stood there, the old abandoned floor of the factory surrounding us with its echos of history, I felt a renewed sense of purpose. The demons that had appeared were a reminder of the dangers that lurked in the shadows, but they were also possibly a catalyst for uncovering the truths that had remained hidden for far too long.

"We'll be vigilant," Wren said, his voice resolute. "We'll keep our eyes open, and we'll be ready for whatever comes next."

I nodded, my resolve unshakeable. "And we'll face Kaelan, too. If he thinks he can manipulate us, he's in for a surprise."

Wren's smile was fierce, a reflection of the determination in his eyes. "That's the spirit, Vale. Let's make sure those damn demons regret the day they decided to cross paths with us."

Chapter Three

Two days later, the gentle patter of rain against the large windows was a soothing backdrop to the solitude that enveloped the loft that Wren and I shared. Our living space, nestled snugly above the bookshop, radiated an aura of enchanting coziness. The apartment's design was a harmonious blend of modernity and warmth, with an open floor plan that seamlessly integrated the living room and kitchen.

The expansive windows that graced the walls allowed natural light to pour in during the day, while in the evening, they framed the world outside like a living painting. The raindrops painted delicate trails on the glass, adding to the apartment's charm. Soft, earthy tones adorned the walls, punctuated by artwork and shelves stocked with well-loved books. The apartment was a haven of tranquility, where the outside world receded, and the comforting embrace of solitude and togetherness coexisted in perfect harmony.

I sat on the couch, a worn book resting in my hands as my fingers traced the elegant script on its pages. The lamplight cast a warm glow, illuminating the room in a soft embrace. A contented purr rumbled in my lap, the old stray cat that had wandered into my life finding comfort nestled against me. Its mangy fur and weathered appearance belied the feline's resilient spirit, and as it blinked up at me with half-lidded eyes, I couldn't help but smile.

The earthy aroma of a lit joint mingled with the scent of rain. Curling tendrils of smoke spiraled upward from between my fingers and danced in the lamplight. I took a drag, the calming effects of the marijuana washing over me in a gentle wave. The apartment was filled with a quiet hum, I had come to cherish the solitude after having none at the Academy all those years.

Wren was off on yet another patrol. The pack had increased their monitoring after the demons had been spotted the night before, their watchful eyes guarding the outskirts of our territory as well as inside the city.

The bond between us was unbreakable, forged through the horrors of our grueling childhood at the Academy, and even in his absence I could feel his presence, a reassuring tether that connected us across the distance.

I turned another page, my focus immersed in the world of my book. The rain continued its gentle rhythm, a lullaby that cocooned me in a sense of tranquility. This was a rare moment of respite, a chance to immerse myself in the written tales that offered escape.

As the words flowed before me, a flicker of movement caught my peripheral vision. The old cat had stirred, its head lifting as it fixed its gaze on the large windows. I followed its line of sight and my heart skipped a beat as I spotted a shadowy figure standing outside in the rain.

A surge of alarm coursed through me, my grip on the book tightening involuntarily. The figure stood still, shrouded in darkness, a silhouette that seemed to blend with the night. My instincts roared to life, a sharp sense of danger prickling at the edges of my awareness.

The cat leapt from my lap, its form disappearing into the shadows as it fled. I rose from the couch, a sense of unease settling over me. Wren was away, and I was alone. But I was no helpless damsel, and the power that flowed through my veins was a force to be reckoned with.

With measured steps I approached the windows, my eyes fixed on the figure beyond. A tangle of emotions churned within me. Whoever stood there had sought me out, and their intentions remained shrouded in mystery.

As I neared the window, my heart raced, the rain-slicked glass separating me from the mysterious figure. My hand rested on the latch, the decision before me a crossroads between caution and curiosity.

With a determined breath, I pushed open the window, the cool night air rushing in to greet me. The stranger turned, their features illuminated by a flash of lightning, revealing dark hair and a wry smile.

"Vale," the stranger's voice was a velvet purr, carried by the wind and rain. "We need to talk."

My wariness deepened, the conflicting emotions of curiosity and distrust warring within me. It was Kaelan. What was he doing here? My mind raced as I considered his words, I had no reason to trust him, yet his appearance carried a sense of urgency that was hard to ignore.

"Not here, downstairs." I hissed. I closed the window, laid my things down, and ran to strap my weapons on. No way was I meeting him without being armed to the teeth.

I rushed downstairs, trepidation snapping at my heels. What could he possibly want now? He had already warned me about the demons this morning, I was sure every Otherworlder within thirty miles knew about them by now, word always travels lightning fast among our kind.

I reached the back door and took a steadying breath, trying to prepare for what lay on the other side. I opened it to find Kaelan already there, waiting, that stupid smirk on his face as his gaze slowly took me in.

"What in the seven realms are you wearing?" His tone was playful as he grinned at me.

I looked down at myself. I had remembered to strap on my knives and axe but had failed to change out of my pajamas, which were covered in colorful cats made to look like sushi rolls. I blushed from my head to my toes as I glared at him.

He looked completely put together in his dark clothes, even dripping wet. As I stood there, gazing up at Kaelan's towering form, I couldn't help but feel a sense of awe wash over me. He stood like a sentinel, his presence was undeniable and captivating. His skin, a lustrous shade of copper, seemed to glow in the faint moonlight, casting a warm, inviting aura that drew me in.

His body truly captivated my attention. Every muscle, every sinew seemed sculpted to perfection, a testament to his unwavering dedication and disciplined lifestyle. His body exuded a silent promise of protection, a sense that he could weather any storm that came his way. And that jawline—it's as if it was carved from marble, unyielding, a physical embodiment of his resolute nature.

Yet, it's his gaze that holds me in thrall. My eyes are inevitably drawn to his dark, almost black eyes—pools of intensity that hold a universe of emotions beneath their surface. His intense gaze seemed to pierce through the depths of my soul, leaving me feeling exposed.

Pushing myself back in the moment, I wouldn't let him know how embarrassed I was as I motioned him inside. The large open space where I trained felt safer than inviting him into my home.

Kaelan followed me, his movements fluid and graceful, the rain leaving a glistening sheen in his dark hair. He was the very embodiment of mystery, his presence a blend of danger and intrigue that I couldn't quite resist. It was infuriating how effortlessly he seemed to unsettle me, how his dark charm worked its way beneath my defenses.

I turned to face him, my axe and knives strapped to my belt, a silent reminder of the power I wielded. The tension in the air was palpable, a charged atmosphere that crackled between us.

"What could possibly bring you here, again I might add, and at this time of night?" I demanded, my voice laced with annoyance. I crossed my arms over my chest in hopes he wouldn't see the old ratty shirt I had on under the button-up top of my pajamas.

He flashed a charming smile, his eyes holding a glint of amusement as he ran his hand through his wet hair. My traitorous heart skipped a beat, a flush of heat once again rising to my cheeks. Damn it, I should be focused on the danger he posed, not the way his wet hair clung to his forehead.

"Impatient as usual, I see," Kaelan quipped, his voice a purr that sent a shiver down my spine. "I must say, you do look rather enchanting when you're armed like that."

I scowled, both at his flirtatious remark and at my own foolish reaction to it. "Cut it out, Kaelan. I'm not here to play games."

His expression turned serious, the twinkle of mischief fading from his eyes. "Very well, Vale. I've come here to warn you about some particularly dangerous demons that have been stirring in the shadows."

My guard didn't waver, but my curiosity was piqued. "Didn't you already warn me about that? What makes this any different than what you've already told me?"

Kaelan's gaze held mine, unwavering and intense, as if searching for something hidden behind my eyes. "This is different because, my dear half-breed, these demons answer to a certain demon lord— one whose power and malice are unlike any other. His influence extends far, and his interest in you is... troubling."

A chill ran down my spine as his words sank in. If that were true, the stakes had just been raised, and the danger I faced was far greater than I had anticipated. Kaelan's presence, his knowledge, and his warning were all pieces of a puzzle I still had not figured out.

I tightened my grip on the hilt of my axe, my resolve solidifying. "Tell me everything you know, demon. No more games."

Kaelan's dark eyes were unyielding, searching mine, as he began to unravel the tapestry of darkness that surrounded us. "Very well," he said after a moment. "There are seven demon lords, each commanding a different territory in Erebus. They are ancient and formidable, their influence extending far beyond our realm."

I listened intently, his words painting a picture of a world far more complex than I had ever imagined. The existence of multiple demon lords was a revelation, and the implications were daunting.

"Blood magic is a rare and coveted art," Kaelan continued, his tone grave. "Even more so now that it hasn't been seen in at least two hundred years. One of the demon lords, known as Zephyrian, has learned of your ability to wield this power."

My heart quickened, the weight of his revelation settling heavily on me. "How could he have known about my blood magic, and why does it matter?"

Kaelan's eyes darkened, the weight of his words carrying a gravity that was hard to ignore. "Zephyrian is a powerful demon, and he has connections that stretch into realms you could scarcely fathom. Anyone near you in Erebus that night could have sensed your blood magic and informed him."

My mind raced, piecing together the puzzle as Kaelan's words painted a chilling picture. Kaelan's voice lowered, his words a stark reminder of the danger that loomed over us. "The demons that roam the mortal realm now are creatures that haven't walked these lands in hundreds of years. Zephyrian has unleashed them, and I fear they were sent to retrieve you."

My grip on my weapon tightened, my knuckles turning white, the weight of his declaration settling like a stone in my gut. The demons' purpose became clear; they intended to capture me and deliver me into the hands of Zephyrian. The implications were unsettling.

"But what does he even intend to do with me? I can barely control my blood magic myself."

Kaelan's gaze softened, a rare vulnerability slipping through his composed facade. "Still, it's a power that he believes could tip the balance of our realms, granting him unparalleled dominion over all three.

"Is that why it's been forbidden for a fae and a demon to reproduce? To stop anyone who can use blood magic from upsetting the balance?" I knew there was more to this than what he had told me. Some missing pieces I wasn't seeing.

"That, my dear, is more about what you are than what you can do."

"What I am? You mean half-fae and half-demon, right?" I searched his face for the answer.

"What you are is a witch." The finality of his words crashed into me. A witch? They weren't real, they were nothing more than a human myth created to prosecute and destroy mortal women and men. The implications of my own heritage were almost too staggering to comprehend. But skepticism gnawed at me, a nagging doubt that I couldn't quite shake.

"Witches are nothing more than myths, tales whispered among mortals," I retorted, my voice tinged with disbelief. "I've never seen any evidence of their existence."

Kaelan's eyes held mine, his sincerity unwavering. "You are wrong, Vale. Witches were very real, and their blood magic was a force to be reckoned with. Over two hundred years ago, the fae and demons— usually locked in conflict— came to a rare agreement. They recognized the threat that witches posed, their ability to wield both fae and demon magic making them formidable adversaries."

I frowned. "So, what happened?"

A somber expression crossed Kaelan's features, his eyes clouded with a hint of something I couldn't quite place. "Working together they sowed distrust among humans, portraying witches as evil beings who threatened the fragile peace on Earth in a carefully orchestrated campaign, they hunted down witches, eradicating them one by one in a manner that left no trace."

My heart sank as I considered the enormity of the betrayal. The systematic extermination of an entire lineage, a genocide orchestrated by the very beings who now sought my power.

"Why did they fear witches so much?" I asked, my voice uneasy.

Kaelan's gaze never wavered. "Witches were a living embodiment of the union between fae and demon, a potent fusion of light and shadow. Their power was unlike any other, and the potential for chaos was too great to ignore."

I swallowed hard, the reality of my existence crashing over me like a tidal wave. "So, I'm just supposed to believe that I'm a witch?"

Kaelan shrugged, his expression now earnest. "Yes," was all he said.

I took a step back, his revelation almost too much to bear. "And you? How do you know all of this?"

A distant look entered Kaelan's eyes, his voice tinged with regret. "I was there, Vale, during those dark times. I witnessed the eradication of witches. I tried to help some of them escape, but I failed, and the memory of that failure has haunted me for centuries."

My skepticism began to waver, replaced by a growing sense of unease and uncertainty. The reality of my identity was a revelation that shook me to my core. I paced back and forth across the worn wooden floor, contemplating everything I had learned.

"So, why are you here now?" I asked, curious but cautious.

Kaelan's expression darkened. "Because, little witch, I couldn't save them then. But I will not fail you now, whether you trust me or not." My breath hitched at the declaration and he continued. "I'm here now to ensure that history does not repeat itself."

As his words sank in, I found myself torn between skepticism and a growing sense of unease at his words. The world I thought I knew had been shattered, and in its place, a new reality emerged— one where my very existence held the key to a power that could very possibly shape the fate of our realms.

It was too much to process, the weight of my own heritage a burden I had not been prepared for. My emotions were a tangled mess, a storm of uncertainty and confusion raging within me. I took a deep breath, trying to gather my scattered thoughts. There were so many questions still unanswered, so much still left unknown. Yet, Kaelan was a mystery. He was a demon, and despite his words, I had no reason to trust him.

"If you expect me to believe that you're on my side then you need to explain to me why I should trust you," I said, my voice filled with doubt. "Why would you betray your own kind for me, a mere half-breed? What's in it for you?"

His eyes darkened, and his jaw tightened as he considered his response. The room seemed to hold its breath, waiting for his words.

"I don't expect you to trust me, yet," he began, his voice laced with a heavy sincerity. "All I can offer is the truth. As for what's in it for me, I've spent centuries trying to rectify the wrongs I've done. If I can save even one life, then maybe my own sins can be absolved."

His words hung in the air, his past sins and the pain he carried palpable. For a brief moment, I could sense the burden he bore, a weight that had shaped him into the being he had become.

My gaze narrowed as I studied him, searching for any hint of deception. There was something genuine in his voice, a raw honesty that touched a chord within me. I could almost feel the sorrow that seemed to weigh on his soul.

The room remained silent, the unspoken tension lingering. Kaelan's revelation had opened up a chasm of uncertainty, and I was left grappling with the enormity of what I had learned.

His dark eyes held mine, his expression earnest, almost pleading. It was an expression that I was unaccustomed to seeing from him. There was something about it, about him, that made me want to believe him, to trust him. But I couldn't, not yet, not until I knew more.

I drew in a deep breath, steadying my resolve. "Okay, let's say I believe you, that you're here to protect me. How can I know that I can trust you? After all, you're a demon, a descendant of the very beings who orchestrated the annihilation of witches. Why should I believe that you're not just after the same thing?"

He stepped forward, his expression solemn. "Because, Vale, the time has come for me to choose a side, and I choose yours."

I took a step back, uncertain, his proximity making my pulse race. He was too close, the intensity of his gaze making my head spin. There was a charged energy between us, a connection that I couldn't deny. I took a deep breath, steadying myself. "Okay, I'll give you the benefit of the doubt, but if you're lying to me, Kaelan, there will be hell to pay."

Kaelan's smirk returned, that familiar glint in his eyes. His words had an eerie weight to them, and I couldn't help but feel a sense of foreboding. There was an undeniable truth in his statement, a harsh reality that hung in the air.

"Oh, little witch, don't worry. There will always be hell to pay," he said, his voice dripping with a dark, almost seductive tone.

His words sent a shiver down my spine. It was as if the flames of his gaze had ignited something within me that I had never felt before—fear and curiosity that made my heart race. There was no denying it and there was no turning back now.

"Now that we have an understanding, tell me how we move forward," I said, trying to regain my composure.

Kaelan's mischievous smile returned, his eyes locked onto mine, their intensity undiminished. "Well, you can start by trusting me," he replied, his tone playful.

I hesitated for a moment, my doubt still lingering like a shadow. "My trust must be earned, not given away freely."

His expression shifted, turning serious as he regarded me. "Fine, then I suggest you learn to use your magic because the only way we can stop these demons is if you're ready."

The weight of his words hung in the air, the urgency of the situation pressing down on me.

I nodded, my determination strengthening with every passing moment. "I'll do my best. Now, are there any other bombshells you need to drop before I head to bed?"

Kaelan's lips curled into a sly smirk, mischief dancing in his eyes. "Just one, Vale. I'm not going anywhere."

I rolled my eyes, irritation and exhaustion bubbling up. "I don't have the time or energy to deal with this right now."

His playful tone persisted. "Oh, I'm sure you have the energy."

I scowled, growing impatient. "Seriously, Kaelan. I have more important things to worry about than your flirtatious comments."

He leaned in closer, his warm breath tickling my ear. "You have no idea just how serious I am." And then, without warning, his lips were on mine.

His lips met mine in a fiery collision, a sensation I couldn't have anticipated. Kaelan's mouth was warm and insistent, his lips moving with an almost magnetic force that pulled me closer. My mind went blank as his kiss sent shockwaves of desire surging through my body. I surrendered to the sensation, a heady rush of longing coursing through me. His fingers tangled in my hair, sending a shiver down my spine.

When we finally broke apart, I was left breathless, my heart hammering in my chest. Kaelan gazed down at me, his expression intense.

"What the hell was that for?" I asked, my voice trembling with surprise.

He smirked, his eyes filled with a hint of danger. "Consider it a promise, little witch."

I blinked, still trying to regain my composure. "A promise? Of what?"

"A promise of what will come," he said, giving me a sultry look before turning to leave and vanishing into the night.

His words hung in the air, leaving me with a sense of both anticipation and doubt. What had I just gotten myself into? I stared at the spot where he had stood, my mind reeling. A promise of what would come? My pulse raced, heat pooling low in my stomach at the thought.

I shook my head, trying to clear the haze of desire that had descended over me. The weight of his warning still hung heavy in the air, the threat of danger looming over me. But the feel of his lips on mine lingered. I could only hope that I was ready for what came next.

Chapter Four

T he soft glow of lamplight bathed the apartment, casting a warm and intimate ambiance over the space. Wren and I sat across from each other, sinking into the comfort of the couch. He had just gotten back from patrol and I was filling him in on what had happened with Kaelan.

I took a deep breath, my gaze locked onto Wren's hazel eyes, filled with curiosity. "So, that's what he told me. Demons are searching for me because of my blood magic. Blood magic I can only do because I'm the firstborn witch in about two hundred years."

Wren's brow furrowed as he processed the information, his fingers tapping a rhythm against the armrest of the couch. "And you're sure that Kaelan wasn't just making shit up?"

I nodded, "I definitely think there is truth to what he told me. But I'd have to be an idiot to trust him completely without any proof."

Wren let out a thoughtful sigh, his gaze distant as he contemplated the gravity of the situation. "And that kiss? What was that about?"

I could feel my cheeks flush with embarrassment, my heart racing as I remembered the electric intensity of the moment. "It...it was unexpected. He caught me off guard, that's all. I'm still confused about it to be honest. "

Wren's lips twitched into a small smile, his eyes filled with amusement. "Well, I won't pretend to understand demons and their charms. But you've got to be careful, Vale. We don't know his true intentions, besides the obvious intention of getting in your pants." He raised an eyebrow suggestively.

I shoved him playfully and nodded, my fingers tracing patterns on the edge of the blanket draped across my lap. "I know, Wren. Believe me, I'm not blind to the risks. But I have a feeling that if he wanted to harm me, he would have done so by now."

Wren's expression softened, his eyes full of empathy and understanding. "I get it, Vale. I'm not trying to tell you what to do. I'm just worried about you, that's all. The last thing we need is some hot demon messing with your head."

I offered him a grateful smile, a mix of emotions swirling within me. "I won't let my feelings cloud my judgment. We need to find out more about Kaelan and why he's involved with all of this."

Wren's gaze held mine for a moment longer before he nodded, a sense of determination in his eyes. "Alright then. We'll figure this out together. But if anything seems off, if you feel even a hint of danger, promise me you'll let me know."

His words warmed my heart, reminding me how lucky I was to have someone like him in my life. Someone who cared about me and had my best interests at heart. "I promise, Wren. I'm not going to take any chances."

The air felt lighter as we settled into a more comfortable conversation, Wren sharing about his night and the different creatures he had encountered during his patrol, there had been more demon sightings. The familiarity of our easy banter was comforting, and I found myself relaxing, the tension in my shoulders dissipating.

Despite the uncertainty surrounding my strange relationship with Kaelan, I was grateful to have Wren's support and friendship. I knew that together, we would figure out what was going on and face it head-on, whatever the consequences.

☾

The first tendrils of dawn stretched across the horizon, painting the sky in hues of soft pink and gold. I lay in bed, my breathing still heavy from the remnants of a dream that had left me unsettled. As I stared up at the ceiling, the fragments of that elusive vision danced at the edges of my consciousness, taunting me with their fleeting glimpses of things yet to come.

Beside me, the old cat nestled on the bed, its fur warm against my skin. It purred contentedly, oblivious to the turmoil of my thoughts. I stroked its fur absentmindedly, the softness a soothing balm against my nerves.

In the dream, I had found myself in a realm shrouded in shadows, an ethereal plane that seemed to exist beyond the boundaries of reality. A figure stood before me, a demon man with eyes that glinted like polished obsidian, his features obscured.

Beside him stood a woman, her presence familiar yet shrouded in uncertainty. Her eyes held a depth of knowledge that seemed to penetrate the very core of my being as if she held secrets that I had yet to uncover. She opened her mouth to speak but I couldn't make out the words. Whispers of her voice echoed in the recesses of my mind, a slight brush of recognition that left me longing for answers.

But the most chilling aspect of the dream was the presence of a looming figure, an evil entity whose malevolence radiated like a toxic aura. Even in the realm of dreams, I could feel the weight of its malice pressing down on me, a sensation that left me paralyzed with dread.

As I lay there, the dream slipping away like grains of sand through my fingers, a fine sheen of sweat coated my skin. I closed my eyes, trying to hold onto the fleeting fragments of that otherworldly vision, desperate to glean some meaning from the chaos.

But dreams were elusive, a realm of their own where reality and fantasy intertwined in ways that defied understanding. As the dream slipped further from my gasp, I let out a frustrated sigh and pushed myself up into a sitting position. My gaze was drawn to the window where the sun was now fully visible on the horizon.

The sight of the morning sun brought a sense of calm, a reminder that despite the mysteries that swirled around me, the world was still turning and the days would keep coming, no matter what. I took a deep breath, trying to clear my head, the memory of the dream lingering like an itch at the back of my mind. I watched the golden rays spill across the landscape, illuminating the world outside.

With a determined exhale, I swung my legs over the edge of the bed and rose to my feet, the cat watching me curiously. "Don't look at me like that," I said with a small laugh. "I've got work to do." The dream may have faded, but the echoes of its message lingered, a puzzle that begged to be unraveled.

I padded across the room, my bare feet whispering across the hardwood floors, and made my way into the bathroom, splashing some cold water on my face. My reflection stared back at me in the mirror, dark circles under my eyes betraying my fatigue.

I let out a sigh, running a hand through my tousled hair. There would be no time for a luxurious bath this morning, I would have to settle for a quick shower and a cup of strong coffee.

I turned the water on, the warmth of the spray washing away the last remnants of the dream, the tension in my body easing as the familiar ritual of getting ready for the day began. I let my mind wander as I went through the motions, the mystery of the dream still nagging at the back of my mind.

As I stepped out of the shower and wrapped a towel around my body, the memory of Kaelan's kiss came rushing back. His lips had been soft and insistent, his touch sending shivers down my spine. Despite the danger, there was something undeniably magnetic about him, a pull that I couldn't deny.

I shook my head, dismissing the thought. Now was not the time to dwell on such things, there was work to be done. I finished drying off and began getting dressed, pulling on my leather pants and jacket. A sense of resolve settled over me as I did. I would not be distracted by Kaelan's charm, no matter how enticing he might be.

As I moved through the familiar motions of starting a new day, the fragments of the dream continued to nudge at the corners of my mind. I brewed a pot of coffee, the soothing aroma filling the air as I stood by the window, gazing out at the city below. The streets were already bustling with activity, the world continuing to turn despite the unknown forces at play.

In that quiet moment, a sense of clarity began to emerge from the haze of uncertainty. I may not know the full extent of what lay ahead, but I would not let fear rule my decisions. Whatever was coming, I would face it with courage and determination, trusting in my abilities to navigate the challenges ahead.

I sipped my coffee, the warmth spreading through me as I allowed myself to contemplate the possibilities. Who were the figures in the dream, and what role did they play in the tangled web that had entwined my life? They were pieces of a puzzle that demanded my attention.

The soft rustle of blankets marked the arrival of a new presence, and I turned my head to find Wren emerging from his bedroom. His dark curly hair was tousled, his expression a mix of morning grogginess and genuine warmth. The cat had moved to the couch and gave him a lazy glance before settling back down with an air of indifference. With him being part wolf, the two kept their distance from each other, not getting along very often.

"Morning," Wren greeted with a yawn, stretching his arms above his head. His green eyes met mine, a hint of concern reflected in their depths. "Did you manage to get any sleep?"

I nodded, taking another sip of coffee. "Yeah, eventually."

His brow furrowed, his eyes filled with understanding. "I could hear you tossing and turning all night. Are you sure you're alright?"

I leaned against the living room's large windowsill, my gaze distant as I considered telling him about my dream. After a moment, I let out a sigh and decided to confide in him. "I had a dream last night, one that left me feeling unsettled."

He tilted his head in a way that reminded me exactly of a wolf, a curious glint in his eyes. "Care to share the details?"

I took a moment to collect my thoughts, searching for the right words to convey the intricacies of the dream. "I saw figures — a demon man, a woman, and something... dark and ominous. I can't be certain, but I believe they are all somehow tied to the mystery of my blood magic."

His eyebrows raised, his curiosity piqued. "What makes you think that?"

"Just a feeling," I shrugged, "A sense of familiarity. The woman...I know her somehow. And the man, the way he looked at me, shrouded in shadows, it was as if he was searching for something within me."

Wren considered my words, his expression thoughtful. "Well, whatever it is, we can figure it out. This morning and afternoon are free for us, no shop to worry about, no wolf pack duties. What do you say we focus on untangling this mess?"

My lips curved into a smile, his words lifting a weight from my shoulders. "I'd like that." He reached out, his fingers brushing against mine in a gesture of silent support.

"Great. We'll start by searching for any clues about those figures you saw. Maybe there's some lore or records that could shed some light on what's going on."

As his words settled over us, I felt a renewed sense of determination. Wren was right — whatever was happening, we would face it together. With his help, I knew we would unravel the mysteries surrounding my blood magic, and I would learn the truth about who I was and why I was so important.

"But first," he continued, "how are you feeling about... last night?"

A surge of emotion welled up within me, a maelstrom of anger, confusion, and frustration. I met his gaze with a fire burning in my eyes, my voice tinged with righteous indignation.

"I feel enraged, Wren. Enraged at the demons and fae responsible for the genocide of my people, for the slaughter of innocent witches who never asked to be part of their twisted war. Enraged that I've been dragged into a conflict that's been raging for centuries, a conflict I didn't choose to be a part of."

Wren's expression softened, his understanding palpable. "Vale, I know you didn't ask for any of this. But you're stronger than you realize, and you're not alone in this fight."

I took a deep breath, the weight of my emotions settling as I looked into Wren's eyes, the unwavering support shining within them. "Thank you. I know I can count on you, and that means more to me than I can express."

Wren's gaze held mine, his eyes were thoughtful as he spoke again. "And what about that kiss? How do you feel about that?"

My heart skipped a beat, the memory of Kaelan's lips against mine flooding back with a mixture of heat and unease. Why had I let him kiss me? I shifted on my feet, my fingers absently tracing the edge of the coffee cup once more.

"It's... complicated," I admitted, my voice carrying a blend of conflicting emotions. "On one hand, there was this undeniable intensity, a connection I can't quite explain. It's like his touch ignited something within me, something I didn't know existed."

Wren nodded, his expression understanding. "And on the other hand?"

A self-deprecating smile tugged at the corner of my lips. "On the other hand, I'm embarrassed and confused. I don't exactly make a habit of kissing random demons I've only known for a few days."

Wren chuckled softly, a warm sound that helped to ease some of the tension in the air. "Fair enough. But emotions aren't always simple, Vale. Sometimes they take us by surprise, lead us down paths we didn't anticipate."

The cat stretched out on the couch, a low purr echoing in the room. I watched the sunlight dance across his black and white fur, the rhythmic sound calming me further. I met Wren's gaze, uncertainty in my eyes. "I appreciate your understanding, Wren. It's just... I can't help but feel a pull towards Kaelan, even though I know I should be wary."

Wren squeezed my shoulder in a comforting gesture. "I get it, Vale. And I trust your judgment. Just remember to listen to your instincts, and don't let anyone push you into anything you're not comfortable with."

A grateful smile spread across my face, the warmth of his friendship filling my heart. "I will, Wren. Thanks."

The cat jumped off the couch, sauntering over to rub against my legs, the sensation of its fur tickling my skin. We both laughed, the mood lightening further. I set the coffee cup down, a sense of calm enveloping me.

Wren cleared his throat, a hint of a smile on his face. "I'm gonna shower and then we can go get breakfast, okay?"

I nodded, smiling back at him. "Sounds like a plan."

With that, he turned and made his way to the bathroom, the sound of the shower turning on echoing through the apartment. I sat down on the couch, the cat settling on my lap. The feel of its purr vibrating against my skin grounded me, my mind slowly clearing.

Whatever the day brought, I was determined to face it with strength and courage. As long as I had Wren by my side, I knew I could overcome any challenge, no matter how daunting.

The cat gazed up at me with its intelligent orange eyes, and I stroked its fur, the simple motion soothing. In the light of a new day, the events of the past few days felt more surreal, almost like a strange dream. But the reality was that a mysterious force was drawing me into a dangerous conflict. It was up to me to find a way to navigate this tangled web of intrigue, power, and politics, or risk losing everything.

☾

With a renewed sense of purpose, Wren and I left our apartment behind, the morning sun casting a golden glow over the city streets. The fall air was crisp, carrying the promise of a new day filled with possibilities. We strolled side by side, the bustling sounds of the city enveloping us as we shared our thoughts.

"So, where do we start?" I mused aloud, walking into our favorite donut shop. "Do we look for more information about witches or try to unravel the meaning behind that dream?"

Wren's lips curved into a contemplative smile, his eyes focused ahead. "Maybe we should start by finding Harker,"

"Harker?" I echoed, the name unfamiliar to me.

Wren's expression held a touch of intrigue as he turned to me. "Harker is a vampire. She's been around for centuries, and she's made it her business to absorb as much history and lore as she can. If anyone alive still knows about the witches or the events you're trying to unravel, it's her."

I furrowed my brows, taking in this new information. "A vampire who's a history buff?"

Wren chuckled a warm sound that seemed to carry a hint of fondness. "More than a history buff. She's practically a living archive of knowledge."

As we ate our breakfast and continued our stroll, the idea of seeking out this mysterious vampire took root in my mind. It made sense — if anyone could shed light on the mysteries that had woven themselves into my life, it would be someone with an extensive grasp of history and the supernatural.

"But how do we find her?" I asked, my curiosity piqued.

Wren's grin was mischievous, his eyes alight with a hint of excitement. "Oh, she's not one to hide. Harker has a... reputation. If we ask around the right circles, we should be able to track her down."

I nodded, a sense of determination settling within me. "Then let's do it."

Wren flashed a smile. "Great, I know of a werewolf dive not too far a walk from here. Someone there will know where we can find her."

The entrance to the bar was marked by a subtle shift in atmosphere — the energy in the air seemed charged, a mix of camaraderie and watchful tension. Wren and I stepped inside, I scrunched my nose at the scent of beer and fur mingling. The dimly lit space was still bustling with activity from the night before. Werewolves gathered in groups, their laughter and banter creating a lively backdrop.

Wren guided me to the bar, his eyes scanning the crowd with a discerning gaze. "I'll be right back," he said, his voice carrying a hint of concern.

"I'll be fine, Wren. Go," I urged him. It was silly of him to worry about how I'd fare in a bar.

He nodded, and I watched as he disappeared into the depths of the bar, his confident stride leading him toward a backroom. Alone at the bar, I leaned against the polished wood, my gaze wandering over the eclectic assortment of patrons.

Before long, my attention was diverted by the arrival of an unnamed werewolf, his gait cocky and his eyes alight with boldness. He sidled up to me and slowly looked me up and down, a lopsided grin playing on his lips. "Well, aren't you a sight for sore eyes?"

I offered a polite smile, not entirely surprised by his drunken attention. "Thanks,"

He leaned in closer, his voice carrying a flirtatious edge. "What brings a beauty like you to a place like this?"

I chuckled softly, my tone measured. "Just passing through."

His grin widened, his confidence undeterred. "You know, I could show you around, make sure you enjoy your time here." His voice was laced with innuendo.

"No thanks," I said dismissively.

His easy charm gave way to a simmering anger, his eyes narrowing at my lack of interest. "Come on, don't be like that," he growled, his tone taking on an edge of irritation.

My hand moved to the knife at my side, a flicker of warning flashing in my eyes. "I appreciate the offer, but I'm not interested."

His lips curled into a sneer, his face contorted with anger. "I'll have you know, I'm a valuable member of this pack. You should be grateful for my attention."

His insult was punctuated by a sudden burst of laughter from a nearby group of werewolves, their mocking voices ringing through the air. "Oh come on, Zane, leave the girl alone."

I met his gaze without flinching, my voice firm and unyielding. "I'm just not interested. There's no need to get angry."

He leaned in closer, his eyes narrowing with a dangerous glint. "Now, listen here you bit—" The last word was cut off in a yelp as I moved quick as lightning, my knife now pressed up against his balls.

"Unless you want to lose these," I said, adding extra pressure for emphasis, "I'd suggest not calling me a bitch." Zane's whole face had gone an impressive shade of purple. "I won't say it again. Back off."

He gulped, his hands up, palms forward in surrender. I pulled back the knife and returned it to my belt, the air crackling with tension.

The bar around us seemed to hold its breath, the tension palpable with the threat of violence hanging heavy in the air. Just as the tension reached its peak, a commanding voice cut through the silence. "That's enough."

I turned to find Wren emerging from the backroom, fire blazing in his eyes. The werewolves in the room seemed to react to his authority, the atmosphere shifting from charged to cautious.

Wren's gaze settled on the werewolf before me, his voice carrying an unmistakable undercurrent of dominance. "Leave, Now."

The werewolf's defiance wavered under Wren's heated stare, with a resentful glare in my direction, he turned and walked away, disappearing into the crowd.

Wren approached me, his eyes softening as he met my gaze. "Why do you have such a knack for trouble?"

I shrugged and gave him a sarcastic smile."Just a natural talent, I guess."

A hint of a smile curved his lips, his eyes alight with amusement.

The adrenaline faded, replaced by a sense of relief. "Honestly, that guy was being a jerk."

He shook his head, his expression exasperated. "Well, that jerk is the Alpha's second. You might want to steer clear of him for the time being."

I snorted, raising an eyebrow. "Second in command and he still can't take a hint? I'm not sure that's an argument in his favor."

Wren chuckled, a warm sound that broke the tension. "True. Anyway, now that I've successfully found you another enemy, are you ready to go see Harker?"

I grinned, the excitement of a new lead lifting my spirits. "Absolutely."

Chapter Five

The air was cool as Wren and I stepped out of the bar. We hailed a cab, the vehicle weaving through the streets of the city until we reached our destination— a dilapidated house in a forgotten corner of the old district. It stood as a relic of ages past.

The house appeared frozen in a state of disrepair, as though its inhabitants moved in one day many years ago and simply never left, allowing the encroaching chaos of the surrounding neighborhood to claim its walls and corners. Ivy crept up the sides of the brick house and its windows were covered in tattered floral curtains, their colors faded with age.

We approached the front door, our steps accompanied by the soft crunch of gravel underfoot. Wren raised his hand, rapping on the door with a resounding knock that seemed to echo through the stillness of the street. Wren's second knock was met with a groan from within, accompanied by the sound of what must have been dozens of papers falling in an untidy cascade. I thought I heard a curse from inside.

"Harker, rise and shine," Wren called out, his voice carrying a blend of familiarity and gentle teasing.

Seconds ticked by, each one stretching out in an intense silence until finally, the door creaked open, revealing a figure whose disheveled appearance mirrored that of her surroundings. Harker stood before us, her features marked by a weariness that seemed to have etched itself into her very bones. Her eyes squinted against the intrusion of the sun, her discomfort clear.

"Wren? What in the Gods do you want?" Harker's voice was a rasp, laden with irritation as she peered out at us from behind the curtain of her long black hair.

"We've got some questions, Harker," Wren replied, his tone measured and respectful. "Ancient lore. We thought you might have some insights."

Harker's expression remained guarded, her ice-blue eyes narrowing as she studied us. The weight of her scrutiny felt like a physical presence, a reminder of her formidable reputation as a keeper of knowledge, despite her bedraggled appearance.

"And you two thought it was a brilliant idea to wake me up in the middle of the day?" Harker's words dripped with sarcasm, her annoyance apparent.

"You haven't changed a bit, have you, old friend?" Wren smiled, his eyes twinkling with mirth.

Harker's gaze flickered between us, a reluctant recognition dancing in her eyes. "Fine," she sighed, a defeated sound. "Get in. And close that blasted door. The light's already making me regret my decision."

With relief and anticipation, we stepped inside, the door shutting behind us with a resounding thud. The interior of the house was dimly lit, the windows covered by heavy but threadbare curtains that muted the sunlight's intrusion. A musty aroma hung in the air, mingling with the scent of old books and forgotten secrets.

Harker led us into a cluttered room, the space dominated by towering stacks of books, scrolls, and piles of parchment. It was a chaotic tableau of knowledge, a testament to Harker's insatiable curiosity and unquenchable thirst for understanding.

"What's this about?" Harker asked, her voice carrying a hint of begrudging curiosity.

"We're looking for information about ancient Otherworlder history," Wren explained. "Something that might shed light on events long past."

Harker's gaze shifted between us, her eyes sharp with scrutiny. "And what kind of history are we talking about here?"

I exchanged a glance with Wren. "The history of witches," I answered, my voice full of trepidation.

Harker's reaction was immediate, her features twisting into a blend of surprise and disbelief. Her eyes locked onto mine, the weight of her gaze almost tangible.

"Witches, you say?" Harker's voice was a hushed whisper, carrying an undercurrent of something I couldn't quite place. "There are some that would say that is a forbidden subject."

I nodded, my heart pounding in my chest. "Yes, they would. But we need to know more about them, about what happened to them."

Harker's gaze held mine, her expression slowly shifting from surprise to something more thoughtful, a spark of recognition in her eyes.

"Come with me," she said finally, her voice carrying a sense of urgency.

Harker led us further into her maze-like house, the dimly lit corridor gave way to another room filled with stacks of books and parchment. The air was thick with the smell of ancient pages, the weight of knowledge and history pressing upon us. My heart raced with anticipation as I absorbed the sight before me.

As we settled into the room, Harker's gaze lingered on me for a moment, a thoughtful expression crossing her features. She seemed to hesitate, as if on the precipice of sharing a revelation. But instead, she began to speak.

"The Otherworlders," Harker began, her voice carrying a somber note, "came to be through the mingling of demons or fae with mortals, their unique heritage granting them a connection to both realms. It was a delicate harmony, a reflection of the interwoven threads of magic that bond our worlds together."

"Witches," Harker continued, her words resonating with deep, ancient wisdom, "are a fusion of realms, a blend of the demon, fae, and the mortal world. Thrice blessed, so to speak."

Her words hung in the air, mystery shrouding the truth she was about to unveil. I exchanged a glance with Wren, both of us anxiously listening to the vampire's words.

"The first witch," Harker continued, her voice a whisper, "was born from the union of a demon and a fae, a union that was rare and forbidden in the eyes of their respective realms."

I watched her carefully. I felt a sense of connection to the ancient tale as if the blood flowing through my veins held the echoes of a past that had long been forgotten.

"She became a witch," Harker explained, her gaze piercing through me, "not by choice, but by circumstance. Raised on Earth, the magic in her blood resonated with the magic of this realm. It was here that she was able to tap into the earth's innate power, a power that demons and fae cannot access."

I listened intently, my mind racing as I absorbed her words. The magic within me, the blood that flowed through my veins, was a reflection of this ancient heritage, a connection to a legacy that spanned centuries.

"Witches," Harker continued, her voice growing stronger, "Became a force to be reckoned with. The first witch lived for over five hundred years, her power growing as she formed the foundation of what would become the witch's hierarchy."

I exchange a glance with Wren, my astonishment mirrored in his eyes. Could I possibly live over five hundred years like the first witch?

"The first witch," Harker explained, her voice tinged with reverence, "formed a coven, known as The Seven. These witches were tasked with overseeing the balance between the realms, with a focus on the Earth and the Otherworlders that inhabited it."

Harker's words held a weight that resonated deep within me, a sense of destiny and purpose that seemed to align with the truths that had begun to unravel in my own life.

"There were two types of witches," Harker explained, her tone carrying a note of finality. "Blood-born witches, those born from the union of demon and fae, possess the ability to wield blood magic. Their power was unparalleled, a force that could manipulate life itself."

My heart raced as her words echoed through the room, a realization dawning upon me. The blood magic that surged within me, the power that had awakened with a raw intensity many years ago, was a testament to this ancient heritage.

"And then there are mortal-born witches," Harker continued, her voice softening, "those born of blood-born witches, who inherit the magic of the Earth and the residual magic within their blood. They could not access blood magic."

Harker's voice held a solemn weight as she continued to weave the tapestry of history before us. "The witches' dominion over Earth and the Otherworlders that resided there became a coveted prize for both the demons and the fae. The delicate balance that had been maintained for centuries began to shift as jealousy and desire consumed them, the Earth too plentiful to let slip from their grasp."

I listened intently, my heart heavy with the weight of the tale Harker recounted. The rise and fall of the witches, and the power struggle, all resonated with the echoes of a past that had left an indelible mark on the world.

"Witches exercised their authority over the Otherworlders, guiding and overseeing their existence on Earth. But as tensions between the realms escalated, a plot was hatched, a sinister alliance between demons and fae."

I felt a chill run down my spine as Harker's words painted a vivid picture of betrayal and treachery. The once steadfast harmony between realms had crumbled, replaced by a thirst for power that sought to obliterate everything in its path.

"They incited violence against the witches," Harker's voice grew softer, carrying a note of sorrow. "Exploiting the fears of mortals, they turned them against the very beings who had safeguarded their world for centuries. Coven by coven, the witches were tracked down, hunted, and extinguished."

My heart ached as I took in the tragic fate that had befallen the witches. The echoes of their sacrifices echoed through the ages, a testament to the strength and resilience of those who had fought against insurmountable odds.

I found my voice, curiosity and sadness driving me to ask, "But why were witches so feared and targeted? What threat did they pose to the demons and fae?"

Harker's gaze met mine, her eyes filled with understanding and sympathy. "Witches possessed a power that bridged realms, an ability to wield magic that was unprecedented. They were a living embodiment of the very balance that demons and fae sought to control. With the witches still living, their control over the mortal realm would never come to fruition."

A sense of indignation rose within me. "How did the demons and fae manage to overcome their power?"

Harker's lips quirked into a rueful smile. "The alliance between the demons and fae was a formidable one. They used manipulation, deception, and the mortal world the witches protected against them. By stoking fear and sowing discord, they managed to turn the tide of public opinion. Soon, nowhere was safe. Mortals turned on neighbors and friends, burning anyone who was thought to be a witch."

"What role did vampires play in the conflict during the witches eradication?" Wren asked.

Harker sighed. "Some vampires supported the witches. Others were content to watch from the sidelines."

Wren shook his head. "Typical. I have no doubt they saw an opportunity."

"Vampires have always been opportunists," Harker agreed.

"And where were you during all this?" I asked her, my eyes studying her face.

"I was a young vampire then. Still learning my way." Her expression betrayed no emotion.

"So you weren't involved in the extermination of the witches?"

"No. I didn't join the fight."

"Would you have fought for the witches if you had known more about their history? About the legacy they had built?" I asked, a hint of accusation in my voice.

Harker smiled sadly. "It's easy to say that in hindsight, but the reality was that there was a lot of uncertainty and chaos back then. And a young vampire, no matter how noble her intentions, is not going to make much of a difference."

My mind whirred with a mix of emotions, the anger and sorrow intertwining as I grappled with the tragedy that had unfolded. The witches, once rulers and guardians, had been betrayed and hunted to extinction.

"Is there any hope left?" I asked, a glimmer of determination in my eyes. "Are there any remnants of the witches' legacy that have survived?"

Harker's gaze once again held mine, her expression a blend of sadness and determination. "The remnants of the witches' legacy are scattered, their knowledge lost to the depths of time. But the threads of their power still linger, waiting for someone with the strength and courage to reclaim what was lost."

Harker's eyes held a distant, contemplative look. She spoke with regret, her voice carrying the weight of the years she had spent seeking answers within the pages of ancient tomes.

"Most of the knowledge of the witches was destroyed," Harker sighed, her fingers delicately tracing the edges of an old scroll. "What little I have uncovered has been fleeting, fragments of a past that remains shrouded in mystery."

She turned her gaze to me, her eyes searching mine with a knowing intensity. "But there is one thing I came across many decades ago, a foretelling of sorts."

With a sense of anticipation, I watched as Harker carefully unfurled the scroll she had been toying with, revealing a script that seemed otherworldly, written in a language that was unfamiliar yet strangely captivating. Her fingers brushed over the text, her voice soft as she translated the words with a reverence that sent a shiver down my spine.

"The First Witch, born from realms entwined, shall rise again."

"The rest, if there is any, is lost." She sighed again, carefully rolling the scroll. The words hung in the air, the weight of their implications settling over us like a whisper from the past. A sense of destiny and purpose seemed to linger within the very fibers of the scroll.

"Why are you so invested in unraveling the mysteries of the witches?" Harker's icy blue eyes bore into mine, her curiosity tinged with a knowing glint.

I hesitated, the truth lingering on the tip of my tongue. In that moment, I felt a connection to Harker, a shared understanding of the truths that remained hidden beneath the surface. I glanced at Wren, who nodded encouragingly.

"I... believe I am a part of this," I admitted, my voice steady despite the weight of my confession. "I am a witch, born of both demon and fae."

Harker's eyes shone in the faint light, her gaze seemed to pierce into me as if she could see the blood magic there. "You are part of something much larger, Vale," she affirmed. "A legacy that was woven long before you were born, a tapestry of power and potential."

She leaned back, her fingers drumming against the scroll thoughtfully. "Demons and fae wouldn't come together lightly, not unless there was a purpose that transcended their differences. You, my dear, are a manifestation of that purpose."

A surge of emotions washed over me, wonder and trepidation. The realization that I was connected to a legacy that spanned realms and centuries was both exhilarating and daunting. The power that coursed through my veins was a testament to the untold possibilities that lay ahead.

As I exchanged a glance with Wren, the bond between us unspoken yet palpable, I knew that our journey had taken on a new dimension. The path we had embarked upon, the search for answers and the reclamation of lost truths, had become intertwined with a destiny that stretched far beyond the horizon.

The legacy of the witches, the prophecy that foretold of their return, and the power that pulled within me — it was all a testament to the intricacies of a world that defied boundaries and expectations. As I looked to Harker, her ancient eyes filled with wisdom and possibility, I couldn't help but feel a sense of determination burning within me, propelling us forward into a future that held the promise of uncovering the mysteries that had remained veiled for far too long.

Chapter Six

Our quaint bookshop, with its aging brick walls, exuded a familiar warmth as Wren and I returned. The fine rain that had started back up on our walk home had ceased, leaving behind an earthy scent that hung in the air. My eyes wandered, finding solace in the sunroom in the back, where our lovingly tended herbs flourished under the gentle light that streamed through the windows.

Juniper bustled about, dusting shelves as I moved to the front desk to organize the day's receipts. The bell at the door jingled and Wren's partner, Donovan, entered, his gaze briefly meeting mine with a smirk before settling on Wren.

"Enjoy your day off while the rest of us take care of business, Wren?" Donovan had grated on my nerves since day one, his blatant lack of respect for Wren apparent. "With these increased demon sightings it *should* be all hands on deck."

"And I'm sure you've been so helpful in that regard, Donovan," I said, rolling my eyes.

Donovan glared at me from the front entrance, but his glare was quickly replaced by a sleazy grin as he looked me up and down. "Well, if it isn't the lovely Vale. Careful, sweetheart, you might get charmed just by looking at me."

"I'd sooner be charmed by a moldy piece of bread." I scoffed, crossing my arms. "What do you want, other than to make everyone's skin crawl?"

Donovan stepped up to the counter and leaned in towards me, his green eyes glinting. "Just thought I'd check up on Wren before patrol. He's been slacking off lately. Can't say the same for you though."

I raised an eyebrow and leaned away from him, grateful there was a counter between us. "Wren might be taking breaks, but at least he doesn't have a stick shoved up his ass."

Donovan sneered and stepped back, "One day that pretty mouth is going to get you in trouble."

"That's enough, Donovan," Wren said, taking a step toward the werewolf. The tension in the air was palpable.

Donovan took another step back, his hands up in a placating gesture. "Let's just get going already, Wren. We've got more important things to do." He narrowed his eyes at me in an accusatory way.

"Go on, then. I'm right behind you." Wren said. Donovan quickly stormed out the front door. Wren turned to me and smirked. "It seems he can't help but get a rise out of you."

I rolled my eyes. "That guy's such an ass. I don't know how you put up with him."

Wren sighed. "He's not all bad, just... abrasive."

I laughed, "Yeah, well, it's no wonder we don't get along."

Wren nodded, his expression amused. "Try not to kill him, okay? The pack needs him, and we don't need any more enemies."

"No promises," I said, grinning. With a quick wink, he left.

◖ ◗

As the daylight's embrace gradually waned, Juniper and I went about our familiar routine of tidying and arranging, each movement brought a calming sense of routine and purpose. The mingling scents of herbs and ink painted an ambiance that was uniquely ours.

With the final chapter of the day closing on the bookshop, Juniper turned to me with a glint of excitement in her eyes. "Hey, Vale, why not join me tonight? I'm heading to a local bar with some friends. It's been a while since you've come out."

It had been some time since I'd gone out with Juniper, or anybody for that matter. Though there had been plenty of offers from guys, mostly Wren's werewolf buddies. My thoughts drifted to Kaelan and that kiss the night before. Wondering for probably the tenth time today what the hell it meant to me.

There was also the fact that there had been multiple demons on the loose recently, all apparently looking for me. Wren would probably tell me it was best if I stayed home.

After a thoughtful pause, I smiled at Juniper. "It has been a while, hasn't it? I'd love to go out."

◖ ◗

The pulsating beat of music reverberated through the dimly lit bar, the air thick with laughter and chatter. Juniper's friends, I had already forgotten their names, chatted animatedly, their voices a blend of excitement and frivolity that clashed with the shadows that seemed to cling to the corners of the room. I sipped my drink, a concoction of mysterious ingredients that matched the atmosphere of the place.

I exchange polite smiles and nods with Juniper's friends, their enthusiasm almost overwhelming. They were sweet, in their own way, but their conversations revolved around subjects that held little interest to me — the latest fashion trends, celebrity gossip, and other topics that seemed as insubstantial as mist. I couldn't help but feel a pang of jealousy at their carefree attitude though, wishing I didn't have the troubles I faced now. The enormity of my situation was staggering.

Turning my attention back to my friend, I found pleasure in Juniper's company. Her lively spirit and genuine enthusiasm were a welcome contrast to the superficiality that seemed to permeate the bar. Our laughter mingled with the music, and for a moment, I forgot the weight of my responsibilities and the lurking shadows of the Otherworld.

But then, as if summoned by fate itself, my gaze was drawn to the far corner of the bar. There he stood, Kaelan, his presence as mysterious as ever. The room seemed to shrink and the shadows gathered in around him. Dark and brooding, his eyes fixed on me with an intensity that sent a shiver down my spine. He leaned against the bar, a glass of whiskey in his hand, the embodiment of seductive allure that was impossible to ignore.

With an apologetic smile, I excused myself from Juniper's company and navigated through the crowd, my heart quickening as I drew closer to Kaelan. The music faded into the background, leaving only the rhythmic thud of my heartbeat.

"Surprised to see you here," I remarked, my tone one of feigned irritation.

Kaelan turned to me, his lips curling into a half-smile that held a hint of mischief, "Is that any way to greet an old acquaintance?"

I arched an eyebrow, unimpressed by his nonchalant response. "Old acquaintance? We've known each other for all of, what, a few days?"

He chuckled, the sound low and enticing. "Time is relative, my dear. And in the grand scheme of things, a few days can feel like a lifetime."

I rolled my eyes, resisting the flutter of anticipation his presence seemed to ignite within me. "Cut the cryptic act, Kaelan. What are you doing here?"

He took a leisurely sip of whiskey, his gaze never leaving mine. I thought about the way those lips felt on mine and a heat rushed to my face. "I was looking for you."

I scoffed, unable to mask my skepticism. "You traveled all the way here just to find me? Somehow, I doubt that."

He leaned in, his voice a velvety whisper that sent shivers down my spine, and had my toes curling in my boots. "Are you accusing me of lying, Vale? I'm wounded." His expression shifted, revealing a glint of mischief. He leaned in even closer, his breath tickling my ear. "Perhaps I've grown a little obsessed."

A retort lingered on the tip of my tongue, but I found myself momentarily distracted by the way his eyes seemed to flicker with hidden intensity. An intensity he focused solely on me. My gaze flickered to his lips, and I suddenly became acutely aware of his proximity. My skin tingled with anticipation, and I couldn't help but imagine what it would be like to bite those lips.

I blinked, pulling myself out of the moment. I cleared my throat and stepped back, trying to regain my composure. "So, are you going to tell me why you're really here?"

He shrugged, a lazy motion. "Like I said, I was looking for you." He smirked, his confidence unwavering. "Tell me, do I need a reason to want to see you?"

I crossed my arms, my facade of indifference waning in the face of his undeniable allure. "I'm not some plaything for your amusement, Kaelan."

His gaze held mine, a playful glint in his eyes. "And yet you still came over here. But if that's the role you'd like to play..." he said, his voice a soft purr.

My heart raced, a maelstrom of emotions swirling within me. I was torn between my instincts to keep him at a distance and the magnetic pull he seemed to exert over me. The energy between us crackled, Kaelan's smoldering gaze held mine, an unspoken challenge in those dark depths.

I couldn't help but play along, a mischievous smile tugging at my lips. "And what exactly are you suggesting, Kaelan?"

I was rewarded by a flicker of surprise in his expression, but it was soon replaced by a wicked grin. "Oh, I can think of a few things."

My breath hitched, his words sending a rush of heat through me. "Then maybe you should show me."

His gaze darkened, a predatory gleam in his eyes. He stepped closer, his body mere inches from mine. He placed his hand on the small of my back, pulling me closer. His lips grazed my neck, sending shivers down my spine. "Are you sure about that, Vale?"

I swallowed hard, my voice barely a whisper. "Maybe."

He chuckled, his breath hot against my skin. "That's not an answer."

I took a steadying breath, trying to maintain a shred of control. "Kaelan, don't play games."

"Who said I'm playing?" His words were a silken promise.

"I don't know what you're getting at." I pulled away, meeting his gaze, his eyes aflame with an unreadable emotion.

He shook his head, an amused smile tugging at his lips. "You really have no idea what effect you have, do you?"

I narrowed my eyes, searching for a hint of his true intentions. "What are you talking about?"

His expression softened, his hand brushing a stray hair from my face. "You have a fire within you, a passion that's intoxicating. It draws people in and makes them want more. Makes them want to be closer."

His words stirred something within me, a flicker of desire that threatened to consume me. I fought against it, clinging to my resolve. "That doesn't explain why you're here."

"I'm here because I want to be. Because you intrigue me, Vale." His admission hung between us and I was lost for words.

I was too busy getting lost in those deep brown eyes that I hadn't noticed that Juniper had walked over to us. "Sorry to interrupt, I just can't listen to those two prattle on anymore."

I shot her a sympathetic smile. "You're not interrupting anything, June. We were just finishing our conversation."

Juniper's eyes darted between the two of us, Kaelan's gaze hadn't moved from me for one second. "Yes, well," she cleared her throat before continuing, "Why don't you walk me home, Vale? It's getting late and I'm tired." Juniper knew I'd never let her walk home at this time of night by herself.

"Sure, let's get going," I said to her, grabbing my things as Kaelan continued to stare. "I'll see you around, I guess."

Kaelan raised his glass and inclined his head in farewell. Leaning against the bar, he watched us walk out, before silently slipping back into the shadows.

☾

The night air was cool against my skin as I walked the familiar path home from Juniper's apartment building, her laughter still ringing in my ears. My thoughts, however, were far from light-hearted, my mind consumed by Kaelan. The memory of his smoky gaze and the feel of his lips on mine played on a loop.

Lost in my thoughts, I turned a corner, only to have my reverie shattered by a figure emerging from the darkness of a side ally. My instincts flared, sending a surge of adrenaline coursing through my veins as I came face to face with a demon.

"Witch," it hissed, the word dripping with malice. This was no ordinary demon— it could speak, and its wicked grin sent shivers down my spine.

Without missing a beat, I reached for the knives concealed within the folds of my leather jacket, my fingers wrapping around the familiar hilts of my weapons. My heart pounded in my chest as I braced myself for the fight about to unfold.

The demon lunged at me, its movements swift and predatory. I sidestepped its attack, my training kicking in as I countered with a well-aimed strike of my knife. The blade grazed its dark hide, a hiss of pain escaping its lips. But the satisfaction was short-lived as the demon retaliated with a powerful swing of its clawed hand.

Pain laced through my side as its claws found their mark, raking against my flesh. I gritted my teeth, determination to stay alive fueling my every move as I parried its attacks. The demon's unnatural speed made it a formidable opponent, and I cursed the absence of my axe.

My knives flashed in the dim light, the dance of steel and shadows punctuated by grunts of effort and the eerie echo of our struggle. I managed to land a few solid strikes, but the demon's resilience was unnerving. Its taunting laughter grated on my nerves.

As the fight raged on, my movements grew more calculated, a strategy forming in my mind. I aimed for the wound on its side I had already landed, exploiting the gaps in its defenses with a relentless barrage of strikes. But even as I fought with all my strength, I couldn't shake the sinking realization that the demon was gaining the upper hand.

A searing pain lanced through my arm as its talons grazed my skin, the sensation almost numbing in its intensity. I stumbled back, my breath coming in ragged gasps as I assessed my options. The demon's wicked smile widened.

Just as despair threatened to take hold, a sudden shift in the shadows caught my attention. From the darkness emerged a familiar figure — Kaelan. His presence was an unexpected relief, and a surge of hope dared to floor through me.

Kaelan moved with fluid grace, his form shrouded in swirling shadows that seemed to dance and writhe around him. In his hands were a pair of gleaming knives, their edges glinting ominously in the moonlight. He was a formidable sight, a force to be reckoned with as he closed in on the demon.

The shadows obeyed his command, swirling and enveloping him in a haze of darkness, making it difficult to track his movements. Kaelan's strikes were precise and deadly, each blade finding its mark with uncanny accuracy. The demon's venomous grin faltered, replaced by a look of shock and fury.

Kaelan's skill and prowess were evident, his every move calculated and deliberate. I couldn't help but be impressed, even as I continued to fend off the demon attacks. A part of me was grateful for his timely intervention, although my stubborn pride compelled me to deny it.

"I had it under control," I insisted, my voice tinged with irritation as I parried a particularly vicious strike from the demon.

Kaelan's amused chuckle resonated through the air, his shadow-wrapped form weaving seamlessly through the chaos of battle. "Your wounds lead me to disagree."

His words were punctuated by the clash of steel against unearthly flesh as we continued to press our advantage. Together, our combined efforts wore down the demon's defenses, leaving it vulnerable to our coordinated assault. I lunged forward with a final decisive strike, the demon let out a tortured shriek before dissipating in a cloud of ash.

The aftermath was an eerie silence, the tension dissolving as quickly as it had emerged. I was left breathless, adrenaline coursing through my veins as I surveyed the scene. Kaelan sheathed his knives as the shadows receded, leaving him standing before me, his expression one of satisfaction.

Before I could utter a word of gratitude, forgotten pain laced through me. Kaelan was at my side in an instant, his gaze intent as he assessed my wounds. My arm throbbed, the superficial cut already beginning to mend thanks to my Otherworldly blood. But the wound on my side was more concerning, a deep gash that pulsed with pain.

Kaelan's touch was surprisingly gentle as he examined the injury, his fingertips tracing the contours of the wound. "It's deeper than it looks," he murmured, his voice tinged with a rare note of genuine concern. "We need to tend to this."

"My apartment." I managed to get out through gritted teeth, a faint sheen of sweat starting to coat the back of my neck.

I leaned against Kaelan as we began making our way, his strong arms offered me much-needed support. The short distance felt longer than usual, my senses attuned to every step, every brush of his body against mine. I could feel the weight of his gaze on me, his features suffused with concern.

We arrived, and as we entered the cat darted swiftly across the room from where he had been perched on the couch, his wary eyes fixed on Kaelan. We crossed to the couch and he helped me lay down gingerly, the leather cool against my skin as I settled against the cushions.

"Where do you keep your first aid kit?" He asked looking around the small apartment.

"In the bathroom, through there," I said directing him.

He disappeared for a few moments before returning, supplies in his hands. He knelt before me, his eyes focused on the task at hand.

"Take off your shirt," he murmured, his voice low and husky.

I hesitated for a moment, caught between the desire to comply and the instinct to resist. The request hung in the air, heavy with unspoken implications. Slowly, I reached for the hem of my shirt, my fingers trembling slightly as I began to peel the fabric away.

The air seemed to thicken as my skin was bared to his gaze, the intensity between us almost suffocating. Kaelan's eyes darkened as they met mine, a smoldering fire that threatened to consume us both. Every brush of his fingers against my skin sent a jolt of electricity through me, the boundaries between us blurring.

Kaelan's hands were deft and sure as he cleaned and dressed my wounds, his touch sending tremors of awareness through me. I winced and let out a small gasp at the throbbing pain.

"Sorry," he said softly, "I don't exactly have a healer's touch."

"It's fine," I assured him. I glanced at the bandages wrapped around my midsection, the stark white contrasting with the golden tone of my skin. I could feel the warmth of Kaelan beside me, the memory of his touch lingering on my skin.

As he finished dressing my wound, the charged silence lingered, the weight of unspoken words hanging between us. I could feel the heat of his body, the magnetic pull that drew us closer despite the rational part of my mind that urged caution.

"This would need stitches if you were mortal. Lucky for you, since you heal so quickly, some steri-strips will work just fine to keep the gashes closed. Just make sure you don't agitate the wound while it's healing."

"Thank you," I whispered, breaking the tension that had woven its way around us.

Kaelan's gaze held mine, a mix of emotions swirling within his dark eyes. "You're welcome, little witch."

With those words, the spell that had bound us began to lift, replaced by a renewed awareness of our surroundings. The first aid kit was closed, the task at hand completed. Yet the charged energy lingered, a testament to the unspoken connection that had formed between us.

I shifted on the couch, my heart still racing as I met his gaze. "I should probably get some rest. My wounds need time to heal."

Kaelan's eyes held understanding. But there was something else underneath it, something dark and heady. Without a word, he closed the distance between us, his presence looming over me like a shadow. His fingers brushed against my cheek, his touch featherlight as if he feared I might shatter beneath his hands.

As his lips met mine, a wave of warmth swept over me. The kiss was slow and gentle, a tender connection that spoke of unshared emotions. I felt a soft sigh escape me, the tension of the past hours melting away in his embrace.

The pain from my side seemed to fade as our kiss deepened, his lips molding against mine with an intensity that raged through me. His touch became bolder, more insistent, and my fingers tangled in his hair as he pulled me closer.

My hands found their way to his chest, feeling the steady rhythm of his heart beneath my touch. The kiss grew fiercer, our passion igniting like a wildfire that consumed us both. The ache from my injuries was forgotten, replaced by a heady rush of desire that pulsed through every fiber of my being.

Kaelan moved over top of me on the couch, and I surrendered to the moment, allowing myself to be swept away by the whirlwind of sensations and emotions that Kaelan kindled within me. Our bodies pressed together, a symphony of heat and need that transcended the boundaries of reason. The weight of the world seemed to disappear, leaving only the two of us entwined in a dance of longing and surrender.

The taste of him was intoxicating, a heady mixture of danger and desire that left me aching for more as I pressed my body against him tightly. A groan escaped his mouth as I wrapped one leg around his waist. His kisses grew more fervent, his touch demanding as he explored every inch of my mouth with a hunger that matched my own.

"Kaelan," I started, but he stopped me with another kiss, this one brief and glancing.

Kaelan pulled away, his breath ragged. He gazed at me with a mixture of longing and restraint, his thumb tracing a gentle path along my jawline. The air around us crackled with an intensity that left me both exhilarated and bewildered. I had never lost control like that with anyone before.

"I have to go," he whispered, his voice a low murmur.

Confusion knitted my brows as I met his intense gaze. "Go? But why?"

Kaelan's expression darkened with a storm of emotions, his features contorted by an internal struggle. "I can't stay, Vale. Not now. It's better if I leave before things go any further. Before you might regret it. And you're injured. When I have you, all to myself, I'd prefer if you weren't hurt." His smile was wistful as he pushed my hair back from my face.

Reluctance tugged at me as I processed his words. It was a bitter pill to swallow, that abrupt departure of the one who had ignited such a passionate fire within me.

But the lingering pain from my wounds and the exhaustion of the fight won out. I nodded slowly. "I understand," I replied, my voice laced with resignation.

Kaelan's fingers brushed against my cheek once more, his touch sending a jolt of electricity through me. "Stay safe, Vale."

He leaned in, his lips grazing mine in a final, lingering kiss before he pulled away and turned to leave. I watched him go, a whirlwind of emotions churning within me as I watched him walk out the door.

Heavy footfalls came from the hallway outside the door and for a moment I thought he changed his mind before the door opened and Wren walked in. They must have passed each other out there right? But Wren gave no indication that he had seen the demon leave.

His eyes held a hint of concern as he took in my bandaged side and healing arm. His gaze swept over the rest of me assessing, my well-being.

"What happened while I was gone?" Wren's voice was steady, but there was an underlying tension in his tone.

My mind raced, trying to decide how much to reveal. "A demon attacked me. It caught me off guard but I managed to take care of it."

Wren's expression remained serious, his wolfish instincts on high alert. "How badly are you hurt?"

I shook my head, offering a reassuring smile. "Nothing that won't heal just fine in a few days."

Relief washed over Wren's features, his shoulders visibly relaxing. "Good. We need to be cautious, especially with the demons becoming more active."

Nodding in agreement, I stifled the urge to tell him about the encounter with Kaelan. It was a secret that I felt uncertain about sharing, a moment of vulnerability that I wasn't quite ready to expose.

As Wren and I exchanged a few more words, I could feel the weight of the evening settling upon me. The intoxicating allure of Kaelan's presence still lingered. An undeniable connection that defied explanation.

With a heavy sigh, I excused myself from Wren's company and retreated into my bedroom. The events of the night swirled through my mind, a whirlwind of emotions and desires that left me both exhilarated and conflicted.

As I lay in bed, the shadows dancing upon the walls, I couldn't help but replay the stolen moment with Kaelan. His touch, his kisses, his overwhelming presence — it all haunted me, an intoxicating reminder of the passions he had stirred within me.

Sleep eluded me as I relived every moment, every touch, every breath. My mind spun with the possibilities, the danger, the thrill of his presence. The memories were bittersweet, a tantalizing glimpse into the forbidden world that Kaelan had introduced me to. Yet, it was also a reminder of the darkness that lurked just beneath the surface, the shadows that threatened to consume him, and perhaps me too.

I wasn't sure how I would ever be able to reconcile the conflicting emotions.

Chapter Seven

The mundane routine of the next week settled over me like a heavy shroud. The bookshop's shelves stood witness to my solitary days, their tales and secrets echoing in the stillness of the sunlit space. As Wren went out on his endless patrols, demon sightings grew more frequent, and the whispers of darkness loomed ever closer.

Tonight, however, was different. The moon hung high in the sky and Wren and I walked down the darkened streets of the city with a purpose —to hunt down a demon that had taken to terrorizing a nearby park after nightfall.

I had met up with Jaks, the old half-demon who posted the bounties, earlier that day. He was as cunning as he was devious, but I knew not to trust his appearance. His calculated act of appearing harmless and absent-minded concealed the mind of a shrewd strategist. He orchestrated the exchange of information and clandestine deals, his fingers never far from the pulse of the nefarious affairs that wove the fabric of the Otherworld.

Jaks' realm of shadows was one I had navigated cautiously, the discordant notes of distrust never far from my mind. "The demon will not be easy prey," Jaks had cautioned, his tone tinged with a note of seriousness. "But I do not doubt that you possess the skill to see it through."

Armed and determined, we stalked through the shadows, our senses sharp and attuned to the slightest hint of any demon. My own senses were sharpened slightly by my half-breed blood though they weren't nearly as sharp as if I had used my blood magic. But with the demons on the lookout for any traces of blood magic, I couldn't risk it tonight.

"Quiet tonight," Wren muttered, his word punctuated by the soft rustling of leaves beneath our feet.

I nodded in agreement, my gaze scanning the darkness for any sign of movement. "Probably out there, waiting," I whispered, not willing to disturb the silence around us.

We continued our cautious advance, our steps silent in the night. As the park came into view, an eerie stillness hung over the swings and slides, a stark contrast to the vibrant laughter that usually filled the air during daylight hours.

"There," Wren's voice was barely more than a breath as he pointed towards a shadowy figure lurking near the edge of the playground, barely discernible from the shadows around it.

The demon's twisted form seemed to writhe in the darkness, its malevolent aura casting an unsettling pallor over the surroundings. With a silent exchange, Wren and I fanned out, our movements synchronized as we closed in on our quarry.

I crouched behind a dilapidated slide, watching as the demon prowled the edges of the playground. Its form was a grotesque amalgamation of twisted limbs and gnarled horns. This creature thrived on the fear it instilled, reveling in the chaos it sowed.

With a nod, Wren and I sprang into action, our movements fluid and determined as we closed the distance. I emerged from the shadows, my knives glinting in the moonlight as I lunged at the demon. It let out a primal snarl, its claws slashing through the air to meet my attack.

Metal clashed against flesh, the sound of our battle echoing through the night. Wren joined the fray, his presence a whirlwind of fury and precision. Together, we performed a seamless dance of combat, our strikes timed to perfection as we sought to subdue our opponent.

The demon proved to be a formidable foe, its agility and strength a testament to the dangers of the supernatural realm. Wren lashed out with his sword and the demon retaliated with a savage swipe, its claws raking across Wren's arm as he deflected the blow. The scent of blood mixed with the acrid demonic tang in the air, fueling the fire that burned within us.

The demon leapt out at me and I countered, my knives slicing through the air in a deadly arc. It dodged with unnatural speed, its inhuman reflexes testing the limits of our resolve.

As we battled, a chilling presence crept over us like a shadow and a second demon emerged from the darkness. Its malicious grin mirrored the wickedness that lay within, and the realization of our dire situation settled over us. My heart began pounding in my chest.

Wren and I shared a glance, our determination unbroken even in the face of this new threat. The park now bore witness to an even deadlier dance as both demons closed in on us.

Beside me, Wren quickly shifted into his wolven form, his red fur taking on a sickly color in the faint glow of the streetlights overhead. Without waiting another moment we charged the two demons, trying to gain the advantage. I was going to murder Jaks for getting us into this mess.

Our movements became a symphony of chaos and control, our strikes fluid and precise as we wove through the onslaught of attacks from both demons.

Wren's wolf instincts guided him, his feral grace a deadly force to be reckoned with. He lunged at the demon in front of him, his ferocity matched only by the creatures' savagery, while I dodged underneath the sharp claws of the demon who swiped at me.

But in a cruel twist of fate, the second demon seized an opportunity, striking with lightning speed. Its claws found their mark, and with a sickening thud, Wren was sent hurtling through the air. Time seemed to slow as I watched, horror and disbelief washing over me. He crashed to the ground with a bone-jarring impact, his body sprawled and un-moving. "Wren!" I cried desperately.

I ran to where Wren lay on the pavement but his eyes remained closed as I shook him in desperation.

The demons closed in, sensing victory within their grasp. My heart raced as I forced myself to my feet, a surge of determination overcoming the shock that threatened to paralyze me. I reached my hand up to my mouth, and bit down, blood welling up from the small bite. Renewed strength rushed through me as the blood magic took effect. No use in hiding who I was from these demons if it got us killed in the process.

With a snarling growl, I launched myself at the nearest demon, my knives a blur of motion as I unleashed a torrent of strikes. The creature bared its razor-sharp teeth, its claws narrowly missing me as I evaded its blows. Each movement was fueled by a desperate need to protect Wren.

I danced through the chaos, every strike an echo of my fierce resolve. The demons fought back with equal ferocity, their laughter ringing in the air. But as the battle raged on, I felt a new surge of strength coursing through me, a primal, feral energy that threatened to break apart my bones if it wasn't unleashed.

It had come down to this. One final, desperate gambit. I could feel the energy surging through my very soul, so I channeled it, allowing it to flow through me like a torrent. As it surged through my veins, my eyes blazed with an otherworldly light. I shouted out with a roar and let loose a devastating wave of power, the force of it knocking the demons off balance.

Using the distraction to my advantage, I lashed out with my axe, cleaving the first demon's head right off as it dissipated.

The second demon regained its footing with unnatural speed, a sinister glint in its eyes. Before I could react, it lunged at me with a ferocity that sent tendrils of fear rippling through me. Its claws sliced through the air, aiming for my throat, but I managed to raise my axe just in time to parry the deadly assault. The impact sent shockwaves down my arms, making my grip on the weapon almost slip. The demon quickly recovered and landed a blow to my head that almost knocked me down. The force of the blow left my ears ringing, and my vision was momentarily blurred.

Summoning every ounce of my strength and willpower, I quickly shook off the disorientation, spinning around just in time to see the demon closing in once more. Adrenaline surged through me as I lunged forward, my axe leading the way. The blade sliced through the demon's leathery hide, a surge of triumph coursing through me as it howled in pain. Its snarls turned to anguished screams as I landed a deadly strike squarely on its side. For a brief, excruciating moment, the demon convulsed and twitched, its form contorted in agony.

With a final, blood-curdling scream, the creature dissolved into nothingness, leaving behind only the fading echoes of its stench. The adrenaline still pulsed through my veins, the taste of victory bitter-sweet as I scanned the area, on guard for any other lurking threats.

I rushed to Wren's side, my heart pounding with relief and fear. His body had shifted back to its mortal form. His breathing was shallow, his body battered but not broken. Gently, I cradled his head in my arms, his eyelashes fluttering as he struggled to regain consciousness.

We had to get moving, my blood magic would draw other demons here, to us. "Wren," I whispered, my voice a desperate plea. Slowly, his eyes opened, his gaze locking onto mine, his eyes were clouded with pain.

"You...you did it," he rasped, a weak smile touching his lips.

I nodded, tears pricking at my eyes. "We did."

Carefully, I helped Wren to his feet, his arm wrapped around my shoulder for support. His weight pressed against me, he was by no means small, and I struggled under him. As we stumbled away from the park, every step felt like an eternity, the weight of my exhaustion pressing down on me.

"We can't go back to the apartment," I said, my voice edged with urgency. "It's too far."

Wren nodded weakly, his features contorted in pain. "Juniper's... her place is closer."

With grim determination, I guided him toward Juniper's apartment building. The walk felt like a marathon, each step an agonizing struggle. Finally, we reached the door, and I banged on it with a sense of urgency.

After a few tense moments, the door swung open, and Juniper's eyes widened in shock as she took in the sight before her —Wren, semi-conscious and bruised, his arm slung over my shoulders.

"What...what happened?" Juniper stammered, her voice laced with concern.

"Demons," I replied. "Can we come in?" My words were a plea.

Without hesitation, she stepped aside, letting us in. Together, we managed to guide Wren to the couch, his breathing labored as he settled onto the cushions. Juniper fetched a blanket and draped it over him, her expression full of worry.

"He's badly hurt," I explained, my voice hushed. "His bones need time to heal, and we couldn't make it home from here with him like that."

Her gaze shifted between us, her concern deepening. "Did you say demons? As in more than just one?"

Wren's eyes fluttered open, his voice barely a whisper. "Later, June. Just...need to rest."

I exchanged a worried glance with Juniper, her eyes filled with questions I couldn't answer just yet. For now, all we could do was wait. I kept watch by the window, every sound and shadow making me tense, my senses on high alert.

As time passed, the weight of my exhaustion began to catch up with me. Juniper sat in a chair nearby, her gaze fixed on Wren as he lay there, his breathing steady but labored as he slept. The room was shrouded in an uneasy silence, the tension palpable in the air.

Her voice broke the stillness, laden with concern. "Vale, what exactly happened out there?"

I let out a weary sigh, my fingers absentmindedly fiddling with her lacy curtains. "We were tracking a demon, one that had been causing trouble at a park after dark. But...things got more complicated than we anticipated."

Juniper's brow furrowed, her eyes wide with anticipation. "Complicated? What do you mean?"

"We found the demon, but then another one appeared," I explained, my voice tinged with frustration. "We had to fight them off together, and it was…intense."

Her gaze never wavered from my face, her curiosity evident. "And you both somehow made it out mostly okay?"

I hesitated, my mind briefly drifting to the surge of energy that had coursed through me, giving me strength and power I hadn't known before. "Yes," I replied, my voice soft. "We managed to defeat them thanks to…something that happened."

"What happened?" She pressed, her eyes narrowing as she scrutinized me.

"It's hard to explain," I admitted, my thoughts still a jumble of confusion and wonder. "I felt this force, this power surging within me, and it helped me fend off the demons. It's what saved us."

Juniper's expression shifted from curiosity to amazement, her gaze fixed on me with a mix of awe and understanding. "That's incredible, Vale."

"Yeah," I murmured, thoughts drifting back to the battle and the inexplicable magic that had surged through me. "It was…something."

Her attention returned to Wren, her eyes full of concern. "Is he going to be alright?"

"He needs more time to heal," I replied, my gaze lingering on Wren's prone form. "But he'll be okay, he just needs to stay here tonight. I think it's safe now. I should head home for the night."

She nodded, her expression worried. "You need to take care of yourself too, Vale."

With a grateful smile, I moved from my spot at the window and made my way to the door. As I stepped out into the cool night air, a sense of weariness settled over me. The events of the evening had left me drained, both physically and emotionally.

The demons were growing bolder, their presence more pronounced with each passing day. It was a reminder that our world was teetering on the brink of a greater conflict, one that threatened to consume everything I held dear. But as I walked through the dimly lit streets, my thoughts focused on the trials that lay ahead, I couldn't help but feel a surge of resilience.

I had faced demons and danger, my blood magic had surged through me like a force of nature, and in the midst of it all, I had discovered an inner strength that I hadn't known existed. As I finally reached my doorstep, I knew that the challenges ahead were daunting, but I was ready to confront them head-on.

With a determined breath, I went upstairs to the apartment, the weight of the night's events heavy on my shoulders. But for now, I would rest, recharge, and prepare for whatever darkness awaited on the horizon. But there was just one problem. I wasn't alone.

Chapter Eight

The apartment felt like a sanctuary, a haven where I could finally catch my breath after the chaos of the night. The dim light cast a soothing ambiance, wrapping me in a blanket of comfort as I kicked off my boots and set my weapons aside. Yet, despite the familiar tranquility, an unsettling sensation prickled at the edges of my consciousness.

A soft rustling sound, barely audible, echoed through the air. My heart quickened its pace, and I instinctively reached for the hilt of one of my knives, my fingers curling around the familiar grip. I moved with calculated precision, my steps silent as I navigated the room, my senses attuned to every shadow and corner.

As I cautiously approached the door to my bedroom, the sense of foreboding intensified, every inch of me stood tense and ready. The blade glinted in the dim light as I slowly turned the handle, bracing myself for whatever awaited on the other side. But just as I prepared to swing the door open, it was yanked away from me.

Startled, I stumbled back a step, my knife raised. My heart raced as my eyes met a pair of intense, dark ones— the brooding gaze of Kaelan. My initial surprise shifted to disbelief and irritation.

"What the hell are you doing here?" I hissed, my voice laced with anger. My grip on the knife loosened, though I didn't lower it yet.

"Nice to see you, too." He quipped, a crooked smile playing on his lips, showing a hint of his fangs.

"I can still stab you, you know," I said, waving the upheld knife a little for emphasis.

He arched an eyebrow, the grin widening as he reached out and grabbed my wrist. My eyes widened as he stepped closer, closing the space between us, my pulse quickening as he moved in.

My mind froze as his body pressed against mine, his chest pressed against my shoulder. I was so focused on the touch, the warmth of his skin that I barely noticed when his free hand grasped the hilt of the blade. With a firm tug, he pulled it from my grasp, his eyes never leaving mine.

My breath caught in my throat as his thumb began to stroke the back of my hand, sending a shiver down my spine. A moment later, he released my wrist and took a step back, the smile never leaving his face.

"Now, is that any way to greet an old friend?" He said, turning the blade over in his hand.

I stared at him in shock, unsure of how to respond. My thoughts were muddled, my focus solely on the way his touch made me feel.

"You know," he continued, breaking the silence. "If I didn't know any better, I'd think you were afraid of me."

"Afraid?" I scoffed. "Of course not."

"Well, you are awfully quiet." He observed.

"Maybe I'm just trying to figure out what the hell you're doing here," I repeated, my frustration evident.

Kaelan's expression turned serious, his features shrouded in an air of urgency. "I found something you need to see."

I stared at him, skepticism and curiosity dancing in my eyes. I hesitated, but after a moment, I sighed. "Fine, talk."

Kaelan stepped back, allowing me space to relax, still on edge from the events of the night. "What happened? Who did this to you?" He asked, his voice concerned as he gazed at my head. I touched my forehead and felt the dried blood there, I must look like death.

"Wren and I went after a bounty tonight, instead of one demon though we got handed two." Kaelan's eyes grew dark. "He was knocked out and I took on the two demons myself."

Kaelan's eyes widened at my words. "Vale, you are absolutely extraordinary," He said with a shake of his head. I blushed at the compliment but didn't comment on it.

"What have you found?" I said, changing the subject.

"I've been chasing rumors, whispers I heard centuries ago. When the purge of the witches began, there were tales of a hidden library, a repository of the most important knowledge that the witches had safeguarded for their eventual return."

My eyebrows furrowed. "A secret library? That sounds awfully convenient."

He nodded. "I've been tracking down leads, and recently I came across something to confirm those rumors."

I crossed my arms, my curiosity piqued despite my reservations. "And what exactly did you find?"

Kaelan's gaze never wavered from mine, "A door, hidden within the keep of a powerful demon lord. A door that reeked of blood magic."

I blinked, my mind processing his words. "Blood magic? So you think this is the door to the library. Why would the witches put something so important in a demon lord's keep?"

A faint, wry smile tugged at the corners of his lips. "Because they knew that even if they fell, the demon's keep would remain standing. They hid it in plain sight, locked in a way that only someone with blood magic could access."

My skepticism warred with the possibility of what he was saying. "And you think this library, if it exists, could help solve my problems?"

Kaelan's intense gaze bore into mine, "You've got to learn more about your magic, Vale. You haven't begun to understand the extent of it."

"And you do?" I asked incredulously.

"I was around when the witches were still in power, I remember the awe-inspiring magic they could wield. The demons won't stop coming after you, you need to be prepared for that."

Uncertainty churned within me. "If this is true, if there's a chance it could help me, then show me."

Kaelan nodded, his expression neutral. "I'll take you to where the door has been hidden. But we need to be cautious, Vale. The demon lord's keep is not a place be to taken lightly."

"Fine, we can go tomorrow then, after I get some rest," I said, clear dismissal in my voice.

He hesitated for a moment, then nodded. With a last, lingering look, he slipped back out the door. I closed it behind him, then leaned against it, my thoughts spinning.

I was not sure what to make of the information that Kaelan had given me. It sounded implausible, yet if there was even the slightest chance that he was right, I had to take it. I could not keep going like this, being constantly hunted by the demons, fearing for my life.

If there was a way to better understand my powers, to master them, then I would do whatever it took to find it. I was sick of feeling like a target, of being a pawn in someone else's game. If the library could give me the knowledge to fight back, then that is where I would go.

❰ ❱

The next day dawned with a sense of urgency, the weight of my newfound mission pressing against my thoughts. Wren's protests still echoed in my ears, his frustration evident at being left behind while I went back to Erebus. I left him in Juniper's care once again. My gaze had lingered on his bruised form, my heart heavy with guilt, but I knew that I had answers waiting for me, secrets that demanded to be unveiled.

The sun hung high in the sky as I stood on the roof of the dilapidated button factory that housed my home and bookshop. Kaelan seemed to materialize out of thin air, a shadowed figure against the backdrop of the cityscape.

"You're prompt," he remarked, his tone laced with a hint of amusement.

I rolled my eyes, a retort quick on my tongue. "I have things to do. I don't have time to wait around."

Kaelan's lips quirked into a faint smile, a glint of mischief dancing in his eyes. "Always the busy witch, aren't you?"

Before I could offer a retort, his hand shot out, fingers closing around my wrist with unexpected strength. Surprise flickered across my features, but before I could react, he pulled me close, our bodies touching. "Hold your breath for this next part," he instructed, his voice low.

Confusion and apprehension churned within me, his grip tightened, and the world around us seemed to shift. Shadows surged forward, enveloping us in a shroud of cold darkness. The sensation was disorienting, the chill creeping over my skin like icy tendrils.

Time seemed to blur, and the wind kicked up around us. Before I could fully process what was happening, the shadows released their hold on us. We emerged from the darkness, standing in a small clearing in the woods. My breath shuddered free and I inhaled deeply, the rush of air filling my lungs. I felt a little nauseous. Kaelan released me and I stumbled back a few steps, my hands on my knees.

"What just happened?" I gasped, glaring at Kaelan whose lips were quirked into a smirk.

"We shifted," he replied, and I raised an eyebrow. "We traveled through the shadows. It's not something I can do with multiple people anymore, but I can manage small distances with one person."

"Where exactly are we?" I asked.

"About three miles outside the city. This portal will take us closest to where we need to be in the demon realm." He said as he began walking through the trees.

We didn't have to walk far, the portal lay nestled underneath two trees that had bent and grown together, creating a natural doorway. A shadowy mist seemed to hang in the air around the curved branches.

"Why is this one different from the one Wren and I accidentally stumbled through that night we met? We didn't even know we had gone through it until it was too late."

"Some portals are fixed points, never moving or fading away. Some, like the ones that crop up on the ley lines, are more volatile, coming and going, sometimes within the same minute. A portal like that is what you went through that night."

"What are ley lines?" I asked.

"Lines of pure power that run through the Earth. The veil between realms is thinner, and magic seeps from the Earth there. " He answered, looking at me with that intense stare of his. "We should get moving."

A surge of both excitement and trepidation coursed through me. The prospect of stepping into the heart of the demon realm again was equal parts thrilling and terrifying. The unknown lay ahead.

Without waiting for my response, Kaelan stepped forward, his hand extending toward me. "Are you ready?"

My heart pounded in my chest, determination and uncertainty guiding my answer. "As ready as I'll ever be."

As our hands brushed against each other, fingers intertwined, we took a collective breath. The portal beckoned, a gateway to a realm of secrets and revelations. With a shared glance, we stepped forward.

The transition from the mortal realm to the demon realm was disorienting, a sensation akin to being plunged into icy water before finally emerging on the other side. My senses were assaulted by the alien environment —the air carried a heavy, oppressive weight, and the very ground beneath our feet seemed to pulse with an eerie energy.

We stepped out of the portal into a dense and ancient wood, its trees towering overhead like sentinels of shadow. Unlike the ever-shifting landscape of the demon realm that I had experienced before, this part of the world was strangely stable. Yet, an unsettling aura of hostility hung in the air, tainting the natural beauty of the woods with an unnerving malice.

As Kaelan led the way, my instincts were on high alert. Every rustle of leaves and every faint whisper of the wind sent shivers down my spine. The woods were alive, not in the way I was accustomed to from the mortal realm, but with a twisted energy that resonated with the dark forces that called this place home.

"The lord's keep is this way, he built it close to the portal so he could gain access to it easily." Kaelan's voice broke through the silence, drawing my attention back to the task at hand. He spoke with a calm resolve as if he was navigating a familiar path. I had to remember that he was one of the creatures that called this place home. Had to remember even when he kissed me.

We moved forward, our steps guided by his memory. Along the way, we caught glimpses of fleeting shadowy forms that shifted and morphed between the shapes of various animals. One a lion now becoming a bird, one morphing from a monkey to a dog, one bounding after the others in the form of a fox.

Kaelan explained they were lesser demons called shadowkin, harmless inhabitants of the shadows that roamed between realms. While they didn't pose a direct threat, their presence added to the eerie atmosphere that permeated the woods.

Our path led us to a large stone bridge that spanned the mouth of a wide canyon. The bridge was built from dark gray stone and appeared to be crumbling in places, yet the overall structure remained strong.

As we crossed the bridge, a faint buzzing filled the air, growing steadily louder with each passing moment. My skin prickled, the sound sending a shiver down my spine. The air took on a sinister aura, the darkness growing thicker. The world itself seemed to grow tense as if preparing for something ominous.

We stopped at the center of the bridge, the source of the noise hovering directly above us. I glanced up and saw a dark mass swirling and churning, a cloud of black smoke suspended in midair.

Kaelan stared up at the anomaly, his expression unreadable. I glanced at him and found him gazing at me with his dark eyes, caution dancing within.

"What is that?" I whispered, unable to take my eyes off the dark shape above.

"I've only heard about it. I have never seen it in person. It's an ethereal rift."

"A rift? What does that mean?" I asked, trying to mask the fear that was welling up inside me.

"It's a tear in the fabric of reality, a passage to another realm not directly linked to this one. That's what makes the demon realm so unstable. These rifts pop up and disappear with little warning, creating portals, and allowing demons and other beings to move between far-off realms with ease. The demons have taken advantage of these rifts to invade the mortal realm."

A shiver ran down my spine. I couldn't help but feel a sense of awe at the power of the rift. The sheer force of nature that was causing such chaos and destruction. And yet, there was a part of me that wanted to reach out and touch it, to experience the raw, untamed power for myself.

Kaelan continued to stare up at the rift, his eyes narrowed, the look on his face was one of suspicion. He turned his attention back to me.

"You should be aware that we are now officially trespassing in the territory of a very powerful demon. This is his domain, and he has the power to strike us dead where we stand."

My breath caught in my throat and my heart pounded wildly. I tried to ignore the growing sense of unease that was creeping over me, the knowledge that we were venturing deeper and deeper into dangerous territory.

"Are you sure this is a good idea?" I asked.

Kaelan glanced over at me, his gaze steady and reassuring. "I know these lands well. We will not be caught unaware. But yes, I do believe that we are doing the right thing. We need the information that the library contains, and if it is truly hidden within the lord's keep, then we have to keep going. The stakes are too high for us to fail."

I nodded, his words easing some of my fears, though not completely. We continued across the bridge, the rift casting its dark shadow upon us.

And then, emerging from the twisted trees, the keep loomed before us — a colossal structure of dark stone and jagged spires, its architecture an embodiment of the maliciousness that had birthed it. The sight was imposing and intimidating, a testament to the power of the demon lord who ruled in the keep.

As we approached the massive fortress, my apprehension grew, the knowledge that the demon lord was undoubtedly lurking within those dark walls filling me with a sense of dread.

The air grew heavy and thick, a hostile aura permeating the surroundings. I could feel the dark energy pulsing all around us, a sinister presence that seemed to seep into the very ground beneath our feet. We paused just outside the keep, our gazes fixed upon its foreboding entrance. The enormity of our task settled upon me.

"We need a plan," I muttered, my mind racing as I considered the best course of action. "We can't just barge in there."

Kaelan's gaze locked onto mine, his expression was contemplative yet determined. "I've been in this keep before. I know a way to get us inside without raising too much suspicion."

My curiosity piqued, and I followed his lead as he guided us toward a small sewer drain hidden beneath a tangle of thorny vines. He climbed in before I could stop him. Sighing, I followed suit.

I followed him into the cramped darkness of the sewer tunnel. The smell was overpowering, but I stifled my discomfort, reminding myself of the greater goal at hand. The tunnel led us deeper, eventually opening into a larger chamber where four different pathways branched off.

Kaelan's eyes narrowed as he surveyed the options before him. "We need to move quickly and we can't afford any missteps. Make sure you stick close to me, no matter what."

He selected a path, his movements confident and purposeful, and I hastened to keep pace with him. The corridors twisted and turned, the oppressive atmosphere making it clear that we were indeed deep within the heart of the demon's lair.

As we navigated the labyrinthine sewers, I kept my wits about me, remaining alert and wary of potential threats. I couldn't shake the feeling that something was wrong.

Then, without warning, a deafening roar shook the walls, the sound sending a wave of dread crashing over me. It was the sound of something immense and powerful. Something that could not be contained. Something that would not hesitate to crush us like insects beneath its foot.

The roar echoed through the corridors, reverberating off the walls and shaking the very foundations of the keep. A chill ran down my spine, and a knot of fear tightened in the pit of my stomach. I knew without a doubt that whatever was making that noise was not a creature that should be trifled with.

I glanced at Kaelan, and the expression on his face told me he was thinking the same thing. He pressed a finger to his lips, signaling for me to remain silent. He pointed to a small grate at the base of the wall. I nodded, following him toward it. He opened it and we found a small side tunnel that we could both squeeze into.

Another roar rang out, closer now, the sound sending a wave of fear rippling through me. My heart pounded, and my palms were slick with sweat. I could feel the panic rising within me but I forced it back down.

The roaring grew louder and more intense. The sound was accompanied by the unmistakable sounds of claws scraping against stone.

I watched, my heart in my throat, as a monstrous beast prowled through the corridor just a few yards away. It was unlike any creature I had ever seen, a terrible amalgamation of scales and teeth and claws. Its hide was mottled and leathery, its head crowned with a row of vicious spikes.

Its eyes glowed with a cold, otherworldly light, and its nostrils flared as it scented the air, seeking its prey. It paused right where we hid and sniffed the air. I was sure we had been found.

Kaelan and I remained frozen, scarcely daring to breathe as the monster prowled past. When it was safely out of sight, we let out a collective sigh of relief.

As the monster's footsteps faded away, a heavy silence fell over the corridor. I glanced at Kaelan, the look on his face revealing his own fear. We had narrowly avoided a dangerous encounter, but the danger was not over.

I swallowed hard, my throat suddenly dry, and nodded at Kaelan, silently urging him to continue on. He took a deep breath and opened the grate, pushing back out into the main tunnel.

We kept going a ways, the tunnel twisting and turning as we walked deeper into the keep. We rounded a bend and suddenly were face to face with a group of demon guards. One of them sneered at Kaelan, its voice dripping with scorn. "Look who we have here, a princeling in the depths of our domain."

Princeling? I noted the insult and the weight it seemed to carry between Kaelan and these demons. His eyes flashed with anger as he turned to me. "Make a run for it, Vale. I'll catch up."

Without hesitation, I did as he instructed, my heart pounding in my ears as I raced down the corridor and up some stairs, the sounds of the demons' pursuit echoing behind me. But then, a sudden sensation washed over me, a disorienting wave that sent my thoughts spiraling into chaos.

My surroundings began to shift and warp, reality itself bending and contorting before my eyes. I stumbled forward, unable to make sense of what was happening. Time seemed to slow to a crawl, and every-thing around me appeared to be moving in slow motion. I felt like I was trapped in a dream, my limbs heavy and sluggish, my thoughts drifting through a fog of confusion. Shapes and shadows danced at the periphery of my vision, taunting and elusive.

I looked down at my hands and they started to melt. I panicked, backing up, and bumping into a wall oozing blood. The blood dripped down on my head and past my eyes, obscuring my vision further. The walls stretched and warped, and the floor seemed to undulate beneath my feet. I struggled to maintain my balance, fighting against the strange pull of the distorted world around me. I could hear the demons gaining ground, their snarls and hisses growing louder.

I had to get away, but what was I getting away from again? I tried to hold onto the thought but I kept slipping away as I grabbed at it.

My surroundings continued to morph and twist, the corridor now stretching into infinity, the ceiling impossibly high and the walls im-possibly far apart. I ran as fast as my legs could carry me, desperate to escape the madness that was closing in around me.

My breath came in ragged gasps, and my lungs burned as if on fire. My heart hammered in my chest, threatening to burst from its cage of bone and muscle. My vision blurred, and my ears rang with the cacophony of my own blood rushing through my veins.

I could hear the demons drawing closer, their foul voices now a constant presence, their taunts and jeers piercing the air. But I couldn't focus on them. I was spiraling deeper and deeper into a waking night-mare.

And then, through the haze of my hallucination, I caught sight of a shadowy form —a fox that seemed to glide effortlessly through the twisting corridors. Intrigued and guided by a strange intuition, I followed the spectral creature, its form leading me deeper into the darkness.

The shadow fox led me through the labyrinth of winding corridors, its movements graceful and deliberate while my own were clumsy from the haze clouding my mind. My heart raced, each step bringing me closer to an unknown destination. As we ventured deeper into the heart of the keep, a sense of unease settled over me, the unnaturalness of the place becoming more pronounced with every passing moment.

Finally, the shadow creature brought me to a dimly lit chamber, but my attention was immediately drawn to the figure seated against an old, worn door—Kaelan, his leg wounded and his expression pained. He was bleeding, and I knew immediately that the injury was serious.

I knelt by his side, the strange haze slowly clearing from my mind, and the gravity of the situation becoming clearer. "What happened?"

He grimaced, his voice strained as he spoke. "Not as bad as it looks. But the demons are close. We need to open this door or we'll be captured."

I followed his gaze to the door, a sense of familiarity washing over me as I recognized the blood magic emanating from it. My mind raced as I considered our options, the urgency of the situation pressing upon us. The sounds of approaching demons grew louder, their footsteps echoing down the corridor.

I hesitated, unsure of how to proceed. Time was running out, and the pressure weighed heavily on me. With desperate resolve, I reached for the door handle, my fingers trembling as I attempted to open it. But nothing happened, the door remained stubbornly closed.

Panic threatened to consume me as the demons drew closer, their presence a looming threat we could not afford to ignore. In a moment of desperation, I turned to Kaelan, and an idea formed in my head. Without hesitation, I pricked my finger on the sharp fang of my teeth, allowing a small bead of blood to well up. Kaelan's eyes widened slightly at the sight.

I touched the blood to the surface of the door, and to my astonishment, the door responded. It swung open willingly, revealing a passage beyond. Kaelan's gaze met mine, relief and admiration in his eyes.

"Quickly," he urged his voice tight with pain. "We don't have much time."

Together, we wasted no time. With Kaelan leaning on me for support, we entered the hidden passage, leaving behind the demons who were hot on our heels. The door closed behind us with an eerie finality, the echoes of the demon keep fading into the distance.

Chapter Nine

T he passage stretched out before us, a hidden conduit through the darkness that seemed to promise escape from the clutches of the demon keep. With Kaelan leaning heavily on me, we pressed forward, our steps echoing softly against the stone walls. The air was thick with tension, the only other sounds were our labored breathing.

As we journeyed deeper into the heart of the passage, I could see the lingering effects of the poison that had tipped the edges of the demon's blades, the slow insidious drag it exerted on Kaelan's once-rapid healing. I cast worried glances at him, my concern a tangible presence that hovered between us.

"Are you holding up?" I whispered my voice empathetic.

Kealan's breaths were ragged, his features etched with pain and determination. "I've endured worse," he replied, his tone tinged with a hint of wry amusement.

The passage eventually gave way to a new space, and my heart skipped and beat as we emerged into the heart of a library —a realm of knowledge nestled within the shadows of the demon keep. The library that stretched out before us was a breathtaking sanctuary of knowledge. Illuminated by a soft, eerie glow emanating from enchanted lanterns suspended from the ceiling, it seemed like a realm suspended between the mortal world and the arcane.

The shelves that lined the walls reached up to towering heights, disappearing into obscurity in the dimly lit upper reaches of the chamber. These shelves were laden with an incredible assortment of texts, scrolls, parchments, and ancient leather-bound tomes, their spines worn and their pages yellowed with age. The air carried a musty scent, a testament to the countless years of accumulated wisdom and forgotten lore.

"Harker would love this," I said with awe.

Tables and worn seats offered quiet refuge amidst the towering stacks, and I guided Kaelan to one of the seats, helping him lower himself carefully. The weight of our recent trials pressed upon us, but the sense of accomplishment in finding the library gave us a glimmer of respite.

Kaelan's weary expression mirrored my own as he settled into the seat, his focus shifting to our surroundings. "So, what now?" I said, casting a concerned glance at his ruined leg.

He cast a thoughtful look around, his voice steady despite the pain he was under. "We need to find the exit. Pocket realms like this usually have one we just have to search for it."

Before I could reply, a voice pierced the air. "That is not always necessarily the case, because right now this one has no exit."

Startled Kaelan and I exchanged wide-eyed glances, our senses on high alert as we tried to locate the source of the mysterious voice. It seemed to reverberate through the air.

And then, as if from the very walls themselves, a figure emerged —a spectral presence that sent a jolt of shock through me. "Holy shit," I uttered, disbelief coloring my voice.

Before us stood the ghostly figure of a woman, her appearance ethereal yet unmistakable. "Who are you?" I managed to squeak out, astonished.

"My name? Oh, it's…" She paused as if searching her memory, "Oh! It's Elara!" She finished triumphantly. Her tone took on a more regal air, "I am the guardian of this library, tasked with preserving its treasures."

Kaelan's brow furrowed with questions. "You're a spirit?" I glanced over at him incredulously at the obvious answer.

"I am, I am the guardian of this library, tasked with preserving its treasures." She repeated.

I raised an eyebrow and glanced at Kaelan again. "You already said that part." I told her.

"Oh, I did? Oh, that's no good." She said fisting handfuls of her hair. After a few moments, she stopped and looked down at me with a smile. This ghost was definitely not all there.

Kaelan and I exchanged bemused glances, a mix of emotions stirring within us. It was an unexpected turn of events.

"Elara," I began hesitantly. "You said something about how this library has no exit. What did you mean by that?"

"Oh, well when you came in the door locked behind you, disappearing from its anchor point in the keep. You'll have to make another one out." She said, matter-of-factly like I just made doors appear every day.

"And how do I do that?" I asked her.

"Oh. Well…you could ask the books," she replied.

"Ask…the books?" Kaelan said hesitantly from his chair.

"Of course! Ask the books and the books will tell you. Wait...are you a demon? Oh, this is bad, the demons weren't supposed to get in here." Elara began floating back and forth between us, pacing I guessed. "Not good at all, Elara, not good at all." She began muttering to herself.

"Well, I can tell she's going to be a great help," Kaelan said, rolling his eyes.

Elara's ethereal presence seemed to flicker with a sense of eccentricity that was hard to ignore, leaving us both intrigued and uncertain of the depths of her knowledge. As she suggested we "ask the books" for help, it became evident that her assistance might be less straightforward than I initially hoped.

Kaelan shifted his weight uncomfortably, his injured leg worsening. I could see the toll the poison was taking on him, his once-proud demeanor now overshadowed by a hint of vulnerability. "We should start looking around."

Elara drifted away towards the rows of books, muttering quietly to herself.

I nodded, my focus returning to his leg, which had begun to fester ominously. The urgency in his voice spurred me into action. I knelt beside him, examining the wound with concern. "You're right, Kaelan. We can't afford to waste time."

As I inspected his wound, I couldn't help but feel a pang of frustration. We were surrounded by books —ancient tomes that held the secrets of countless spells and incantations— and yet, we were at a loss for where to start. Elara's guidance to "ask the books" left me feeling a bit bewildered, unsure of exactly how to proceed.

"Maybe she's not speaking literally," Kaelan offered, his voice laced with discomfort. "Perhaps there's a specific book we need to find."

I considered his words, realizing the possibility that Elara's guidance might be more straightforward than metaphorical. With a determined nod, I stood up and approached one of the shelves, scanning the spines and trying to decipher their potential relevance to our predicament.

"I think I've got it," I murmured to myself, spotting a book that seemed to stand out from the rest. I grabbed the tome and opened it to a page in the middle, staring down at the words. "Can you show me a spell to heal demon poison?" I felt a sudden shift in the air as a book tumbled from the shelf and landed at my feet. I couldn't help but chuckle at the absurdity of the situation. "Well, that's convenient."

Kaelan's gaze followed my movements as I retrieved the fallen book and opened it, revealing the pages within. It didn't take long for my eyes to find the passage that held the answer we sought — a way to use my blood magic to heal Kaelan. However, one detail left me puzzled, and I turned to Elara with a questioning glance. "It says here that he needs to 'take some of my blood.' What does that mean?"

Elara's eyes sparkled with a mischievous glint as she responded, "Oh well, it's quite simple. He needs to drink some of your blood, of course."

My eyebrows shot up in surprise, my gaze shifting to Kaelan. The idea seemed both bizarre and strangely intimate, yet desperation fueled our need for a solution. Turning back to Elara, I took a deep breath and nodded. "Right. Thank you." It seemed prudent to thank the ghost.

With newfound determination, I closed the book and returned to Kaelan's side. "It's not ideal but it might be our only option." I met his gaze, my voice filled with resolve. "Are you up for it?"

Kaelan's hesitation was palpable, his internal struggle written across his features. "It's not as easy as you might think, Vale. I could easily end up hurting you. And this, it means something different to me than it does to you. Blood sharing shouldn't be taken lightly."

I could sense the depth of his conflict, the intimate significance of the act combined with the potential danger it posed. Yet, as I looked into his eyes, I knew that there was no other way out of this predicament. His leg needed to heal, and my blood held the key to that solution.

"Kaelan, I know it's not a great solution," I began softly, my voice shaking despite my calm demeanor. "But we don't have a choice. We're both trapped here, and we need each other's help to find a way out. I can't do this alone."

He met my gaze, his turmoil evident, and for a moment, it seemed he might refuse. "Alright." He said finally.

I took out one of my knives, and carefully sliced open a portion of my wrist, Kaelan's gaze remained fixed on the crimson liquid welling up. I held my wrist out to him, offering a lifeline that bridged the gap between us. Still, he hesitated, clearly conflicted. "It's just a little blood, Kaelan, it's really not a big deal."

With trepidation, he leaned forward, his lips brushing against my skin as he tentatively took the offered blood. The sensation was both intimate and strangely surreal, a connection forged through the ancient magic that flowed through me.

I could feel my blood magic flowing into him, strengthening him, and a surge of power coursed through me, igniting my instincts. My heart pounded in my ears, adrenaline flooded my veins, and a strange heat blossomed in my core.

Without warning, he pulled back, his eyes alight with an almost wild expression, his voice barely a whisper. "More."

My own breath quickened, his desire a tangible presence that hung between us. I was caught off guard, unprepared for the intensity of his response. "Kaelan," I said softly, "are you okay?"

"I need more." His voice was almost a growl, his body trembling with restraint. I could feel his control slipping, his instincts threatening to overwhelm him.

I stared at him for a moment, trying to understand the depth of his need, and the intensity of his reaction. He seemed almost like a different person, his primal urges driving him.

Without warning, he reached out and grabbed my arm, pulling me closer, his grip strong. A shudder ran through me, the air thick with anticipation and uncertainty.

I was powerless to resist, my body responding instinctively to his touch. The heat within me intensified, spreading through my limbs and igniting a fire deep in my belly.

"Kaelan," I said his name breathlessly, a soft gasp escaping my lips. He didn't respond, his focus fixed on my wrist, his mouth drawing deeply from the wound.

My mind raced, trying to process the intensity of the situation, the danger of it. His eyes flashed up at me, filled with hunger and a dark intensity.

"Kaelan, stop," I urged, my voice shaking. But he seemed lost in a blood-induced trance.

Desperation surged within me, and I raised my voice, calling out to him once more. "Kaelan, stop! You're taking too much!"

Finally, his head snapped up, his eyes wide and completely dark, filled with a look of confusion that shifted slowly to realization. He pulled away, breaking the connection, and we both stared at each other, breathless and shaken.

For a moment, silence hung in the air between us, the weight of what had transpired settling over us. Kealan's leg began to heal before our eyes, the wound closing and mending, a testament to the potent nature of my blood magic.

As the healing magic took effect, Kaelan's dark eyes still stared into mine, his expression one of pure guilt. His words came out in a broken whisper, filled with shame.

"I'm so sorry, Vale."

"It's okay, I'm fine," I assured him, my voice steady despite the rapid beating of my heart.

"Never again." He said gravely, his expression darkening. "You're never doing that for me again."

The aftermath of the blood sharing left us both slightly shaken, our emotions and vulnerabilities laid bare. My breath came a bit quicker than usual, the blood loss affecting me more than I anticipated.

The cut on my wrist was already starting to heal, I wrapped it with a strip of gauze I had in my waist bag. I leaned against one of the nearby shelves, a bit unsteady on my feet, and met Kaelan's gaze once more. He had been watching me with that guilty look on his face.

I'd deal with that later, right now we needed a door out of this place. With a renewed sense of purpose, I called out, "Elara? You still here somewhere?"

To my surprise, the ghostly figure of Elara shimmered into view once again.

"Well, what happened here?" Elara chimed, looking between the two of us, her voice carrying a sing-song quality. "Oh you healed the demon, I wasn't expecting that. That was a pretty risky move, everyone knows how tasty demons think witches' blood is."

"It was your idea!" I retorted, throwing my hands up and rolling my eyes.

"Oh, dear, yes well, always a price to pay, isn't there?" She started to turn as if she had completely forgotten we were even there.

"Wait!" I called out. She stopped and turned back around, a confused look in her eye. "I have questions. Why was this library created?"

Elara's spectral form seemed to shimmer with a touch of solemnity, her memories perhaps surfacing through the layers of her long ethereal existence. "The library, my dear, was created to safeguard the most crucial knowledge and magic for the eventual return of the First Witch. It holds the threads of our legacy, preserving the arcane secrets that would ensure our resurgence."

"The First Witch?" I asked, hoping I didn't already know the answer.

"The first witch reborn, the first witch to come. You." She answered, tilting her head to the side curiously. There was such a sense of finality in her words that I shuddered, remembering the line that Harker had shown me.

"And who were the creators?" I pressed.

"The coven known as The Seven," Elara responded, her voice carrying a hint of reverence. "Each member was a paragon of power and wisdom. They saw the storm on the horizon and sought to ensure that even in the darkest times, the light of our craft would endure."

Kaelan's gaze remained fixed on Elara, his expression one of fascination and curiosity. "And what can I find in here, exactly?" I asked.

Elara's form seemed to shimmer with an almost mischievous air as if she were privy to a grand secret. "Everything you require, my dear. Incantations, ancient spells, and rituals, it's a reservoir of power waiting to be tapped. Our greatest secret."

As Elara spoke, I couldn't help but feel a sense of awe and anticipation. The library held the key to a source of knowledge that could potentially tip the scales in my favor.

But there were other matters at hand before I delved into all that had been left for me. With determination, I turned my attention to the towering shelves of books that surrounded us. Taking a deep breath, I addressed the library itself in a clear voice, "I need information on how to create a doorway out of here and back to the mortal realm."

As if in response to my request, the air seemed to shimmer with a subtle energy, and three books thumped to the ground in front of the shelves they had been sitting on. Kaelan and I exchanged a glance, that would take some getting used to. Moving cautiously, we reached out and took hold of the books.

"I'll look through these two, you look through that one," Kaelan said, sitting back down in a chair. I sighed and sat down as well. How was I ever going to sift through all this knowledge? It would take a hundred years to read it all.

The words and symbols danced before our eyes as we poured over the pages, looking for anything that would help us. The urgency of the situation seemed to fuel our focus, though Kaelan kept glancing up at me from his books.

Amidst the sea of information, his voice finally broke the silence. "I think I've hit a roadblock, here." He murmured, his gaze fixed on a particular passage.

"What do you mean," I asked, scooting over to better see the book he had open.

"It says here that after we create the door, we need to anchor it to a specific point in a realm. Just like how it was anchored here for all these years."

I raised an eyebrow, confused. "Anchor it? To where my place?"

Kaelan's eyes met mine, his expression thoughtful. "Your apartment won't do. It's not warded, and anyone could stumble upon the door, including the demons who are after you. And now that you've broken the blood magic ward that was placed on the door, I'm sure they'd be able to get in."

I considered his words, nodding in understanding. "So, where then?"

A faint smile tugged at the corner of his lips. "How about my house?"

I blinked in surprise, not expecting his response. "You have a house?"

Kaelan's gaze was sad for a moment. "It used to belong to witches, before...well, before they were found and murdered. I've been taking care of it since. And it's warded against detection, it's safe."

As his words sank in, I couldn't help but feel curious. Kaelan's past, his connection to the witches, took on new layers of complexity. And here he was, offering a solution that could potentially save us both. The secrets of his past took on new hues, each shade revealing a facet of his character I hadn't previously fathomed.

We returned to the task at hand, searching the pages of the tomes for elusive instructions that would help us create the door. After what felt like an eternity of scanning text and deciphering cryptic passages, I finally came across the passage we needed.

"I think I've found it," I said, my voice laced with excitement and relief. I quickly read aloud the steps we needed to take. "We have to draw a new door with chalk, anoint it with blood magic, so I'm guessing more of my blood, concentrate on the anchor point, and then knock three times." I guessed spells didn't have to be complicated for them to work.

Kaelan's attention was immediately drawn as I explained the process. With a sense of urgency, we gathered the necessary materials, which Elara found for us in a desk drawer, and moved to a clear space on the wall.

As I prepared to draw the door Kaelan began to describe his house in vivid detail. His words painted a picture of a grand white manor nestled deep within a sprawling forest, standing elegant but solitary. I could see it as he spoke, almost like he cast his own spell.

As you approached along a meandering gravel path, the manor gradually emerges from the verdant tapestry of towering trees.

It boasted a two-story facade, its white walls standing in stark contrast to the vibrant greens of the surrounding flora. Imposing columns frame the entrance. The symmetrical design of the manor lends a send of balance and poise to the structure, while its large grand windows reflect the dappled sunlight. A sprawling veranda wraps around the front of the manor, and sturdy balustrades adorned with intricate carvings line the edges.

His detailed description allowed me to focus my concentration on the intended anchor point, channeling my energy and intention into the magic we were about to perform.

With the chalk in hand, I began to sketch the outline of a door on the stone wall. Once the door was complete, I pricked my finger, allowing a few drops of blood to fall on the outline. The surface seemed to shimmer briefly in response. And then, together, we knocked three times.

For a heartbeat, uncertainty hung in the air, the library around us holding its breath as if caught between realms. But then, responding to my conjured magic, the chalk outline began to glow, its light spreading and expanding until it took on the form of a plain wooden door.

I reached out, my hand trembling slightly as I gripped the doorknob. A surge of apprehension washed over me —had we succeeded? Was this truly our escape, or had something gone wrong?

With a deep breath, I turned the knob and pulled the door open.

Before us stretched a hallway, bathed in soft illumination. The walls were adorned with ornate tapestries, and the air carried a sense of comfort and safety that contrasted starkly with the perilous realm we had just left behind.

Kaelan and I exchanged a glance, our eyes meeting in silent affirmation. We had done it. The door had materialized, and on the other side lay the passage to Kaelan's house —our sanctuary, our escape.

Chapter Ten

As we stepped through the threshold of the portal, the transition from the spectral library to the tangible world of Kaelan'shouse was accompanied by a sense of grounding relief. Night had fallen and the moonlight cast an ethereal glow on the hallway that stretched before us. The chill of the evening air was a soothing balm, washing over me.

The door clicked shut behind us, sealing our connection to the library. In its wake, I found myself standing in Kaelan'shouse, my senses reeling from the whirlwind of events we had experienced. As I stepped into the hallway from the portal, I was immediately struck by the sense of history that permeated every corner of the residence.

The hallway itself was wide and inviting, its walls adorned with ornate, antique wallpaper that had aged gracefully over the years. The moonlight streaming in through tall, arched windows cast a soft, ethereal glow that accentuated the intricate patterns of the wallpaper. The windows were framed by heavy, velvet curtains, which added to the old-world charm of the house.

Kaelan's voice, with its underlying warmth and invitation, pulled my focus back to the present. "Would you like to stay the night? It's a little ways back to the city, and I can't shift you there in my state."

The offer caught me by surprise, my mind racing as I considered the implications. Was it simply a practical suggestion, or was there something more behind it? I tried to gauge his intentions, searching his expression for a hint of what lay beneath the surface.

But his gaze was steady, betraying no sign of anything but the desire to extend a basic courtesy. After all, we were both exhausted and would benefit from a night of rest before we made our way back to the city in the morning.

It was the logical choice, yet somehow, I found myself hesitating, my mind filled with doubts and uncertainties.

Before I could give it too much thought, the words spilled from my lips. "Yes, thank you."Kaelan's answering smile was a flash of fangs. "I just need to give Wren a call first."

"Of course, take all the time you need," he replied, gesturing for me to follow him into a grand living room.

I pulled out my phone and dialed Wren's number, my nerves thrumming with anxiety as I waited for him to pick up. The familiar voice of my friend greeted me through the connection, the sound of it instantly bringing a sense of relief.

"Vale, where are you?" Wren asked, concern lacing his tone. "I've been worried sick about you. Did you find the library?"

I gave him a quick rundown of the day's events, leaving out the more intimate details, like healing Kaelan.

Wren's sigh was audible. "You had me worried. But I'm glad you're okay. So are you coming home then?"

"I am. But not yet, I'm staying the night at Kaelan's." The words sounded strange as they left my lips, but Wren didn't miss a beat.

"Oh, I see." There was a hint of amusement in his voice. "So you'll be having fun spending the night at the hot demon's house, huh?" Wren's mischievous tone added a playful edge to his response.

Color rose to my cheeks, caught off guard by the suggestive remark. I caught Kaelan's eye, a smirk playing on his lips, and realized he could hear everything Wren was saying. "Okay, that's enough Wren, gotta go bye," I said quickly before he had another chance to say anything. I hung up the phone and glanced at Kaelan. "Oh, don't let it go to your head." I retorted and his smirk deepened.

He chuckled, amusement dancing in his eyes. It had become evident that beneath his dark and mysterious exterior lay a touch of lightheartedness, a quality I hadn't fully anticipated.

"How about I prepare some food for us? I'm sure you could use something warm to eat, especially after..." he paused and cleared his throat, clearly nervous about something. "After you gave me your blood."

A wave of embarrassment swept over me at the reminder of our shared intimacy, the memory of his lips against my skin and the feel of his tongue caressing my wound. The intensity of it lingered in the air between us, palpable and raw.

Kaelan averted his gaze, his discomfort evident, and the tension in the room intensified.

I broke the silence, trying to bring us back to the present. "Food sounds good. But you don't have to cook, don't go through all that trouble just for me." I said, though I wasn't sure if I was trying to be polite or whether I was feeling anxious about the thought of sharing a meal with him.

"I insist, besides, I'm sure you must be starving after such an eventful day. You can wait here if you want, or you can follow me and keep me company in the kitchen." He said, gesturing towards the hallway. I nodded, following him wordlessly.

The warm glow of Kaelan's kitchen embraced us as we stepped into its comforting confines. The soft glow of the gas lamps he lit cast fleeting shadows on the walls that seemed to dance. The scent of lavender and lemon, a simple yet inviting aroma, enveloped the room as Kaelan moved with fluid grace, gathering the necessary ingredients.

"I have some leftover soup and bread from a previous meal. It won't be a grand feast, but I hope it suffices," Kealan's voice carried a note of gentle reassurance as he prepared the meal. His hands moved with easy familiarity.

"Would you like a drink? Although, I haven't got anything besides maple whiskey and water." He asked as he placed the soup bowls on the counter.

I hesitated, then nodded. Maybe a drink would help me relax.

Kaelan grabbed two glasses and poured a generous amount of whiskey into each one, before offering one to me.

The amber liquid was smooth and mellow, the taste of whiskey spreading through my mouth, leaving a warm, lingering sensation in its wake. I took a deep breath, trying to ease the tension that had settled in the pit of my stomach. His movements were efficient, betraying an inherent skill that belied the effortless elegance with which he cooked. I watched as he sliced the bread, his hands working with a practiced precision that was both efficient and precise.

A sudden warmth spread across my face as I caught myself staring, and I averted my gaze, my attention turning to the surroundings instead. I scanned the room, admiring the rustic beauty of the decor. The old, oak table, the wooden countertop, and the brick walls adorned with copper pans and pots made it all feel so quaint and cozy.

The scent of the soup wafted through the air, filling the space with its aroma. I inhaled deeply, allowing the fragrance to carry me away, my senses reveling in the simple pleasure.

As the soup simmered in a small pot, Kaelan and I settled into the rhythm of conversation, recounting the events that had transpired within the spectral library and the monumental task that lay ahead—the daunting endeavor of deciphering the wealth of knowledge that had been dropped at my feet.

"How in the seven realms are you planning to tackle all of that?" He questioned me.

Leaning back against the kitchen counter, I allowed my thoughts to unfurl, the weight of the task ahead not lost on me. "I have an idea. There's someone I know, a vampire named Harker. She's incredibly knowledgeable and might be willing to help me. It won't be easy, but it's a start."

As the meal was ready, we settled into companionable silence. I savored each spoonful of the hearty soup, the flavors a soothing balm to both body and soul. Kaelan's watchful gaze did not escape my notice, his eyes tracing the contours of my face with a quiet intensity that stirred something within me.

With a contented sigh, I placed the empty bowl before me. As my gaze lifted to meet his, a subtle heat colored my cheeks. Kaelan smiled a slow, lazy grin that sent a shiver of anticipation through me. He sipped at his drink, his eyes never leaving mine. The silence that had settled between us was both intimate and charged, the air thick with the undercurrent of unspoken emotions.

"Would you like to be shown to the guest rooms?" Kaelan's question, posed with a gentle tone, was met with a nod of affirmation.

He led the way through the hallways of his house, our footsteps whispers against the still night. The guest room he showed me to exuded an air of tranquility, the soft illumination casting a warm embrace using the space.

The room was spacious, with high ceilings adorned with delicate, intricate moldings that spoke of the craftsmanship of a bygone era. The walls were adorned with vintage floral-patterned wallpaper that had aged gracefully, lending the room a timeless appeal. In the soft moonlight that filtered through the lace curtains, the patterns seemed to come alive, casting subtle shadows that danced across the room.

A large, four-poster bed with a canopy dominated the center of the room. The bed was draped in sumptuous, deep-colored fabrics, giving it an air of regal elegance. The headboard was intricately carved with floral motifs, a testament to the artistry of the past.

As we stood in the threshold of the room, an unspoken tension lingered between Kaelan and me. Our gazes met, a current passing between us. Kaelan's voice, a gentle murmur, broke the silence that hung in the air.

"Vale," he began, his tone concerned, "about what happened in the library. Sharing your blood with me was reckless. You can't afford to take such risks."

I met his gaze, my brow furrowing slightly as I processed his words. The gravity of our actions in that moment weighed upon me, the implications of blood magic and its intimate significance threading through my thoughts. "What did you mean by what you said? That the blood sharing would mean different things to either of us." I inquired, a note of curiosity mingling with the traces of embarrassment that danced within me.

Kaelan's eyes held a depth of understanding, his response measured and composed. "In the realm of demons, as well as in the realm of the fae, blood sharing is a deeply intimate act, reserved for lovers. It holds significance beyond the mere exchange of power. To demons, it's a binding of souls, an act of vulnerability and trust."

A blush tinged my cheeks, the realization of the cultural nuances of both realms washing over me. I nodded, the intensity of his gaze igniting a mix of emotions within me. "I understand. But it was a necessary risk. Given the circumstances, we did what we had to do."

Kaelan's agreement echoed through his nod, his eyes searching mine for a fleeting moment before he turned to leave. Yet, an invisible thread seemed to tether him to the space between us, his hesitation palpable. His hand rose, tucking a single strand of my hair behind my ear with a touch so gentle it sent shivers down my spine. His fingertips trailed along my cheek, the sensation a tantalizing dance upon my skin.

And then, in the breathless space between heartbeats, his lips captured mine in a fervent kiss. The world around us fell away, replaced by the dizzying rush of sensations that pulsed between us. The kiss was an explosion of emotions, a whirlwind of desires and tensions that had been building up inside us since the moment we first met.

Time seemed to stretch, the touch of his lips kindling a passion inside me that blazed with a fierce intensity. My fingers curled into his soft black hair and his hands roamed my body freely, moving to cup my backside.

The kiss was a powerful force that swept us away, an intoxicating combination of passion and desire that engulfed us wholly. Kaelan's lips moved against mine with a purposeful fervor, each touch threatening to carry me away. My head spun with the taste of him, stirring an aching deep within me. The more I had, the hungrier I grew for more, consumed by this potent elixir.

His fingers, warm and possessive, traced a trail down the curve of my neck, sending shivers of anticipation in their wake. With a gentle yet insistent touch, he pulled me closer, his body pressed against mine in an intimate embrace that erased any distance between us. The air seemed to thicken, heavy with the weight of unspoken emotions that hung between our shared breaths.

As the kiss grew wilder, a current of electricity surged through me. The fire within me burned hotter with every pounding heartbeat. Our tongues moved in a seamless rhythm, a dance of passion and vulnerability that spoke volumes without a single word. I lost myself in the sensation, allowing the world around us to blur into insignificance as the boundaries that separated our bodies dissolved.

His scent, a tantalizing mix of woodsmoke and maple whiskey, surrounded me. The touch of his fingertips, trailing along my jawline and down the curve of my spine, ignited sparks on my skin. A soft, almost imperceptible moan escaped my lips, a testament to the overwhelming intensity of the moment.

He pushed me back against the bedroom door roughly and I let out a small gasp at the unexpected movement. He ran his hand up my leg and lifted it to his waist letting out a low growl as I ground my hips into his. I could feel the hard length of him through his pants. "Naughty girl." he purred. I felt myself shiver at the sound of his voice, and I arched my neck to give him better access. His teeth grazed my neck in response, his tongue lapping at the small scratch they left there.

My hands reached for the buttons on his shirt, but he grabbed them in one hand and pulled away. His eyes were dark with desire and I felt like I was melting under his gaze.

I gave up trying to reach for the buttons and instead slid my fingers over his chest, tracing the outline of his muscles, the rise and fall of his breaths. I leaned forward and pressed my lips to his neck, sucking lightly. He growled, and his hand tangled in my hair, tugging my head back gently so I was looking at him.

"Vale," My name sounded like pure sin on his lips. He kissed me again and I realized he must have been holding back before because this kiss was wild and rough. Our tongues came together, tasting each other, exploring. I felt his hand slide down and grab my breast, squeezing it gently. I moaned into his mouth as I felt his finger brush against my nipple. He sucked my lower lip between his teeth and bit gently. I gasped, and he released my mouth. "I'm not going to stop unless you beg me to." He said, and I breathlessly nodded my consent.

He stepped back and I saw the hunger in his eyes. He unbuttoned his shirt, letting it fall open, revealing his muscled torso. I leaned forward and traced my tongue over his collarbone, and then down the valley between his pecs. He let out a low groan when I licked around his nipple, circling it with my tongue. I heard him groan again, louder this time, and he pulled me tighter against him.

I looked up at him, and he smiled a wicked grin, watching me intently. "Do you have any idea what I've wanted to do to you?" he asked, his voice husky. In one fluid movement, he picked me up and slung my legs around his waist, carrying me to the large four-poster bed. "You're so beautiful," he said as he gently laid me down and dropped to his knees before me. He pulled off my shirt and let it fall to the floor, exposing my breasts to his hungry gaze. He ran his thumb over my peaked nipple, teasing me until I cried out.

He smirked and then leaned forward and took my nipple into his mouth, sucking hungrily. I moaned, arching my back. He switched to the other side, biting it playfully, before trailing kisses down the slope of my stomach. He unhooked the button of my jeans and slid them down past my knees and then over my feet, dropping those to the floor as well. He grabbed my leg in his hands and began kissing the skin at my ankle trailing up, up, up until he got to my inner thigh, he stopped for a moment and looked up at me, smirking. I almost came undone at that heated look.

He slid his finger down the very center of me and I arched my head back. "So wet for me already." He purred.

Hooking his fingers down the front, he quickly slid my panties off. I held my breath, waiting for what would happen next. I felt him push my legs apart draping one leg over his shoulder, and then he was kissing me there, his tongue swirling in circles as he devoured me. "You taste even better than I imagined, witch," he whispered against me.

I whimpered softly as he sucked my clit between his lips and he chuckled in response, his hot breath tickling my skin. He slid a finger inside of me and I gasped. He pushed it in and out slowly, flicking his tongue over that sensitive bundle of nerves.

I ground into his face as he crooked his finger upward hitting just the right spot and sending shock waves rippling through my body. I cried out as he slid another finger in, stretching me slightly. He started moving his fingers faster, harder. I writhed against his hand and mouth and he groaned, his fingers still curling inside of me.

I felt my body tensing, felt my release rising, and I moaned again, jerking wildly. "That's it, Vale. Fuck my hand." He said, his voice husky. I threaded my fingers through his hair, gripping tightly as my body went higher and higher. "Come for me."

He pushed his tongue against my clit and I broke apart.

"Oh gods, Kaelan!" I cried out through my release. My head kicked back as I let out a strangled gasp. It shot through me like a lightning bolt, radiating outward from my center. I gasped, eyes clenched shut, muscles spasming in ecstasy. I felt as if I were floating, my mind and body filled with a kind of bliss that I'd never experienced before. I felt Kaelan's hands still on my hips, his mouth still circling me, and all I could do was whisper his name in a ragged voice.

The bed creaked as he rose to move over the top of me, his arms holding his weight as he leaned down to kiss me. I could still taste myself on his lips as he dipped his tongue in my mouth. He tasted like a perfect mix of desire and temptation, and I could feel myself melting into him, succumbing to the pleasure of his mouth on mine.

"You are absolutely mouth-watering, little witch," he whispered against my lips before pulling away.

I stared up at him through my lashes breathlessly, captivated by the intense desire in his eyes. His gaze smoldered with passion and I felt my heart quickening in my chest as he stared down at me.

I wanted nothing more than to give in, to surrender myself to the sweet, dark pleasure of his touch, but the rational part of me was screaming to put on the brakes. I was playing with fire and I knew it. This was not what I came here for, but how could I resist him? How could anyone?

He shifted off of me and got up, reaching down for his shirt. I propped myself up on my elbows. "Where are you going?" I asked incredulously.

"I think it's best that you get some rest now, Vale." He said kissing me softly.

"You won't stay?" And maybe continue where the night left off. I thought to myself.

"Not tonight," he said softly, catching my chin in his hand and caressing my bottom lip. "After the day we've had we both need the rest."

I sighed. He was right, of course. Today had been eventful, and I was exhausted. I was sure he was as well, though he didn't seem to show it.

With a nod, he turned and walked toward the door, and I didn't stop him. The moment the door closed behind him, I fell back onto the pillow, my head swimming with everything that had happened. My thoughts lingered on the memory of his kiss, the heat of his skin against mine.

I couldn't believe what had just transpired between us. A few days ago, I would never have imagined being in such a position, alone with him in this room. Even a few hours ago, it would have seemed impossible. But now, lying here, still flushed and aching from his touch, I couldn't deny the desire that burned within me. I closed my eyes and took a deep breath, willing myself to calm down.

Later as I lay staring up at the ceiling I still wasn't sure if I should have stopped him from leaving or not. But it was too late to go after him now.

With a sigh, I rolled over and closed my eyes, willing sleep to come. As I drifted off, I thought back to his words earlier, and the way his gaze had captured mine. "You are absolutely mouth-watering, little witch." Those words echoed in my head long after sleep had taken me.

Chapter Eleven

Sunlight filtered through the curtains, casting a warm golden glow over the guest bedroom as I stirred from sleep. The lingering traces of dreams faded, replaced by the reality of a new day. With a languid stretch, I rose from the comfortable bed and quickly dressed.

Stepping out of the bedroom and into the hallway, I followed the inviting aroma that led me to the kitchen. A delectable display welcomed me at the scene: Kaelan stood in the midst of a range of ingredients, skillfully preparing a wonderful breakfast. The sizzle of bacon, the rich aroma of brewing coffee, and the clatter of utensils combined into a harmonious chorus that seemed to chase away the remnants of the previous night's trials.

"Good morning," Kaelan greeted me with a warm smile, his eyes alight with a playful glint. He was obviously a morning person. "I thought a proper breakfast might help make up for last night's less-than-stellar dinner."

I smiled, taking a seat at the table. "Well, I appreciate the effort. This looks amazing." I spread butter on a biscuit fresh from the oven and took a bite.

He placed a plate piled high with eggs, bacon, sausage, and biscuits in front of me, and I couldn't help but marvel at the spread. As we dug into the meal, conversation flowed naturally between us.

"So, what's the plan for today?" Kaelan asked between bites.

I paused with my fork halfway to my mouth. "Honestly, I'm not entirely sure. I want to go visit Harker and see if she'd be willing to help me sort through everything we found in the library. It's a monumental task, and I could use all the help I can get."

Kaelan nodded thoughtfully. "Sounds like a good idea. I can shift you back to your apartment so you and Wren can go talk to her."

I arched an eyebrow, a playful smile tugging at my lips. "And what about you? What will you be up to today?"

He grinned, a mischievous glint dancing in his eyes. "Oh, you know, just typical demon things. I might cause a little chaos here and there, stir up some trouble."

I rolled my eyes with a chuckle. "Right, of course. Have fun with that."

As we finished our breakfast and cleared the dishes, a sense of ease settled between us. It was as though the weight of our respective worlds had temporarily lifted, allowing us to simply be present in the moment.

With a glance at Kaelan, I stood up from the table. "Alright, ready to shift me back?"

"There is just something I need to do first," he said, coming to stand in front of me.

"What—" My words were stopped by his sudden kiss. Unlike the fervent kisses we had shared last night, this one was gentle and teasing, but it still made my toes curl in my boots. The familiar sensation of heat ached low in my belly as his lips moved against mine.

He pulled back and stared down at me with a small smile, his hands still resting on either side of my face. "That was just in case."

"Just in case what?" I asked, smiling ruefully.

"Just in case you forgot how intoxicating you are," he answered playfully. "Close your eyes."

I closed my eyes and felt the now familiar sensation of shadows enveloping me, the world around me shifting and warping. When I opened my eyes once more, we were back in the familiar surroundings of my apartment. The transition was seamless, and I looked up at Kaelan with a grateful smile.

"Well, you two look cozy." I looked over at the werewolf on the couch, who was grinning like a fool, and rolled my eyes. Still, I took a step back from Kaelan who was looking at Wren through narrowed eyes.

I turned back to Kaelan and he placed a finger under my chin, angling my head up to look at him. "Good luck today," he said softly.

As he spoke those words, his gaze seemed to hold a hint of something more, a depth of emotion that stirred a subtle flutter within me. But before I could decipher it, the moment passed, and Kaelan's form wavered, dissolving into the shadows as he shifted away.

Wren let out a low whistle of appreciation. "Now that's a cool trick." I chuckled and punched him on the shoulder playfully. Wren sat up on the couch, stretching his arms above his head before swinging his legs over the edge. "Well, now I can guess what you two got up to last night."

"It's not like that, you perv!" I shouted at him, throwing a throw pillow in his face. "We didn't even have sex." I sighed, plopping down on the couch beside Wren. Why had he left last night? There was no indication of why Kaelan wouldn't want something like that from me, and yet he still left.

"So, you're telling me nothing happened then?" Wren said, raising an eyebrow. "Because something has definitely changed between you two."

"No, something happened. Look, I'm done talking about this with you right now." I nudged him playfully with my shoulder, we were as close as we could be but talking about my sex life when I didn't even have it figured out was the line for me.

"How are you feeling, by the way?" I asked him. He looked much better today, I would forever be grateful for our supernatural healing. I needed to remember to thank Juniper as well.

He gave me a reassuring nod. "Much better. I'll be back to normal today. Now, tell me what the hell happened to you in hell." I laughed despite the terrible joke.

"Well we almost got captured and killed, but we found the library. Oh, and it's haunted by a ghost, so that was unexpected." Wren's eyes widened at my words, his features a mix of shock and confusion.

"Okay, you need to start from the beginning then, because I am genuinely confused." He sat back and listened intently as I recounted the events from the previous day up until when we made the door that anchored the library to Kaelan's house. Talking through it all helped me process it better.

"So a real freaking ghost, huh? And here I thought I was the one that had news." He was really stuck on the whole ghost situation.

"What do you mean by news? What happened?"

"There were three demon attacks the night before last, and two more last night. All involved groups of people. There was a fire involved during one attack." I sat up straight in shock. "The apartment complex that burnt down housed nothing but Otherworlders."

Demon attacks weren't completely unheard of, it was fairly common for a mortal or Otherworlder to wind up hurt or missing. But attacks on groups, specifically on groups comprised solely of Otherworlders, spoke to a disturbing change of tactics by the demons. They were growing bolder and more dangerous.

"The alpha is taking in wounded wolves, but he's leaving any other Otherworlders to fend for themselves," Wren explained, his frustration evident.

I frowned, a sense of indignation welling up within me. "That's not right. They shouldn't just turn their backs on those that need help."

Wren nodded in agreement, his eyes reflecting the same sentiment. "I don't agree with it either. But, I might have a solution. What if we offer the displaced Otherworlders refuge here? We have enough room in the old button factory. We could fix it up a little and provide them with shelter, it wouldn't be much but it's better than being out on the streets."

My eyes brightened with hope, a small smile tugging on my lips. "That's not a bad idea. Do you think Juniper would want to help? This kind of stuff is usually right up her alley." Juniper was always volunteering at the mortal homeless shelters in the city, and she spent a good amount of time at the animal shelters as well.

"Yeah, we should talk to her about it later when she gets here," he said as he got up and went to the kitchen to make coffee.

With a shared sense of purpose, Wren and I discussed the plan further. The idea of turning the old factory into a sanctuary had ignited a spark of excitement within us both. As we talked, it became clear that this was a path we were committed to pursuing. Wren's determination mirrored my own.

"There is something else I need to do today though," I said.

Wren regarded me curiously, "What is it?"

I hesitated for a moment, "I need to go see Harker again, I want to ask for her help in sorting through all the books we found in the library."

Wren's eyebrows lifted in surprise, "That's a brilliant idea. Harker would kill to have access to all that knowledge."

Wren suggested we call a taxi to get to Harker's place quicker so I reached for my phone and dialed the number.

The taxi arrived promptly, and we climbed in, the city passing by in a blur as we made our way to Harker's house. I stared out of the window, lost in thought, contemplating everything that had happened recently. My finding of the library opened doors to new possibilities, but it also unveiled a host of challenges that demanded our attention.

"Vale," Wren's voice broke through my thoughts, and I turned to look at him.

"Yeah?"

Wren glanced at me with concern in his eyes. "Everything alright?"

I sighed softly, knowing that I could confide in him. "I can't help but feel guilty. Those demons that are supposedly looking for me... they're hurting people now."

He regarded me with understanding, his expression sympathetic. "Vale, you can't shoulder the weight of the world's problems. You didn't ask for this situation, and you certainly didn't ask for demons to start wreaking havoc. Feeling guilty over things that are out of your control won't help anyone."

His words made sense. It was a reminder that I needed to focus on what I could do rather than dwell on what I couldn't change. "You're right Wren. I know I can't control everything, but I still feel responsible in some way."

Wren reached over and gently squeezed my hand, offering a reassuring gesture. "It's natural to feel that way, but we'll figure this out together, just like we always do." I managed a small smile, grateful for his unwavering support.

As the taxi continued on, I felt a sense of clarity wash over me. Wren's words served as a reminder that I shouldn't allow guilt to consume me— not when I had more important things to worry about.

We arrived at Harker's house, still as charmingly rundown as ever. With determined resolve, we banged on the door, our persistence eventually coaxing a grumpy Harker to answer. She greeted us with a mixture of annoyance and curiosity, clearly displeased at being woken during her preferred nighttime hours.

"What's all this racket about, huh?" Harker grumbled, squinting under the bright sunshine.

"We've got a proposition for you," I said, meeting her gaze with a knowing smile. "Trust me, it's something you'll want to hear."

Harker's interest was piqued, albeit reluctantly. She allowed us inside her dimly lit abode, her annoyance shifting to begrudging curiosity. As we settled in, I began to recount once again the story of the library —its purpose, its significance, and the monumental task that lay ahead.

With each word, Harker's eyes seemed to light up like stars in the night sky. The prospect of diving into the depths of magical knowledge and arcane secrets held immense appeal to her insatiable curiosity.

"I'm in," she declared eagerly, a rare spark of enthusiasm lighting up her features. "This sounds like a challenge worth sinking my fangs into."

I grinned, pleased to have gained her interest. "There is one small thing, though."

Harker's grin began to slide off her face, replaced with worry.

"The library is currently inside a demon's house."

"Oh, that won't be stopping me," Harker said as she began to gather up books from random stacks.

"What are you doing?" I asked, watching her flit about.

"I have to pack, of course. I'll be staying where the library is, I think." She said matter-of-factly. Kaelan was going to just love that idea.

With Harker's agreement to join us, we made our way back to the apartment. She had donned a pair of dark sunglasses and a wide floppy hat to shield herself from the intrusive daylight. Her casual and confident demeanor didn't waver, even as we walked through the entrance to the bookshop. I couldn't help but admire her ability to navigate the mundane world with such ease, especially when she usually spent her time immersed in archaic texts.

As we stepped into the bookshop, we were greeted by the sight of Juniper behind the counter. Her surprise was palpable as her gaze settled on Harker, who was smiling at her, fangs flashing. I could practically see the gears turning in her mind as she processed the existence of the vampire standing before her. Her knowledge of the supernatural world had expanded due to her connections with Wren and me, but encountering a vampire in the flesh was an entirely different matter.

"Juniper, this is Harker, she'll be helping me out for a while. Wren can catch you up on everything I'm sure." I said to her. I was anxious to get back to the library.

She nodded her head in understanding, though her eyes still lingered on the vampire. Harker didn't seem bothered in the slightest and merely offered a friendly wave.

Harker's inquisitive eyes turned to me, her voice laced with curiosity. "So when can we expect this demon to return and take us to his home?"

I shrugged, my lips curling into a wry smile. "Your guess is as good as mine. He tends to operate on his own schedule.

"Well, we shall just wait then. I assume your apartment is upstairs, yes?" And with that, Harker strode off without another word said to any of us.

❨ ☽

Kaelan's return was marked by a subtle shift in the air. His presence filled the room, full of intrigue that seemed to draw everyone's attention. I glanced over at him as he walked in, his eyes meeting mine with a look that sent a shiver down my spine.

"Hey," I greeted him. I realized I was relieved to see him, but I was still uncertain about what our time together meant. This whole library door situation was sure to complicate matters.

"Miss me?" he smirked, his voice deep and full of amusement.

My eyes narrowed as I took in his smug expression, his cocky demeanor making my pulse race.

"Hardly," I retorted.

He laughed, the sound echoing through me.

"I guess I'll just have to try harder, won't I?"

Harker took a step forward, her gaze locked on Kaelan. "I assume you're the demon."

He raised an eyebrow. "I am. Who are you?"

"Harker. Vampire. Librarian. Aquarius, etc." She said bluntly, not seeming to care what Kaelan thought about her.

He looked over at me and I just shrugged my shoulders. I could have warned him, but then I would have missed seeing his face.

Steeling myself for what came next I breathed in deeply before saying, "She's willing to help me with the library, but she's planning on moving in while we work on the project...to your house."

Kaelan's eyebrows shot up in surprise, his expression shifting from curiosity to something akin to alarm. "Absolutely not."

Harker, who was apparently never one to back down from a challenge, crossed her arms and met Kaelan's gaze with a steely look. "Look, demon boy, I'm not going to be sitting around waiting for you to ferry me around all the time. I need to be at the center of it all, and that means staying at your place. If you say no, then I'm out, and good luck sorting through that massive library without my expertise."

He glanced at me, and I just grinned, leaving the decision to him. I wasn't sure if it would be better or worse if Harkermoved in, but she seemed convinced that it would be a positive arrangement.

His resistance seemed to crumble in the face of Harker's fiery resolve. He sighed and ran a hand through his hair, clearly torn between his instincts and the practicality of the situation. "Fine, you can stay," he conceded, albeit with visible reluctance. "But you'll be responsible for your own...meals and other needs. I'm not your personal servant."

Harker's lips curled into a triumphant smirk. "Deal."

With an agreement reached, Kaelan turned his attention to the logistics of transporting us to his house. It was decided that Harker and I would be shifted one by one, while Wren and Juniper remained behind. Wren was needed out on patrol anyway now that he was healed.

As Kaelan's shadows enveloped us, the world blurred around me, and I found myself standing within the walls of Kaelan's home.

The air was charged with a sense of anticipation, and as Kaelan and I stood alone, our eyes locked. It was as if the intensity of our emotions had reached a breaking point, and without a word, he pulled me into a passionate kiss. The world around us faded away as I pulled at the front of his jacket and his arms wrapped around me, leaving only the sensation of his lips against mine and the overwhelming rush of longing and desire that flowed between us.

The kiss deepened and Kaelan's hand snaked up my back to tangle in my hair, pulling me even closer. When we finally broke apart, breathless and flushed, he whispered against my lips, "I couldn't stop thinking about you."

A soft smile tugged at the corners of my mouth, my heart racing in response to his words. "Even though you saw me this morning?"

He chuckled, his gaze filled with mischief. "Even though." He sighed and grazed his hand down my cheek. "I'll go get the vampire now."

I chuckled as he shifted away, watching the two of them squabble was going to be entertaining.

Chapter Twelve

Harker and I stood at the entrance to the grand library, staring in awe at the vast array of books and scrolls that filled its shelves and corridors. The library was a veritable treasure trove of knowledge and secrets, and both of us were eager to commence our exploration.

"How do we even begin?" I asked, feeling somewhat at a loss.

Harker gave me a reassuring smile. "We'll start with the oldest books first," she said. "That way, we can work our way backward and get a better understanding of what lies within these walls. The oldest books often contain the most valuable information."

As we walked further into the room, the hush of carpet beneath our feet seemed to amplify the sense of awe that enveloped me. But my wonder was momentarily interrupted by an unexpected presence — the ghostly figure of Elara, who materialized before us.

"Whoa," Harker murmured, taken aback by the sight before us.

"Yeah, sorry. I forgot to mention the ghost." I apologized ruefully.

"The fact that you forgot a whole damned ghost speaks volumes about what you've probably been through since we last spoke." I chuckled softly at her correct guess.

Elara's gaze held a blend of curiosity and irritation as she addressed us. "Ah, another unexpected guest. First, a demon, and now a vampire. My, my, the library certainly has become more diverse."

I shot Harker an amused look at Elara's words. "She has a habit of speaking her mind," I told her.

Elara responded with a huff, her form dissolving into a mist that swirled around a nearby bookshelf. Harker and I glanced at each other, sharing an amused look.

Harker's eyes were alight with curiosity as she picked up an ancient book and flipped through its pages. "I've seen my fair share of impressive collections, but a secret magical library is on a whole other level."

I nodded, my gaze sweeping across the shelves. "To think that all of this was successfully hidden for generations. The witches who created this place had to have been truly devoted to preserving their legacy. And I'm the one who gets stuck with it all, fate has a cruel sense of humor."

Harker chuckled at my words. "If I had to guess, you were chosen because you have the strength to carry this weight, and you're also stubborn enough not to give up. There are few who could take on such a task and succeed. And I intend to help you do so."

While Harker began to immerse herself in the vast array of tomes, I turned my attention inward, seeking a connection with the library itself. Closing my eyes briefly, I wondered if this place could guide us.

"There is one other thing about this library that I haven't shown you yet," I said, leading her deeper into the rows of shelves.

"What's that?" she replied.

I smiled at her. "The library has a consciousness of its own. I've discovered that the library has a sort of will. It will lead me to what I need, and I have a sense that it will do the same for you, too."

"How?" she asked incredulously.

"Library?" I began, feeling slightly foolish. "Can you show me exactly where I should start?" A few moments passed as I held my breath.

Harker's skeptical voice broke the silence. "You really think this library can answer something so vague—"

Before she could finish her sentence, a book fell from a shelf with a soft thud. Her skepticism turned to astonishment, and I couldn't help but grin at the library's unique way of responding.

"Okay, I stand corrected," she admitted with some amusement. "That's exactly how it works, apparently."

I sat down at the table in the center of the room and opened the book that had fallen for me. It was a book about blood magic. Spells, incantations, stories about how it'd been used in the past, all right here laid out for me. But there was a problem.

Harker observed me from a nearby table, her fingers tapping thoughtfully against the wooden surface. Finally, she broke the silence. "Find anything interesting?"

"Sort of," I mumbled. "A good deal of these spells here don't say anything about spilling your own blood, which is the only way I've ever been able to access mine." The only time I'd ever really used blood magic was for little stuff like enhancing my senses, the only other time had been to heal Kaelan, and they all had to do with drinking my blood. So how had these witches accessed their magic?

Harker's lips curved into a thoughtful smile. "It's because these witches had proper training, someone guided them along. Spilling your own blood was a shortcut, a way to access your power without truly understanding it."

I turned my attention back to the book, absorbing Harker's words. "It makes sense that I've been using a crutch this whole time."

Harker's voice was gentle as she spoke. "Don't be too hard on yourself. You're still learning and now you have access to this library and the wisdom it holds, you have the opportunity to truly master your blood magic."

A flicker of hope rose in my chest. Maybe I could truly unlock my full potential. I was determined to learn everything the library had to offer.

(☽

Some hours later, I palmed my weary eyes. I had managed to read three more books on blood magic. I could tell you how to light a fire. I could recite five different incantations by memory. But I still didn't know how to access my blood magic without using my own blood. "Okay, I need a break."

Harker's head jerked up from behind the stacks of books she was barricaded in like she had forgotten I was there.

"Okay, I'll be here," she said from her perch inside her tower. She reminded me of a wise old owl.

Leaving the library, I wandered the expansive halls of Kaelan's house, marveling at the grandeur. I let my thoughts wander, musing about where Kaelan could possibly be. It wasn't long before distant noises caught my attention, drawing me toward the source.

As I approached a set of double doors, the sounds grew louder. Intrigued, I pushed the doors open and stepped inside to find Kaelan in the midst of an intense workout. His sculpted muscles glistened with sweat as he executed various moves with precision.

He noticed me watching and paused, smirking playfully. "Enjoying the show?"

I rolled my eyes but couldn't help a small smile. "You could say that. What's all this about?"

Kaelan wiped the sweat from his brow with a towel before walking over to me. "Just blowing off some steam. How's the research going?"

I let out a sarcastic huff. "Oh, just great. Tons of fun learning I know nothing about my magic and deciphering centuries-old handwriting."

He chuckled. "Sounds like you could blow off some steam too. How about a little sparring practice?"

I raised an eyebrow, surprised by his suggestion. "You want to fight me?"

He nodded, his eyes sparkling with mischief. "No weapons, just fists and feet. It might help you relax."

I hesitated for a moment, not sure if I was up for it, but then a grin tugged at my lips. "Alright, why not? But don't expect me to go easy on you."

Kaelan's lips once again curved into a smirk. "I wouldn't want you to."

We took our positions on the mat, ready to begin our sparring match. Despite the playful tone, it was clear Kaelan had the upper hand. Being over six foot tall, his size and strength gave him an advantage so I would have to rely on my speed to level the playing field.

We began to circle each other, trading blows and feints, each trying to land a decisive hit. I used my speed to my advantage, slipping around Kaelan and dodging his jabs. He kept up the pressure, his fists like hammers against my body when he did manage to land a few hits.

As the fight continued, I managed to catch Kaelan off guard a couple of times, earning a surprised chuckle from him. Kaelan's shift in attitude was sudden and unexpected. All signs of playfulness had vanished and he was now all business. He lunged forward, easily side-stepping my attacks and closing the distance between us with long strides of his powerful legs. Before I could react, he grabbed me in a tight bear hug, pinning me down on the mat beneath him.

I struggled against his grip for a few moments, but ultimately I knew it was a lost cause. His weight held me down firmly and I realized that this fight was over.

I huffed, slightly out of breath, and shot him an annoyed look. "Alright, I get it, you win."

Kaelan chuckled, his chest rising and falling with exertion. "You're not so bad yourself. You're fast and scrappy."

I pushed against him playfully, trying to free myself. I only ended up wriggling against him. He made a low noise in the back of his throat and looked down at me.

He leaned down closer. "Careful, now," he whispered, his mouth moving down my neck, I shivered as I felt his hot breath. "With this position and the way you're moving, I might start getting different ideas."

I stopped moving at all, staying perfectly still as I felt his teeth graze my neck.

"Do you always get distracted so easily?" I asked breathlessly, his resulting chuckle vibrating against my skin.

"Only around you, little witch," he said kissing up my neck. He traced his tongue along my jawline and nipped at my ear with his teeth. That curl of heat in my belly rose and I arched my head under his touch.

He shifted slightly above me and that's when I knew he was thoroughly distracted because all it took was a twist of my hips and our positions were reversed, with me on top of him. He let out a slightly startled sound as I stared down at him triumphantly, a huge grin on my face.

"Who's the winner now?" I asked smoothly as I pressed a knife to his neck.

"We said no weapons," he said staring up at me, a crooked smirk etched on his face and the hint of a fang poking out. "But please, continue I'm having a thoroughly great time with this position."

I growled at him and maneuvered off, sheathing my knife. He chuckled from where he still lay on the mat and got up.

He stood there for a moment, staring down at me with a look in his eyes I couldn't quite place. "Would you like to take a walk with me?"

The question caught me off guard but I nodded my head and took his hand as he offered it to me.

As Kaelan and I wandered through the grounds surrounding his house, I couldn't help but be captivated by the tranquil beauty of the landscape unfolding before us. The world seemed to slow down, allowing us to savor each moment in this idyllic setting.

The tall trees that surrounded us swayed gently in the breeze, their leaves rustling and whispering secrets to one another. Sunlight filtered through their branches, creating a mesmerizing dance of light and shadow on the forest floor. Shafts of golden warmth pierced the canopy, illuminating patches of wildflowers and ferns that grew beneath the protective canopy of nature.

The house itself, a magnificent 200-year-old mansion, stood proudly as a testament to history and resilience. Its weathered facade exuded an air of grandeur that had withstood the test of time and it seemed to watch over the estate with a sense of quiet authority.

As we strolled further, Kaelan led me to a majestic tree that stood as a sentinel at the edge of a small clearing. From one of its sturdy branches hung a beautifully crafted two-person swing, its ropes weathered and aged, yet strong and inviting. The swing swayed gently in the breeze as if beckoning us to take a moment to relish the serenity of this place.

I couldn't resist the allure of the swing, and with Kaelan's encouraging smile, I approached it. The picture-perfect scene unfolded before me: the lush greenery, the dappled sunlight, and the grandeur of the mansion in the distance. With a sense of childlike joy, I took a seat on the swing, feeling the rough texture of the rope in my hands.

"These grounds are beautiful," I remarked, genuinely in awe of the natural beauty that surrounded us.

Kaelan smiled, a touch of warmth in his eyes. "I've always found solace in these woods. They've been a sanctuary for me for a long time."

He settled onto the swing, and we sat side by side, the gentle creak of the rope filling the air. It was a moment of quiet companionship, a stark contrast to the dangers and uncertainties we faced. Amid the chaos and upheaval, it was a momentary oasis of peace, and I cherished every second of it.

As we swung back and forth, Kaelan's demeanor softened, and I could sense a more relaxed side of him that I hadn't seen before. It was as if the weight of the world was momentarily lifted, leaving room for a genuine connection between us.

Kaelan's voice broke the silence. "There's something about you. Something that draws me in. I can't quite explain it, but there's a part of me that feels...whole when I'm with you. It's like you're the missing piece of the puzzle."

His words were filled with honesty and sincerity, and they touched me in a way I hadn't expected. My heart skipped a beat, and I couldn't help the smile that spread across my lips.

Kaelan's gaze lingered on mine, a tenderness in his eyes that was both exciting and intimidating. It was a moment filled with possibilities, and I wondered what it all meant.

The soft touch of his fingertips on my cheek snapped me out of my trance. He gently cupped my chin, his thumb tracing along my lower lip. A shiver ran down my spine, and my heart rate picked up.

"Kaelan..." I breathed, unable to finish my sentence as he closed the distance between us, capturing my lips in a searing kiss.

The kiss was gentle at first, his lips brushing softly against mine, but then the intensity increased, the passion building until it consumed us both. His arms wrapped around me, pulling me closer as our bodies melted together, the heat and hunger overwhelming us.

We finally broke apart, our breathing heavy as we stared into each other's eyes. My heart was racing, and I could feel his doing the same.

Kaelan rested his forehead against mine, his voice low and husky. "You make me want things, things I never thought I could have."

My stomach did a somersault at his words.

I saw a shadow flicker across the corner of my vision and my stomach dropped. Panic surged through me, the fear of encountering another demon making my pulse race. But as the figure emerged from the shadows, my fears subsided. It was the same shadowkin fox that had guided me to the library during the haze of that twisted mind trap.

"Kaelan, do you see that?" I whispered, pointing to the shadowed fox.

He followed my gaze and nodded. "I've seen it around. It's been waiting for you to notice."

The fox approached us cautiously, its dark form shifting and weaving with an otherworldly grace. Memories of its aid flooded back, the sensation of being guided and protected.

"I've met this creature before," I murmured, my voice filled with awe. "You've seen it around?"

Kaelan's expression remained calm and knowing. "Nothing that happens in the shadows escapes my awareness. It seems this one has taken an interest in you."

The shadowkin fox regarded me with an intelligent grace, and a sense of recognition passed between us. It had sensed what I was, a witch born with unique potential.

"Hello again," I said softly, extending my hand to the fox.

With cautious curiosity, the fox drew closer, its body swirling with a mass of ever-shifting shadows. My hand passed through its form like a dark swirling mist. There was a sense of reassurance in its presence.

"Why is it here now?" I asked Kaelan, wondering if he knew the reason.

He paused for a moment, seeming to consider the question carefully. "I think it's your familiar. Long ago, when the witches were still in power, a few of them had familiars. But I've never heard of a demon familiar."

"A familiar?" I looked back at the shadowkin, my mind reeling. I suddenly sensed a slight connection between us. Yes, it was faint but it was there. I was taken aback at this sudden unspoken decision between the two of us. Not sure what having a familiar entailed. "Tell me more about familiars. What was their purpose?"

"Protection and companionship mostly, I believe. I'm not an expert on this subject though. Maybe there is something in the library that can help."

The library. Yes, I would definitely be paying it a visit. My familiar — the word sounded foreign and strange. I wasn't sure what this would mean, but I was willing to accept the help that was offered.

With one last glance at the fox, I rose from the swing. Kaelan stood beside me, and as he reached out his hand, I took it, feeling the warmth of his touch. There was a sense of safety in his presence, an anchor amid the turbulence of my life.

As we walked back toward the house, I marveled at how much had changed since I had met him in Erebus.

Back in the library, Harker gave no indication that she saw or cared about the small fleeting shadow of a fox now playfully chasing after my own shadow. She gave no indication that she even knew I was there as she happily continued reading one of the many scrolls housed within the library.

I stood amid a row of shelves, my eyes scanning the books for any sign of one related to familiars. Frustration began to creep in as I realized that my search was coming up empty.

"Library, can you give me a book about familiars?" I asked deliberately, hoping to learn about my new friend. But after waiting a moment it was clear none were about to shoot out at me from their shelves. "Elara?" I called curiously.

"You called for me?" A voice chimed from behind me, causing me to nearly jump out of my skin. I turned to see the ghost, who looked somewhat put out at being there.

"Yes," I replied, my frustration evident. "I'm trying to find a book about familiars, or anything that might mention them."

Elara's gossamer form settled beside me, her wispy appearance contrasting with the solidity of the books around us. "Familiars?" She replied, glancing down at the shadowy form now curled in a dark corner. "Well, dear, I'm afraid there won't be any books about them here."

I blinked in surprise. "None at all? But why?"

Her gaze took on a distant quality as she recalled times long past. "Familiars were a rare and intimate aspect of witchcraft, even during the height of our power. Those who had them considered their bond sacred and kept their secrets closely guarded. It was a way to honor and show respect to their familiars, ensuring that the information they shared remained between the two of them."

"So, definitely no books on the subject, then?" I asked, both disappointed and intrigued by the notion.

"No, my dear," She replied with a soft smile. "Familiars were a personal connection, one that mirrored the very soul of a witch. The details of that bond were considered too precious to be written down and shared. The secrets of familiars were only passed on from one witch with a familiar to another."

As Elara spoke, the mystery surrounding my new friend deepened. It was both frustrating and fascinating to think that such a significant aspect of witchcraft has been shrouded in secrecy, hidden even from the pages of the magical library. I couldn't help but feel curiosity and a tinge of disappointment at the thought that familiars were elusive even in a place of such boundless knowledge.

"How am I supposed to learn about familiars if there's nothing written about them?" I asked, running my hands through my hair in frustration.

Her smile was warm and knowing. "Don't fret, now that your bond has been made you'll learn soon enough."

I titled my head, intrigued by her words. "You had a familiar, didn't you?"

Her eyes took on a faraway look, a mixture of fondness and wistfulness. "Yes, I did. A loyal and mischievous raven named Orion. He was a mirror of my spirit, reflecting my strengths and weaknesses."

Curiosity burned through me as I absorbed her words. "So, familiars are reflections of a witch?"

Elara nodded, her diaphanous form seeming to shimmer with memories. "Exactly. Your familiar is a manifestation of your very soul, chosen by the threads of destiny itself."

A question that had been lingering in my mind found its way to my lips. "What does it mean then that a demon has become my familiar?"

Her smile remained gentle and reassuring. "The nature of your familiar doesn't inherently define your own nature, dear. It's a connection that carries its own mysteries and lessons. Don't view it as a negative thing, embrace it as an opportunity to understand yourself on a deeper level."

I nodded, taking in all she was saying. "And how does the bond between a witch and her familiar develop?"

Her eyes sparkled as she continued. "Over time, as you and your familiar grow together, you'll begin to sense the magical bond between you better. Familiars often act as guides, protectors, and companions. Some witches even used them as spies, gathering valuable information from afar. Their presence can also help alleviate the loneliness that comes with the longevity of the witches."

With a newfound understanding of familiars and what my own would bring me, I turned my attention to another burning question. Elara had provided me with so much insight, and I felt a genuine connection with her. But there was a mystery surrounding her own existence.

"There's something else I'm curious about," I began, failing to keep the intrigue out of my voice. "How did you end up here, as the guardian of the library?"

Her ghostly form seemed to shimmer as she settled into a more contemplative stance, her eyes filled with memories that spanned beyond the boundaries of the library's walls. "That is a tale with its roots buried in both sacrifice and duty," she began.

As I listened, her words wove a story that was both captivating and heart-wrenching. "When the library was nearing its completion," she continued, "the coven known as The Seven required one final element to ensure the library's potency and protection."

I leaned in, my curiosity piqued. "And that element was what?"

A bittersweet smile graced Elara's lips. "Me. I was chosen to be a part of a powerful ritual that would bind me to the very essence of this place. My role was to become the final thread that would weave together the library's magic and its guardianship."

I couldn't help but feel a mixture of awe and sympathy for the path that had led her here. "What happened during the ritual?"

Her gaze turned distant as if she was reliving those moments from long ago. "The ritual was intricate, it required a sacrifice. I was killed by The Seven, and my life force was woven into the very fabric of the library's existence, my bones sealed within its walls."

Her words hung heavy in the air, a testament to the weight of her sacrifice. I was horrified. "So, your bones are what grant the library its magic?" I inquired.

She nodded, her expression a mix of resignation and pride. "Yes, my bones are a vessel of power, intertwined with the spells and enchantments that keep this place alive. I am forever bound to the library."

As I absorbed the significance of her story, I couldn't help but feel a deep respect for the role she had undertaken. "You gave so much to ensure the library's existence," I said softly.

Her gaze met mine, a hint of warmth in her ghostly eyes. "It was my duty, my purpose. And though my afterlife is one I regret sometimes, I find solace in preserving the legacy of witchcraft."

I nodded, my admiration for her growing stronger with each passing moment. Her story was a reminder that every aspect of this magical realm had been shaped by individuals who were willing to sacrifice for the greater good.

As the weight of Elara's tale settled within me, I found myself determined to unravel the mysteries of the library and the world of magic it held. My curiosity sated, she flitted off to a distant shelf, muttering to herself as if she had forgotten entirely what we had just discussed.

Chapter Thirteen

"Are you ready to head back?" Kaelan asked as we stood in his kitchen, his voice a comforting presence amidst the sea of thoughts that tugged at my mind.

I looked at the shadowkin, its eyes gleaming with an eerie intelligence. "Will my new friend be able to follow us through the shadows?" I inquired, hoping that our newfound connection would extend beyond realms.

Kaelan nodded with a knowing smile, wrapping his arms around me and pulling me close. "Oh, most definitely. Shadowkin can traverse the shadows with ease, just like I do."

"Are you sure you're not a shadowkin then?" I teased him playfully. "Maybe you're bonded to me as well, and that's why you can't stay away."

He chuckled and kissed my forehead affectionately. "I just might be, little witch."

As the shadows began to envelop us, I couldn't help but wonder about the possibilities that lay ahead. What surprises would my new relationship with the creature bring?

Once we were back in my bedroom, I turned to Kaelan with a wistful expression. I didn't want our time together to end. "You know, I wouldn't mind keeping you here a while longer," I said, a smile tugging at the corner of my lips.

Kaelan's eyes darkened with desire. "What did you have in mind?" he asked, his voice taking on a husky tone.

My pulse quickened, my skin prickling with anticipation. "Well, we could pick up where we left off the other night," I suggested, remembering how heated things had gotten between us.

He moved closer to me, his hands settling on my hips. "I like the sound of that," he murmured, his breath warm against my neck.

The heat of his body pressed against mine, and I melted into him, my skin tingling with desire. As his lips met mine in a searing kiss, my thoughts began to fog over, my body surrendering to the sensations that consumed me.

He sighed as he pulled back reluctantly. "I really do need to go."

I frowned, trying to hide my disappointment. "Where do you always disappear to?"

Kaelan looked conflicted, and it was clear there was something he wasn't telling me. "It's just a small task that I must attend to. Nothing you need to concern yourself with."

His response was vague and unrevealing, and it only made me more curious about what he was up to. But I knew that pressing him would only result in more evasive answers, so I simply nodded.

"Well, I'll be here if you need me," I said, trying to mask my hurt.

He gave me a regretful smile, his eyes searching mine. "I know. I'm sorry. I'll see you soon."

And with that, he disappeared into the shadows, leaving me alone with my thoughts.

I couldn't help but wonder what it was that Kaelan was hiding from me. And I couldn't help but worry that whatever it was, it was something that could threaten the fragile bond we had formed.

I took a deep breath and tried to shake off the uneasy feeling that lingered. There was nothing I could do but trust that Kaelan would tell me the truth when he was ready.

Wren's presence in the apartment pulled me from my thoughts, and I greeted him with a smile as I walked into the living room. "Hey, you're back."

Wren nodded with a smile and his eyes drifted over to a shadowed corner, where my new familiar lay curled up in a ball. "What is that?" He asked in shock.

"Oh, that's a bit of a story," I replied. I introduced them, recounting how the shadowy animal had guided me through the treacherous mind trap in the demon lord's keep and had then apparently taken a liking to me, following me ever since. "I guess it wants to be a part of all this." I mused.

Wren observed the creature, who was now leaping at shadows playfully, with interest. "Does it have a name?"

I chuckled softly, realizing I had not even wondered that myself. "I'm not sure, Elara told me her familiar's name was Orion. Maybe I'm meant to give it a name."

"You should name it after the goddess of night, Nyx." He suggested. It was as good a suggestion as any, and I liked it.

I turned to the shadowkin in the corner. "How do you like Nyxen, little one?" The shadow fox just stared at me with gleaming eyes, but I could sense a faint acceptance from it, I wondered if that was the bond between us that I could feel.

"So, how's everything going with the factory?" I inquired, eager to hear about the progress he and Juniper had made.

Wren leaned back against the couch, a satisfied smile on his face. "We've been getting the main floor ready for the Otherworlders. Juniper's done an amazing job organizing everything. I got the word out through a connection of mine. We've even had a few people arrive already."

"That's fantastic," I replied, my excitement growing. "It's good to know that there's a safe place for them to go."

He nodded in agreement. "Yeah, and a couple of the women who've come have offered to help out at the bookshop during their stay. Juniper was thrilled to have the extra hands."

The image of Juniper surrounded by a community of supportive individuals warmed my heart. "I'm glad Juniper will have some company, with us running off at all hours of the day and night. And it's wonderful that they're already forming connections."

Wren's gaze met mine, his expression filled with a sense of purpose. "We're making a difference, Vale. It might not be on a grand scale, but it matters."

I smiled, grateful for the steadfast determination that Wren and Juniper brought into my life. "You're right. Every small step counts."

As the night grew darker, and the apartment quieted down, Wren and I each retreated to our rooms, looking forward to the day ahead. We exchanged our good nights before parting ways.

❨ ☽

The following morning, I woke up with a renewed sense of purpose. The anticipation of meeting the Otherworlders who had sought refuge in our sanctuary filled me with nervousness and excitement. With a determined spirit, I joined Wren in the living room, where he was sipping on a cup of coffee.

"Ready for the day?" He asked, his eyes bright with enthusiasm.

I nodded, my resolve strengthening. It was time to meet the Otherworlders.

"Shall we?" I asked Wren.

"Let's do it." He replied happily.

With a shared determination, we left the apartment and made our way down to the main floor of the factory. The large open space was now bustling with activity, as people moved around, or sat around makeshift sleeping areas, conversing in small groups.

As we entered the main area, I caught sight of Nyxen lurking in the corners, his form blending almost seamlessly with the darkness. I approached him and whispered, "Stay hidden today. I don't want to overwhelm the newcomers."

He looked at me in what seemed to be understanding before melting into the shadows, his presence disappearing from view.

Wren and I began making our way through the crowd, and he started introducing me to the Otherworlders who had sought refuge here. There were all sorts of beings —half-fae, half-demons, even a vampire had made it into the mix. Some of them approached me with gratitude, expressing their thanks for the haven. I felt a mix of emotions, humbled by their appreciation and determined to do whatever I could to help.

"I want you all to know that it was Wren's idea," I said, deflecting the praise toward him. "He's the one who saw a need and took action."

Some of them looked at Wren with newfound respect, and he shrugged, offering a humble smile in return.

As we continued talking to the Otherworlders, I noticed a figure who seemed to hold an air of leadership among the group. His presence commanded attention, and I could tell that others looked to him for guidance. Wren noticed my gaze and guided me over to him.

"Vale, this is Jason," Wren introduced.

Jason extended his hand, his grip firm as he shook mine. "Thank you for opening your doors to us. We've been through a lot, this is just the end of a string of bad luck. It means more to us than you know."

I nodded, sincerity in my voice. "I'm glad we could offer some help. How are you holding up?"

Jason sighed, his expression wary but determined. "I took care of most of the folks in that building that burned down. I'm trying to get as many of us here as I can. We need this."

"I'm here to support you in any way I can," I assured him.

Wren chimed in. "Looks like they've got breakfast started if you all are hungry."

Jason smiled, a glimmer of hope in his eyes. "Thank you. We'll gladly take any help we can get right now. Though some of us are a little apprehensive, the world has left them slow to trust." That was understandable, the life of an Otherworlderalone in the mortal realm could be a difficult one.

As the morning unfolded, Wren and I pitched in to help serve breakfast for everyone, before sitting down to join them in the meal. The sense of unity and purpose at that moment was palpable. I felt a deepening connection to these people, all of us bound together by the shared struggles we faced as Otherworlders.

As we ate breakfast and shared stories, I couldn't help but feel that we were indeed making a new beginning. This sanctuary was only the first step, but it was an important one. By coming together and standing united, we were taking a stand against the forces that sought to destroy us.

( )

After Wren and I left the bustling main floor of the factory, we made our way to the cozy haven of the bookshop. The atmosphere here was quieter, more intimate, as Juniper explained the ins and outs of the bookshop to the two Otherworlder women who had graciously offered to assist her. As we approached, Juniper was in the middle of explaining the categorization of different books, her enthusiasm evident in her animated gestures.

One of the Otherworlder women, a young half-demon with vibrant green eyes, listened with rapt attention. Her gaze was fixated on Juniper as if absorbing every word of her explanation. I can't help but smile at the scene, watching as Juniper imparted her passion for books to another eager soul.

As Juniper finished her explanation, the other woman, a half-fae with intricate tattoos adorning her arms and slightly pointed ears, stepped forward. She hesitated for a moment, then spoke with gentle confidence. "My name is Ava. I have a strong affinity for herbs and natural remedies. If it's alright, I'd love to help with the herbs in the shop."

Juniper's eyes lit up with genuine delight, her enthusiasm infectious. "That would be wonderful! We have a variety of herbs and plants, and your expertise would be a welcome addition to the shop."

Ava nodded, her smile warm. "I'm glad to contribute in any way that I can."

I was struck by the camaraderie that was forming among these diverse individuals, each bringing their unique talents and abilities to the table. It's a stark reminder that even amid uncertainty and upheaval, there was a sense of unity and purpose that can bind us together.

Juniper continued to talk animatedly with the women. It was heartwarming to see how welcoming and inclusive our small community was becoming. As we've worked to provide a haven for Otherworlders who had nowhere else to go, it was clear that we were creating a space where everyone could contribute and thrive.

A thought crossed my mind, a fleeting idea that perhaps this was the start of something much larger —a movement that could change how the different realms interact and cooperate. It was a grand vision, and while it may have been ambitious, I couldn't help but feel a sense of determination and hope.

As Juniper continued to instruct the two Otherworlder women, Wren and I stood by, watching with satisfaction as the new members of our little community found their place and contributed their skills.

I checked my phone, realizing it was time to leave for the library. With a few quick taps, I sent Kaelan a message letting him know I was ready and to meet me on the roof shortly. I was eager to dive back into research and learn what Harkermay have uncovered.

Just as I was about to head for the door, a sudden shift in the atmosphere captured my attention. The entrance bell chimed, announcing the arrival of new visitors. My steps faltered as my eyes settled on the trio that just walked in. Two men and a woman, their aura radiating an Otherworldly presence that set them apart from the rest of the room. Their beauty was striking, almost ethereal, and their presence commanded attention.

The woman was radiant, her beauty beyond that of mortal women. Her face was heart-shaped, and her lips were ruby red. The second man was slight of frame, his shoulders wide but his waist narrow. His hair and beard were golden, and his eyes were the color of stormy seas. The third and final member of the trio was a warrior. His muscular frame was imposing, and his demeanor was confident and self-assured. His hair was the color of raven feathers, and it hung down to his shoulders in thick waves. His eyes were hard and his stare was penetrating.

Juniper paused mid-conversation, her gaze flickering to the newcomers. Ava's eyes widened in awe and even Wren seemed taken aback. I could hardly blame them —the trio looked completely out of place in the background of a modern bookshop.

The woman of the group spoke first, her melodic voice carrying a note of reverence. "Vale."

I blinked, my surprise mingling with curiosity. These three were definitely fae, full-blood fae. "Yes, that's me. Can I help you?"

The golden haired man standing beside her stepped forward, his features sharp. "We've been searching for you."

Wren and Juniper exchanged panicked glances, the question in their eyes mirroring my own. "Searching for me?" I repeated.

The third member of the group, the obvious warrior, spoke up. "Forgive us, but you bear a striking resemblance to someone we lost many years ago — someone who was very dear to us."

My heart skipped a beat as a strange sensation of anticipation washed over me. "Who is that?" I inquire cautiously.

The woman's eyes met mine with a mixture of hope and sorrow. "Our beloved princess, who vanished without a trace twenty-four years ago."

My breath catches in my throat. "And you think I'm her?" This obviously was not possible, I hadn't even been born yet.

The second man shook his head solemnly. "No, but there is no mistaking the resemblance. You could be the daughter of our lost princess."

The revelation sent shockwaves through me and uncertainty and curiosity swirled within me. The others were silent, their expressions a mirror of my own astonishment.

"We understand this may be overwhelming," the fae male continued, his voice gentle. "But if you are indeed her descendant, it would bring us great joy to reunite with you and bring you home."

I listened to their words, my heart racing as I processed the implications of what they were saying. The thought of being connected to a missing fae princess, of a lineage I know nothing about, was both intriguing and unsettling. I exchanged a quick glance with Wren, who came to stand by my side, his presence a reassuring anchor amidst the uncertainty.

Despite the aura of grace and sincerity that these fae exuded, I couldn't ignore the undercurrent of wariness within me. It's not just my instincts as a witch that have me on guard — it's the knowledge that there's a deep history between my kind and the fae, one marked by betrayal, conflict, and the eradication of the witches who came before me.

"Thank you for your words," I replied cautiously, trying to remain diplomatic, my gaze steady. "However, I must admit that this is all quite sudden, and I need time to process."

The woman nodded, her expression empathetic. "Of course, we understand. We didn't mean to overwhelm you."

As she spoke, I sensed a shift in their approach. They seemed to be probing, trying to gauge my reactions and emotions. It was almost as if they were reading between the lines, looking for something beneath the surface. My guard rose even higher as I guessed that their intentions might be more complex than they were letting on.

The blonde man's next words confirmed my suspicions. "We know that you are not purely fae. Your blood is mixed, a blend of different realms."

I couldn't help but raise an eyebrow at this revelation. It hinted at their desire to manipulate my emotions. If they felt I might be torn about going with them due to my mixed blood, they were sorely mistaken.

I decided to test the waters and confront their intentions head-on. "It's interesting that you're suddenly showing so much interest in me. Could it be that you've learned I'm a witch?"

The woman looked momentarily surprised, her eyes narrowing just slightly before she regained her composure. "The fact that you are a witch, and your forbidden heritage is no matter to us."

"And yet," I pressed on, "you seem to have conveniently forgotten about certain details. Like the role the fae played in the persecution of the witches."

Their composed demeanor wavered, a flicker of surprise and unease passing across their faces. It's another confirmation of my suspicions —they were not expecting me to be aware of the history that connected our two worlds.

"We acknowledge that there were dark times in our history," the woman admitted, her voice tinged with regret. "But we also believe in the possibility of reconciliation, of forging a new understanding between our realms."

I couldn't deny that the idea of reconciliation was tempting, and to know more about this woman they assumed to be my mother, but my skepticism remained strong. The wounds of the past run deep, and while I was willing to consider the possibility of unity, I wouldn't do so blindly.

"I appreciate your interest in me and your persistence," I began, my voice firm. "But the decision is mine to make, and I've chosen not to go with you."

The fae exchanged glances, disappointment and frustration evident on their features. It was clear that they had anticipated a different outcome, probably one where I would willingly embrace my fae heritage and return with them.

Before the tension could escalate further, the chimes to the shop rang out again, drawing our attention. Kaelan stepped in, his expression dark and stormy and his presence a welcome interruption.

The fae's reactions were immediate and visceral. Their expressions twisted into a combination of disdain and anger, all directed at Kaelan. "Demon," the third male hissed. "It must be you who has been poisoning her mind against the fae and her rightful home."

Kaelan's dark eyes were thunderclouds, but his tone was steady. "I told her the truth, nothing more. Her choices and opinions are and will always be her own." He walked over to where I stood and glared at the trio.

The tension in the room was palpable, the air heavy with unspoken resentment. It was a clash of different worlds, histories, and beliefs that had been deeply ingrained in both fae and demon cultures.

"I appreciate your concern for me," I interject, my voice calm but resolute. "But my choices are not based on anyone else's influence. They are a reflection of my own beliefs."

The fae's disappointment is clear, the woman stepped forward again, her eyes glinting with determination. "Vale, we are your people."

"No," I say firmly, meeting her gaze with steely resolve. "My people are here, these Otherworlders in the mortal realm."

"If that is your final decision, we will take our leave." The blonde male answered. "But just know, our king requires your presence in the fae realm, and he will not stop at sending just us to get what he wants."

Their message was clear — this encounter was far from over, and they were determined to ensure I fulfilled their expectations, regardless of my feelings on the matter.

Kaelan's instincts kicked in immediately, his demeanor shifting into a protective stance. His voice took on a low, threatening quality as he addressed their words. "Is that a threat?" He questioned, the very air around him crackling with tension. Shadows started to swirl around the room. His eyes gleamed with an intensity that made it clear he was standing a hair's breadth away from unleashing his fury.

A faint smirk tugs at the corner of my lips at his protective display. I appreciated his readiness to defend me, but I also wanted to avoid confrontation within the confines of my shop. "Easy, Kaelan" I interjected, placing a hand gently on his arm. "No need to turn this place into a battleground."

The fae didn't seem fazed by Kaelan's aggression, a fact that I found very stupid, as he was practically vibrating with rage under my touch. Instead, they offered one final ominous statement —that their king's desire for me to join them is unwavering. Their words hung in the air like a storm cloud.

They all turned swiftly to leave, the door chimes sounding strange in the light of the current situation.

Once they were gone, everyone in the room seemed to release a heavy sigh at once. Juniper finally ushered Ava and the other woman out of the room and into the green room. Her voice was a whisper telling them to forget about what they'd just witnessed, how it would be better for everyone that way.

My shoulders slumped from the weight of the encounter. Kaelan and Wren's reassuring presence brought me a measure of comfort. Kaelan's hand found mine and gave it a gentle squeeze. I met his gaze, my expression worried.

"I don't like this," I admitted, my voice concerned. "Both the demons and the fae are after me. It's...a lot to handle."

Kaelan met my gaze with a steady look, his tone comforting. "Yes, it is. But you're not alone, and you're not defenseless."

A determination kindled within me, a renewed resolve to hone my abilities and control my magic. With both the demon realm and the fea realm after me, it was clear that I couldn't afford to be unprepared. I gave Kaelan a determined nod.

"You're right," I replied, my voice firm. "I need to get better at this—controlling my magic. I won't let their threats control me."

Kaelan gave a curt nod, the storm clouds still swirling in his eyes. Wren placed a comforting hand on my shoulder, his eyes full of worry. I took a deep breath, my resolve steadying as I prepared for whatever lay ahead.

Chapter Fourteen

The weight of the encounter with the fae lingered in the air, a reminder that my world had suddenly become a battleground between realms. I found myself lost in thought, my mind spinning with questions about my past, the woman the fae claimed to be my mother, and the dangerous forces that now converged on me.

Wren's comforting voice broke through my reverie, his calm presence a balm to my anxious thoughts. "You don't need to worry about them, Vale," he assured me, his tone steady. "We've faced tougher challenges before."

Kaelan, on the other hand, remained contemplative, his expression calculating. "You should consider staying at my house for a while," he proposed, his gaze fixed on me. "Until you can put up wards around the shop and factory, that is." His solution could potentially keep me safe, even if it came with its own set of complications.

I hesitated, torn between my sense of duty to the Other-worlders and the realization that he might have a point. His words cut to the heart of the matter — my vulnerability. The fae and demons both sought me out, and my current location was far from secure.

"But the Otherworlders..." I began to protest, my voice trailing off as Kaelan held up his hand.

"Wren and Juniper seem to have things under control," Kaelan pointed out, his tone gentle but firm. "Your safety comes first. With the rise in demon attacks, it's only a matter of time before they find their way to the factory. And if the fae can locate you so easily, demons won't be far behind."

Wren's nod of agreement echoed Kaelan's sentiments, and I found myself begrudgingly swayed by his logic. The prospect of ensuring my own safety was undeniable, even if it meant temporarily leaving behind the haven we had created for the Otherworlders.

With a sigh, I relented, offering a reluctant agreement. "Fine, I'll go." I conceded, my gaze flickering between Kaelan and Wren. "But just for a little while. I won't be away for long."

Kaelan's lips curled into a small, teasing smile. "Don't worry, you won't be lonely," he remarked, a hint of mischief in his eyes. "You'll have Harker for company."

I couldn't help but respond with a wry smile of my own. The prospect of spending extended time with Kaelan was both tempting and unnerving. Our connection, the undeniable tension between us, was a constant presence and I was acutely aware of the potential complications it could bring.

With the decision made, Wren excused himself to inform Juniper of the plan, leaving me to head upstairs to the apartment and gather the belongings I'd need for my stay at Kaelan's house. I stepped into the familiar space of my room, surrounded by the comforts I'd grown accustomed to —my books, my bed, and the aura of the place I called home. The first real home Wren and I had.

Kaelan followed me and as I began to pack I noticed his thoughtful gaze roaming around the room. His demeanor was different from what I was accustomed to —a mix of concern and contemplation. I paused in my packing and looked at him curiously. "Is something wrong?" I asked, my voice soft.

Kaelan's eyes met mine, and he let out a sigh as if releasing a weight he'd been carrying. "I didn't think the fae would catch wind of you so quickly," he admitted, his expression frustrated. "They must have spies in the demon realm— they heard the whispers about your existence."

I frowned, the pieces of the puzzle not quite making sense. "But how did they find out my name?" I wondered aloud, the mystery deepening.

Kaelan's gaze remained locked on me, something I couldn't quite decipher clouding his eyes. "They most likely know more about you than you think," he said slowly, his words laden with meaning. "And they'll be relentless in their pursuit. We'll need to be cautious."

As his words sank in, a revelation hit me like a lightning bolt. My eyes widened, and I looked at Kaelan with a sudden realization. "Jaks," I said, my voice frustrated. "It must have been him."

Kaelan arched an eyebrow, clearly taken aback by my statement. "Who is Jaks?"

"The half-demon who hands out the bounty contracts. He's always hated me. He's the only one who could have given the fae that kind of information. He's the link between the demon realm and the mortal one, and he's known for gathering intelligence."

Kaelan cursed under his breath, clearly sharing my concern. "It's possible. And if it was him, we need to find out what exactly he's told them."

Without further hesitation, Kaelan turned on his heel and headed for the door. "I need to talk to Wren about this," he said, his voice edged with fury. "If Jaks has betrayed you, we'll make sure he pays for it." Jaks was in for a visit from Wren —one that wouldn't end well for him if my suspicion proved correct.

Kaelan swiftly descended the stairs with a determined stride. I stood in the doorway to my room, watching his back as he disappeared from view.

Moments later, I could hear their voices in low, serious tones. The topic of Jaks, my suspicion, and the possibility of his betrayal were the core of their conversation. Wren's assurances that he would investigate and uncover the truth were met with Kaelan's firm resolve. I felt a mixture of gratitude and unease — their concern for my safety was evident, but the realization that someone like Jaks might have played a role in the web was disconcerting.

As their voices faded into the background, I turned my attention back to the task at hand. I finished packing my essentials and ensured everything was in order. Kaelan's reminder that we needed to leave brought a renewed sense of urgency. I thought about Nyxen and re-alized I hadn't seen him since our conversation in the bookshop.

Curiosity got the better of me, I called out to him softly, "Nyxen?" The name felt strange on my lips, but it was beginning to take on a familiarity. I scanned the room, my eyes searching for any sign of movement. And then, from behind my bookshelf, a shadow stirred, taking form into the sleek figure of a fox.

Nyxen's shadowy form slipped out from behind the bookshelf, his eyes fixed on me with an attentive gaze. He emitted a low, rumbling purr-like sound, an indication of his understanding.

I approached him slowly, crouching down to his level. "We're going to Kaelan's house," I whispered, hoping he could comprehend my words. "Will you come with us?"

As if to confirm his understanding, Nyxen padded closer to me, his insubstantial form brushing against my fingers as I extended my hand. His cool touch was strangely comforting, and I could feel it as the sense of connection between us deepened.

With a final glance around my apartment, I stood up and took a deep breath. Spending time at Kaelan's house was both thrilling and nerve-wracking. I remembered what happened the last time I spent the night at his house, and a blush rose to my cheeks at the vivid memories of our encounter.

Nyxen followed at my heels as I descended the stairs. As I reached the lower level of the factory and walked into the bookshop, I found Kaelan and Wren engrossed in their conversation about Jaks. Their expressions were serious.

Kaelan glanced up when he heard me approaching, his eyes softening as they met mine. "Ready to go?" He asked, his voice concerned.

I nodded, trying to quell the emotions swirling within me. "Yeah, let's do it."

Wren's gaze shifted to me, and he offered a nod of his head. "I'll get to the bottom of this, Vale. Don't worry. Just go learn those wards quickly."

I appreciated Wren's determination to uncover the truth about Jaks, and I know he wouldn't rest until he had answers. With a final nod in his direction, I turned my attention back to Kaelan. As he walked towards me, a warm smile tugged at his lips, erasing some of the tension that had hung in the air.

Kaelan's hand slipped into mine, his touch sending a comforting jolt through me. Without a word, he pulled me close, our bodies pressed together.

"Do you always have to hold onto the people you shift with you?" I asked him, curious.

"Not at all, I just use it as an excuse to touch you." He said, smirking.

Shadows shifted and swirled around us, enveloping us in a protective shroud. In a heartbeat, the world around me blurred and twisted, the sensation of shadow shifting taking hold.

The disorienting sensation lasted only a moment before I found myself standing in Kaelan's grand house. The familiarity of the surroundings eased my racing heart, and I looked up at Kaelan.

"Thanks for this," I said softly, my voice laced with genuine appreciation.

Kaelan's smile was warm and understanding. "You're always welcome here, little witch."

◖ ☽

The day after my arrival at Kaelan's house dawned with anticipation and uncertainty. As I navigated the unfamiliar territory of my own conflicted emotions, I found myself pondering over the unexpected dynamics of Kaelan and me. He had been surprisingly reserved since my arrival, not making any overt advances or suggestive comments. While a part of me appreciated the respectful space he was giving me, another part was perplexed by the sudden change in our interactions.

Lost in my thoughts, I wandered to the library and sat down across from Harker. I wondered if she had slept much the past few days. The task of cataloging the library had consumed her, she was eating up the knowledge she gained. Last night, she had offered to help me try my hand at some spells this morning, saying she had found a few simple ones.

"Ready to get started? I want to go to bed before long. Elara was in here all night rearranging books and muttering curses." Harker looked to where the ghost was fussing over a shelf of books with disdain.

I nodded and stood up, heading to the middle of the room where she had placed a single red candle. I sat on the floor before the candle and crossed my legs, getting into a relaxed position. Harker began reading aloud from an old, weathered book, her voice echoed with ancient wisdom. The blood magic spell should be relatively simple, I was to conjure a small flame and light the candle.

I focused inward, trying to call forth that part of me that could control the blood magic. I pictured a flame softly dancing on the candle wick, I held my breath until my face began to turn blue, but to no avail. I had yet to be able to use my blood magic without spilling my blood.

A flicker of frustration crossed my features as I watched Harker read another passage, her expression filled with understanding. Suddenly, Elara appeared beside me, her spectral form emanating a stern energy.

"Conjuring flames? In a library!?" Her voice held a reproachful tone as she cast a disapproving look in Harker's direction.

Harker rolled her eyes, clearly unimpressed by Elara's chastising. "Vale is trying to learn here Elara, something maybe a fellow witch such as yourself should help her with."

Elara huffed, crossing her arms. "I will not have you setting my precious library ablaze, especially not for the sake of practicing reckless spells."

"Oh, go haunt a bookshelf," Harker said dismissively.

I sighed, frustrated with my lack of progress. "I just can't seem to get it to work."

Harker closed the book with a decisive thud. "Maybe it's time we explore a different avenue of magic."

I glanced at her curiously. "What do you mean?"

Harker leaned forward, her expression thoughtful. "As a blood-born witch, you have access to two distinct forms of magic: blood magic and spirit magic."

I frowned, processing her words. "Spirit magic?"

Harker nodded, her eyes holding a glint of knowledge. "Yes, I've been reading about it here." She walked back over to the table and picked up another well-worn book. "While blood magic emanates from within," she read aloud. "Spirit magic is the essence of the Earth itself. It's the magic that brought the original witches into existence, fusing the energies of both demon and fae."

I leaned back against the floor, absorbing her explanation. The revelation opened up a new realm of possibilities, one that extended beyond the confines of my preconceived notions of magic.

"This spell I found here," she said turning pages of the book, "Is for unlocking doors, maybe we can start there. It's got a pretty simple incantation, so you don't have to sit there and stare at the door like you did with the candle."

I shot Harker a piercing look but held my tongue. "It's worth a shot, does it say anything about how to tap into spirit magic?"

"No, all it says is that you pull forth power and say the incantation." She finished, reading out of the book once more.

"I guess it's worth a shot. Read me the incantation and I'll memorize it then go find a locked door to try it on."

Armed with the incantation Harker had shared, I walked through Kaelan's house in search of a suitable challenge. It wasn't long before I found an old-fashioned door that seemed to call out to me, its intricate lock serving as the perfect canvas for my experiment.

Standing before the door, I took a moment to steady my thoughts. I could feel the weight of my own expectations pressing down on me, the desire to succeed in this new form of magic nearly overwhelming. With a determined breath, I began to recite the incantation, the words flowing from my lips like a melody.

But as the final word left my mouth, the lock remained stubbornly unmoved. Frustration bubbled up within me. I gritted my teeth, trying to suppress the surge of irritation. I had hoped that spirit magic would come more naturally to me, that I could tap into the Earth's energy effortlessly.

Yet, even in the face of failure, a stubborn fire burned within me. I tried the incantation again, my voice steady and determined. Still, the lock didn't budge. I clenched my fists, my frustration intensifying with each unsuccessful attempt.

Stepping back from the door, I closed my eyes and took a deep breath. I needed to calm myself down, to find a way to channel the spirit magic within me. I placed a hand on the door and focused on the feeling of the worn wood beneath my fingertips.

With each breath, I visualized the energy within me, a pulsating force centered around my heart. It was as if a dormant muscle was flexing for the first time, awakening with newfound strength. I let the sensation grow, allowing the energy to flow through me, connecting with the very essence of the Earth.

Opening my eyes, I looked at the lock once more, a quiet determination in my gaze. I whispered the incantation, my voice filled with intent. As the words left my lips, I reached out and touched the lock with my fingertips, feeling a surge of energy flow from me into the mechanism.

And then, just like that, the lock clicked. The door swung open, revealing the room beyond, some kind of study. A triumphant shout escaped my lips as I jumped in the air, pumping my fist with unbridled joy. I had done it.

As I stood before the open door, a sense of wonder washed over me. It was as if I had tapped into an innate source of power, a wellspring of untold potential. The sensation in my chest, that connection to the Earth's energy, was like nothing I had ever experienced before.

I couldn't believe the rush of adrenaline, the thrill of accomplishment, that came with being able to unlock a door. The simple act had a profound impact on me, making me feel empowered and capable. And most importantly, it gave me hope that I could indeed master this new form of magic.

With newfound confidence, I closed the door and turned to leave the room. Only to come face to face with a bemused Kaelan. Caught in a moment of surprise, my heart skipped a beat as I realized I must have appeared as if I were snooping around his house. I felt a rush of heat to my cheeks and quickly cleared my throat.

"Hey there," I said, my voice tinged with awkwardness. "I promise I wasn't snooping or anything."

Kaelan's lips curled into an amused smile, his eyes dancing with playful curiosity. "Snooping, huh? I'm not so sure about that."

He leaned casually against the doorframe, his posture relaxed. I couldn't help but feel a mix of embarrassment and self-consciousness under his gaze. I was like a deer caught in headlights, and I could not seem to shake off the feeling that I had intruded on his space.

Kaelan's amusement softened into genuine interest as he asked, "So how did you manage to get into the room? I only saw the jumping up and down part."

A surge of excitement bubbled up within me, and I found myself animatedly sharing the details of my recent achievement. I told him about the feeling in my chest, the connection I had to the Earth, and how the door had finally unlocked after my third attempt. As I spoke, Kaelan's eyes lit up with enthusiasm, and his genuine interest made my heart race even faster.

He was just as excited as I was, and before I could second-guess myself, a burst of boldness overtook me. Without thinking, I leaned in, grabbing his face in my hands, and pressed my lips to his, the contact sending a jolt of electricity through me. It was a quick kiss, almost glancing.

When I pulled back, a mix of surprise and desire darkened Kaelan's eyes. I couldn't help but wonder if I had crossed a line. If I had misread the signals he had been sending by keeping his distance. The uncertainty gnawed at me, and I averted my gaze for a moment, my cheeks flushed.

"I...I'm sorry if I overstepped," I stammered, my words a mixture of regret and confusion.

Kaelan's hands gently tilted my chin upward, forcing me to meet his gaze once again. His expression was a blend of surprise and something else, something that mirrored the emotions swirling within me.

"Don't be sorry," he said softly, his thumb brushing against my cheek. "You never have to apologize for kissing me. I might have been keeping my distance out of respect for your space, but that doesn't mean I don't want to be kissing you at every opportunity there is."

His admission sent a warm rush through me, and I found myself drawn to him once more. He tugged at my hips, pulling me closer.

The magnetic pull between us was undeniable, and in that moment, I knew that my kiss had merely opened the floodgates of what we had both been feeling.

As our lips met once more, time seemed to stand still. The initial spark of contact ignited a fierce blaze of desire between us, a fire that had been smoldering beneath the surface for far too long. Kaelan's lips were warm and firm against mine, his touch sending shivers of electricity coursing through my veins. Our mouths moved against each other, a dance of longing and pent-up passion. I could feel the weight of every unspoken emotion, every shared moment, fueling the intensity of the kiss.

Kaelan's hands were no longer restrained, his touch roaming across my body with a possessive urgency. His fingers brushed against my skin, igniting a trail of sensations that left my senses reeling. Every touch, every caress felt like a declaration. I pressed up against him, letting his touch consume me.

As the kiss eventually ended, we pulled back, both of us breathless and flushed with desire. It was a raw and unrestrained connection, a reminder that there was something between us that went beyond the ordinary.

Kaelan's voice broke the silence, soft and tinged with a hint of reluctance. "You should go back to the library before I decide I no longer want to be a good guy and take you in this hallway." His words sent a thrill through me, a shiver that raced down my spine and settled in my core. I bit my lip, unable to suppress the grin that spread across my face.

I nodded, my own voice a whisper as I replied, "You're right, I should let Harker know about my progress."

We stood there for a moment longer, our eyes locked in silent understanding. The fire between us had not dimmed, but for now, duty called. With one final lingering glance, I turned and left, my heart still racing from the intensity of our shared kisses.

Back in the library, Harker greeted me with a knowing look. Her expression was a mix of satisfaction and surprise as I told her of my success.

"What did I tell you? Spirit magic is much easier for you than blood magic. You've got a stronger connection to it. We can start training you for more intense spells. Maybe even see if we can get you a better handle on your blood magic since that's where you got your start."

I couldn't stop the grin that spread across my features. "Thank you, Harker. Truly, I could not have gotten this far without you."

She waved away my words. "It's nothing. I'm happy to be here."

The warmth of her kindness, her dedication, was enough to bring a lump to my throat. I was grateful for her presence in my life, and her support.

"Now," she said, clapping her hands together, "let's get started on some more spells."

Chapter Fifteen

The next few days flowed by like a river, carrying with it a sense of uneasy calm. Wren's call had confirmed my suspicions about Jaks' betrayal, and his rough handling at Wren's hands was a satisfying retribution. I continued to immerse myself in the world of spirit magic, my bond with Harker growing into something like friendship as we delved into the ancient spells and incantations. Each day, I felt a surge of strengthening power coursing through me, it felt exhilarating.

My lessons were intense and demanding but I relished every moment of them and soon I was confident enough to try out some simple rituals on my own.

Elara and Harker's clash of personalities was becoming a daily spectacle in the library. The two strong-willed women fought over how to organize the books, their arguments sometimes escalating into full-blown shouting matches. One particularly trying day, Harker's sleep-deprived frustration led to a fierce showdown that echoed through the house, leaving me caught between exasperation and amusement.

Kaelan was a calm amongst the chaos. Our stolen moments were calming oases compared to the storm surrounding us, and we allowed our defenses to slip away for a few moments of peace. The warmth of his touch and the electricity of his kisses reminded me of the depths our connection went, even as I grappled with the uncertainty that lingered beneath the surface.

One evening, as the sun set in a blaze of orange and pink hues, I found myself standing by one of the large bay windows, lost in thought. The gentle breeze ruffled the curtains, and the tranquility of the scene before me belied the whirlwind of emotions inside. The questions that had been gnawing at me couldn't be ignored any longer. I needed to know more about Kaelan — his past, his motives, everything that led him to this point.

Turning away from the window, I made my way to a cozy sitting room where Kaelan was engrossed in a book, a glass of whiskey in his hand. His gaze lifted as I entered, a smile gracing his lips. It was the same smile that had ignited sparks between us, a promise of something more.

"Hey," he greeted softly, closing the book and setting it aside.

I took a deep breath, my resolve firm. "Kaelan, there's something I need to ask you."

He nodded, his expression curious. "Of course, what's on your mind?"

I hesitated for a moment, gathering my thoughts. "I realize that I don't know much about you — your past, your experiences. And I think it's important that I do. Especially if we're going to...continue this." My words were cautious, but my intent was clear.

Kaelan's gaze held mine, his eyes unreadable for a moment before he sighed and leaned back. "You're right. It's only fair that you know."

Kaelan's voice was tinged with resignation and vulnerability as he recounted his intricate lineage. "My mother was a blood-born witch, my father is one of the seven demon lords." My mind reeled at the revelation that he was not entirely a demon, that he had some fae in his bloodline. His admission made my earlier doubts seem trivial, as I realized the depth of his own internal struggles.

"That makes you a..." I trailed off, unable to fully comprehend the magnitude of what he was revealing.

"A prince among demons," Kaelan finished with a faint, wry smile. "But a very insignificant one, in the grand scheme of things."

His story unfolded, painting a vivid picture of his life in the shadows —a life that had been shaped by a cutthroat demon court and the fierce competition among his own kin. The darkness that had surrounded him was palpable, and I couldn't help but feel a pang of sympathy for the young Kaelan who navigated those treacherous waters alone.

"For a while, I gave into the darkness. I embraced the anger and hatred, letting it consume me. I did some things, terrible things, that I'm not proud of. I was feared by many, I even killed some of my own siblings to climb higher in the court. But as I grew older, I realized I had a choice," Kaelan continued, his gaze distant as he recalled his journey. "I met a witch, my aunt, who taught me I could either succumb to the cruelty and ruthlessness that was expected of me, or I could strive to be something different."

His transformation from a creature feared by many to a man who sought compassion and humanity was nothing short of remarkable. The witch he had met, the one who had shown him a path beyond his darkness, had left an indelible mark on his soul. I found myself captivated by his words, by the intricate layers of his past he was peeling back for me.

"When the demons and fae turned on the witches, I chose to help many of them. Eventually, we were all caught and the witches I was with, the ones who owned this house, were killed. When my father learned of what I had done he threw me in his dungeons for five years as punishment. When he finally freed me he bound the majority of my powers and banished me from his court forever."

I felt horrified by his words. His admission of being stripped of his strength, of being restricted by metaphorical chains made me realize just how much he had sacrificed for his beliefs — even if it meant giving up a part of himself in order to protect those who needed him most.

"I'm sorry that you went through all of that," I whispered, my voice heavy with empathy for all he had endured.

Kaelan's gaze met mine, his dark eyes reflecting the shadows of his past, the weight of the burdens he had carried alone. There was an undeniable strength and determination in his voice as he replied, "Don't be. It was a choice I made willingly. But meeting you has been a turning point. You've shown me there's more to life than just surviving."

Our eyes locked, the air between us thick with unspoken emotions. The layers of Kaelan's past were now laid bare before me, and in that moment, I felt an even deeper connection to him. His pain, his struggles, and his determination to do the right thing were an echo of my own. He understood what it was like to fight for what you believed in and to endure hardships that tested you to your very core.

I moved to him from where I stood by the door and climbed into his lap, straddling him. A look of surprise crossed his face before his eyes darkened and his arms went around me. "I'm glad you shared this with me," I said softly as I leaned into him, my hands tangling in his hair.

Kaelan's lip curved into a seductive smile, a desire in his eyes that had fire curling low in my belly. "Thank you for listening," he murmured his nose gently nuzzling my neck. "It means more than you know."

The distance between us dissolved, our lips meeting in a fiery and passionate kiss that left no room for doubt or hesitation. Our tongues swirled together, sending electric currents through my veins. The world around us faded into the background as the intensity of the moment consumed us.

When the kiss finally broke, the air between us seemed charged with a new energy. I leaned in, pressing a trail of kisses down the strong column of his neck, feeling the thrum of his heartbeat against my lips. The low growl that rumbled from deep within his chest was a testament to the effect my actions were having on him, a primal response that sent a shiver down my spine.

"Careful," he warned, his voice a husky whisper. "Unless you want me to rip your clothes off and take you right here."

A mischievous smile curved my lips as I met his gaze, my fingers trailing lightly over his chest. "And what if that's exactly my plan?"

His eyes darkened with desire, full of longing and caution. In that moment, it felt like the space between us held a tangible energy, charged with raw and undeniable attraction. The boundaries that had separated us before were now blurred, and the tension that had simmered between us for so long was ready to be acknowledged.

Before I realized what was happening, Kaelan swept me up in his arms, my legs wrapping around his waist and my dress hiking up as he rose out of his chair. His lips met mine with a ferocity that he hadn't unleashed before, claiming every part of my mouth. He began leading us to a part of the house I hadn't been to yet, his lips moving against mine without pause.

I knew he was taking me to his bedroom. I knew it and I didn't care. He stopped in front of a well-worn wooden door and pushed me roughly against it.

My hands went to his shoulders as he pressed himself against me, his tongue invading my mouth once more. I moaned softly, my hands running through his hair. He pulled back slightly, his eyes blazing into mine with dark desire. "What do you want, Vale?" he asked, his voice rough.

"I want you," I whispered, my voice smoky with heat. He chuckled darkly and opened the door behind me. I could feel him hardening against my stomach as he walked up over to the bed, and my body responded in kind, heat curling low between my thighs.

"You're so responsive, little witch," he said, his hand sliding down to cup my ass. I gasped when his fingers slid between my thighs, rubbing over my panties. "So wet for me already, aren't you?" he murmured against my lips.

"Yes," I said breathlessly.

He laid me down on the bed and moved over top of me, "I've wanted this for a long time, wanted you so badly." His fingers moved against me and I arched my back, pressing myself against his hand. "Tell me what you want, Vale," he said, my name like a prayer on his lips.

I shivered under his touch, "I want you inside of me."

Kaelan growled deep in his throat as he pulled my dress off, letting it fall to the floor. He looked down at me hungrily for a moment before pulling me to the edge of the bed. His hand moved back to my panties, his fingers lightly stroking right down the very center of me. I let out a small gasp. He groaned against my mouth, and his fingers pressed against my clit. I whimpered softly at his touch and he smiled against my mouth at the sound.

Without warning I flipped us over, switching positions to where I was now on top of him. He let out a bemused chuckle that quickly died off as he realized I was pulling his pants off, he lifted his hips enough for me to pull them down over his thighs. His dark eyes smoldered and held my gaze as I drew my fingers over the soft material of his underwear and over his hard length. I closed my hand around him through the fabric, and his entire body jerked in response. I eased my hand under the band on his underwear, gripping him and pulling him free, my thumb smoothing along the glistening head. "Gods," he hissed through his teeth.

"The Gods won't help you here, demon." I teased him.

I curled my hand around him and I moved along his length, his hips jerking slightly at the contact. He was so big and so hard under my palms as I drew my hand up and down languidly. Strands of my silver hair fell over my shoulder and against my face as I lowered my head.

My tongue caressed the tip of his head and his hips jerked once again, my breath quickened to match his. I licked all the way down and back up, his fingertips brushing against my cheek as he watched me with stormy eyes.

Our gazes locked, and I don't think he breathed as I closed my mouth over the head of his cock. Kaelan's entire body reacted, his hips lifted and his back arched as I drew him into my mouth, and he let out a groan. I took him in as far as I could, my tongue swirling over his skin, and used my hands on the rest of him. The salty taste of him was like an aphrodisiac. I greedily sucked on him, thoroughly enjoying the reactions his body had to what I was doing. His hands reached down and wound through my hair gently.

He wasn't pushing me, he wasn't trying to set the pace or make me go faster. It was as if he were using his grip on me as an anchor. I bobbed my head up and down on his length, taking him deep and sucking hard before pulling him free.

"Fuck, Vale, that mouth," he grunted, his voice hoarse with desire.

I smiled and licked his tip before sliding back down onto him, my hand still stroking him as I worked him into my mouth. Kaelan's fingers tightened in my hair, and his hips began to thrust. My own arousal grew, and I was aching to be filled by him.

His breathing was ragged as he tried to control himself. "Fuck," he growled again before lifting me up and roughly tossing me on the bed. "Do you know just what I'd like to do to you?" I could guess, and I was sure he had every intention of showing me. I lay back and watched as Kaelan tore his shirt off over his head, the muscles rippling beneath his bronzed skin. He was built like a warrior, strong and solid. My gaze drifted down his chest and across the ripples of his abs, landing on the thick length of him.

He knelt between my legs and pulled off my panties, the cool air caressing my wet heat. I could feel his eyes on me, watching the rise and fall of my chest, his lips slightly parted. He propped my legs up on the bed, folding them at the knees so I was displayed before him. He dragged his tongue clean up the center of me and my head dipped back as I let out a startled gasp.

His tongue slid between me and lapped at the moisture pooled there, his thumb rubbing against my clit. He growled deep in his chest at the taste of me, and I could hear the rustle of fabric as his other hand worked himself. My heart was pounding wildly, and I had to grip the sheets as a wave of pleasure washed over me.

Kaelan moaned against me, the sound sending a shock-wave through me as he sucked my clit into his mouth, nipping with his teeth. My hand reached up to my breast, kneading it as he devoured me. "Do you like seeing me on my knees before you, little witch?" he asked, his words rumbling into my very core. He gave me another slow lick from base to top, and as he reached my clit, he slid a finger into me. I bowed off the bed, and he thrust his finger in again before adding another one.

The pleasure was overwhelming, and I couldn't help but writhe against him, begging for more. Kaelan's fingers curled inside me, hitting a spot that made me cry out and clench around him.

"That's it," he purred. "I want to see you fall apart, Vale."

His mouth found my clit again, and his tongue traced circles over it. His fingers continued to pump in and out of me, his pace increasing. He sucked hard, and his fingers crooked up, hitting that perfect spot again.

"Kaelan," I breathed, my muscles tensing deliciously as I felt my climax already rising. He kept his hand where it was and came up to kiss me again, I could taste myself on his tongue.

"How do you want it?" he asked breathlessly, thrusting his fingers into me again so that I cried out.

"Hard," I gasped.

"Thank fuck," he swore and then I felt his tongue again, past my clit, up my stomach, to my breasts, until he was over me, and I opened my legs to him. Kaelan pulled away and I could see the hunger in his eyes, the need for release. He slid off the bed and discarded his boxers, and I couldn't help but watch the way his muscles moved under his skin. He was absolutely breathtaking.

He lowered himself into the cradle of my thighs, kissing my neck as I felt the very tip of him press against my entrance. I pulled his face to mine and kissed him savagely, my tongue scrapping over his teeth as I pressed our mouths together.

Kaelan broke away, his voice barely a whisper, "Are you ready for me, little witch?"

"Yes," I panted, my hips shifting, trying to get him closer. I reached down and gripped him, guiding him to me.

As he slipped in slowly, fire erupted within my body. I moaned into his mouth as he eased himself in inch by inch, filling me up wholly until he was fully seated at the base. He was large enough that I felt the sweetest pain and he remained there unmoving for a moment while my body grew accustomed to him. His care and gentleness snapped me free of any restraint, I gripped his ass, my fingernails biting down. He groaned as my silken, blazing heat gripped him tightly, and he began to move over me. He pulled out all the way and then slowly, so very slowly eased back in. He withdrew again, lowering his head to watch his cock slide out of me, gleaming, and then watched as he entered me again.

"Kaelan," I breathed again, urging him on.

His self-control seemed to give out at the sound of his name on my lips and he thrust his hips roughly, pushing me across the bed. He thrust again and again, and I cried out as I writhed beneath him. I needed more, needed him to be deeper. Kaelan shifted, and the change in angle was perfection. The tip of him hit a spot inside of me that had me seeing stars. He must have known because he angled his hips so that he hit it every time. His thrusts became harder and more urgent. His eyes never left mine, and I was drowning in his gaze.

He withdrew from me and flipped me on my stomach, I lifted my ass in the air and presented it to him. His tongue licked over me again, and my body jerked at the unexpected contact. Kaelan grabbed me by the neck and gently pulled me up onto all fours, I heard the low rumble in his chest. His hand ran over the curve of my ass and gave it a rough smack before sliding down between my thighs, finding the sensitive bud. His other hand pressed on my lower back, pushing my ass up even higher.

He grabbed my hips and plunged into me, driving all the way down to the hilt. He pumped into me roughly as I panted and grabbed the headboard for support. Every time he drove into me, the friction of his body against my clit sent a wave of pleasure through me. His hips began to snap forward in quick succession, and his grip on me tightened. Kaelan leaned down, his lips grazing the back of my neck. He trailed kisses down my spine as he pushed in and out of me, his pace steady and unforgiving.

He circled his arms around my waist, pulling me up until I was seated on top of him, my back pressed against his chest. One hand palmed my breasts while the other wrapped around my throat as I moved up and down. He bit my neck enough to leave a mark and I could feel the electricity growing within me. Kaelan pinched my nipple, and I ground down onto him, my inner muscles clenching.

His hips snapped upward and he growled, his hands gripping me so tightly I was sure they would leave bruises. A sheen of sweat broke out over his forehead, his dark hair sticking to his face as he continued his relentless assault. The sounds of our bodies colliding was drowned out by the pounding of blood in my ears and the ragged panting that escaped my lips.

Kaelan was lost in the rhythm of our bodies moving together, and when he spoke, his voice was rough and low. "Touch yourself for me, little witch."

My fingers slid down my belly and I began to circle my clit, the tension rising. "Yes," he moaned as he watched me, "just like that."

He thrust harder, his grip on my hips tightening as his body slammed into mine. "Vale," he gritted out through his teeth, he was as close as I was.

The friction, the pressure, and the pleasure were all mounting and I felt myself reaching the brink of release. My walls clenched around him and he groaned, his fingers digging into me. Kaelan's hand went to my jaw, turning my face to his as he kissed me roughly. My fingers sped up as I rode him and the tension within me grew.

I moved over him faster and harder, and my release barreled into me. My entire body shuddered, and I shouted out his name, not caring who heard me. My body contracted, and his hips continued to snap forward. He was unrelenting as I came around him. He growled, his hands gripping my hips hard. I was still riding out my own orgasm when he reached his peak. He thrust so hard I nearly screamed, his own release finding him as he climaxed with me, growling savagely.

Kaelan's arms tightened around me, holding me against his chest as his hips slowed. My head lolled against his shoulder, and I could feel the pounding of his heart. The demon's chest was heaving, and he pressed a kiss to the top of my head, his grip loosening slightly. He held me there until our bodies were done shaking, then gently lowered me to the bed. He collapsed beside me and we lay there panting, trying to pull ourselves back together. He rolled over and brushed some stray hairs away from my face before cupping my head in his hands and kissing me gently.

"Vale," he began, his eyes glinting, "That was..." He shook his head as words escaped him.

"I know," I agreed breathlessly, trailing my hand down his chest.

He chuckled, "I wasn't finished." He brushed his thumb along my cheekbone and the gesture was so tender and affectionate, so unlike anything I thought a demon was capable of, that I could only stare at him. "You are exquisite," he said, his gaze never leaving mine.

"You're not too bad yourself," I teased.

He grinned and pulled me close, wrapping his arms around me.

"Stay with me tonight, Vale," he said, his voice low.

I nodded, "Alright."

"I didn't scare you, did I?"

"No, why would you?" I asked, confused.

"I don't usually...let go like that. It's been a very long time since I've had anyone in my bed." He said, his fingers trailing down my neck as he looked down at me.

"I've never been with a demon before, you're certainly different from the stories."

He smiled, his eyes dancing. "We aren't all the same."

"Will you stay with me?" he asked gently, as if he were worried what my answer would be.

"Yes," I told him, smiling, and the relief was clear on his face. I didn't think I could walk back to my room even if I wanted to.

I lay there with him, enjoying the silence and the feeling of being in his arms. I had no idea what time it was, but I didn't really care.

I snuggled close to his body, my eyes growing heavy with sleep as the warmth of his embrace soothed me into a peaceful slumber.

Chapter Sixteen

The dream realm unveiled itself before me, a mysterious tapestry woven with threads of darkness. Wrapped in the comforting embrace of Kaelan's arm, I had slipped off to sleep, only to be plunged into a world of foreboding visions. Shadows danced at the periphery of my awareness, beckoning me toward a figure that stood at the heart of the darkness. The figure was a woman whom I faintly recognized, clothed in a long black dress, the gossamer folds of her skirt blowing in an ethereal wind.

Recognition struck me like a lightning bolt, my memories merging with those of the past. I had encountered her before, in fragmented dreams that felt like forgotten echoes. This time I found myself drawn to her presence, compelled to inquire about the mystery she represented.

"Who are you?" I asked, my voice carrying a note of apprehension.

The woman regarded me with ancient eyes that seemed to hold vast knowledge within them. Her response was cryptic, a riddle. "I am like you, but not you. We are the same, yet different."

The words hung in the air, echoing through the void that surrounded us. My instincts flared to life, this was the First Witch. A shiver ran down my spine as I realized who she was.

As if sensing my thoughts, the First Witch's gaze bore into mine, and I felt as if she were peering into the very depths of my soul. "You are unprepared for what's to come," she intoned, her voice carrying an eerie resonance that seemed to reverberate through me.

Curiosity bubbled up within me like a tempest, and I couldn't help but question her about the future she hinted at. "What is to come?" I asked, urgency and trepidation lacing my words.

The First Witch's response was a mere shake of her head, her lips forming a melancholic smile. It was clear that the specifics of the future she foresaw were not meant to be shared, leaving me to grapple with the uncertainty that loomed ahead.

Our time within the dream world was fleeting, a fragile bridge connecting the conscious and the subconscious. With a heavy sigh, the woman seemed to communicate that our discourse needed to be swift, our connection short-lived. Her words held a sense of urgency.

"You must wake, Vale." She murmured, her voice a whisper carried on the winds of the dream realm. "Find me in the world of the waking, call to me, there we may converse beyond these veiled confines."

Understanding dawned upon me, the gravity of her message sinking in. The dream realm was but a glimpse, a prelude to a conversation that needed to take place in the physical world. The mysterious First Witch had something to impart to me, something so vital that she had made her way into my dreams.

As the dream realm's threads unraveled around me, the woman's figure began to fade into the obsidian void. A sense of urgency pulsed within me, a determination to heed her message and seek her out once I returned to the waking world.

With a small gasp, I stirred from the depths of slumber, my eyes fluttering open to the soft illumination of Kaelan'sbedroom. The dream's echoes lingered in my mind, a resonant reminder of the encounter with the First Witch. As the sun's rays painted the room with a gentle morning light, a sense of purpose settled within me, mingling with the uncertainty of what was to come.

I found myself entwined in Kaelan's arms, his presence a comforting reassurance amidst the lingering remnants of the dream realm. As I stirred, his lips brushed against mine in a soft kiss, and his voice, laden with sleep, greeted me with a gentle, "Good morning."

"Good morning," I replied, my tone carrying a mix of emotions that I couldn't quite hide.

His inquiry was expected, his concern genuine. "What's wrong?" He asked, his gaze searching mine.

I took a moment to gather my thoughts before sharing the haunting encounter with the First Witch. Kaelan's eyes never wavered from mine as I recounted the conversation.

Silence hung in the air for a heartbeat, his fingers gently tracing patterns on my arm as he absorbed the weight of my revelation. Finally, he spoke, his voice a soothing balm against the tempest of emotions swirling within me. "You should heed the message," he said, his eyes unwavering. "But how do you find a witch who lived millennia ago?"

I sighed, the enormity of the task ahead weighing on me. "I don't know," I admitted, my voice full of doubt.

His hand found mine, his touch grounding me. "We can figure it out together," he said, determination flickering in his eyes.

With his support, I gathered my resolve and rose from the bed, grabbing my discarded dress. As I slipped the garment over my head, I heard the rustle of fabric behind me and felt the heat of Kaelan's gaze on my body. Despite the gravity of the situation, a small smile tugged at my lips as I turned around and found his eyes roaming my body, a mischievous glint in them.

As he sauntered over to where I stood, I couldn't help but admire the way the morning sun lit his body, accentuating his toned muscles and giving his dark hair a silky shine. I bit my lip, my eyes raking over him hungrily, a blush creeping up my cheeks at the sight.

He smirked, his voice teasing. "If you keep looking at me like that, we're never going to get out of here."

"Is that a bad thing?"

"Not necessarily, but we do have a rather urgent task ahead of us."

I sighed, my mind conjuring up the vision of the First Witch. "I guess I'll have to start by looking into summoning spirits," I mused, my thoughts racing as I considered the possibilities. "Maybe there's a way to call her forth, even if she lived millennia ago."

Kaelan nodded in agreement, his expression thoughtful. "The library might have some information about summoning rituals," he suggested. "It's worth a shot."

With his suggestion in mind, we made our way to the new heart of the house —the library. The air within was charged with the energy of countless tomes, a repository of knowledge waiting to be discovered. I was surprised when we didn't find Harker still there, the sleep deprecation must be getting to her. I felt excitement and trepidation, a yearning to unravel the secrets that might hold the key to reaching the First Witch.

With Kaelan by my side, I delved into the pages of ancient texts, my fingers trailing over the words that held the potential to guide me on this extraordinary journey. As the hours passed, my focus remained unyielding, my determination unwavering.

The story of the First Witch and the rituals that could bridge the gap between our realms slowly began to unravel before me. Each page turned was a step closer to understanding that complex interplay between the realms of the living and the spirits that existed beyond.

Kaelan's presence provided a sense of stability amidst the sea of words and incantations. With his help, we pieced together the fragments of knowledge that might enable me to reach out to the First Witch, to breach the barriers that separated our worlds.

As the day turned to evening, I closed one of the books with a sigh, my mind swirling with newfound information. Kaelan's hand found mine, his touch a reassuring connection. "We're making progress," he said, his voice laced with determination.

I nodded, emotions coursing through me. "Yes, we are," I agreed, feeling the weight of the journey ahead.

"Why don't you go get some rest while I make dinner? You probably could use some." He offered, his concern evident in his words.

The idea of a break was tempting, and I nodded in agreement. "That sounds like a good plan," I replied, my gaze lingering on him for a moment before I turned to head towards my room.

As I stepped from the library, I felt a swirling of emotions— gratitude for Kaelan's presence, determination to uncover more about the First Witch, and a sense of anticipation for the days to come. We had begun the journey to summon the spirit of the First Witch, and it was an expedition unlike any other. There was no map, no compass to guide us, but with the knowledge we had gathered, and the determination we both possessed, I was confident that we would find a way.

Yet, my moment of contemplation was cut short by my phone ringing.

With a furrowed brow, I answered the call, the voice on the other end immediately recognizable as Wren's. His urgency was palpable as he replayed his news. "A group of demons attacked the factory tonight. No one was killed, but some were seriously hurt." My heart skittered to a stop in my chest, the factory was supposed to be safe without me there. My heart clenched at the thought of danger befalling those under our care.

Panic surged through me, and I ended the call with a swift promise to be there soon. I rushed to the kitchen where Kaelanwas, my words tumbling out in a rush. "The factory was attacked by demons."

Kaelan's eyes darkened with concern, his features hardening as he took in the information. Without hesitation, I called out for Nyxen and he stepped out of a nearby shadow, his head cocked to the side curiously. His presence was a silent reassurance.

"Can you shift us to the apartment's roof?" I asked, turning back to Kaelan. He nodded and began to cross the room towards me. "Wait, there's something I need to find first." Without waiting for a response from him, I turned and sprinted to the library. Harker was there now, already positioned behind a tower of books.

Without sparing her a second glance I stepped up to the center of the library. "I need a book on healing with spirit magic," I said to the dusty shelves and a moment later the resulting book plopped onto the floor, its pages splayed open at an awkward angle from the fall.

"What's going on, Vale?" Harker asked from her perch as I bent down to scoop up the book.

"The factory has been attacked," I repeated. "There are people injured and I plan on helping them." I began rifling through the pages of the book, looking for the page that could help me.

"I'm coming with you," Harker said unexpectedly. I looked at her in surprise and she shrugged her shoulders. "Guess that means I like you. I'm in this with you now."

I studied her for a moment and then offered her a soft smile, her offer of friendship overwhelming me slightly. "Thank you, Harker. I mean it."

I turned back to the book and finally found the page I needed, it was a simple incantation, I could almost weep with relief.

"Vitality's flow, magic's embrace,
Bind and mead in healing grace.
From earth to sky, let energies blend,
Wounds undone, strength ascend."

I read the incantation aloud two more times, memorizing it quickly. Spirit magic consumed a lot of energy from me, but hopefully, it wouldn't end up being too much for me tonight.

I put the book back quickly and motioned for Harker to follow me back to the kitchen where Kaelan and Nyxen waited. Kaelan had strapped on several weapons while I was in the library, including a gleaming black sword strapped to his back.

With Harker coming Kaelan would only be able to shift us one at a time, so I turned to Nyxen. "Nyxen, I need you to shift me to the apartment's roof, can you do that?" A silent affirmation gleamed in his dark eyes. Good, I hadn't been completely sure that my familiar could accomplish shifting us both.

"I'll see you there," I said turning to Kaelan and Harker and they both nodded their assent.

The shadows began to wrap around me, and their images faded from my sight. In moments, I was transported to the familiar rooftop, the night air carrying a sense of urgency. A breath later Kaelan and Harker were there are well. I raced downstairs, the two of them close on my heels, our steps quick and determined. As we entered the factory's main floor, my eyes scanned the scene, searching for Wren in the chaos.

And there he was, Wren, a stalwart figure amidst the turmoil. As he caught sight of me, relief washed over his features and he crossed the room quickly to meet me. My voice trembled as I spoke, "Wren, what happened?"

Exhaustion etched his features, but his gaze was steady. "About five demons showed up out of nowhere and started attacking everyone. Luckily Donovan and I were here after our patrol and managed to fight them off with the help of some of the Otherworlders."

My eyebrows shot up at the fact that Donovan had stuck around to help and Wren continued. "We managed to take down three before the rest fled. Some have a few minor scrapes but it's Jason who might be in trouble. And June is hurt too."

The weight of Wren's words settled heavily on my chest. Juniper, always the steadfast and caring soul, was also injured. My concern for her welled up, but I knew I needed to prioritize the more immediate situation. I nodded to Wren, determination settling into my features. "Take me to Jason," I said firmly, ready to do whatever I could to help.

Wren led me to a cot where Jason lay, his breathing labored and a deep gash marring his side. My heart clenched at the sight, guilt washing over me. If only I had managed to put up those wards faster, but I was too busy enjoying myself with Kaelan.

Kneeling beside him, I examined the extent of his injuries. The wound was deep, the mark of demon claws, and it was clear that he needed immediate medical attention. There was only so much his supernatural healing could do, and it wasn't fast enough. I knew that my spirit magic had the potential to heal, but the task ahead was daunting.

"What are you going to do, Vale?" Wren asked curiously.

"I'm going to try and heal him. I've never done it this way before so I'm not sure what will happen or if I can even manage it." I replied, my words shaky and unsure.

With a steadying breath, I focused on the energy within me, that invisible muscle flexing in my chest. I recited the incantation in a whisper, every word laced with intent and hope. As I channeled my spirit magic into Jason's injured side, a faint glow surrounded the wound. I heard Wren let out a small gasp behind me.

The magic worked, I could feel the energy knitting together the torn flesh, repairing the damage inflicted by the demons. But the process was draining, a surge of fatigue washing over me as I continued to pour my energy into the spell. Jason's breathing steadied, his features relaxing as the magic worked its wonders.

When I finally released the spell, the glow faded and I pulled back, my chest heaving with exertion. I looked at Jason's side to find the wound had closed completely with only a raised pink scar remaining. The sight left me in awe of the power that flowed within me, exhilaration and exhaustion coursing through my veins.

Jason stirred and blinked in surprise, disbelief etched across his features. "What...how?"

Wren's eyes held a mix of wonder and gratitude as he answered for me. "Vale healed you with her magic."

Around us, the gathered Otherworlders exchanged whispers of amazement. But I could only spare a fleeting smile before my energy levels plummeted, the aftermath of the healing spell taking its toll on me. I swayed slightly, the room spinning for a moment as I fought to remain upright.

Kaelan was quick to steady me, concern evident in his eyes. "Vale, you need to rest."

I nodded weakly, my chest heavy with fatigue. As the room slowly came back into focus, I met Wren's gaze, my voice a mere whisper. "Make sure Juniper's taken care of."

Wren assured me that they were attending to her, and I allowed myself to be led away from the scene by Kaelan and Harker, my body heavy with the aftermath of my magic. As we climbed the stairs to my apartment, every step seemed to require an almost superhuman effort. My legs felt like lead, and my vision began to blur around the edges.

By the time we reached the apartment, I could barely stand on my own. Kaelan and Harker guided me inside, their concern palpable. I sank onto the edge of the nearest chair, my head spinning as I struggled to keep my eyes open. Kaelan's strong arms wrapped around me, and before I could protest, he effortlessly lifted me into his arms.

"You shouldn't be walking in this state," he murmured, his voice laced with worry as he carried me toward my room. I leaned into his warmth, my exhaustion making it difficult to form coherent thoughts.

As he gently laid me down on my bed, I let out a soft sigh of relief. The softness of the mattress cradled my tired body, and I closed my eyes for a moment. Kaelan's voice reached me through the haze, urging me to rest and assuring me he would take care of everything while I slept.

I managed to crack a small, tired smile. "Pretty inconvenient, my body giving out on me so quickly."

Kaelan's fingers brushed a strand of hair from my forehead, his gaze warm with understanding. "You're just beginning to tap into your magic. Building up your endurance will take time. I'm sure it's normal to feel drained after using such powerful spells, especially when you're new to them.

I nodded weakly, grateful for his reassurance. He pulled the covers over me, tucking me in with a gentle touch. "Rest, Vale. You've done more than enough tonight."

As my eyes closed, the last thing I felt was Kaelan's presence lingering beside me, his protective aura soothing and comforting. The exhaustion that had been weighing me down finally overtook me, and I slipped into a deep sleep, my dreams a jumble of images and emotions from the night's events.

Chapter Seventeen

The faint smell of coffee drifted to my nose, rousing me from sleep. The light filtering through the curtains indicated that it was late in the afternoon. My body felt significantly better than the night before, and as I stretched, I was surprised by how rejuvenated I felt. However, the moment was interrupted by a familiar voice, and as I turned, I found Wren sitting in a chair nearby.

"Good afternoon, sleeping beauty," he greeted with a faint smile. "You've been out for about sixteen hours. I wanted to make sure you were recovering well."

I sat up slowly, my gaze shifting between Wren's concerned expression and the room around me. "Sixteen hours? I guess I was more exhausted than I thought."

Wren nodded. "Considering that powerful magic you used, it's not surprising. But you're looking much better."

I swung my legs over the side of the bed, testing my balance. Wren cautioned me to be careful. I nodded in acknowledgment but felt confident in my ability to move. "I feel alright, just still a bit tired maybe."

"I'm glad to hear that," Wren said, a note of relief in his voice. "Everyone's downstairs, getting things back to normal after last night."

At the mention of the demon attack, the events of the previous night came rushing back to me, and my worry and anxiety returned. I took a deep breath, gathering my thoughts. I wanted to see how the injured were faring and check on the factory.

I was anxious about the attack. This was supposed to be a place of safety, a refuge for the Otherworld community. Yet, the factory had become a target. It seemed the demons were relentless, determined to make their point.

The uncertainty of what lay ahead weighed on me, but I knew I needed to remain focused, to find a way to protect those under my care. With that thought, I stood up, feeling determined.

"Let's go check in with everyone," Wren suggested, standing and holding out his arm.

"Thanks," I murmured, linking my arm through his. He smiled, leading me out of the room.

Wren followed beside me as I headed out of the room and down the stairs to the main floor. There, I found Juniper tending to some of the Otherworlders, her expression a mix of concern and determination. She was tending to a small child with a cut on his cheek, applying a salve and then gently kissing the top of his head. The child's eyes lit up at the attention, a sweet smile on his lips. I approached her, and without a word, enveloped her in a tight hug. Her arms wrapped around me, her embrace a comforting presence. "Hey," she whispered.

My voice was muffled against her shoulder. "I'm so sorry, Juniper. I should have been faster with the wards."

She pulled back slightly, looking at me with a gentle smile. "Vale, none of this was your fault, and thanks to what you did for Jason, everyone is safe."

I sighed, realizing she was right. I offered a small smile in return. "I guess you're right," I told her, but I still felt guilty as I looked her over. Her arm was bandaged and there was a huge bruise on her head.

"I could heal these for you, June." I offered, touching her head lightly.

"Absolutely not. I can heal just fine on my own, and you don't need to lose all your strength again."

Before I could protest, Jason approached us. His posture was a bit stiff, likely from his recent injuries. He met my gaze with a mixture of gratitude and something else I couldn't quite place.

"Vale," he began, his voice sincere, "I wanted to thank you for what you did for me last night. If it wasn't for you, I don't know what would have happened. I'd probably be dead."

I felt a sense of warmth in my chest at his words. "You don't need to thank me, Jason. I'm just glad I could help."

He nodded, his gaze shifting between Juniper and me. He cleared his throat before continuing. "Well, I owe you one."

Juniper chuckled, nudging Jason playfully. "You owe her more than one. Now go rest please, you look like you could use it."

Jason huffed, but his eyes sparkled with affection. "Okay, okay. I'm going. Don't you two get into trouble without me."

As Jason walked away, I turned back to Juniper, my expression serious. "Are you sure you're okay? I mean, you got hurt too. You should rest."

She shrugged off my concern, though her eyes held a glint of appreciation. "It's nothing major, just a few scrapes. But I appreciate your concern."

I let the matter drop, knowing that she was strong enough to take care of herself. Still, the thought of her injuries left a bitter taste in my mouth. Being mortal, Juniper had no real reason to want to help the Otherworlders, yet she did so happily.

I looked around the room, seeing that everyone seemed to be taking care of themselves, and I breathed a sigh of relief. It was clear that the Otherworlders and Juniper were strong, resilient people. They had endured many challenges and would no doubt continue to do so.

As Juniper excused herself to check on the others I turned my attention back to Wren, "What happened to Kaelan and Harker after everything calmed down?" I asked.

Wren scratched his head, looking a bit amused. "Well, they stuck around for a few hours and made sure everything was secure. Harker was grumbling about needing to learn more about wards and protections. Then they headed back to Kaelan's house, I think she was itching to get back to the library, she wouldn't let Kaelan stay to watch over you."

I nodded. It seemed like Harker's determination to ensure our safety had only grown stronger.

As I walked through the factory, I noticed everyone's lingering gazes on me. The news of the healing magic had spread. Some looked curious, others wary. It was a reminder that my true nature was no longer hidden. They knew about my magic. The thought crossed my mind that not all of them might be trustworthy, but I pushed the thought aside. If the demons and fae already knew about me, it was futile to keep the truth concealed.

I made my way into the bookshop, and I spotted Ava tending to the herbs in the backroom. She looked up when she heard me entering and gave a tired but genuine smile.

"Hey," I said, stopping in front of the door. "Are you doing okay?"

Ava nodded, wiping her tattooed hands on her apron. "Yeah, thanks to Wren and the others who fought off the demons. They were really brave."

"You're right, they were," I agreed with a small smile.

Ava turned back to the herbs, carefully placing the dried plants in labeled jars. The sight of the familiar flowers and leaves brought a wave of comfort. I moved to her side, helping her with the work. The repetitive motion was soothing, and the smell of the herbs was calming.

After a few moments of silence, Ava spoke up, her voice soft and hesitant.

"So, is it true that you can use healing magic now? That you healed Jason last night?"

I paused, looking over at her. I knew the truth would spread, but I wasn't sure how everyone would react. I swallowed hard, nodding.

Ava's eyes widened her expression one of surprise and awe.

"That's incredible," she breathed. "To be able to use healing magic, that's an incredibly precious gift."

I shifted uncomfortably, not quite knowing how to respond. "It's still new to me, and it takes a lot of energy. But I'm grateful for the ability to help."

Ava studied me for a moment, her eyes searching mine. "You're a special person, Vale. I'm glad to know you."

I felt my cheeks heat at her compliment, and I shook my head. "I'm just a regular person, trying to do what's right."

Ava gave a small smile, returning to her work. "You're much more, I want you to know that."

I didn't know how to respond, so I remained silent, continuing to help her with the herbs.

How in the world was I going to ensure all these people's safety? Could any wards I place really be enough to protect them if the demons came back?

We spent the rest of the day helping clean up the damage from the attack and checking in on everyone. As evening approached, Wren and Juniper approached me. "So what are you planning to do now?" He asked, crossing his arms and leaning against the checkout desk.

I took a deep breath before answering. "I had a dream about the First Witch, and she told me I need to contact her in the physical realm. I have no idea how to do that, but I'm hoping I can find something in the library."

Wren listened attentively, his expression thoughtful. "That's a good place to start. If you need any help I'm sure Harker would be more than willing."

I nodded, grateful for his support. "And besides that, I also want to find a spell or ritual to ward the factory properly. I can't keep hiding at Kaelan's place forever. I need to ensure everyone's safety and have a way to come and go without risking too much exposure."

"Just be careful and don't push yourself too hard. We saw how drained you were last night. It's important to find a balance." Juniper said.

I sighed, realizing that she was right. "You're right, June. I'll be more mindful of my limits. I can't afford to exhaust myself like that again. If I overextend, I might not have the strength to protect anyone."

Wren's expression softened with understanding. "We're all here to support you. Just remember that."

I knew the path ahead wouldn't be easy, but I was determined to do whatever it took to keep our makeshift family safe. I couldn't afford to falter, not when so much was at stake.

I was eager to get back, so after bidding farewell to Wren and Juniper, I called Nyxen forth. His shadowy form appeared from the shadows behind the desk and Juniper nearly jumped out of her skin. I had forgotten I hadn't introduced the two of them.

Juniper blinked rapidly, clearly startled.

"What is that?!" She gasped.

I laughed, feeling a little sheepish. "I'm so sorry, June. This is Nyxen. He's my familiar."

Nyxen regarded her with a curious expression, tilting his head slightly.

"Your familiar?" Juniper echoed, her voice a bit shaky.

I nodded, feeling a little guilty for startling her. "Yes, my familiar. He's a shadow spirit. It's hard to explain, but he's sort of bound to me."

Juniper's eyes widened as she absorbed the information.

"Well, that's certainly unexpected," she finally said.

I chuckled, knowing it was an understatement.

"Yes, it is. But he's been a big help to me," I replied.

Nyxen preened, and I had a feeling he enjoyed being appreciated.

"So, he's like your spirit guide?" Juniper asked, seeming a bit more at ease.

I shrugged, not entirely sure how to describe it. "Something like that."

Nyxen nodded, looking pleased with the comparison.

We all three looked to the shadowkin, and I swore I could feel a brush of consciousness from him against my mind. I was slightly shocked but decided to file that way for later.

With a final glance at the bookshop, Nyxen shifted me back, the sensation of darkness enveloping me briefly before revealing the familiar surroundings of Kaelan's sitting room.

I found my way to the library where I expected to find both Kaelan and Harker. To my surprise, only Harker was present, engrossed in a book as usual. I frowned slightly, wondering where Kaelan had gone after shifting Harker back.

"Harker," I began, my tone thoughtful, "have you seen Kaelan? I figured he'd be waiting for me here."

Harker looked up from her reading, her gaze meeting mine. "After shifting us back, he seemed quite restless. I think he mentioned he had some matters to attend to."

I nodded, still curious but not wanting to pry further. "Alright, well I guess I'll just start researching on my own then."

Harker closed her book with a decisive nod. "I'll do what I can to help as well. What exactly are we looking for?"

I proceeded to lay out my plans—finding a ritual or spell for placing protective wards around the factory and searching for a way to contact the First Witch. Harker listened intently, her focus unwavering for once.

"I'll start delving into ways to communicate with the spirits," Harker offered. "You can begin searching for information on wards."

I appreciated her dedication to our cause. With a nod, I replied, "That sounds like a good plan. Let's see if the library can offer us any guidance."

Turning my attention to the massive collection of books around us, I addressed the room itself. "Oh, mystic library," I paused, looking to Harker for her reaction. She gave a small chuckle but didn't look up from her book.

"I need a book that provides detailed information on placing protective wards." I continued.

In response to my request, a book slid off the shelf and fell to the floor with a soft thud. Harker flinched noticeably, she hated when the library did that, preferring to find the books herself so the library wouldn't harm any of the tomes. I walked over, bending down to retrieve it. A smile crossed my lips as I realized the library had once again provided me with exactly what I needed.

Bringing the book over to the table, I settled in and began flipping through its pages. The text was rich with diagrams, symbols, and instructions for creating wards of varying complexity. I scanned the contents, absorbing the knowledge within, while occasionally jotting down notes in one of Harker's small notebooks nearby. It would probably be helpful to start my own notebook with the different spells and incantations I use. My own modern grimoire of sorts.

I felt determined as I delved deeper into the text. The events of the past few days had driven home the fact that I needed to be prepared for any threat that might arise. This was only the beginning, and I couldn't afford to hold back anymore. It was time to face the danger head-on.

Hours passed as I meticulously read and absorbed the information within the book. Occasionally, I looked up to see Harker engrossed in her own research.

Eventually, after much reading and careful consideration, I found a warding spell that seemed suitable for our purposes. I looked over at Harker, a sense of accomplishment evident in my eyes.

"Harker, I think I found a way to provide the factory with additional protections. It should work to keep the demons out, and even if they manage to break the barrier, we should have enough warning to mount a defense or escape."

Harker closed the book she was reading and turned to me with a determined expression. "That's great, Vale. What do you need us to do?"

I took a deep breath, mentally preparing myself for the task ahead.

Just then, the library door opened, and Kaelan strode in. I looked up, surprised to see him return. He hesitated for a moment as if deciding whether or not to share whatever news he might have.

I, however, was not one to wait. "Hey, where have you been?"

His expression was weary as he spoke, running his hands through his thick hair. "I went to the demon realm to gather some information. I needed to find out who was behind the attack on the factory."

I leaned forward, my curiosity piqued. "And did you find out?"

Kaelan's gaze met mine, his eyes reflecting his concern. "It was Zephyrian. He wants you, Vale."

A surge of anger and fear welled within me. Zephyrian's relentless pursuit was infuriating, but it also fueled my determination to stand my ground. "He won't get me. I won't let him succeed."

Kaelan nodded in agreement, his expression dark. "We won't let him."

As I rose from my seat and gathered my notes, I felt a sense of urgency. There was no time to waste, especially with the looming threat of Zephyrian and his demons. I looked at Kaelan, determination clear in my eyes.

"I need to gather up some supplies then we can head back to the factory to place these wards," I said to him and he nodded.

The shelves were stocked with a variety of magical tools and ingredients, a testament to the depth of knowledge and resources that the library held. With my supplies in hand, we left the library and made our way through the house. Kaelan paused our progress with a touch, and his lips met mine in a passionate kiss. It was a moment of intensity, his emotions and desires for me evident.

Breaking the kiss, he held me close, his eyes studying my face with longing and concern. His voice was gentle as he asked, "Are you sure you're okay after last night? You used a lot of energy, and I don't want you pushing yourself too hard with these wards."

I smiled at his concern, grateful for his thoughtfulness. "I'm alright, Kaelan. Really. But thank you for looking out for me." I took a deep breath and focused on the task ahead. "Now, let's get these wards in place. I want to make sure the factory is as protected as possible."

The shadows wrapped around us as Kaelan pulled me closer, and the world went dark.

Chapter Eighteen

As moonlight glittered through the windows, tinting the room in cool hues of blue and silver, Kaelan and I descended the stairs from my apartment, our steps quiet. The bookshop's atmosphere felt charged, determination and uncertainty hanging in the air. Wren was out on patrol, and Juniper was preoccupied with the well-being of the Otherworlders, leaving us in solitude to execute the critical task at hand.

"I have to gather some herbs first," I said to Kaelan before going to the sunroom in the back of the shop. Once there I hurriedly looked for the dried rosemary and mugwort I needed, I had already grabbed the cedar stick the ritual called for from the library.

I walked back to the front of the shop and began burning the herbs in a small bowl, walking around the entire space until it was filled with haze. The dried herbs released their fragrant plumes as they burned, cleansing the space of any negative energy. I set the bowl down on the floor and took out seven white candles from my bag and laid them out in a circle, lighting each one in a clockwise pattern.

With the candles aligned and lit, I felt the energy in the room shift. The soft glow of the candles' flames danced, casting shadows that seemed to sway to an inaudible rhythm. I took my place at the center of the circle, the candles encircling me like silent witnesses to the magic I was about to wield.

I looked to Kaelan, excitement, and trepidation thrumming within me. "Midnight is said to be an optimal time for this ritual. The convergence of natural energies is believed to enhance its effectiveness."

I retrieved my notebook, its pages filled with meticulously transcribed incantations and sigils. "This part might require precision," I murmured to Kaelan, my voice quiet. I pulled out a small, silver-bladed knife— the instrument that would allow me to infuse blood magic into the spell. The subtle prickle of anticipation ran down my spine as I prepared myself.

A measured, controlled cut on my forearm prompted a smell wellspring of blood, it was a small sacrifice that the spell required. The crimson blood, glistening in the candlelight, held the essence of my life force, a potent offering to the magic I was about to wield.

Gathering my focus I dipped my finger into the pool of blood and began anointing each candle with a sigil that I carefully copied from my notes. I could feel the soft currents of my magic intertwining with the vital fluid as I drew. The room seemed to hum with energy.

Seven symbols for seven candles— a calculated sequence that represented the intricate balance between protection and magic. With each precise stroke of my finger, the connection between the symbols and the candles seemed to strengthen, building an ethereal bridge that would soon be fortified by an incantation.

And then the moment arrived— a conflux of power, intent, and ancient wisdom. As I sat surrounded by the carefully arranged candles,

I drew upon the energies around me and within me, reciting the incantation with a voice that resonated with purpose.

"In the midnight's shroud, with sigils drawn so tight,
I ward this sacred space against the demon's blight.
Inscribed in shadows, symbols of ancient might,
I banish all darkness, protect through the night.

By moon's eerie glow and stars' celestial light,
I summon divine strength, my barrier ignite.
Let demons recoil, my powers take flight,
In this enchanted circle, we stand in the light."

The words echoed in the room, each syllable carrying a weight that echoed through the space. As I finished, I felt an almost electric surge coursing through my veins, a current of energy intertwining with the blood magic I had invoked.

A sudden and unexpected tremor reverberated through the room, a response to the heightened energies I was invoking. A few items fell from the shelves, a testament to the sheer intensity of the magic that was being woven. My heart raced as I realized the power of what I was achieving, the significance of the ancient spell taking hold.

A surge of energy seemed to emanate from my very core, pulsating outward in a wave of raw magic. The room vibrated, resonating with the forces I had harnessed. I was at the epicenter of this magical whirlwind, my connection to the blood magic solidifying as it surged through me and into the factory around us.

With a shuddering exhale, I felt the magic take hold, spreading out like a protective shroud over the bookshop and factory beyond. The wards, imbued with the energy of the ritual, formed an intangible barrier, an unseen fortress guarding against unwanted intrusion.

As the room settled, the lingering traces of the ritual's energy gently subsided, leaving behind a tranquil air charged with the scent of herbs and the resonance of magic. I turned to Kaelan, my chest swelling with pride at what I had accomplished.

With a nod of satisfaction, I sealed the spell by blowing out the seven candles one by one, extinguishing their flickering flames. As each flame winked out, a sense of accomplishment settled within me—a reminder that the efforts I invested in safeguarding our haven were worth every ounce of energy.

After concluding the ritual, I rose from my spot on the floor, my legs feeling a touch unsteady from the potent magic I had just invoked. Kaelan, ever vigilant, rushed to my side, concern etching his features as he reached out to steady me. His proximity sent a jolt through me, the thrumming energy of the magic still pulsating within my veins, intermingling with a different, more primal heat.

His hands were on my arms, his gaze locked onto mine, I reassured him with a gentle smile. "I'm not drained, Kaelan. Actually, I feel...quite charged. Kind of exhilarated. The ritual went better than I expected, and the blood magic made the wards much stronger than they would have been otherwise."

He smiled, relief evident in his eyes. "I'm glad you're not exhausted after all that."

I felt the energy from the ritual flowing through me, the magic and blood mingling together in an intoxicating mix. It was a rush like no other, my body felt hot and pent up.

Kaelan's touch left an imprint on my skin, his closeness only serving to fuel the flames of desire burning within me.

"Kaelan..." I breathed, my voice heavy with need. "I think the blood magic has left me feeling... a bit worked up."

"How can I help?" He asked, confusion crossing his features.

I could feel the heat rising in my cheeks, my pulse quickening as his fingers trailed down my arm, leaving goosebumps in their wake. "I think you know how," I replied, my tone laced with suggestion.

The words had barely left my lips when I found myself enveloped in a rough, unrestrained kiss. Kaelan's mouth captured mine with a fierce urgency that mirrored the intensity of the magic we just witnessed. The sensation of his lips moving against mine sent sparks of desire through me, mingling with the residual magic's hum. Every part of me felt alive with electricity.

My fingers wound into his dark hair, holding him close as the kiss deepened. The potent blend of magic and desire created an addictive cocktail that surged between us, our shared heat stoking a fire that defied the boundaries of our surroundings.

Kaelan broke the kiss breathlessly, turning me around and pushing me up against the wooden counter of the bookshop roughly.

"I want you," he growled, grinding his hips into mine. "Now." His hands slid down my body, over my breasts, cupping them, squeezing gently as he pulled me tight against him. I arched my back, grinding my backside against him.

I moaned in response, feeling my nipples harden under his touch. He leaned forward, nibbling at my neck and shoulder with those deliciously sharp teeth, his lips brushing against the shell of my ear.

"You're intoxicating," he whispered, sliding his hand between us, down the front of my pants as he began rubbing my clit through my panties.

"Kaelan..." I breathed, arching my back even further, wanting him inside me now, even though anyone could walk in on us at any moment. He chuckled softly, biting my earlobe.

"Shh..." he murmured, his voice low and husky. "You don't want anyone to hear us, do you?"

His fingers continued to rub slow circles around my clit, driving me mad with need. I bit my lip, trying desperately to keep quiet as he brought me closer and closer to the edge.

I felt his fangs graze my skin, sending a jolt of pleasure through me. I couldn't help but moan, which only spurred him on. He pulled my panties aside and pushed two fingers inside me, curling them against my g-spot, making me gasp and writhe beneath him.

I whimpered, grinding against him, wanting nothing more than for him to take me right here on the countertop. He kneeled, sliding my pants down to my knees. I felt his warm breath on my skin as he moved his head lower, licking along my leg, making me gasp. "Mmm..." he murmured, kissing my inner thigh, "You smell so sweet."

I could feel his fangs grazing the tender skin, making me shiver. He continued kissing and licking my thighs, making his way slowly up to my aching center. He pushed the lace of my panties aside and licked up the length of my slit, sending a wave of pleasure through me. I arched my back and pushed myself towards his mouth. He chuckled, licking me again, teasing me.

I moaned, gripping the edge of the counter tightly. He slipped his fingers back inside me, curling them again and again while he licked and sucked on my clit.

I gasped, biting my lip as the muscles low in my belly began to tense. "Please..." I begged, bucking against his hand. "Please..." He smiled, sliding his finger out of me.

"What do you want, Vale?" he purred.

I looked back at him, eyes wide, heart racing, breathing heavily. "I want you to fuck me, Kaelan. Hard and fast, right here." I said, my voice steady. He smiled again, slipping off my clothes the rest of the way.

He stood and unbuckled his pants, pushing me down on the counter, my ass in the air. He stroked himself, rubbing up and down my entrance, teasing me with just the tip. I pushed back against him, trying desperately to take him inside me.

I groaned, writhing against him. "Kaelan..." I pleaded again. He growled low in his chest and then thrust his cock inside me roughly. I cried out, tightening around him, feeling every inch of him slide into me.

"So fucking tight." He growled, gripping my hips. He withdrew almost all the way before plunging back inside me, filing me completely.

"Gods, you feel so good," he groaned, his cock throbbing inside me. I bit my lip, trying not to cry out as he began to move inside me. His strokes were slow and powerful.

I moaned again, lifting my hips to meet his thrusts. "Fuck me, Kaelan," I breathed, "Fuck me like you mean it." He groaned, pounding me hard, reaching up to place his hand around my throat. Every cell in my body screamed out in pleasure, the blood magic mingling with my desire. He pounded me harder and faster, deeper and deeper. I could feel my orgasm building, my pussy tightening around him.

I gripped the edge of the counter, holding on for dear life as he fucked me. I could feel the muscles low in my belly begin to contract, the familiar warmth building deep inside me.

He thrust his fingers into my hair, gripping it tightly as he fucked me hard and fast. His cock throbbed inside me, filling me completely. I was so close, so ready. I cried out, moaning and panting, not caring who heard.

"Oh gods," I cried out, "I'm gonna come." I felt him tighten his grip, his pace quickening, and knew he was close too. He slammed into me one last time, finding his release, as my body shook and clenched around him. I threw my head back, crying out as the most intense orgasm ripped through me. It was like nothing I had ever felt before, and it lasted for what seemed like hours. My entire body shuddered, and I collapsed against the counter, completely spent.

Kaelan was breathing heavily, his hand still buried in my hair, his cock still buried deep inside me.

He wrapped his arms around me, holding me tight. We stayed there for a moment, our bodies pressed together, both breathing heavily. Then he slowly pulled away and turned me back around.

He kissed me passionately, I could still taste myself on his lips. His tongue tangled with mine, his hands roamed all over my body.

He broke the kiss and looked at me, a devilish smirk playing on his handsome features.

"Well that was unexpected."

I grinned back, laughing breathlessly. "Tell me about it."

We kissed again, long and slow, savoring the moment, before I reached down to retrieve my discarded clothes. We had just had sex in the bookshop, where anyone could have heard or seen us, the thrill had definitely heightened the experience.

Kaelan buttoned his pants as I pulled mine on, "Come on, we still need to see about contacting the First Witch." He sighed, reality slowly fading back in as the glow from sex left us.

"You're right," I said, gathering up the candles that had been knocked over in our frenzy. I couldn't help but smile at the thought of what had just happened. It was reckless and impulsive, and oh so very satisfying.

I could get used to this.

As I finished clearing away the remnants of the ritual, I turned back to Kaelan, a renewed sense of purpose coursing through me. "Let's get to work."

CHAPTER NINETEEN

After the successful warding ritual and the fiery passion that had followed, I had spent a restful night in my apartment. The wards held strong, a testament to the magic I had woven. The morning light spilled in through the windows, illuminating the room in hues of gold. I dressed quickly in a pair of jeans and an oversized sweater, ensuring my weapons were in their proper places.

As I made my way downstairs, I encountered Wren, his weariness evident in his posture. He had just returned from a night of patrolling, the weight of his responsibilities in his expression. I greeted him with a small smile.

"Hey, Wren." I offered as he stifled a yawn. "Long night?"

He nodded, rubbing his eyes with the back of his hand. "Yeah, it's been a busy one. You're up early."

"We got the wards up last night," I explained to him. "Nothing awful happened on patrol I hope."

"No, but there were a lot of demon sightings. At least seven that were reported." Seven demons in one night was still troubling.

I explained my plans for the day, and the intent to visit the library and consult Harker about contacting the First Witch. Wren's expression was thoughtful as he listened intently.

"Well, before you dive into all that, maybe you should check in on the Otherworlders," he suggested. "See how everyone is holding up. They'll appreciate it."

With a nod, I made my way to the main factory floor, greeted by the sounds of quiet conversation and the scent of coffee.

As I walked through the area, several Otherworlders approached me, their expressions full of gratitude and respect. They thanked me for my efforts to save Jason, knowing the tremendous influence it had. I humbly accepted their words, not quite sure how to respond to the praise.

Soon enough, Jason came forward, offering me a cup of coffee which I gladly took. "Hey, Vale," he greeted, genuine warmth in his voice. "Wren told me about the wards you're planning to place. Have you done it yet?"

I met his gaze steadily, appreciating his concern. "Yes, I placed them last night, you guys should have a lot less to worry about now."

He sighed, a weight visibly lifting off his shoulders. "Thank you for all you've done for us." He said, placing a hand on my arm.

"Anyone would have done the same," I said.

"No, they wouldn't have." He replied, giving my arm a soft squeeze before turning away.

Entering the bookshop, I called out softly for Nyxen, who promptly emerged from the shadows, his dark form moving gracefully toward me. I asked him to transport me to Kaelan's place, and as the shadows enveloped me, the world shifted. I emerged from the shadows in the house, my purpose clear in my mind.

The library beckoned, and within its walls, Harker was engrossed in her research, her notes scattered across the table. "Oh, Vale!" she exclaimed, excitement and eagerness evident in her voice. Her discovery seemed to have lit a fire within her, and I couldn't help but share in her enthusiasm.

"Hey, Harker," I greeted with a warm smile as I approached. "You look like you've made some progress."

Harker nodded enthusiastically, gesturing to the notes before her. "I've found a wealth of information on contacting the dead. It's like piecing together a puzzle, but I think I've got something that might work."

As we talked, Elara made her presence known, her spectral form appearing with a hint of irritation. She floated near Harker, her incorporeal gaze fixed on the books scattered about. "Do you have any idea how long it'll take me to put all these back in order?" she complained.

Harker's response was as impertinent as ever. "Well, it's a good thing you're dead then, you've got forever to do it."

I was amused by their banter but turned back to the notes she had presented me with. Harker explained the ritual she had uncovered, detailing its steps and significance. As she outlined the process, a sense of anticipation grew within me.

"That sounds promising," I said, studying the notes with interest. "Let's give it a shot."

Harker's grin widened, and for a moment, we shared a mutual excitement. I was ready to delve into the ritual and seek guidance from the spiritual realm. As we continued to discuss the details and preparations, Harker's enthusiasm was contagious.

"We'll need to wait for the upcoming full moon," Harker interjected, a note of anticipation in her voice. "It's in four days, the alignment of the moon's energy will enhance the connection."

I nodded, absorbing the information. It was undoubtedly worth it if waiting for the right cosmic alignment would grant us a stronger link to the First Witch. The coming full moon held the promise of unveiling secrets from the past, and I was eager to unlock the mysteries it held.

☾

Later that night, my sleep was abruptly shattered by Wren's frantic shaking, pulling me from dreams to the stark reality of the night. His wide eyes and trembling urgency made my heart race as I sat up, fully awake in an instant.

"Donovan found out the demons are targeting you," Wren's words rushed out in a tumble, his voice laced with worry. "He went to the alpha, Rafe, and now he wants to hand you over to the demons to stop the attacks. They are on their way now."

The shock of his words jolted me further awake, the gravity of the situation settling heavily upon me. "Gods damn that Donovan!" I cursed. I never liked him and now my safety was on the line.

In a heartbeat, I was on my feet and dressed, donning the leather clothes and weaponry that were second nature to me. A cold knot of fear settled in my gut as the implications of Wren's revelation washed over me. Adrenaline surged through my veins as I mentally prepared for whatever was to come.

"What do you plan on doing?" Wren asked, his eyes fixed on me, concern etched across his features.

"I'm going to confront them. If Rafe thinks he can just hand me over to the demons, he's got another thing coming." I said, my voice laced with anger.

Wren's expression darkened. "But if you stay here and they find me, I'll have to follow the alpha's order whether I want to or not. I'll be physically compelled, Vale."

Just then, the sound of footsteps and low voices filtered through the still night air from outside. Wren moved to the window, peering cautiously through the glass while keeping himself hidden. I moved to look as well.

"Wait," he whispered urgently to me, his eyes locked on the approaching figures.

Four werewolves approached the factory, I recognized one as Donovan. My captures here to take me away. I felt the urge to storm out and face the confrontation head-on. But Wren's firm grip on my arm held me back. My muscles tensed as I hesitated, about to do something reckless.

Donovan's deep voice called out in the night. "Vale, we're here to escort you to Rafe. Come out, it'll make this easier on everyone." His words dripped with arrogance, and I knew he was relishing the moment.

The four werewolves approached, their posture hostile, eyes locked on the place that had become my refuge. I felt a pang of anger, how dare they show up here. "You can't keep hiding, Vale," Donovan's voice boomed. "If you won't come out, then we'll drag you out."

Just as I went to move, the heavy doors leading into the factory below creaked open, revealing a determined group of Otherworlders led by Jason. They stepped out, forming a line that seemed to echo defiance against the approaching werewolves. My heart fluttered at the sight of them standing there. "No one by that name here," Jason replied cooly, his tone unflinching.

The werewolves growled low, the tension between the groups building. I could feel the energy shift, a crackle in the air that was terrifying.

Donovan was not deterred. "We know she's here, half-breed," he sneered. "We can smell her. So, if you'll just bring her out, we can settle this."

"This isn't a negotiation," Jason countered. "Vale isn't leaving."

Donovan's expression hardened. "Last chance. Bring her out or we'll take her."

"You're not welcome here," Jason stated, his words firm and resolute. "Leave now, or there will be consequences."

The two groups stared each other down, neither willing to back down. I could feel the power emanating from the werewolves, their muscles taut and ready for a fight. The moment was electric, and I knew a violent clash was imminent. I held my breath, my heart pounding as I watched the standoff unfold before me.

"Wren, I can't just stand here and let them get hurt because of me." I hissed under my breath. But Wren's grip on my arm didn't lessen.

"Look," he whispered back.

Then, as if answering the call, more Otherworlders began emerging from the factory, forming a united front. The odds shifted rapidly as the group swelled to nearly twenty, a show of unity that left me awestruck. The werewolves hesitated, seeing their disadvantage in numbers.

As moonlight bathed the scene, the werewolves seemed to recognize the futile battle they were on the brink of.

Donovan glared at the crowd but relented. "You're making a mistake," he warned, his voice low and threatening. "Rafe will not tolerate this insubordination."

"And you're a coward," Jason retorted. "Turning on your fellow Otherworlder just to please the demons."

Donovan snarled, his anger flaring at the accusation.

"If you're not man enough to take her by force, then just leave," Jason said, his tone final.

Donovan hesitated for a moment, his rage simmering just below the surface. He knew he was outnumbered and outmatched. Finally, with a frustrated growl, he turned and stalked away, the other werewolves following behind.

As the tension dissipated, I felt my legs wobble beneath me. The overwhelming support of the Otherworlders left me humbled and grateful, their unspoken promise of protection a powerful reminder that I wasn't alone in this fight.

"Vale, you need to get out of here. Go back to Kaelan's house, now." Wren says urgently, jerking me back to the present. I nodded my head in assent but hesitated a moment.

"What are you going to do about all of this? Is it safe for you back with the pack?"

Wren hesitated, his eyes clouded with uncertainty. "I can't show back up at the pack right now. I need time to decide."

I nodded in understanding, albeit reluctantly. "Just...let me know when you've figured things out. I'll be there when you need me."

He nodded back, his gaze fixed on mine with determination and guilt. "I will."

I cast a fleeting glance around the room, the familiarity of it now tinged with uncertainty. "Make sure to thank Jason and the Otherworlders for me."

Wren's expression softened, a hint of a smile touching his lips. "I will, Vale. Be safe."

With that, I summoned Nyxen from the shadows and we shifted back to Kaelan's house.

I entered Kaelan's room, my heart still racing from the recent events, and found him sleeping shirtless. The soft moonlight filtered in, casting gentle shadows across his features. As the door creaked open, his reaction was immediate— he bolted upright, grabbing a knife from the nearby table in a swift, practiced motion.

His tense posture eased as his eyes met mine, and the knife was lowered with a sigh of relief. "Vale," he muttered, his voice concerned. "What's going on?"

I moved further into the room, my anxiety now tinged with exhaustion. The night's events had taken a toll on my nerves, and the weariness seeped into my bones. I recounted the events that had transpired, my emotions a chaotic jumble. He listened intently, his expression shifting from shock to anger.

Kaelan's brow furrowed and his eyes darkened into storm clouds. "They think they can just waltz in and take you?" he demanded.

I nodded, comforted by his desire to protect me. "They tried, but the Otherworlders rallied together and scared them off."

Kaelan's fingers tightened around the hilt of the knife and his eyes blazed with a fire. "They won't get away with this," he growled, his words a fierce promise.

Even in the midst of my turmoil, his unwavering support warmed my spirit. I moved closer to him, the shadows seething in the corners of the room as they mirrored his dark mood. "Wren thinks I should stay here, with you, until things calm down."

Kaelan's gaze softened as he reached out to cup my cheek. "Then you'll stay," he affirmed, his thumb brushing gently against my lips. "I won't let anything happen to you."

Relief and gratitude washed over me, and I leaned into his touch. The tension that had knotted in my shoulders slowly began to unwind. "Thank you."

His fingers traced a soothing pattern on my skin, his eyes locking onto mine. "Always, little witch."

He leaned down and wrapped his arms around me, pulling me close and pressing his lips against mine for an impassioned kiss. His lips claimed mine with a sense of urgency, and I could feel his possessiveness in the way his hands curled around me. It was as if the events of the night had awakened something primal in him, a need to reassure himself that I was here, safe and close.

Breaking away from the kiss, Kaelan's gaze held mine, desire and restraint in his eyes. "Vale," he murmured, his voice husky.

I took a moment to catch my breath, my heart racing in sync with his. "Yes?"

A playful smirk tugged at his lips. "Would you like to sleep with me?"

A laugh escaped me as I realized his implication. "Yes, that sounds good. I'm exhausted." I said, getting up to take off my leather jacket and pants. I crawled back into bed beside him, in nothing but my t-shirt and underwear.

He chuckled, his fingers brushing a strand of hair from my face. "Undressing in front of me like that could easily lead to other things."

I rolled my eyes, a smile tugging at the corners of my mouth. "You're insufferable."

Kaelan pulled me close, his arms enveloping me in a warm embrace. "You love it," he teased.

With a playful swat on his arm, I settled in beside him on the bed, letting the weariness of the night wash over me. The events of the evening seemed to fade into the background as we snuggled close, finding solace in each other's presence. The moon cast a soft glow through the window, illuminating the room in a gentle embrace. As the weight of the day lifted, I closed my eyes, finding comfort and warmth in the arms of the demon prince who had unexpectedly become a source of strength in my life.

Chapter Twenty

As consciousness slowly returned to me, I became aware of the strong arms wrapped around me, the warmth of Kaelan's body pressed against mine. It was a comforting embrace that had become all too familiar, a reminder of the bond that had grown between us. The morning sun peeked through the drapes, covering the room in a gentle, comforting light.

As I stirred, Kaelan's eyes opened, his gaze immediately finding me. A fond smile curved his lips, and he murmured a sleepy, "Good morning."

I returned his smile, my heart fluttering at the sight of him. "Morning," I replied, my voice soft and filled with contentment and affection.

Leaning down, Kaelan brushed his lips against mine in a gentle and lingering kiss. It was a sweet and tender gesture that sent a rush of warmth through me.

"You look beautiful in the morning," Kaelan whispered against my lips, his fingers tracing patterns on my back.

I couldn't help but roll my eyes at his compliment. "You're a liar," I teased, my tone playful, knowing full well my hair was a rat's nest of tangles.

His laughter rumbled softly. "You caught me," he said sarcastically, his eyes dancing with amusement.

The sheets were a tangle around us, as tangled as the connection we had forged. My fingers reached up to gently cup Kaelan's face, drawing him closer. Our lips met once again, this time with a hunger that belied the tranquility of the morning. It was a passionate and electric kiss, our desires intertwining in a way that left me breathless and wanting more.

The kiss seemed to go on forever, and as it did, the outside world melted away. All that remained was his lips pressing against mine and the sound of my racing heart in my ears. There was an urgency in our connection, a need to explore and express the emotions that had grown between us.

My fingers threaded through his hair, pulling him even closer as my heart raced in response to the intensity of the moment. Every touch, every brush of our lips, seemed to fan the flames of desire that surged between us like a crashing wave.

Reluctantly, we eventually broke apart, our breathing mingling as we gazed into each other's eyes, neither of us wanting to break the spell hanging over our heads. An unspoken understanding hung between us, a knowledge that we were treading on the precipice of something greater.

"Vale," Kaelan whispered, his voice husky with longing.

I offered him a half-smile, my cheeks flushed with embarrassment and excitement. "Sorry," I murmured, my fingers tracing a pattern on his bare chest.

Kaelan's chuckle was a deep resonant sound. "No need to apologize," he assured me, his thumb gently brushing my cheek.

With a soft sigh, I settled back against the pillows, Kaelan's arms still wrapped around me. The connection between us remained tangible, a current of energy that pulsed beneath the surface.

"We should probably get up," I mused, the practicality of the day ahead nudging at my thoughts.

Kaelan's fingers continued their soothing trail along my skin. "Or we could stay like this for a little while longer," he suggested, his eyes warm and inviting.

I smiled at him, my gaze wandering over his handsome face. I ran my hand up his chest, enjoying the feel of his smooth skin. I loved the way he smelled, like woodsmoke and the maple whiskey he liked to drink. It wasn't just the scent of him that made me melt. It was everything about him— his smile, his laugh, his eyes.

"You're being very distracting," he teased, his voice husky with desire. The sound of it sent a chill through me. I grinned at him, kissing his chest lightly. "And that's not helping," he chuckled, leaning down to kiss me again.

I wrapped my arms around his neck, sighing happily as our lips met. His hands moved to my waist, pulling me closer. With our bodies pressed together I could feel the heat from his body against mine.

His breath hitched, and I knew he was feeling the same things I was. My heart pounded in my chest, and I felt heat curling low between my thighs. He groaned, pressing his hips forward.

He leaned down, nipping at my lower lip. I opened my mouth, letting him slip his tongue inside. I moaned softly, my hips moving restlessly. I wanted more. I needed more, needed him.

He pulled back and began trailing kisses along my neck, coming up to nibble on my ear. I felt like I would combust under his touch.

His hands moved to cup my ass, squeezing gently. "Gods, Kaelan," I whispered, my head falling back. I could feel myself getting wetter, desperate for him.

I didn't want to ever stop what we were doing. I didn't want to move away from him, wanted to stay here forever. I wanted to have this moment with him and many, many more moments. Wanted to experience all of him.

His hand moved to my panties, his fingers trailing over the bundle of nerves there. He pushed them aside and ran a finger up the very center of me. "You're always so wet for me, little witch." He purred.

I moaned softly, my hips moving against him. I couldn't get enough of him. I never wanted him to stop touching me. His finger slid into me, and I gasped, arching my back. He pushed another finger inside, curling them upward, hitting that spot inside me. I cried out softly, my hands tightening in his hair. I couldn't believe how good it felt just to be touched by him.

I needed him, needed him to fuck me, to own me. He thrust his fingers in and out of me, and I moaned loudly. He rubbed my clit in gentle but tantalizing circles and my hips bucked against his hand.

He kept rubbing me, pushing me higher and higher. I heard him groan, his fingers still moving inside me. I felt the pressure building low in my stomach and tried to hold back. I wanted to enjoy this.

I wanted to savor every delicious moment of it. I didn't want to lose control. I needed to come, needed to be fucked. I needed to feel him deep inside me. But I cried out, my orgasm washing over me. My body tightened around his fingers. I felt the waves of pleasure pulse through me, my legs trembling. He kept thrusting his fingers in and out of me and I moaned his name loudly, my eyes closing.

I felt him grow harder against my leg. He kissed me hard, his fingers still moving inside me. I felt him pull his fingers out of me, and I whimpered, wanting more. I watched, wide-eyed as he brought those fingers to his mouth and sucked on them greedily. "Mmm," he moaned softly.

He nipped at my neck, and I shuddered. He rolled us over, bringing me on top of him. He looked up at me, his eyes dark with desire, while I smiled down at him. I leaned down, kissing him softly, my tender breasts rubbing up against the fabric of my t-shirt.

I felt his hands slide under my shirt, running up my sides. He pulled my shirt off, and his hands moved across my exposed skin. I groaned, loving the feel of his hands on me. I ached my back, exposing my breasts. He raised his head, taking one of my nipples into his mouth, sucking on it. I cried out, my hands running through his hair.

He sucked harder, his tongue flicking across my nipple, and bit down. I moaned, feeling myself getting even wetter. I wanted him to make me come again, wanted to feel him moving inside me.

I reached down between his legs and grabbed the length of him through his thin pants. He jerked slightly at the sudden contact, and I grinned mischievously. I pulled his pants down, exposing his hard cock. I shifted down further on the bed and licked at the glistening tip.

I flicked my tongue across the head, tasting him. I moaned, loving the feel of him in my mouth. I wrapped my hand around him, stroking him slowly and he groaned, his hands gripping my hair.

I took him deeper into my mouth, sucking hard on him. I moved my head up and down, my hand stroking him faster. He groaned even louder, his hips rising off the bed. I pulled my mouth away, looking up at him. His eyes were closed and his head arched back, his face flushed with passion. I licked my lips, the taste of him lingering there.

I stroked him faster, the slick sound filling the room. I watched his face, watched the pleasure etched on his features. I felt the warmth pooling in the pit of my stomach, my arousal growing. I kept stroking him, my grip tightening. He groaned loudly, his hips thrusting upward.

I reached back and slid my panties down, moving forward and straddling his waist. He grabbed his cock in his hand and I guided myself down onto him, feeling his thick length filling me. I cried out, my eyes closing as he entered me. I pressed my hips down, grinding against him.

I moaned, feeling him so deep inside me. I started rocking my hips, fucking him. He moaned, grabbing my waist. I leaned down, kissing him hard, and felt him thrust up into me, making me cry out.

I rode him harder, my hips slamming down onto his. I felt his hands in my hair, holding me down. I broke the kiss, crying out his name, and riding him even faster.

"That's it, baby. Ride me." He breathed, his hands moving down to grab my ass, lifting me. I moaned, feeling him going even deeper. He lifted his hips up and down, his cock sliding in and out of me. I felt his teeth bite down on my neck, his hand tightening in my hair. I cried out, my body trembling. I felt him cumming, his cock pumping into me. I moaned, and my orgasm rushed through me.

I slammed down onto him, feeling his cock twitch inside me. He held me down as we gasped for breath, our hearts racing. I collapsed against him and he kissed me softly, his fingers running through my hair. We lay there for a while, our bodies touching. I loved being with him like this.

I sighed happily, rolling off him. I turned to my side, curling up next to him, feeling a sense of peaceful satisfaction. Kaelan's hand found mine, his fingers entwining with mine as he whispered, "That was an amazing wake-up call, little witch."

A soft, genuine smile graced my lips as I met his gaze. "I aim to please," I murmured teasingly. His lips met mine again, a soft lingering kiss that seemed to convey so much more than words ever could. As sleep started to tug at the edges of my consciousness, I closed my eyes, feeling the world around us fade away.

But just as I had drifted back off, my phone began ringing insistently on the nightstand. I groaned softly, reluctantly pulling myself from the warm cocoon of Kaelan's arms. I reached over and grabbed my phone, seeing Wren's name on the caller ID. With an anxious feeling building in the pit of my stomach, I answered the call, holding to phone to my ear.

"Hey, Wren," I greeted, trying to shake off the remnants of sleep.

"Vale, you need to come to the apartment," Wren's voice sounded urgent on the other end. "I've made a decision about the pack, and it affects all of us."

I nodded, even though he couldn't see me. "I'll be there," I replied, my curiosity piqued.

"Good," Wren said, his tone serious. "See you soon."

As I hung up, I turned back to Kaelan, his demon hearing having caught every word. I sighed and placed the phone back on the nightstand. "Wren needs me to come to the apartment," I explained anyway, feeling intrigued but concerned.

Kaelan's expression was curious as he met my gaze. "We should go then," he suggested, his fingers brushing a strand of hair away from my face.

I nodded, and with a final lingering kiss, I reluctantly pulled away from the comfort of his bed. Together, we got dressed. He pulled me close as we shifted back to my room in the apartment. As we entered the living area, Juniper was already there, sitting on the couch with a cup of tea in her hands.

"Hey, Juniper," I greeted her with a small smile.

"Morning, Vale," she replied, her tone serious.

Wren left his room and walked into the living room, I could tell by the tense atmosphere that something important was about to unfold. Wren stood there, his posture determined, Juniper's expression mirrored his.

"What's going on, Wren?" I asked as we approached them.

Wren took a deep breath, his gaze steady. "I met with some of the wolves from my pack last night, werewolves who don't agree with Rafe's decision," he began, his voice resolute. "There are enough of us that I can challenge the alpha."

Surprise washed over me as my mouth fell open. The implications of his words were significant— a challenge to the alpha's authority was a serious matter among werewolves. My mind raced, processing the gravity of the situation.

Kaelan's presence beside me was a steady source of support, and I felt the reassuring touch of his hand on my back. "What happens if you win?" he asked, his voice steady.

Wren's expression hardened. "If I win, I become the alpha, and the rest of the pack either submits to me or leaves. And we can finally put an end to the reckless decisions that have been endangering everyone."

The weight of his words settled over me like a heavy blanket. My mind raced, grappling with the implications of his decision. The idea of Wren challenging Rafe, of putting his life on the line, was something I couldn't accept. I felt a knot of protest forming in my chest, and before I could think, the words tumbled out of my mouth. "And what if you don't win? What happens then?"

Wren's gaze held mine, his eyes reflecting the gravity of the situation. "If I don't win, I'll be banished from the pack, along with those who stand with me. Or worse, I might not survive. And if I'm not there to protect you, they'll undoubtedly try to take you again."

Kaelan's growl rumbled through the air, the fierce protectiveness in his eyes evident. "I'll die before I let that happen," he declared, his voice low and dangerous.

I felt anger and fear welling up within me. "Wren, you can't do this," I protested, my voice tinged with desperation. "You can't put yourself in danger for my sake."

Wren's jaw clenched, his resolve unyielding. "Vale, you don't understand. This is long overdue. Someone needs to step up and challenge Rafe. The pack deserves a better leader who doesn't put the wants of himself over the needs of the rest of the Otherworlders."

My frustration surged, and I raised my voice, the emotion crackling in my words. "Let someone else do it then. You can't risk your life like this!"

A hint of exasperation entered Wren's expression. "Vale, listen. This isn't just about you, it's about the entire pack. I've been waiting for an opportunity like this for a long time. Rafe's decisions have put us all in danger, and I can't stand by any longer and watch him make bargains with demons."

My hands clenched into fists at my sides, my heart torn between my concern for Wren's safety and my understanding of his perspective. "But what if something happens to you? What if you die?" I whispered, my voice breaking with emotion.

Wren's voice softened, his gaze steady. "I won't let that happen. I'll do everything in my power to make sure I come out of this alive."

Kaelan gripped my shoulder, his voice firm as he spoke up. "We'll stand by you, Wren, if we must. But Vale's right, there has to be another way."

Wren's eyes flickered between us, his gaze determined. "I appreciate your concern, both of you. But sometimes, the only way to ensure everyone's safety is to take a risk."

My breath shuddered, my heart heavy with conflicting emotions. I wanted to protect Wren, to shield him from harm, but I also understood the necessity of his decision. A sigh escaped my lips, and I looked at Wren, my eyes pleading. "Just promise me you'll be careful. Promise me you'll come back."

Wren's expression softened, and he reached to take my hand in his. "I promise, Vale. I'll do everything I can to make sure I come back to you."

As his words settled over me, I couldn't shake the feeling of dread that lingered. The path ahead of us was filled with doubt and uncertainty. While I knew Wren's intentions were noble, the outcome was far from guaranteed.

I looked at Wren with determination burning in my eyes. "I need to be there with you. I can't let you face this alone."

Wren opened his mouth to protest, but I held up my hand, cutting him off. "Don't even try to argue. I'm not letting you do this without me."

He sighed, his gaze conflicted. "Vale, it's dangerous. The werewolves could easily grab you as leverage."

I squared my shoulders, my resolve unwavering. "Trust me. No one's going to be capturing me. And if they try, I'll kill them. I can handle myself."

Wren's eyes bore into mine, searching for any sign of doubt or hesitation. After a moment, he nodded solemnly, the acceptance clear in his expression. "Alright, but you have to promise that you'll stay close and safe. I won't be able to focus on the challenge if I'm worried about you."

I held his gaze, my commitment mirrored in my eyes. "I promise. I'll stay close and I'll do everything I can to ensure both of us make it out of this."

Chapter Twenty-One

The next day the library's atmosphere was heavy with tension as I flipped through dusty tomes and scrolls, my frustration growing with each fruitless page turn. I was determined to find something— anything— that could give Wren an edge in the impending fight against Rafe. The stakes were high, and I couldn't bear the thought of him going into such a dangerous confrontation unprepared.

Harker, seated at a nearby table surrounded by notes and arcane symbols, glanced up as I let out an exasperated sigh. "Still no luck?"

I shook my head, the weight of my concern evident in my expression. "Nothing useful so far. I've scoured through so many resources, but there's no clear advantage to give Wren."

Elara, perched on a nearby shelf, chimed in with a mischievous grin. "If you're not finding anything useful, perhaps a different approach is in order."

I shot her a confused look. "What do you mean?"

Elara glided down from the shelf and approached me, her dark eyes gleaming with a mixture of amusement and something else—something more cunning. "Vale, not all witchcraft is passive. There's plenty about it that can hurt, or even kill."

My brows furrowed as I processed her words. "You mean...you're suggesting that I use darker magic to harm Rafe?"

Elara shrugged, her tone nonchalant. "I'm just saying that if you really want to help Wren, you might have to think outside the box."

My mind raced, torn between the desire to do anything to aid Wren and the ethical implications of using dark magic. I glanced at Harker, who was listening intently, her expression a mix of curiosity and caution.

"Harker, what do you think?" I turned to her, seeking her guidance.

She sighed and ran a hand through her hair. "From what I've read about it, dark magic comes with serious consequences, and the price can be steep. It can corrupt and consume those who wield it. It's a path that's difficult to turn back from."

I nodded, understanding the seriousness of her words. My heart felt heavy with the moral dilemma before me. Could I truly bring myself to use magic that could potentially cause harm or worse? And even if I could, what price would I have to pay?

As I pondered these questions, Elara retrieved a book from a darkly lit corner of the library and handed it to me. "Here, take a look at this. It might give you some ideas."

I took the book from her, my fingers brushing against its old leather cover. Opening it, I was met with a plethora of spells and rituals—some that promised protection, others that held a far darker promise.

Elara's voice was low as she spoke. "Sometimes, survival requires making tough choices. But just remember that every action has consequences."

I turned my gaze back to the book, the weight of the choice ahead heavy on my shoulders. The fight that Wren was about to face was dangerous and potentially deadly, and the desire to help him was overwhelming. But could I really embrace the darker side of magic to do so?

As I delved into the pages, my heart raced with uncertainty. The line between right and wrong had never felt so blurred, and I knew that whatever path I chose would come with its own set of sacrifices.

(☽

The moon hung high in the inky sky as we gathered in the dimly lit bookshop, the air heavy with anticipation. Wren, Juniper, Kaelan, and I stood around, our faces anxious. The moment I had been fretting over all day was finally here.

We had spent the day making preparations, and now we were waiting for the wolves who supported Wren to arrive. The tension in the room was palpable as we discussed the plan once more, ensuring that every detail was in place.

Wren's gaze was focused, his jaw set as he spoke. "The wolves who support me will be here any moment. We've already informed those at camp to be ready."

Juniper, her expression tense, nodded in agreement. As if on cue, Jason entered the room, his presence commanding attention. "Wren, I've spoken to the others, and many of them are willing to join you. They want to stand by your side and ensure justice prevails. They remember your alpha turning us away when we needed help."

Wren's eyes softened with gratitude. "Are you sure about that? It could get ugly."

"They are committed, and so am I," Jason said, his tone filled with resolve.

"Thank you." Wren's voice was filled with sincerity and appreciation.

We all went outside, where a group of Otherworlders had already gathered. A few came up to Wren and offered him some reassuring words, grasping him on the back. The wolves began to arrive not long after. Their faces bore a mixture of resolve and worry, but their loyalty to Wren was unwavering. As we waited for the time to move, Wren took a deep breath, his voice steady.

"Tonight, we take a stand for our pack, for justice, and for all those who have suffered under Rafe's reckless rule. We go into this knowing the risks, but also knowing that we can't stand idly by any longer. I want to thank each and every one of you for being here with me, your loyalty will not be forgotten."

I felt a surge of admiration for Wren's determination. He was risking everything for the chance to bring about change for them and for me. Risking it all to put an end to the dangerous decisions that had been endangering not only the wolves but also the people we cared about.

With everyone gathered, our group set off towards the wolf camp just outside of town, the weight of our purpose heavy in the air. It would be a brisk four-mile hike to the camp. The moonlit path stretched ahead, a winding journey that would lead us to a pivotal confrontation. The wind whispered promises of change, of the hope for a brighter dawn. We were stepping into the unknown, with hearts that beat with a shared purpose and a hope that our efforts would bring about the change we so desperately sought.

I glanced over at Wren, his features sharpened by the shadows cast by the moonlight. His expression was filled with determination, a quiet resolve that had driven him this far. I knew the burden of responsibility he carried. The weight of his decisions and the future of the pack rested on his shoulders. But he didn't hesitate, didn't waver in his conviction. He was willing to risk everything to make things right, to ensure a brighter future for all of us.

A chill ran through me, and I shivered, my nerves getting the better of me. The path was silent, the night air cold and still. No sounds came from the forest, as if the world were holding its breath, waiting. We continued forward, our footsteps crunching on the leaves, the only sound piercing the silence.

My heart raced, apprehension coursing through my veins. This was it. Everything was coming together, the pieces finally falling into place. But there was no way to predict the outcome. The risk was great, the stakes higher than they'd ever been. But there was no turning back now.

We arrived at the campsite, the tents illuminated by lanterns, casting ominous shadows across the landscape. The camp was nestled up against the forest, its tall trees standing like guards against the cold night. The tension in the air was tangible, the wolves alert and ready for what was to come.

As our group entered the wolf camp, the sentries stationed at the edges became aware of our presence and issued warning growls that rippled through the night air. One by one, wolves emerged from their tents, their eyes fixed on us with wary expressions. Some watched with open hostility, their lips curled into snarls, while others nodded in acknowledgment of Wren's presence, showing solidarity with his cause.

We navigated through the sea of onlookers, our steps resolute, until we reached the camp's center where Rafe's huge tent stood. Wren's voice rang out, commanding and determined. "Rafe! Come out and face the consequences of your actions!" As we waited, a hush fell over the crowd. My heart thudded in my chest, anticipation coiling tightly inside me.

A moment later, the flap of the tent was pulled aside, and Rafe stepped into view, his stance relaxed and a mocking grin on his lips. His eyes flicked over our group, taking in each member before landing on Wren. "Well, well, what do we have here? The mutinous pup and his band of misfits."

Wren's jaw was set, his gaze unyielding. "I'm here to challenge you, Rafe. It's time to put an end to your reckless decisions and dangerous alliances."

Rafe's laughter echoed through the camp, a taunting sound that reverberated in the night air. "You think you can stand a chance against me, pup? You're amusingly naive."

Wren's voice remained steady. "I'm more than capable of dealing with you, Rafe. Your actions have crossed a line, and it's time someone held you accountable."

The air surrounding us was tense as their confrontation unfolded. But then, Rafe's attention shifted, and his gaze locked onto me. His grin turned wicked. "Look what we have here," He chuckled, a sinister sound. "Boys, capture the half-blood bitch. Don't bother with the others for now."

My heart raced as I saw wolves advancing toward me, their eyes hungry and eager to please their alpha. I drew two of my knives preparing to fight when Kaelan stepped in front of me, his presence imposing and his expression lethal.

"Careful, Rafe," Kaelan's voice dripped with a cold warning. "Laying a finger on her would be your last mistake."

The wolves hesitated, their aggression momentarily halted by Kaelan's commanding demeanor. His smirk held a dangerous edge. "If you're looking for a fight, I've been itching for one. Feel free to make my day."

Rafe's grip on the situation seemed to falter as the tension between our groups grew. The wolves looked at each other, unsure of what to do, their uncertainty apparent.

Rafe growled, his irritation growing. His eyes narrowed, a flicker of rage igniting behind them. His voice was a low growl, his anger seething. "This is a disgrace. I shouldn't have expected anything else from the lot of you."

He looked at the wolves around him, and they flinched under his gaze, their posture becoming submissive. He sneered, a contemptuous look on his face.

Wren's voice cut through the charged atmosphere. "That's enough. This isn't about them; this is about you and me, Rafe. Are you willing to face my challenge, or are you just a coward who hides behind his pack?"

Rafe's arrogance remained undeterred. He laughed again, a cocky smile playing on his lips. "A coward, you say? I could easily have the rest of my pack rip you to shreds. But I don't want your death to be that easy. Besides, a fight is long overdue, and I'm looking forward to putting you in your place."

The crowd gathered around us, forming a circle that felt like an arena. Anticipation hung heavy in the air as shouts began to rise from the crowd, eager for bloodshed.

Facing each other, Wren and Rafe stood as if they were to only two people in the world. Rafe launched into a speech, his words dripping with disdain. "Now watch this, this is what it looks like when a true alpha puts down a mutinous mutt. Watch closely, because this is the fate that awaits you all. The fate of the weak, and the disloyal. You all serve at my mercy, and if you don't, then I'll destroy you without hesitation. This is the price of your insolence. I won't show you mercy, or sympathy. You will kneel before me and beg for forgiveness, and if I find you undeserving, then I will kill you." His eyes locked onto mine as he spoke, and rage turned my vision red. A part of me knew I could end all this right here and now.

Wren's voice cut through Rafe's speech. "Enough talking. No more excuses. It's time for us to settle this once and for all."

And then they transformed. They shifted into their wolf forms in a blur of fur and muscle. Rafe's massive body turned into a great black-and-grey beast, while Wren's russet-colored fur gleamed in the moonlight.

The crowd watched with anticipation as the two wolves faced off. Rafe's words had fueled his confidence, while Wren's determination was etched into every line of his form. They circled each other, snarls echoing in the night air. Rafe'sdeclaration of victory hung in the air, but Wren's eyes blazed with defiance.

The crowd was whipped up into a frenzy as they lunged at each other, other teeth bared and fur flying. The clash of fangs and muscles echoed through the camp. My heart pounded in my chest, each blow sending a jolt of anxiety through me.

Wren's fighting prowess was evident, his moves calculated and strong. But Rafe was no weak opponent, his own strength and skill evident with every snap and twist. Their blows clashed, but neither seemed to gain the upper hand.

And then it happened, Rafe's jaws snapped shut around Wren's neck, shaking him with a ferocity that made my breath catch. Wren struggled within Rafe's grip, his growls of pain echoing through the night. With a mighty effort, Wren managed to break free, stumbling away, his russet fur matted with blood.

Fear clenched my heart as I watched, my hands balled into fists at my sides. The sight of Wren's blood ignited a dark fire within me, tempting me to act, to unleash a spell that would level the playing field.

But I hesitated, and the fight raged on. Wren was wounded but undeterred, his eyes still fixed on Rafe.

Wren and Rafe continued to battle, their growls and snarls mingling in the night air. Wren managed to land a few more blows, his russet form moving with agility. A moment of triumph flashed across his eyes as he lunged forward, jaws snapping shut around Rafe's foreleg.

Rafe let out a painful yelp, his strength faltering for an instant. Enraged, he cast a glance towards the wolves crowding behind him and motioned them forward. Chaos erupted as the wolves under his command shifted and launched into the fray, attacking the group that had come in support of Wren. Shouts and snarls filled the air as the battle spread in every direction.

Amidst the chaos, Wren and Rafe continued to clash, their forms weaving in and out. Wren looked winded, his movements showing signs of exhaustion, but he still managed to deliver a powerful blow that sent Rafe stumbling back.

As the fighting swirled around me, I found myself trapped in a whirlwind of danger and confusion. I desperately tried to keep track of Wren, my heart pounding with every strike he landed and every hit he took. But the roar of battle was overwhelming, and my surroundings became a chaotic blur.

Suddenly, a black-furred wolf broke through the fray, his yellow eyes locked onto me with a predatory glint. Instinct took over, and I reacted without thinking, drawing a knife from my belt and stabbing it into the wolf's side just as he lunged. The wolf let out a yelp of pain and fell to the ground, lifeless.

My breath caught in my throat as I stared at the fallen wolf, my hands trembling with shock. I had taken a life and defended myself in a brutal moment of survival. The weight of what I had done settled heavily on my shoulders, but I couldn't afford to dwell on it.

More wolves closed in, snapping me out of my daze. I faced down the next threat, a brown wolf and a white one. Adrenaline surged through me as I evaded their lunges, my body moving on instinct. Through the roar of the chaos, I could hear the sound of Rafe and Wren fighting, their snarls and growls punctuating the disorder around me.

A moment of panic washed over me when the white wolf caught hold of my jacket and threw me to the ground. I scrambled to my feet, my heart hammering, and saw the brown wolf closing in, his lips drawn back in a snarl. With nowhere to run, I did the only thing I could think of—I threw one of my knives at the wolf.

To my surprise, the blade lodged itself deep in his throat, causing the wolf to stagger backward, blood gushing from the wound. I didn't hesitate, pulling the second knife and throwing it, the blade landing deep into his heart. The brown wolf crumpled to the ground, dead.

I had managed to take down the brown one, but before I could fully react, a third wolf lunged at me from behind.

Pain seared through my shoulder as teeth clamped down viciously. I screamed in agony, struggling against the hold, the white wolf saw this as an opening and drew near. Just as the panic threatened to overwhelm me, a flash of movement caught my eye. Kaelan appeared at my side in an instant, his snarl cutting through the chaos. He moved like swift death, the shadows swirling around him.

With an unhesitating, brutal motion, he impaled the attacking wolf on his sword, ending its life with cold efficiency. The wolf's grip on me released, and I stumbled away, breathing heavily and clutching my injured shoulder. Before the white wolf could come another inch closer he grabbed it by the scruff of its neck and slit its throat. Dark red blood splattered across his face.

Kaelan's eyes, like thunderclouds, locked onto mine. "Are you alright?" he demanded, his voice rough with tension.

I nodded with a grimace on my face, the blood spilling from my shoulder. "I can make it."

His fingers brushed against my cheek, a gentler touch among the turmoil. "Stay close to me," he ordered, his protectiveness evident in every word. I nodded, my heart still racing as we navigated through the confusion surrounding us. Otherworlders and wolves clashed in fierce combat, some wolves clashed with other wolves. The roar of battle and the scent of blood threatened to overwhelm my senses.

"We need to find Wren," I said, my voice shaky. Kaelan nodded, his grip on his weapon tightening as he led the way, clearing a path through the battling wolves. I felt a surge of fear and resolve, the urgent need to reach Wren and help turn the tide of the fight.

As we pushed through the throng, my heart sank at the sight that awaited us. Wren was locked in a desperate struggle with Rafe, his russet form battered and bloodied. Rafe seemed to have the upper hand, his jaws dangerously close to Wren's throat. Desperation gripped me as I realized Wren was on the brink of losing.

Unable to stand by and watch, I made a split-second decision. Ignoring the consequences, I summoned the dark magic I had learned, my voice rising above the chaos. "Confusio mentis, obscura sensus!" I yelled, the incantation carrying my intent. Kaelan looked at me curiously as I shouted. The spell took effect causing Rafe to become dizzy and disoriented, his movements faltering as confusion clouded his mind.

Unaware of my intervention, Rafe stumbled, presenting a vulnerable moment. Seizing the opportunity, Wren lunged forward, clamping his jaws around Rafe's neck and shaking vigorously. The sickening sound of bones snapping echoed through the air as Wren snapped Rafe's neck, ending the challenge.

The wolves around us took notice, and gradually, the fighting began to subside. The fighting gave way to an uneasy silence as Rafe's lifeless body fell to the ground. The wolves, both those loyal to Rafe and those who had supported Wren, stared in shock at the outcome.

Wren shifted back to his human form, his body battered and bruised, barely able to stand. His gaze met mine, exhaustion and triumph in his eyes. The significance of his success was palpable in the atmosphere, as well as the uncertainty of what could come next.

Wren brought himself up to his full height, his bloodied form emanating a commanding presence. His voice rang out, addressing the assembled wolves with authority. "I've slain the alpha, and by right, the title is now mine. Submit to me or suffer banishment from this pack!"

The wolves loyal to Wren immediately lowered their heads in submission, acknowledging his new status as their alpha. Some of the others begrudgingly followed suit, their resistance fading in the face of Wren's victory and the unity of his supporters. However, a few defiant stragglers remained standing, their eyes burning with resentment and pride. I noticed Donovan was among those who remained standing, his gaze full of loathing.

Wren's voice was unwavering as he addressed those who hesitated. "Traitors have no place in this pack. From this moment on, you are all banished. We do not welcome those who can not stand united."

He stood there a moment longer, his gaze sweeping over the wolves before him with authority and dominance. Then slowly, he turned, and his steps faltered. I moved forward quickly, my arms reaching out to catch him. At the same time, another figure approached, a female werewolf with chocolate-brown eyes and dark skin. Together, we helped Wren, supporting his weight as we guided him toward the alpha's tent.

Kaelan followed closely behind, his concern evident. As we entered the tent, the gravity of the moment hung in the air. The camp had turned into a battlefield and now transformed into a scene of upheaval, the old order overthrown, and a new leader emerging from the ashes.

Chapter Twenty-Two

Inside Wren's new tent, the atmosphere was heavy with exhaustion. We helped Wren down into a chair and his body slumped weakly, displaying the toll of the intense battle he had fought. My cry of alarm filled the air as I beheld the extent of Wren's injuries.

"I'm...okay," He managed to rasp, his voice strained but resolute. His eyes met mine, pain shining in his gaze.

His admission didn't ease my worries. My eyes scanned his form as I took in the gashes and bruises that marred his skin, the way he held his side gingerly as if he had cracked ribs, and the blood that stained his pants from a particularly horrible leg wound. I could see that his body was struggling to heal itself from the multitude of injuries, his supernatural healing abilities hindered by the sheer extent of the damage.

Kaelan, ever vigilant, knelt in front of Wren, his experienced eyes assessing his wounds. "You've taken quite a beating," he remarked, his tone filled with concern. "These wounds, especially the leg injury, might not heal as swiftly as they should."

Wren's lips twitched into a tired smile. "Well, not every battle can be a swift victory, can it?"

My determination flared as I looked between Wren and Kaelan. "Everyone, give us some space," I declared, my voice firm. "I'm going to help heal Wren."

Kaelan's eyes widened in surprise. "Vale, you've lost a lot of blood already. Healing him might drain you completely."

I shook my head, a determined glint in my eyes. "Not if I use blood magic."

Kaelan's concern deepened, his hand moving to cup my cheek. "It's too risky, Vale. Your blood loss—"

I cut him off with a determined gaze. "I won't let him suffer like this. And I know what I'm doing."

Wren, his curiosity piqued, looked at me. "How is this healing different from the healing you did on Jason?"

I took a steady breath, my gaze steady on Wren's. "I can heal you by using my blood. You'll have to drink it; my magic will mend your injuries. It's a powerful but controlled way to help you without draining me."

Kaelan's unease was palpable, though he kept his thoughts to himself. I could tell that my sharing my blood with anyone was something he hadn't anticipated, and the thought of anyone else partaking in such an intimate connection with me made his possessive instincts surge.

Wren's brows furrowed. "Vale, I can't—"

"Wren, you can't afford to be weakened right now. You need to lead your pack and show strength. I won't let you face this challenge in your current state." I said sharply. I was not going to allow Wren to refuse. I knew his stubborn nature well, and I did not doubt that he would rather bear his injuries than take the risk. But I was not about to let him suffer unnecessarily, and I knew the risk of my magic was well worth it.

The female werewolf, who had been quietly observing, stepped forward, her voice supportive. "She's right Wren. This is a pretty dangerous time for new alphas, you need to be at your full strength."

Wren hesitated for a moment longer, then nodded in agreement. "Very well. Let's do it."

I nodded and drew one of my knives, the metal blade glinting in the lamplight. Wren's gaze flickered down to the knife, his expression guarded.

Kaelan moved closer, his voice low and his eyes filled with concern. "Are you sure you can handle this, Vale?"

"I know what I'm doing, Kaelan. Trust me."

Kaelan's concern was evident in his eyes, but he nodded, albeit reluctantly. "Just be careful."

I took a deep breath, steadying my nerves. With a small cut on my wrist, I offered my blood to Wren. He hesitated, his eyes fixed on the wound, and then he pulled my arm gently towards him. His lips met the wound tentatively, tasting the magic woven into my blood. I felt a shiver down my spine as he drank, his initial hesitance giving away to a more fervent need. The sensation was strange yet intimate as if he was consuming not just blood but a piece of my soul.

Before my eyes, Wren's injuries began to mend. The gashes closed, the bruises faded, and the strength slowly returned to his battered form. But as his healing progressed, I could feel myself growing wobbly, the blood loss taking its toll. Still, I held on, my gaze unwavering as I watched the transformation unfold.

Kaelan's strong presence suddenly appeared by my side, and his voice broke through the gathering haze in my mind. "That's enough, Wren."

Wren's eyes met Kaelan's, and he released my arm, the magic of my blood in full effect. I stumbled a little and Kaelanwas there, his hands cupping my face, his concern palpable. It was as if no one else existed as he held me close, looking deep into my eyes.

"I told you," he murmured, his voice worried. "It would take too much from you."

I tried giving him a reassuring smile. "I'm fine. I'm not as weak as I look."

His eyes roved over my form, taking in the pallor of my skin and the slight tremble of my hands. "I'm still worried."

"Don't worry, Kaelan. I can take care of myself." I told him firmly.

Wren's voice drew our attention back to the situation at hand.

"Vale," Wren said, his voice thick with emotion. "Thank you. You're amazing."

"You're welcome," I said, smiling.

Wren slowly rose from the chair, his gratitude evident in his tired eyes. Then he turned to the female werewolf by his side, introducing her as Venna, his new second in command. She gave me a respectful nod, a silent acknowledgment of the role I played tonight.

But Wren's gratitude was followed by his concern. He glanced back at me, his expression softening. "You should rest now, Vale," he urged gently. "The wound on your shoulder is bad, and no one else can heal you like you've done for me."

Kaelan stepped forward, offering his assurance. "I've got her," he said, his eyes never leaving mine. "Go meet with your pack. I'll take care of her."

Wren nodded, a weighty seriousness in his gaze. Before he could leave, though, I stopped him with a smile, trying to inject a touch of light-heartedness into the heavy air. "Hey, alpha," I teased playfully, despite the fatigue that tugged at my senses.

Wren paused, a slight smile touching his lips.

I reached up and pulled him down towards me, and brushed a kiss on his cheek. "Good luck."

However, the weight of the situation wasn't lost on anyone. Just as were were about to find a moment of respite, Jason entered the tent with somber news. He informed us that the Otherworlders that survived were gathering the fallen to give them a proper send-off before returning to the factory. My heart sank at the thought of lives lost in the unnecessary turmoil.

"How many?" I managed to ask, dreading the answer.

Jason's gaze was sympathetic. "About eight of them."

Eight lives were cut short by the violence that had unfolded here. It was a sobering reminder of the price we paid for standing up against the darkness. Wren's decision was clear, and he and Venna left the tent with determination in their steps.

After they were gone, Jason spared me a lingering look, his eyes reflecting the weight of our shared experiences. Then he, too, left the tent, leaving Kaelan and me alone amidst the aftermath of the battle, the echoes of pain and loss ringing in our ears.

Kaelan's hands found their way to my face once more. His touch was gentle but filled with concern. His words held both pride and worry, a testament to the rollercoaster of emotions that this day had brought forth. "You are so incredibly brave, little witch," he said softly. "But also incredibly foolish. You have to start respecting your limits."

I nodded weakly, acknowledging his point. I had acted on impulse, driven by my determination to protect those I cared about, but I hadn't considered the consequences of pushing myself too far, and truthfully in that moment with Wren, I hadn't cared.

Guiding me over to a chair, Kaelan's protective instincts were palpable. He left me sitting there and quickly located a first aid kit within the expansive confines of the alpha's tent. Returning to my side, he instructed me to take off my ruined shirt. I was going to run of out decent clothing at this rate.

Gingerly, I removed my shirt as instructed, wincing at the pain radiating from my injured shoulder. Kaelan's gaze was focused, assessing the wound seriously. Despite his concern, he spoke with a reassuring tone, letting me know that the injury was already starting to mend. With careful hands, he cleaned the wound, his touch both gentle and skilled as he wrapped my shoulder in gauze.

He finished dressing my shoulder and I thanked him with a kiss. He remained on his knees before me, his hands cradling my face. His eyes bore into mine, a mix of emotions swirling within them. "I'm glad you're okay," he murmured, his voice a tender whisper. "But when I saw you being hurt, all I wanted was to tear those wolves apart for what they did to you. I would have killed them all without hesitation."

I met his gaze with a small shiver at his admission. "I know, Kaelan. But I'm fine," I assured him, wanting to ease his worry. "You don't need to be so ready to fight every battle for me."

He leaned in, his lips brushing mine with a lingering kiss. It was a connection forged from the shared intensity of the day, a silent exchange of emotions that spoke more than words ever could.

As he pulled away, his eyes bore into mine with a gravity that seemed to pierce through the chaos around us. His voice was low and intense are he declared, "Even so, I will never stop fighting for you. I would cut a bloody path through countless lives for you. I would walk through hellfire for you. Burn for you, destroy my soul for you, if that's what it took to keep you safe. I need you to remember that, no matter what."

A wave of emotion washed over me at his fierce declaration, and my heart beat faster at the sincerity of his words. His devotion was all-encompassing and I knew then that there would be no escaping him, no denying his claim on me. The thought slightly terrified me.

He stood up, helping me to my feet. "We should go," He said softly, "We should pay our respects to the dead."

My throat was tight as I followed him outside. The bodies of the fallen had been lined up and covered in blankets. As the survivors gathered around, I realized how deeply this victory had cost us all.

Kaelan stood beside me, his presence a comfort amidst the somberness of the occasion. We listened as Wren, now alpha, spoke about the sacrifice of the fallen. Their names were listed, their contributions praised, and their bravery honored. As we stood, listening to the list of the dead, I could feel my emotions rising. Tears burned at my eyes, my throat tightening with the reality of what we had experienced.

I had never imagined the cost of being in the midst of such violence, and the pain of losing the innocent was raw and fresh in my mind. As I looked around at the faces of those gathered, I could see the same emotions mirrored in their eyes. We had all been scarred by this day, our wounds still raw and tender.

I could feel Kaelan's presence beside me, and I knew that he, too, was feeling the weight of the loss. He had lived through many battles, and seen countless lives lost, but that didn't make it any easier.

His hand slipped into mine, a silent gesture of comfort and solidarity. I laced my fingers through his, holding on tightly as we remembered the fallen and honored their sacrifice.

"Come on," he said in a whisper as he pulled me back into the tent. "You need to rest and your presence here isn't needed anymore." He pulled me close and the shadows settled around us as we shifted back to the apartment. The familiar surroundings brought a sense of relief, but also a reminder of the challenges we still faced. Waiting for us was Juniper, her worry evident in her expression. She jumped at our sudden appearance, her concern spilling forth in a rush of questions.

I let out a tired sigh as I recounted the events of the fight, and how Wren had emerged victorious against the odds. Juniper's relief was evident, her exhaustion apparent as she sank into the couch. The weight of the day's tension seemed to melt from her shoulders.

Despite the lingering worries of the night, I knew that we had succeeded in our mission. Wren was now alpha, his pack was free from the oppression of Rafe, and the darkness was pushed back once again.

And I couldn't help but feel a glimmer of hope amid the turmoil. We had taken a stand and we had triumphed. Even though the war was far from over, I felt like we had made a dent in the darkness, and for the first time in a long time, I felt a genuine sense of hope.

Kaelan stepped forward, his offer to take Juniper home carrying an unspoken promise of safety. She hesitated for a moment, then nodded, accepting his hand. They shifted away, leaving me alone in the apartment.

As I stood there, the old cat padded over, its presence a comforting reminder of the little moments of normalcy that still existed within our chaotic world. He purred as he curled around my ankles, and I crouched down to pet him.

The room was quiet now, the adrenaline of the day slowly ebbing away. I couldn't help but think about Kaelan's words, about the fierce protectiveness he held for me.

Kaelan shifted back from Juniper's apartment. My weariness settled heavily on me as I sat on the edge of the bed, the events of the day taking their toll. Kaelan came over and settled beside me, his presence a comforting anchor amidst the lingering chaos.

"Are you okay," he asked again, his concern evident in his eyes as he looked at me.

I managed a faint smile. "Just tired. It's been quite a day."

He nodded in understanding, his hand finding mine and giving it a reassuring squeeze. "You should get some rest."

I looked at him with gratitude. "Will you stay with me?"

A tender smile crossed his lips, his eyes warm. "Of course. I'll be right here all night."

With his assurance, I got up and moved to get dressed for bed, peeling off my bloodied clothes and replacing them with my sushi cat pajamas, washing up quickly in the process. As I stepped out of the bathroom, I found Kaelan lying on the bed, his shoes and bloodied shirt discarded to the side. He chuckled as he noticed my choice of sleepwear, and I couldn't help but tease him.

"These are your favorite, huh?" I said with a playful smirk, striking a pose.

He let out a laugh, his gaze lingering on me. "I think you would look sexy in an old potato sack."

I laughed and replied, "But you haven't seen me in my flimsiest, laciest pair of silk pajamas yet."

His eyes darkened at the thought, a hint of desire flickering in them. Though I couldn't deny the thrill that raced through me at the intensity of his gaze, I playfully rolled my eyes at him.

He patted the space beside him, and I crawled into bed, settling down with my head on his chest. His fingers found their way to my back, tracing soothing patterns as a sense of serenity washed over me. The gentle rise and fall of his chest beneath me was relaxing and before long the exhaustion caught up with me.

As Kaelan's fingers continued their comforting movement, I drifted to sleep, wrapped in his arms and the promise of safety he brought. In that moment, there was nothing but the sound of his steady heartbeat and the reassuring touch that bound us together.

Chapter Twenty-Three

I was awoken by the soft rays of sunshine playing across my face, the shadows cast by the trees outside dancing on my skin. Kaelan and I lay wrapped in each other's arms. The exhaustion from the previous night's events had taken its toll, and we had both slept deeply, seeking solace in each other's embrace. My old cat lay at the foot of the bed, blinking at me sleepily.

As I stirred awake Kaelan shifted beside me. His lips brushed against my nose, and he greeted me with a soft, sleepy smile. "Hey there, sleepyhead. How'd you sleep?"

A contented sigh escaped my lips, and I stretched slightly against him. "Soundly. I guess we both needed it."

He chuckled, the sound rumbling beneath his breath. "Definitely. It was an eventful night."

I was about to lean in to kiss him when I noticed something strange. The tips of my fingers on one hand had turned an unsettling shade of black. Confusion surged within me, and I pulled my hand back, staring at it in disbelief. "What...What happened to my hand?"

Kaelan's brow furrowed in concern as he pulled my hand closer to inspect my fingers. "I don't know. It's like they're stained or something."

I felt a rush of unease, my heart beating faster as I tried to rub the dark hue off my fingers. It was as if I had been dipped in ink, the color refusing to fade. "I can't get it off. What in the world is this?"

Kaelan's voice remained steady, though I could sense his worry. "Maybe it has something to do with your magic. You've been using it quite a bit lately. You should ask Elara about it. She might know what's going on."

Nodding, I quickly got out of bed, my movements a little frantic. "Yeah, you're right. I need to find out what this is."

We both hurriedly got dressed, Kaelan washed up in the bathroom while I continued to try and scrub the black stains from my hands. Despite my efforts, the color remained stubbornly present. It was a disconcerting feeling, a reminder of the mysteries that often came with my magical abilities.

Kaelan emerged from the bathroom, looking at my hand with a furrowed brow. "Ready to go?"

But before we headed out, I realized that I wanted to check on the Otherworlders downstairs. I knew that many of them had been wounded during the chaos of yesterday, and the thought of their pain tugged at my heart.

"Actually, I'd like to see how the wounded are doing before we leave," I told him, my voice tinged with worry.

He nodded understandingly. "Of course. Let's go check on them."

We made our way down to the main floor of the factory, and the sight that greeted us was sobering. Wounded Otherworlders were lying on cots, and the air was heavy with pain. Juniper was there, as expected, tending to those in need with her usual dedication. She really was the heart of our group.

As I looked around, I couldn't help but feel a pang of sadness. Eight of our allies hadn't made it through the battle, and their absences hung in the air like a heavy cloud.

Ava approached me, her expression determined. "I've been able to provide some help by offering up some of the herbs I had been cultivating. They're being used to treat the wounded, which makes me feel like I'm doing my part." She said, smiling at me.

I smiled gratefully back at her. "That's wonderful, Ava. Thank you for helping out."

She nodded, her brown eyes glinting with a hint of pride, before returning to her tasks.

Jason, always vigilant, noticed me and walked over with a concerned look. "Vale, how's everything with Wren?"

I shook my head, feeling a twinge of unease. "I haven't heard from him yet. But I'll let you know as soon as I do."

He nodded, his gaze shifting to my hand. "What happened to your hand?"

Quickly, I hid my stained fingers behind my back, hoping he didn't notice my unease. "Oh, just a little accident. I spilled some ink."

Jason accepted my explanation with a nod before returning to his duties.

Kaelan stood beside me, his hand resting gently on my lower back. "Are you okay?"

I nodded, though a cloud of concern still hung over me. "Yeah, I just...I wish I could have done more to prevent this." I said, gesturing around me.

He rubbed my back reassuringly. "You did plenty, Vale. You helped Wren when he needed it most."

It took me a moment to realize he was talking about healing him and not about the dark magic I had cast on Rafe.

With the decision to check in with Elara, Kaelan and I shifted back to his house. We wasted no time as we made our way to the library, our hands tightly entwined. Harker was nowhere to be seen, likely tucked away for her daylight slumber.

"Elara," I called, my voice carrying a mixture of urgency and concern.

The air in front of us shimmered, and the witch materialized. Her sharp gaze immediately fell on Kaelan, a glint of distrust present. "You brought the demon back," she stated, her eyes narrowing.

Kaelan's response was laced with amusement. "It's still my house."

Not wanting to waste any time, I held out my hand, showing Elara the blackness that had marred my fingertips. "Look at this. What's happening to me?"

Elara's gaze shifted from my hand to my face, her expression now more serious. "The consequences of your actions. Didn't I tell you that every choice has a price?"

Kaelan seemed confused, his brow furrowing. "What are you talking about?"

Elara addressed him while keeping her eyes on me. "Dark magic is not without its cost. The more significant the magic, the heavier the price. The blackness on her fingers is a manifestation of those consequences."

Understanding dawned on me as Elara's words sank in. I looked at the blackened tips of my fingers, dread filling me. "Will it go away?"

Elara's response was disheartening. She shook her head, her expression grave. "No, Vale. As you continue to use dark magic, the blackness will spread. I've known witches whose entire bodies were covered in that darkness. And it changes them, twisting them into something darker, something wrong."

I felt a shiver run down my spine at the implications of her words. I had dabbled in dark magic out of necessity, not fully comprehending the price I would pay. And now, as I stared down at my tainted fingers, I realized that my choices were altering more than just the outcome of spells— they were changing me from within.

Kaelan's concern shifted to a tinge of anger as he looked at me. "When and why did you use something as dangerous as dark magic?"

I took a deep breath, knowing I had to be honest. "It was during the fight. When Rafe was about to defeat Wren, I panicked. I cast a small dark magic spell to disorient him, to give Wren a chance."

His eyes flared, and he spoke with an edge to his voice. "Vale, do you even understand what you're playing with? It's not some weapon you can wield without consequences."

I felt a defensive knot forming in my chest. "I know that now, Kaelan. But at that moment, I didn't see any other way. I had to do something to help Wren."

Kaelan's anger was discernible as he responded, his voice laced with frustration. "Blindly using magic you don't understand, putting yourself at risk... You think that's helping?"

His words struck a chord, and I couldn't deny the truth in them. He was right— I had acted recklessly, thinking only of the immediate problem and not considering the bigger picture. I couldn't bring myself to regret helping Wren, though. I knew I would do it again if I had to do it over.

But I wasn't ready to back down. "Everything I've done is to help the ones I care about, Kaelan. Healing the wounded, protecting those I care about. I don't regret it."

"And who's going to help you when you're the one in trouble? There are no other witches around to save you from the messes you get into." He retorted, his voice still carrying an edge.

His words stung, a harsh reality I couldn't ignore. I looked at him, frustration and guilt swirling within me. "From now on, I swear to be more careful with my magic. I am aware of the consequences of misusing it, and I won't make that mistake again."

His gaze held mine for a moment longer, and then he turned abruptly, leaving the room. I stood there, feeling the weight of his anger and my own mistakes settling heavily on my shoulders.

Elara's voice broke the silence. "Demons, always so volatile."

I glanced at her, frustration welling up. "Thanks for the insight, Elara. It's really helpful."

She shrugged, unbothered. "I do what I can."

Exhaling a sigh, I shook my head and followed Kaelan's path, my guilt trailing behind me like a shadow.

I left the library and headed towards Kaelan's room, the uncertainty of his anger gnawing at me. As I entered, I found him pacing back and forth, his frustration noticeable. "Kaelan," I said softly, attempting to break through to him.

He didn't immediately respond, his gaze fixed on the floor. I wasn't going to let him avoid the conversation, so I stepped closer, took his hand, and repeated his name with more urgency. Finally, his eyes met mine, revealing the turbulence of his emotions.

"I'm sorry," I began, my voice sincere. "I didn't mean to anger you or act so recklessly. It was foolish, and I know that now."

He let out a sigh, his anger dissipating as he took my head in his hands. "Vale, you have no regard for your own safety. You are more valuable than all the people you have supported in the past."

I looked into his dark eyes, understanding the depth of his concern. "I understand why you're angry and I apologize. I'll be more mindful in the future. I won't let my spur-of-the-moment decisions place me in harm's way."

He nodded, relief and lingering worry in his eyes. He pulled me close and kissed me, the tension between us slowly melting away. "What's the plan now?" he asked, his voice a gentle rumble against my lips.

I smiled mischievously, an idea forming. "Well, we have a few hours before Harker wakes up, and I could really use a shower."

He grinned back, his tone playful. "Can I join you?"

I nodded, my heart skipping a beat at his words. "Absolutely."

With a sense of renewed closeness and understanding, we headed to the bathroom together, ready to wash away the stress of the day and rekindle the connection between us.

Hours later, I found myself back in the library alongside Harker. We were poring over her research notes, the room dimly lit by a few strategically placed candles. The task at hand was immense— finding a way to contact the First Witch for guidance and assistance. I couldn't shake off the feeling of urgency that had settled upon us since the events at the wolf camp.

My phone buzzed on the table, and I glanced at the caller ID— it was Wren. I picked up and stepped aside. "Hey, how are you holding up?" I asked, concern lacing my words.

Wren's voice carried a hint of exhaustion, but also resolute determination. "I'm managing. The pack is a mess, but we're working on restoring order."

I empathized with him, knowing the immense challenges he must be facing as the new alpha. "It's not easy, I'm sure."

He chuckled darkly. "No, it's not. But I know it's worth it—for my pack and for you."

My heart warmed at his words even as a pang of guilt twisted inside me. I looked down at my blackened fingertips. If only he knew the lengths I had gone to, the dark magic I had wielded, to help him win the challenge. But I pushed that thought aside and focused on our conversation.

"I'm glad you're okay, Wren. And I'm always here to help," I reassured him, though a layer of unease lingered beneath my words that I hoped he didn't pick up on.

"Vale, I can't thank you enough for being there for me, for helping me when I needed it most," he said sincerely.

A heavy sigh escaped me. "You don't have to thank me. I'll always be there for you."

As we said our goodbyes, I hung up the phone, feeling a mix of emotions swirling within me. Harker's inquisitive gaze met mine, and I knew I couldn't hide anything from her. "What's on your mind?" she asked.

I hesitated, then confessed, "Wren doesn't know the full extent of what I did to help him."

Harker's brows furrowed in concern and she glanced down at my darkened fingertips. "You used the dark magic, didn't you?"

I nodded, my gaze falling to the floor. "Yes, I did. He doesn't need to know—it won't change anything now."

Harker's expression softened, and she stepped close, placing a hand on my arm. "Just be cautious, Vale. Dark magic always comes with a price, and secrets have a way of resurfacing."

I nodded in understanding, a weight settling over me. "I know," I said looking at my hand. "But I know it was worth it."

With a thoughtful nod, Harker left me to my thoughts and returned to her research. As the minutes ticked by, the anticipation for the upcoming ritual only grew stronger. I paced the floor anxiously, my footsteps echoing in the quiet library.

"Are we all set for tomorrow night?" I asked, my voice carrying a hint of nervousness.

Harker glanced up from her notes, a glint of excitement in her eyes. "Yes, we're as prepared as we can be. The necessary items are ready, the incantations are laid out, and the timing should be perfect with the full moon."

I sighed in relief, a small smile tugging at my lips. "Good. I just wanted to make sure we have everything in place."

Harker's smile mirrored mine as she closed her notebook. "You're being responsible, Vale. It's important that we're ready for this. If it goes wrong, well, let's just say it won't be very pretty."

I nodded in agreement, the gravity of the situation not lost on me. "Is there anything I should do to prepare myself?"

Harker leaned back in her chair, thoughtful. "Just make sure you don't eat anything a few hours before the ritual. The connection with the First Witch might make you a bit queasy."

I chuckled softly. "Got it. No big meal before the magical rendezvous."

Harker chuckled along with me. "Exactly. Aside from that, just stay focused and be open to the connection. The First Witch will guide you through the rest."

"Okay," I said, taking a deep breath. "I can do that."

Harker's expression softened as she regarded me. "You're stronger than you think, Vale. And I have a feeling this ritual is going to be easy."

I appreciated her encouragement. "Let's hope so. I really need her guidance right now."

"Then we'll be ready when the moon rises tomorrow. Rest well tonight." She said.

"Thank you, Harker," I said sincerely. "I'll see you tomorrow."

With a nod, we parted ways for the night, each of us carrying the weight of our preparations and the hope for what the upcoming ritual might reveal. As I left the library excitement and trepidation coursed through my veins. The moon's ascent tomorrow held the promise of answers— and with them, the potential to shape the course of our journey.

Chapter Twenty-Four

The sun was dipping below the horizon, painting the sky with hues of orange and pink as the full moon began to ascend. Harker, Kaelan, and I stood outside Kaelan's house, the anticipation tangible in the air. My heart raced with excitement and nervousness as I prepared for the ritual ahead. Kaelan stood nearby, his presence a comforting reassurance in the gathering darkness, there to make sure I didn't become too drained from the spirit magic.

Harker had meticulously drawn a circle on the ground in silver dust, and I stepped into its confines with purpose. Four black candles were strategically placed at the cardinal points— North, South, East, and West. As I glanced around, I could feel the weight of the moment settling upon me.

With a nod from Harker, I ignited the candles one by one, their eerie glow casting dancing shadows across the ground. Closing my eyes, I inhaled deeply, grounding myself in the connection between the moon and the spirit world. I could feel the energy humming around me, a harmonious blend of natural and supernatural forces.

As I began to recite the incantation, the words flowed from my lips like a melody of ancient secrets. Each syllable held intention, a beckoning to the elusive presence I sought to summon.

"Beneath the full moon's glow, in whispered incantation,
I conjure The First Witch, ancient incarnation.
From realms unknown, you shall heed my invocation,
Awaken, spirit, with wisdom's illumination.

With moon's silver halo as our guiding constellation,
Let your spectral presence grace this sacred location,
In the name of magic's craft, I seek your revelation."

With the final word spoken, a hushed expectancy fell upon the surroundings. The very air seemed charged with an otherwordly energy, a sensation that sent shivers down my spine. I stood there, palms upturned, in breathless anticipation as I felt the threads of magic weave around my intent.

As I opened my eyes, I sensed a shift— a subtle change in the atmosphere, as if the veil between realms had thinned. I was the conduit, the bridge between the tangible and the ethereal, and a surge of power coursed through me. My heart raced in tandem with the rhythm of the night, a symphony of connections converging in this sacred space.

The candles responded to my invocation, their flames leaping higher. The circle seemed to pulse, a heartbeat echoing through the earth beneath my feet.

In the space between heartbeats, I felt it— a presence, an echo brushing against my senses. It was as if a realm beyond the mundane had brushed against my consciousness, revealing layers of existence that transcended the visible world. I was connected, part of a delicate dance between realms.

My hands reached out toward the candles, fingers outstretched as if grasping for the very essence of magic itself. A soft breeze whispered in response, playing with strands of my hair like ethereal fingers. The boundary between the physical and the mystical blurred, and I stood poised on the threshold between worlds.

The moon, fully ascendant now, cast its silvery radiance upon me. I felt its energy flow through me, intertwining with my own. I was a vessel, a vessel for truths waiting to be uncovered. I stood, rooted in my purpose, a conduit between the earthly and the divine.

With unwavering clarity, I voiced my intent, "First Witch, I call to thee." I intoned, my words reaching beyond the physical realm. I placed a small moonstone, dried acacia, and dandelion leaf in a small silver bowl before me, setting it aflame. As the flames flickered to life, a fragrant scent wafted on the breeze. The offering was a bridge, a gesture of goodwill and respect to the spirit I sought to commune with.

Closing my eyes, I envisioned a misty veil, a boundary between realms that rippled like a gossamer curtain. In my mind's eye, I saw the veil thinning and parting, an Otherworldly passage materializing to welcome the spirit I called upon. The air around me hummed with magic, the energies converging to create a portal between worlds.

With a tingling sensation brushing against my skin, I knew that the veil was responding to my summons. Mist began to coil at my feet, tendrils curling and spiraling like wisps of silver smoke. I felt a presence, like a whisper against my senses, and I called out the second incantation.

"Beneath the full moon's grace, I conjure with might,

The First Witch, ancient spirit, appear this night.
Share your ancient wisdom, secrets held so tight,
In this sacred space, let your presence ignite."

And then, as if the veils of reality itself had parted, she was there before me. The First Witch emerged from the mists, her form unearthly and graceful. Dressed in a flowing black gown that seemed to absorb the moonlight, her silver hair cascaded like liquid metal, so similar to my own hair. Her eyes held ancient knowledge and a spark of curiosity, a reflection of lifetimes lived beyond the veil.

We stood there, bathed in the moonlight's glow, a connection woven between realms. The First Witch's presence enveloped me, her energy thrumming around me. A sense of awe mingled with reverence as I stood in the company of such an ancient force.

Her words, a resonance that transcended the material world, echoed around us. "You've done well to summon me, daughter of realms," Her voice carried the weight of knowledge. As the moonlight kissed the earth, the First Witch's form seemed to shimmer, both present and ephemeral. A sense of urgency pressed upon me, the awareness that the magical currents I harnessed were steadily drawing upon my energy.

"You are here with a purpose," she continued. "But you are unprepared for the trials that await you."

Her words were a sobering reminder of the challenges ahead. "I know," I said with trepidation. "I'm ready to learn, to grow stronger."

Attuned to the subtle currents of magic, I felt the drain on my energy, a gradual siphoning. The temporal nature of this encounter compelled me to press further, to seek guidance while I still had the chance.

"What must I do to prepare?" I asked, my voice edged with an eagerness to embrace the path laid before me.

The First Witch's gaze held mine, her eyes like pools of ancient knowledge. "You require a teacher, someone to guide you, to impart power beyond your current grasp."

The implications of her words sent a shiver down my spine. "A teacher," I echoed, my mind racing to comprehend the magnitude of what she was suggesting. "But who? All the witches are gone."

The First Witch's response was cryptic, her word laden with a gravitas. "Your teacher stands before you," she declared, gesturing toward herself.

Confusion washed over me as I glanced at Harker and Kaelan, their expression mirroring my own incredulity. "Wait," I stammered, grappling to make sense of her words. "You mean yourself?"

The First Witch's presence remained unyielding. "Yes," she confirmed, her voice an echo that transcended space and time. "For you to access the wisdom and power you seek, my spirit must merge with yours."

Her revelation bore down on me, a realization that sent shockwaves through my being. My heart beat wildly in my chest, and I looked from the First Witch to my companions, seeking their support in this moment of profound uncertainty."Let me make sure I understand," I said, my voice trembling slightly as I addressed the mysterious figure before me. "You want to merge your spirit with mine? So you can teach me?"

The First Witch's ethereal form shimmered, her gaze unwavering. "Yes," she affirmed, her words carried on the wind. "With our spirits entwined, I can guide you and bestow upon you the knowledge and strength you seek."

The energy within me continued to wane, an undeniable reminder that time was slipping away. Every second counted, and I pressed on, my mind racing to absorb the magnitude of what was proposed. "But...what happens to me? To us?"

The First Witch's words echoed in the darkness. "It will forever bind us in a symbiotic union. You will be strengthened, but there will be challenges, and you will carry a part of me within you."

A gnawing sense of uncertainty swirled within me as I considered the gravity of her words. "What if I decline?" I asked, my voice wavering with doubt.

Her response was direct, her gaze unyielding. "To refuse this opportunity would be to face your trials defenseless, lacking the tools and guidance you desperately need. It would be foolish on your part to decline."

My mind raced, grappling with the implications of her revelation. What lay ahead? What were the challenges she spoke of? I had so many questions and she held the answers I sought.

"I cannot reveal the future to you," The First Witch responded to my unspoken query as if she could read my thoughts. "Trust in the path that led you here and know that I am offering a chance to be prepared."

Doubt and uncertainty warred within me, a storm of emotions swirling beneath the surface. I took a deep breath, my heart heavy with the weight of my decision. The First Witch's words hung in the air.

"We're running out of time," I whispered, feeling the strain of the spell on my energy.

The First Witch's presence seemed to shift, a sense of finality settling around us. "Think on my offer, Vale. If you decide to proceed, seek out the blood magic spell within the library. It will be your choice to make. I pray you make the right one."

Before I could voice another question, the First Witch's form began to dissolve, her essence receding like a retreating tide. "Wait!" I called out, reaching out instinctively, but she was already gone, leaving me standing there in the moonlight's embrace, a myriad of emotions and uncertainties churning within me.

The spell's energy released its hold, and I stumbled slightly, my balance disrupted by the sudden shift. Kaelan was by my side in an instant, his strong arms steadying me. I assured him that I was all right, relieved that this time the drain from the spirit magic wasn't as severe as it had been before.

Harker's concerned gaze was fixed on me, his curiosity palpable. "What are you going to do?" she asked, her voice a whisper.

I took a deep breath, my mind racing as I tried to gather my thoughts and emotions. "I'm not sure of anything yet," I said, my words heavy with the gravity of the encounter.

Kaelan's eyes darkened with anger. "You can't seriously be considering this," he said, his voice laced with doubt.

I turned to him, my heart heavy with the knowledge of the choices that lay before me. "It's not just about me," I replied, my voice soft but resolute. "There's more at stake here, and if this can help us—help everyone— then I have to consider it."

His frustration was evident as he ran his hand through his hair. "And what about you? What about the toll it can take on you, have you thought about that?"

Torn between the gravity of the situation and Kaelan's impassioned concern, I felt a surge of emotions welling within me. "Of course, I've thought about it," I said, my voice tinged with frustration. "But we can't ignore an opportunity like this. We need every advantage we can get."

Kaelan's eyes locked onto mine, a mixture of worry and desperation in his gaze. "You have no regard for your own life, do you? You keep putting yourself in harm's way without thinking of the consequences."

I sighed, my heart aching at the truth in his words. "It's not that I don't care," I began, my voice softening. "But sometimes sacrifices have to be made."

His gaze bore into me, a pleading intensity that tugged at my heart. "Vale, please don't do this," he implored, his voice filled with raw emotion.

I met his gaze, my own emotions mirroring his. "I have to at least consider it, Kaelan," I said my voice steady but trembling slightly.

He sighed as he ran a hand through his hair again. "Fine," he relented, but I knew this wasn't the end of this conversation.

As the spell's aftermath left me feeling drained, Kaelan gently scooped me up in his arms. He carried me toward the house, his steps sure and steady. Harker followed closely, concern etched on her features. As Kaelan laid me down to rest, I closed my eyes, the events of the night swirling through my mind. The decisions ahead loomed like shadows, their outcomes uncertain, but the conviction to protect those I cared for remained unwavering.

Chapter Twenty-Five

I slowly roused from a night of strange dreams and restless sleep in Kaelan's guest bedroom. His absence was notable, and I couldn't deny the tension that lingered between us after last night's heated conversation. I needed some space, some time to gather my thoughts and emotions before I was ready to face him again. With a sigh, I pushed myself out of bed and got dressed, a knot of uncertainty gnawing at the pit of my stomach.

The decision to visit Wren felt like a welcome escape, a chance to distance myself from the complexities that had unfolded. As I stepped out of the guest bedroom, I found myself alone, the house eerily quiet. I pushed my worries aside and called Nyxen from the shadows.

My familiar happily bounded from the shadows behind the curtains hanging from the windows. I smiled at the strange creature, holding my hand out and running it through his insubstantial form. He let out a low rumbling sound close to a cat's purr.

We shifted directly into Wren's new tent just as he was stirring awake. Mine and Nyxen's sudden appearance seemed to startle him, and a chuckle escaped my lips as he blinked at me, bleary-eyed and disoriented.

"You're going to have to get used to my unconventional entrances," I joked, a playful smile tugging at my lips.

Wren managed a half-hearted chuckle, his gaze sharpening as he took in the situation. "Right, the shadow-shifting thing. Keeps things interesting."

A genuine grin broke free as I approached him. "Exactly."

I watched him sit up, the morning light filtering in through the tent's opening. The alpha mantle rested heavily on his shoulders already, and my heart went out to him. I had an inkling of how challenging this role had become, and I was here to see how he was holding up.

I walked into the makeshift kitchen. Pouring some water into a pot, I started preparing coffee, its aroma filling the air. The process felt soothing, grounding me. I settled down beside Wren on his cot.

"So, how's life as the new alpha treating you?" I inquired, my tone carrying genuine curiosity.

Wren sighed, his gaze distant for a moment before returning to me. "It's a rollercoaster, honestly. Settling disputes, handling challenges to the pack's hierarchy, trying to better the community— it's a lot to juggle right now."

Handing him a mug of coffee, I met his tired eyes. "Sounds like a true test of leadership."

He took a sip of the coffee, his expression grateful. "Definitely, one I'm determined to succeed at."

With a nod of understanding, I leaned back against the tent wall. "I have no doubt you will."

The conversation shifted, and Wren's eyes lit up as he began discussing his plans as alpha. The determination in his voice was evident as he spoke of helping more Otherworlders as well as wolves, opening the pack and the factory to those in need.

"I want to provide a haven for them all," he said, his gaze unwavering. "A place where people can find refuge and community, despite the challenges."

His goals were lofty. I admired his commitment to making a difference and was struck by the strength he exuded as he faced this new role head-on. Leaning into the moment, I found myself offering a genuine smile.

"That's a noble mission, Wren. And I believe in your ability to achieve it."

Wren's expression softened, gratitude and determination etched into his features. "Having you here means a lot."

The warmth of his words enveloped me, and I nodded in response. "I know the road ahead will be a hard one, but you'll do great things, Wren. You're going to change lives." Wren's genuine smile softened the weight of my uncertainty from the past few days.

"Thank you, Vale. For everything," he said, his gratitude shining through.

Wren proposed taking me on a tour of the camp to show me some of the changes he had already implemented. As we made our way out of the tent, a flash of light drew our attention, and my eyes landed on Venna who was walking towards us, a small smile tugging at her lips.

"Hey, Venna," I said warmly, returning her smile.

She stopped before us, a glimmer of mischief in her eyes. "Hey, Vale." She glanced at Wren. "And Alpha," she said, nodding in deference.

Wren shook his head, his expression amused. "Just Wren is fine."

"Alright," she said with a grin. "Well, I was just coming by to see if you needed any help today. I'm happy to lend a hand."

"Actually," Wren said, glancing at me. "We were just going to take a tour of the camp. Would you like to join us?"

"Sure," Venna replied. "I'd love to."

I smiled at Venna, appreciating her easygoing presence. As we began walking, I asked about her plans now that Wren was alpha. She explained that she wanted to help him in any way she could, and was determined to make a positive impact on the community.

As we continued our walk, I noticed the change in the camp. The atmosphere was brighter, the mood lighter. Wolves walked around, their posture relaxed and their smiles genuine. It was clear that the former alpha's oppressive presence was gone. The empathy in Wren's actions was evident as he pointed out the daycare set up to support families in need of childcare and the preparations for the food bank to aid those facing hunger. I couldn't help but be impressed by his swift and thoughtful responses to the challenges before him.

"You've accomplished so much in just a short time," I remarked, my admiration genuine.

Wren chuckled softly, his gaze humble. "It's a start. We have a long way to go, but it's a step in the right direction. These people are my responsibility now, and they deserve a better future."

I nodded, my lips curving into a smile. "You're a good leader, Wren."

We continued the tour, Venna pointing out the various improvements and changes that had been implemented since Wren's rise to alpha.

As we strolled through the camp, Wren's question about the ritual brought my thoughts back to last night. The uncertainty of what lay ahead with the First Witch left me torn, and I knew I needed to share my experience with Wren. Vennaexcused herself and Wren and I continued our walk alone.

I took a deep breath, deciding to confide in him. "Wren, the summoning... it was different than what I had anticipated," I began, trying to come up with the words. "The First Witch wants to merge our spirits— to mentor me, share her power, and prepare me for what's to come."

Wren's eyes widened, surprise evident on his face. "Merge your spirits? What does that even mean?"

I continued, my voice tinged with the complexity of my emotions. "It would mean that part of the First Witch's essence would become a part of me. We'd be connected in a way that I don't fully understand. But she would be there to guide me."

Wren's brow furrowed as he processed the information. "That's...a lot to take in. And what does Kaelan think about all this?"

A sigh escaped me, my thoughts heavy with the memory of our recent argument. "He's strongly against it. He believes it's dangerous, that I'd be sacrificing a part of myself and end up becoming something different."

Wren's concern was evident as he regarded me. "And what do you think?"

I looked at him, my inner conflict reflected in my eyes. "I'm torn, Wren. On one hand, I can't deny that I need help—I need to be prepared for whatever challenges lie ahead. The First Witch kept talking about 'trials to come.' But on the other hand, I worry about what it would mean for me. I'd be giving up a piece of myself, and I'm not sure I'm ready for that."

Talking about this made me feel better and I felt a renewed sense of gratitude for having him in my life. As we walked through the camp, uncertainty churned within me. The trials ahead were shrouded in mystery, and the path I chose would shape my destiny in ways I couldn't yet comprehend.

I could feel Wren studying me as we walked, his thoughts clearly weighing the situation. His words were measured and careful. "Vale, if you ask me, it sounds like a big risk. I know how much you need help, but merging your spirit with someone else's? That sounds dangerous."

I couldn't deny the wisdom of his words. My emotions were tangled, the complexity of the decision weighing on me. As we rounded a corner, a group of kids playing tag caught my eye. They laughed and ran, their eyes bright and their expressions carefree. The innocence in their faces made me ache, and I wondered if I would ever be able to live such a simple existence.

A knot formed in my stomach as I thought about what Kaelan had said about me becoming something other than myself. But even worse was the thought of standing by and watching the darkness take over. I couldn't just turn a blind eye while the world fell apart.

"Wren, the darkness is only growing," I began, my voice soft but resolute. "If I'm supposed to defeat it, I need help. I'm not ready for what's coming, and I can't afford to ignore that."

I met Wren's gaze, his eyes reflecting the same gravity as mine. We both knew the stakes were high, the future uncertain.

"Vale, I trust in you to be able to make the right call here," he said, his expression earnest. "All you need to do is trust yourself too."

A sad smile tugged at my lips. "Easier said than done, Wren."

He nodded, a small smile lifting his own lips. "I know. But I believe in you."

My heart warmed at his words, and I hoped they would be enough.

❨ ☽

The soft glow of lamplight cast a warm ambiance throughout my apartment, illuminating the shelves lined with books, as I sat on the worn-in leather couch. The scent of sandalwood incense lingered in the air, mingling with the faint aroma of the coffee I had brewed earlier.

Seated on the couch, I was surrounded by a sea of cushions and throws that reflected a spectrum of deep, rich hues. A book lay open on my lap, its pages bathed in the soft lamplight. The story within transported me to another world, a welcome distraction from the weight of the decisions that loomed over me.

I took a drag from the joint nestled between my two fingers, the tip glowing like a small ember in the dimness. Exhaling a stream of smoke, I watched it curl and dance in the air. The smoke carried with it a sense of release, a temporary respite from the burdens that had been occupying my mind.

Lost in my book and the tendrils of fragrant smoke, I momentarily forgot the weight of the world outside. It was a brief interlude of solace, a pause before the storm that would undoubtedly come when I made my final decision.

A knock on the door interrupted my thoughts, and I wearily rose to answer it. To my surprise, Kaelan stood there, his appearance disheveled, his usually strong demeanor softened by exhaustion. I couldn't help but notice the weariness etched into his features.

"Hey," I greeted softly, concern lacing my voice. "You look like you haven't slept."

His eyes met mine, fatigue and frustration in them. "I haven't. Not since the summoning."

I stepped aside, inviting him in. He entered, his steps heavy as he moved to the couch and slumped down onto it, burying his head in his hands. The sight of him in such a state pulled at my heartstrings. I closed the door behind him and joined him in the living room, sitting nearby.

"Kaelan, where have you been?" I asked gently.

He let out a sigh that carried a weight of its own. "I've been in the demon realm, getting into fights, looking for trouble. Anything to drown out the noise in my head."

My concern deepened as I took in his exhausted appearance. The turmoil within him seemed to mirror my own. His next question caught me off guard, and I couldn't help but feel the vulnerability in his words.

"Have you made a decision about the First Witch?"

I leaned back, the smoke from my joint still curled in the air. "I'm torn, Kaelan. I need the help. But merging spirits? What does that even entail? I still need time to think."

His frustration was unmistakable as he ran a hand through his tousled hair. "What's there to think about? You should just say no and be done with it. We'll face whatever comes our way together."

A big part of me wished I could do just that, to forget this whole issue ever arose. "It's not that simple, Kaelan."

He let out a frustrated exhale, his emotions raw. "You realize the First Witch could easily be manipulating you, right? She wants access to your body, your mind."

I met his gaze, my own frustration mingling with his. "I don't think it's that straightforward. She didn't seem conniving."

He scoffed, his voice edged with disbelief. "You're trusting her words? You have no idea how these ancient spirits operate. They have their own motives."

My irritation flared, and the tension between us heated. "And neither do you."

We stared at each other, emotions swirling in the air between us. The weight of the decision hung heavily over our heads, and neither of us had all the answers. As the silence stretched, I couldn't help but wonder if there was a middle ground— a choice that took into account both of our concerns.

"I don't want to make this decision alone," I admitted softly, my voice laced with uncertainty.

He sighed, his frustration beginning to subside. "You won't be alone. No matter what, I'll be there with you."

His words were a balm to my pain, easing some of my anxiety. "No matter what?" I echoed his promise, my voice soft but searching for a depth of understanding.

Kaelan's gaze met mine. "I promise."

A fragile smile tugged at the corners of my lips, the weight of my indecision momentarily lifted by his support. As he sat there, the lines of worry etched on his face seemed to soften, replaced by genuine sincerity.

We both rose, drawn together by a shared need for connection amidst the turmoil. Our embrace was soothing as if our worries were being exchanged and dissolved in the warmth of our closeness. Kaelan's arms encircled me, holding me as if to shield me from the uncertainties that loomed on the horizon.

We lingered there. I could feel his heartbeat against my chest, a steady rhythm that mirrored the steady presence of him in my life. A deep exhale escaped Kaelan as if he were releasing the tension that had gripped him.

I held him just as tightly, my fingers clutching the fabric of his shirt as if grounding myself in his unwavering presence. The world outside may have been chaotic, full of choices and consequences, but here, in this embrace, there was a simple truth that held us together.

As we finally pulled away, our eyes met once more, carrying the unspoken understanding that had formed between us. Kaelan's gaze held affection, a silent reminder that no matter what lay ahead, we were in this together. And for now, that assurance was enough to quiet the storm within me.

Chapter Twenty-Six

Two days later I still hadn't reached a decision.

The atmosphere was tense as I took out my frustration on the wooden dummy in Kaelan's training room. The room was adorned with various weapons, from swords and staffs to daggers and throwing knives, hanging on the walls or placed neatly in weapon racks. The dim lighting created shadows that danced around the room as I moved, giving the space an almost eerie ambiance. My breath came out in ragged exhales, mingling with the sound of my punches and strikes landing on the dummy.

With each strike, I tried to drown out the whirlwind of thoughts spinning in my mind. The weight of the First Witch's offer pressed heavily on me, and I couldn't shake the feeling that I was standing at a crossroads, unsure of which path to take. Was it worth the risk? Could I truly trust her intentions? My thoughts were jumbled, and my emotions were a storm of doubt and uncertainty.

As I continued my assault on the dummy, the sound of footsteps and the creaking of the door caught my attention. Harker entered the room, her presence a calming influence against my inner chaos. She took a seat on the floor, her ice-blue eyes fixed on my movements. I paused, catching my breath, and looked at her.

"You're really giving that dummy a workout," Harker remarked with a half-smile, her voice carrying a hint of amusement.

I released a heavy sigh, my frustration overwhelming. "I can't make a decision, Harker. It's like I'm stuck in this never-ending loop of 'what ifs.'"

Harker's gaze, full of sympathy, was steady as she observed me. "It's not an easy choice. Merging spirits with the First Witch is a significant commitment, one that could change the course of your life. That's pretty heavy no matter which way you look at it."

I leaned against the wall, my hands resting on my hips as I met Harker's gaze. "I know. But what if it's the right choice? What if it's the only way to be ready for whatever comes next?"

Harker's expression softened with understanding. "I can't decide for you, Vale. It's your path to choose."

I went back to venting my frustration on the training dummy, feeling the rhythmic pounding of my fists against the rough fabric as a small outlet for the chaos within. Harker's presence was comforting, a reminder that even amid my inner turmoil, I had those who cared about my well-being.

She watched me for a moment before her thoughtful words broke through my concentration. "Have you tried asking the library for more information? Specifically about spirit merging?"

I paused my strikes, my breaths heavy as I considered her question. "I did try, but all I found was the spell itself. No explanations, no guidance."

Harker's brows furrowed in thought. "That's odd. The library usually provides more context. It's strange for it to lead you to a dead end like that."

I nodded, my frustration deepening. "It's exasperating. I need more information before I can make a decision."

Harker's gaze never left me. "Have you thought about asking Elara?"

My eyes widened at the suggestion. "I...I hadn't thought of asking Elara," I admitted. Why hadn't I thought of that before? Elara, being a former witch herself, might have insights of knowledge about spirit merging that I hadn't considered. The possibility offered a glimmer of hope.

Harker smiled gently. "Sometimes answers can come from unexpected sources. Elara might have knowledge that could help you make a more informed choice."

The weight of my indecision still lingered, but the idea of seeking guidance from Elara sparked a renewed sense of determination within me. I knew I couldn't keep grappling with this decision on my own. With Harker's support and the possibility of seeking knowledge from Elara, I was determined to find the clarity I so desperately needed.

"Let's go ask her now," I said eagerly.

Harker and I made our way to the library, my heart beat with anticipation and nervousness. I called out for Elara, and she appeared from behind a bookshelf, looking at me curiously.

As I explained the situation and the First Witch's proposition, Elara's expression shifted from curiosity to surprise, her eyes widening as I recounted the events. When I finished speaking, there was a moment of silence, and then Elara spoke, her voice a whisper that seemed to hold more weight than mere words.

"I do know about spirit merging," she said, her voice tinged with a hint of hesitation.

I leaned forward, my heart racing with hope. "Tell me everything you know, Elara. Please."

Elara hesitated for a moment, her gaze distant as if she were reliving memories that were both painful and profound. "Spirit merging is a forbidden and ancient magic. It involves binding two spirits together and sharing thoughts, power, and essence. It's...volatile magic."

My brows furrowed as I tried to process her words. "Volatile? What do you mean?"

Elara's gaze met mine, her eyes carrying a depth of understanding that seemed beyond her nature. "Magic, in itself, can be unpredictable, and using too much of it can have dire consequences. But spirit merging takes it to another level. It's a risky endeavor, Vale, with the potential to backfire and consume the one attempting the merge."

My heart sank at her words, the weight of the decision pressing down on me even more heavily. "So, there's a chance I could die if I go through with it?"

Elara nodded solemnly. "Not just die, your soul would be obliterated. The merging of two spirits is a delicate and dangerous dance. It requires balance, control, and a deep understanding of the forces at play. Many who attempted it in the past paid the ultimate price."

The room felt suffocating, the enormity of the choice before me echoing in the silence. As Elara's words settled over us, I couldn't help but feel a sense of dread. The promise of power and guidance from the First Witch was alluring, but the potential consequences were too great to ignore.

I swallowed hard, absorbing Elara's words as they sank in like heavy stones dropped into a still pond. "What is it like to have your spirit merged with another?" I asked, my voice shaky.

Elara's gaze seemed distant again, lost in memories that were far removed from the present. "When two spirits merge, they become intertwined in a way that's difficult to describe. It's as if you're sharing a part of your very soul with another being. You have to give up a piece of yourself to take on a piece of them."

Harker shifted beside me, her expression one of empathy. "And the bond, once formed, is permanent?"

Elara nodded solemnly. "Yes, permanent and irreversible. The two spirits become connected on a profound level, and their fates become intertwined."

I couldn't help but think about what this meant for me, for the First Witch, and for the path I was contemplating. A surge of conflicting emotions washed over me— hope for the potential strength and guidance, fear of the unknown consequences, and the weight of making a choice that would impact the rest of my life.

Harker's voice broke through the heavy silence, her words laced with concern. "Vale, this decision…" she stopped and shook her head. "You'd be altering your very being, forever."

I nodded slowly, my mind a whirlwind of thought and emotions. "I understand that, Harker. But the First Witch's offer, as horrifying as it is, is tempting. I just get this feeling of urgency, like something is about to happen and I'm not prepared for it."

Elara's ethereal form seemed to shimmer with empathy. "The allure of power is strong, especially in times of uncertainty. But remember, Vale, power comes at a price, and the consequences of such a decision could shape your destiny in ways you can't foresee."

I looked down at my blackened fingers as she spoke. I now knew something of the consequences of magic I didn't fully understand. I knew that whatever path I chose, would change the course of my life in ways I couldn't fully comprehend. But was the risk worth the reward?

Just as I was about to ask more questions, a surge of panic washed over me like a chilling wave. It was as if an invisible thread connected me back to the factory, and that thread was being violently pulled. I knew that this unfamiliar sensation could only mean one thing; my wards had been breached.

"Harker, something's wrong," I said urgently, my voice betraying the fear that flooded through me.

"What's happening?" Harker asked, her voice tense.

"The wards at the factory...they've been triggered," I managed to say, my mind racing as I grasped the severity of the situation. My mind raced through all the possibilities. Was it an attack? Were the Otherworlders already in danger?

Without hesitation, I sprinted to my room, Harker close behind, and strapped on my weapons, sliding into my well-worn leather jacket as I moved. My fingers trembled slightly as I tightened the laces of my combat boots. "Go tell Kaelanwhat's happened," I shouted to Harker, who took off running. I called out for Nyxen who materialized beside me with a low, urgent growl as if sensing my distress.

"Shift us to the factory, Nyxen," I said, my voice firm as I met his shadowy gaze.

In an instant, the darkness enveloped us, and the world seemed to twist and morph. When the sensation ceased, I found myself standing at the entrance of the factory, a scene of chaos before me.

Smoke billowed in the air, the acrid scent stinging my nostrils as I took in the sight of flames licking at the edge of the building. Screams and cries for help filled the air, along with the sound of shattering glass. Otherworlders were scrambling, some desperately trying to extinguish the flames while others engaged in battle against a menacing and grotesque demon.

The demon stood tall, its hulking form draped in tattered, charred cloth that barely concealed its twisted and snarled body. Its skin was a sickly shade of ashen grey, marred with grotesque welts and scales. Its eyes glowed with an unnatural, malevolent light, and its mouth stretched into a sinister grin, revealing rows of jagged, razor-sharp teeth.

Time seemed to slow as I took in the scene, the urgency and instinct to protect surging through me. Without hesitation, I drew my weapons—my axe in one hand and a dagger in the other. I quickly pricked my finger and sucked on the digit, my blood magic overwhelming me momentarily before I grew accustomed to it. At the smell of my blood, the demon whipped its head around to look at me, momentarily distracted. It was definitely here for me.

I rushed forward, my heart pounding with determination and dread. The clash of battle filled the air, the harsh scent of smoke mingling with the metallic tang of blood. The demon's eyes fixed on me, its sinister grin widening as it anticipated the fight ahead.

My muscles tensed as I closed the distance between us, my weapons glinting in the blazing light of the fire. The demon moved with a speed I had never encountered before, its movements almost a blur. I ducked and dodged frantically as it lunged at me, its claws slashing through the air with deadly precision. My axe clashed against its monstrous claws, sparks flying as the metal rang out with the force of the impact.

Among the chaos, I saw an Otherworlder charge at the demon, their desperation driving them forward. The demon's speed proved its advantage, and with a swift swipe of its clawed hand, it sent the Otherwordler hurtling backward. They crashed to the ground with a sickening thud, the impact silencing them forever.

"Get back!" I shouted, my voice mixed with fury and desperation, my heart aching with the loss. The others hesitated, fear and uncertainty in their eyes, before they retreated, leaving me alone to face the demon.

My focus narrowed as I assessed the demon's movement, searching for any opening. Its claws sliced through the air again, and I barely managed to twist away, feeling the rush of wind as the tips grazed my back. Pain erupted as the claws left a searing trail along my skin and a cry of pain escaped my lips.

I gritted my teeth, pushed past the pain, and lunged forward while the demon was still close. My dagger found its mark, sinking into the demon's side. A guttural growl echoed from its twisted throat, its grin contorting into a snarl. It swung at me again, its claws aiming to rend my flesh, but I managed to duck and roll to the side, narrowly avoiding the deadly strike.

As I rose to my feet, I met the demon's glowing eyes with unwavering determination. This battle was far from over, and despite the odds stacked against me, I couldn't afford to back down. Not when there were so many depending on me.

The battle raged on, the demon's onslaught relentless and unyielding. I could feel my muscles protesting each movement, my fatigue setting in as the pain from my back throbbing relentlessly. Despite the odds, I knew I couldn't let the demon win. I couldn't allow the lives of the Others to fall victim to its viciousness. I refused to fail.

With renewed vigor, I lunged forward, my axe arcing through the air and slicing through the demon's arm, eliciting a pained howl. Before it could recover, I struck again, my blade finding its mark, buried deep within the demon's chest. It staggered back, its twisted features contorting with rage and agony. I pulled out my dagger and moved to step out of reach. But I was too slow and the demon's claws struck again, this time lacerating my arm, the searing agony surging through me. I grunted, gritting my teeth against the pain, determination keeping me standing.

Summoning every ounce of strength I had left, I lunged forward, my dagger aiming true for the demon's face. It snarled as the blade found its mark, a gash running across its twisted features. The strike was enough to hurt, to weaken it, but not enough to end the battle.

Just when it felt like I was slowing down, my moments becoming sluggish, salvation emerged from the shadows. Kaelan's sword gleamed in the firelight as he leaped into action, striking at the demon with precision.

Wren, with a swift shift in forms, came to stand beside me, his growl resonating with fierce determination. The demon hesitated, the balance of power now tipping in our favor. But it was far from defeated. With a surge of fury, it unleashed its full force, its claws and teeth a whirlwind of danger.

I raised my axe just in time, blocking the demon's blow with a loud clang. Kaelan moved in tandem with me, his curved sword weaving a dance of deadly strikes. Together, we held our ground, the combined strength of our efforts forcing the demon to retreat momentarily.

In that moment of respite, Wren seized his opportunity. With a powerful leap, he lunged at the demon, latching onto its leg. The demon let out a roar as its balance was thrown off, crashing to the ground with a heavy thud. Its struggle was fierce, its claws slashing and teeth snapping, but we pressed our advantage, attacking with renewed ferocity.

Each strike was a testament to our determination and unity. With Wren's tenacity, Kaelan's skill, and my own resolve, we managed to overcome the odds. Together, we wore down the demon's defenses until, at last, it let out a final, anguished wail and collapsed under the weight of our assault.

The tension in the air finally eased, replaced by the heavy exhales of breath and the backdrop of the factory's shattered remains. We stood there, triumphant but battered, but we had prevailed against the darkness that had threatened us. As the adrenaline began to ebb away, I felt the magnitude of the battle's toll settle upon me, my body aching and my senses dulled by the relentless struggle.

My heart pounded in my chest as panic surged through me. The battle was won, the demon defeated, but the aftermath was a grim reminder of the cost we had paid. My gaze swept over the factory, the shattered windows and scorched walls, the signs of the havoc that had been unleashed. Otherworlders were picking themselves up, tending to injuries, and surveying the wreckage with weary eyes.

Then, a voice shattered the tense atmosphere. Someone called out that Juniper was missing. My heart dropped like a stone in my chest, dread tightening its grip. Without hesitation, I rushed toward the back room of the bookshop where Juniper would run to with the children if there was any danger, my mind racing, my breath coming in shallow bursts. Kaelan and Wren followed closely on my heels. I had to find Juniper, had to make sure she was safe.

As we burst into the room, the sight before me struck me like a physical blow. Juniper lay on the floor, bloodied and broken, her life force fading rapidly. The children were huddled in a corner sobbing loudly. Wren gasped and began yelling Juniper's name, the sound was muffled in my ears as my blood surged wildly through me. He called for help, and Ava quickly came to herd the children from the room, but not before tears welled up in her eyes as she beheld Juniper. She had been hurt, but she had still managed to protect the children from a literal monster.

Horror clamped down on my chest, a raw, gut-wrenching pain that threatened to consume me. I fell to my knees beside her, my fingers trembling as I gently cradled her in my arms.

"Juniper," I choked out, my voice heavy with sorrow. Her eyes flickered weakly, the light in them dimming as she struggled to speak. Kaelan stood there motionless as he witnessed the scene. I could see the pain etched across her features, and desperation clawed at me.

My hands moved almost of their own accord, reaching for one of the knives at my belt. With hurried, trembling movements, I slashed open my arm, the blade biting into my skin. I was about to offer her my blood, to heal her, to save her. But before I could act, before I could offer her the lifeline she needed, her breathing grew shallower. Her heartbeat became faint and erratic, and her eyes lost their light, staring vacantly up at the ceiling.

Time seemed to slow, every heartbeat thundering with dread. The words she tried to speak were a whisper, too low to make out. And then, with a final, ragged breath she was gone. My heart stuttered for a moment before shattering completely, the weight of loss crushing down on me.

I held her lifeless form in my arms, my eyes blurred by tears, my chest aching with a pain I couldn't put into words. The room seemed to close in around me, the weight of the battle, the devastation, and now this loss pressing down on me.

My heartache manifested in a guttural cry that tore from my throat, a raw, primal expression of grief that threatened to consume me. Juniper, my friend, my confidante, was gone. The pain of loss bore down on me, suffocating and relentless. The knife I had meant to use to save her now lay forgotten on the floor, its purpose unfulfilled.

Desperation took hold of me, a frantic need to bring her back, to undo the irreversible. With trembling hands, I pressed my cut arm to her pale lips, begging the universe, the very essence of magic, to grant me the impossible. But the blood that flowed from me held no miracles, and Juniper remained unmoving, her heart forever stilled.

My sobs intensified, a chorus of pain that echoed off the walls, mingling with the anguish that surrounded me. I clung to her lifeless form, rocking back and forth in a futile attempt to soothe the agony tearing through my soul. The room blurred in my vision, my grief narrowing my focus on the loss that had torn a hole in my heart.

Through the haze of my tears, I felt a presence near me. Kaelan's arms enveloped me, pulling me away from Juniper's body with a gentle but firm touch. My resistance was weak, my strength all but drained by the torrent of emotion that raged within me. I clung to him, my fingers gripping his leather jacket as if he were my lifeline in this storm of despair.

I leaned into him, my sobs wracking my body as he held me. The pain was insurmountable, a gaping wound that seemed impossible to heal. Wren stood nearby, his shock evident in his eyes, his heart undoubtedly heavy with the weight of the loss as well. At that moment, there were no words to offer solace, no actions that could undo what had been done.

Time blurred as Kaelan guided me through the haze of grief, his presence a steady anchor in the tumultuous sea of emotions. He lifted me into his arms and carried me up to my apartment, the familiar surroundings now marred by the scent of smoke and the lingering aftermath of the battle. My limbs felt heavy, this pain seemed unbearable.

He took me into my room and sat me down on the bed. My body felt numb, my mind distant and detached from reality. Kaelan's touch was gentle as he began to remove my blood-stained clothes, taking note of the wounds I had endured, his movements wordless and filled with a quiet understanding. I allowed myself to be led to the bathroom, my resistance replaced by an emptiness that had settled deep within me.

Kaelan turned the shower on and pulled me in. He got in as well, not bothering with his clothes. The water in the shower was warm and soothing as it cascaded over me, but I couldn't feel it, my body felt far away. Kaelan's hands moved with care, washing away the remnants of battle, the blood that clung to my skin like a haunting reminder. I stood there passively, his touch an anchor in a world that had lost its color.

He guided me out of the shower, wrapping me in a towel as if shielding me from the harshness of reality. He sat me down gently on the bed. The numbness persisted, aching in every fiber of my being.

He went and grabbed the first aid kit and began wordlessly dressing my already healing wounds. I was detached from the pain I felt from them, numb and distant, the loss of Juniper overpowering any other senses. When he was finished, he went and retrieved a change of clothes for me. He helped me into the soft cotton clothes before pressing me gently down on the bed, pulling the covers over my shaking body.

Kaelan changed into dry clothes from Wren's room before returning to my side, his arms a sanctuary as he pulled me into his embrace. I clung to him, the dam of emotions I had been holding back finally breaking free.

The sobs that wracked my body were unrelenting, a torrent of grief that I had been unable to express until now. Kaelanheld me, his chest a solid anchor as I let my pain flow freely. The hours passed, my tears staining his borrowed shirt, my anguish pouring out until there was nothing left. I cried for Juniper, for the loss of a friend who had offered me kindness and compassion. I cried for the future that was stolen, for the life that had been taken too soon. And I cried for the pain, the agony that gripped my heart, and refused to let go.

Exhaustion eventually overcame me, my sobs dwindling into quiet whimpers as the light outside shifted to dawn. I drifted into a restless slumber, wrapped in Kaelan's arms, finding solace in his presence even amidst the heartache. The darkness of sleep claimed me, offering a temporary respite from the overwhelming pain that had consumed me.

Chapter Twenty-Seven

As Kaelan shifted slightly beside me, I blinked away the remnants of sleep, my mind still heavy with the weight of grief. The previous day's events echoed in my thoughts, and I struggled to find a foothold in the world that had shifted so drastically.

Kaelan's voice broke through the silence, concern etched across his face. "How are you feeling?" he asked, his eyes searching mine for any trace of true emotions.

I managed a small nod, my voice a hoarse whisper. "I'm okay."

He studied me for a moment, his lingering pain evident in his gaze. He swung his legs over the edge of the bed, his movements deliberate as he rose to his feet. Without a word, he retrieved some clothes for me from my dresser. The simple act of him caring for me warmed a corner of my heart that felt like it had turned to ice.

Sitting up slowly, I allowed him to help me get dressed. Every movement felt mechanical as if I were operating on autopilot. My body moved, but my mind remained numb, the rawness of my emotions simmering just beneath the surface.

Once dressed, I let out a sigh and ran a hand through my knotted hair. "Where's Wren?" The worry for my friend tugged at me, a reminder that he too was grappling with the loss of Juniper.

Kaelan turned his gaze to me, his expression somber. "He left a message on your phone late last night. He went back to the wolf camp after helping the Otherworlders. I think he needed some time alone."

I nodded, a pang of understanding mingling with my concern. Wren was processing his own grief, likely in solitude. I felt a twinge of guilt that I had not been able to provide him with the support he needed last night.

Kaelan moved closer, his fingers brushing gently across my cheek. "Vale, it's okay to not be okay," he said softly, his voice a soothing balm to my fractured spirit.

Tears welled in my eyes, threatening to spill over the dam I had built. I leaned into his touch, the vulnerability of the moment leaving me exposed. "I know," I admitted, the words catching on a fragile breath.

He cupped my face, his thumb wiping away a stray tear. "You don't have to bear this burden alone," he said, his voice tender.

I closed my eyes for a moment, savoring his warmth. Then, with a deep breath, I opened my eyes and met his gaze, the depth of his emotions mirroring my own.

The corners of his lips tugged upward into a smile, and the sight brought a small glimmer of light to the darkness that had taken hold of me. It was a reminder that, even in the darkest of times, there was still beauty to be found, and hope to be had.

With a gentle squeeze, Kaelan released his hold on me and stepped back, his gaze scanning the room. My attention shifted, and I realized the state of disarray the room was in. Blood-stained clothes littered the floor, the first aid kit was strewn across the bed, and the smell of smoke was still thick in the air.

Before I could protest, Kaelan moved around the room and began gathering the discarded items. He paused, glancing at me with a raised brow.

A hint of a smile crept onto my lips, and I let out a breathy laugh. His care, his thoughtfulness, his willingness to do whatever was needed, was a salve to my aching soul. I joined him, and together we made short work of the mess.

When we were done, I paused, taking in the sight of the clean room. Kaelan watched me, his presence calming. I could feel the warmth and safety emanating from him, a reminder that I wasn't alone in this.

Stepping forward, I wrapped my arms around him, leaning my head against his chest. His embrace enveloped me, and I felt a wave of relief wash over me. The loss was still fresh, the grief a painful reminder of the price we had paid. But the comfort, the security, and the affection I felt with Kaelan gave me the strength to face this new reality.

❨ ☽

The day seemed to stretch endlessly, an expanse of time marked only by the weight of grief that refused to loosen its grip. I had remained in bed, my thoughts a jumble of memories and regrets. Kaelan had been a constant presence, his quiet support a lifeline in the sea of sorrow.

As night began to fall, casting long shadows across the room, a determination stirred within me. I couldn't allow myself to drown in my own sadness. Slowly, I pushed the blankets aside and swung my legs over the edge of the bed. Kaelan, who had been lying next to me, sat up straight.

"Vale," he murmured softly, an unasked question in his tone.

I looked at him, my resolve firm. "I can't stay in bed forever," I said, my voice steadier than I had anticipated.

He nodded, smiling sadly. "No, you can't. But you also shouldn't push yourself before you are ready."

I reached for the edge of the bed and pushed myself to my feet, wincing at the pain in my back, my limbs feeling heavy from hours of inactivity. Kaelan stood as well, his presence a reassuring anchor as I took tentative steps toward the dresser. I reached for my worn leather boots, my fingers brushing against the familiar texture.

As I was about to put them on, my heart constricted at the sight of dried blood marring the leather, Juniper's blood. A stark reminder of the events that had unfolded. Kaelan's swift action drew my attention as he took the boots from my hands, disappearing into the bathroom to clean them.

Moments later, he returned with the boots, their surfaces now free of the haunting stains. I slipped them on, the simple act a signal of my determination to move forward, even amid my unrelenting sorrow.

Standing up straight, I took a deep breath, the cool evening air filling my lungs. I could feel the grief that still clung to me, a burden that was hard to bear. But as I looked at Kaelan, the understanding in his eyes, the support he offered without a word, my resolve strengthened.

My heart ached, the hole in it a gaping wound that would never fully heal. But I knew that with time, and the support of the people who cared about me, I would be able to live with the grief. I would be able to carry the memories of Juniper and the impact she had on my life. And in time, I would be able to look back and celebrate the life she lived, and the love she had shared.

I would continue to fight for a better world, a safer place for all those who called this realm home. I would carry the memories of Juniper and her unwavering faith in our mission, the courage and strength she displayed even in the face of death. And I would continue to love, to find joy in the small things, to live in a way that honored her memory.

I would continue because that was what she would have wanted, and that was what would honor her sacrifice. I would continue, not just for myself, but for everyone who had been touched by her light, her laughter, her love.

I would continue, not because I was okay, but because I was stronger than the grief, the pain, the loss.

I pulled in a shaky breath. "Can you shift me to the camp?"

Kaelan gave me a nod and a warm smile, his gaze full of understanding.

I closed the distance between us, his arms coming around me, cocooning me in warmth and comfort. Kaelan pulled me close and tucked a strand of hair behind my ear. Cupping my face gently, as if I would crack like porcelain under his grip, he leaned down and placed a tender and claiming kiss on my lips as we shifted to the werewolf camp.

He was still kissing me as the world came back into focus. He pulled back and looked deeply into my eyes, searching still for the roiling emotions within. He reluctantly let me go and we faced the camp. The autumn night air was crisp, carrying with it a sense of life that contrasted sharply with the lingering weight of my grief.

Kaelan reached down, entwining his fingers with mine. My hand fit in his like it was meant to be there. My heart fluttered at the simple gesture, the warmth of his touch a balm to the raw, aching wound of loss.

We walked through the camp, the atmosphere calm. The scent of smoke was thick in the air, mingling with the aroma of a bonfire. People milled about, their expressions somber, their movements subdued.

As we approached the main campfire, I saw some members of the pack sitting in a circle, their faces illuminated by the warm glow.

Venna glanced up as we approached, her eyes betraying her lingering worry. She rose to her feet, her posture tense. She spoke first, his voice strained.

"Vale," he said, his tone a mix of concern and uncertainty. "How are you?"

"I'm okay," I managed, the lie coming more easily than expected.

Kaelan's grip on my hand tightened, and I felt his silent support, a steady presence. I glanced up at him, the depth of his emotions reflected in his eyes.

Venna studied me, her gaze piercing. After a moment, she nodded. "That is good to hear," she said, her tone softer.

I swallowed the lump in my throat, my emotions threatening to spill over. "Is Wren here?"

"Yes, he returned early this morning."

"May I speak with him?" I asked, a sudden urgency gripping me.

"Of course," she replied, stepping aside.

I squeezed Kaelan's hand before releasing it, and he gave me an encouraging smile. Wren's tent stood in the middle of the camp, silhouetted against the moonlit sky. I made my way towards it, Kaelan by my side. None of the sentries stopped us or announced our approach, they already knew who, and what, I was. My heart raced as I came closer, uncertainty mingling with the anticipation of seeing Wren again.

Before I could reach out to announce our presence, the tent flap was pushed aside, and Wren stepped out. His eyes met mine, and a mix of emotions flashed across his face— surprise, relief, and something else I couldn't quite identify.

"Vale," he said, his voice a whisper carried on the night breeze.

I stepped forward, meeting him halfway. The air was thick with unspoken words, the weight of our shared loss tangible between us. Without a word, Wren pulled me into a fierce hug and I clung to him as if he were the one who had been ripped from my life violently.

We held each other for a moment, a tangle of emotions swirling between us. Then, slowly, Wren pulled away, his eyes meeting mine. The sorrow in his gaze was a reflection of my own and I knew that he understood my pain, that he shared it.

The silence stretched between us, the weight of grief an oppressive force. Wren reached out, his hands holding my face gently. The tenderness of the gesture was a sharp contrast to the intensity of his gaze.

"Vale, I'm so sorry," he said, his voice barely above a whisper.

I swallowed the lump in my throat, the grief a bitter taste on my tongue. "Me too," I said, the words catching in my throat.

Wren's expression softened, and he pulled me into another hug, his arms a solid presence. I clung to him, my anchor in the sea of sorrow.

After a moment, I pulled away, the weight of my emotions threatening to spill over. Wren studied me, his concern was evident. "Are you okay?"

"Yeah," I said, the lie coming more and more easily as I spoke it.

"Are you sure? You went through a lot yesterday. And the last couple of days have been..." he trailed off, his voice laced with pain.

"I'm not okay, not yet," I admitted the words leaving a bitter taste in my mouth. "But I will be."

He gave me a small nod, his gaze intense. "You're not alone, Vale," he said, his words a reminder.

"Neither are you," I said, the truth of the words echoing between us.

"I know," he said, the corners of his lips tugging upwards into a small smile. "I have you, and that means everything."

A rush of emotions washed over me, the weight of the past few days bearing down on me. The tears came before I could stop them, streaming down my cheeks.

Wren stepped forward, his arms wrapping around me once again. He held me as I cried, the sobs wracking my body. I held onto him, the grief a physical presence that threatened to overwhelm me.

"Come on, Vale," he whispered. "Let's get inside."

The interior of Wren's tent was spacious, with soft rugs covering the ground and various seating areas scattered around. Moonlight filtered through the fabric, casting a serene glow that held a semblance of solace. We settled onto a comfortable couch, our heavy loss hanging in the air.

Wren's grip on my hand was steady, a lifeline of connection against the turmoil. We exchanged glances, our eyes saying more than words ever could. The comfort of his touch was a balm against the ache in my heart.

As moments passed in silence, the enormity of our grief felt almost tangible. There were no words that could mend the wound that had been opened, and yet, being together in that moment felt like a small respite from the storm.

The heaviness of the silence was broken when I found my voice, the question I had been carrying within me demanding to be spoken. "When is her funeral?"

Wren's expression remained somber as he replied, "Tomorrow, at dusk. We're organizing a service here at the camp. We'll honor Juniper and the two others who lost their lives." His voice wavered slightly, a testament to the weight of his own sorrow.

I nodded, my gaze dropping to my lap as I absorbed the information. Juniper deserved to be remembered, to have her memory etched into the hearts of those she had touched. The thought of the fire, her body and the others being laid to rest in its flickering embrace brought a bittersweet ache to my chest.

"Have the Otherworlders who were at the factory started settling in yet?" I asked. I no longer trusted my wards to keep them safe.

Wren nodded. "They arrived this afternoon."

"That's good. At least they'll be safer here," I said, my voice subdued.

Wren's gentle reassurance filled the silence, "It's not your fault, Vale. None of us could have predicted what happened, and if you hadn't been warned, if you hadn't shown up when you did, I'm sure there would have been more bodies to burn."

Those words struck a cord deep within me, and the well of emotions that I had been trying to suppress burst forth like a dam breaking. I felt a surge of anger and helplessness, the weight of my inadequacies crushing down on me. In a split second, my emotions transformed into a storm that consumed me, I jumped up from the couch and began to scream.

"Of course, it's my fault!" I cried out, my voice shaking with raw emotion. "My wards failed, Wren. They thought they were safe. They thought they were protected. But they weren't, and now Juniper and two others are dead because of me! If I had known more magic, if I had been better at it, they would still be alive. I let them down, and now I have to live with the fact that my actions, or lack of them, led to their deaths."

The waves of grief, anger, and frustration crashed over me, drowning me in their intensity. I collapsed onto the couch, burying my face in my hands as my body shook with sobs.

Kaelan moved beside me, wrapping his arms around me in a comforting embrace. My cries and shouts mixed together, my words choked by the overwhelming swell of emotion. "They could have been here," I managed to get out between my sobs. "They could have been safe at the camp. But they weren't. I let them down. They thought they were safe, but they were caught in the crossfire of the demons who were after me. Not once, but twice. How can I even face them now?"

Kaelan's grip tightened, his voice soft and soothing as he tried to console me in my distress. He held me close, letting me release the pain and guilt that had been pent up inside me.

Then, Wren knelt in front of me, taking my head in his hands, his gaze piercing through my turmoil. His voice held a firmness that cut through my cries, his words strong and direct. "It's not your fault, Vale." He repeated it, his tone unwavering. "You can't shoulder the actions of others. You can't take on their blame."

His words struck a chord within me, and even amidst my sobbing, I began to listen. He continued, his voice intense, "Juniper wouldn't want you to blame yourself like this. She would want you to remember her with love and honor, not with guilt."

The sound of Juniper's name hung in the air and my breath hitched. The raw emotions were still spilling over, but his words began to chip away at the wall of self-blame that I had built around me. Wren's words were like a beacon of hope, dragging me back from the depths of my sorrow.

Wren held me tightly and I began to realize that while the pain of losing Juniper would never truly fade, I couldn't let it consume me. Not when there were those who cared for me and I needed to stand strong despite the trials and tragedies that life threw our way.

I nodded reluctantly, Wren's words finally starting to break through the fog of despair that had clouded my mind. The tears continued to fall, but they weren't as consuming as before. Wren's presence, his unwavering support, was like an anchor keeping me from drifting too far into the abyss of grief.

His words were a call to action, a reminder that I couldn't let my pain paralyze me. I sniffled, wiping my tears with the back of my hand as I listened intently.

"The Otherworlders saw what you did last night, taking on that demon by yourself. They still believe in you and in your ability to keep them safe. You can't let this darkness swallow you whole."

It seemed surreal considering how broken I felt at the moment. But his conviction was infectious, and his words carried a weight that resonated with me.

"You're right," I managed to say, my voice hoarse from crying. "I can't let this break me completely."

Wren's sad yet supportive smile tugged at the corners of his lips. I chuckled softly through my tears and shook my head, disbelief mingling with gratitude. "When did you become so gods damned commanding?" I teased, though my attempt at humor was tinged with sadness.

He held my gaze, his eyes softening. "In times like these, we all need to find strength within ourselves and each other. We'll get through this, Vale. We'll honor Juniper by continuing to fight, for her and for all of us."

As his words settled over me, a sense of determination began to emerge from the depths of my grief. Tomorrow's service for Juniper loomed, a final farewell to a dear friend. But in the wake of that, I could see the path forward more clearly. With Wren and Kaelan beside me and the bonds of our united front, we would forge ahead, even in the face of darkness.

Chapter Twenty-Eight

As I stood before my vanity mirror, I fiddled with the small black earrings I held in my hand. My reflection stared back at me, weariness shining in my eyes. The short black dress I'd chosen for the occasion clung to my form. I slipped the earrings into my ears, the simple act bringing a sense of finality to my preparations.

Kaelan sat on the bed, his eyes fixed on me with an intensity that seemed to pierce through my facade. He was dressed head to toe in black, his sharp suit making him look like a different person. His unwavering attention had been both comforting and slightly unsettling since yesterday. I appreciated his concern, yet it also highlighted my vulnerability and my struggle to mask my inner turmoil.

I turned to face him, offering a small smile. "What do you think?" I asked, gesturing to the dress and the simple black heels I'd chosen to complete the outfit.

Kaelan's lips curved into a faint smile, but his gaze held a touch of sadness. "You look beautiful," he said softly, his voice laden with unspoken emotions.

I nodded, my fingers nervously smoothing down the fabric of the dress. "Thanks," I murmured, the weight of the impending funeral settled in my gut.

As the hour approached dusk, anxiety began to build within me. This would be the first time I faced the Otherworlderssince the attack, the first time I would see the grieving faces of those who had lost loved ones. I worried that they would look at me with blame, and see me as the cause of their pain, just as I blamed myself.

Kaelan stood up from the bed and approached me, his hand reaching to gently brush a strand of hair behind my ear. "You don't have to do this if you're not ready," he said softly, his concern evident.

I shook my head, resolve welling up within me. "I need to," I replied, my voice steady despite the nerves that fluttered in my stomach. "I need to face them, to honor Juniper and the others who were lost."

Kaelan's gaze softened, his thumb caressing my cheek gently. "Just remember, I'll be right by your side if you need me."

His words gave me a sense of comfort and assurance that I didn't have to carry the load alone. With a deep breath, I nodded, summoning the strength to face what lay ahead. Together we would honor the fallen and find a way to forge ahead, even in the midst of our grief.

Without a word, Kaelan shifted us to Wren's tent in the camp. As we materialized within the spacious tent, Wren was already there with Venna, his green eyes meeting mine, full of pain. Harker stood beside him as well, her presence a quiet source of support in the solemn moment that awaited us. Wren stepped up and wrapped me in a comforting hug before pulling back and looking at me.

He had donned a black suit as well, the sharp lines and careful tailoring giving him a composed yet somber appearance. As I complimented him, a faint smile tugged at his lips, a small flicker of gratitude in his gaze. I smoothed down his jacket with a gentle touch, a gesture that carried both affection and a wish for strength.

"Are you ready?" He asked, his voice gentle but laced with concern.

I exhaled slowly, my breath trembling ever so slightly. "As ready as I can be," I replied, my words a testament to the emotional turmoil that still churned within me.

With our resolve bolstered by each other's presence, we stepped out of the tent into the heart of the werewolf camp. The sun was sinking below the horizon, casting a golden glow that gave the camp a serene yet mournful ambiance. Tents of various shapes and sizes were arranged in orderly rows, each housing members of the pack, and now, the Otherworlderswho had sought refuge here.

As we walked, I noticed the faces of the wolves and Otherworlders, each wearing expressions of solemn respect. Some stood in small groups, murmuring among themselves, while others stood alone, lost in their thoughts. Lanterns flickered to life, casting warm pools of light that cut through the encroaching darkness.

The smell of aged wood hung in the air as we reached the designated area where the pyres would be lit. Stacked logs and kindling had been prepared, waiting to be ignited in honor of those we had lost. The flames would carry our grief, our memories, and our love for Juniper and the others beyond the veil of life and into the realm of spirits.

The crowd had started to gather. The five of us stood side by side, our presence a testament to unity in the face of tragedy. The weight of our collective loss was staggering, but we stood strong, resolute in our determination to remember the fallen. And as the sun dipped below the horizon, surrendering to the night, a hush settled over the camp, a quiet and reverent acknowledgment of the pain that had brought us all together.

Wren's deep voice resonated through the gathering, his words carrying the weight of his emotions and the shared sorrow of those who had come to pay their respects. He stood tall, his eyes scanning the faces of the gathered crowd before he began to speak.

"Today, we gather to honor the lives of those we have lost," Wren began, his voice steady but laced with a raw vulnerability. "Each name we say, each memory we hold, is a testament to the lives that were lived, the hearts that beat with passion, and the bonds that were formed."

He paused, his gaze briefly locking onto mine before he continued, "Juniper, Ford, and Adrik— each one of them brought their light into our lives, and their absence casts a shadow that touches us all."

Wren's voice wavered and he took a deep breath, gathering his strength to continue. "Juniper was a healer, her compassion extending to every being that crossed her path. Ford, a guiding spirit, provided wisdom and counsel beyond his years. Adrik, young and spirited, reminded us of the vitality of life and the potential for growth. They will all be deeply missed."

As he spoke, the wind seemed to carry his words to every corner of the camp. The flames from the lanterns danced in response, joining in the solemn scene.

"Our hearts are heavy, burdened by the weight of grief and the unanswered questions that lie before us," Wren's voice rang out, filled with sorrow. "But let us not forget that it is in times like these that our strength is tested, our bonds are forged, and our resilience shines."

He paused, and the silence that followed was profound, a collective pause to remember those who were gone. Then, Wren's voice rose with renewed conviction.

"We will not be broken by this tragedy. We will not let the darkness overshadow the light that still burns within us. We will honor the memory of Juniper, Ford, and Adrik by carrying their spirits forward in our actions, in our unity, and our unwavering commitment to one another."

A solemn murmur of agreement spread through the crowd, a testament to the unity that Wren's words had inspired. His gaze met mine once more, his eyes shining with both grief and a quiet hope.

"And so, as we gather around these pyres, let us remember the lives that were lived, the love that was shared, and the impact these individuals had on our world. Let their memories be a beacon of light in the darkness, guiding us through the challenges that lie ahead."

With those final words, Wren's voice softened, the weight of his emotions evident in every syllable. He stepped back, allowing the stillness of the moment to settle over us all, as the flames of the lanterns cast their gentle glow on our faces, a tribute to the lives that had been lost and a reminder of the strength that remained within us.

As Wren's words hung in the air, three figures stepped forward, each holding a torch that flickered with a solemn light. One by one, the torches were lowered, and the flames caught on the carefully arranged pyres. Juniper, Ford, and Adrik'sbodies were soon engulfed in the beautiful yet haunting dance of fire, the orange and gold flames casting shadows and light in a mesmerizing display.

The hushed crackling of the fire accompanied the silence that enveloped the camp, a collective reverence for the lives that had been lost. The flames danced higher as if reaching towards the stars to carry the spirits of the departed souls from this realm to the next.

Amidst the luminous display, I found myself lost in a quiet moment of contemplation. My heart was heavy with grief, yet there was also a glimmer of hope— a reminder that even in the face of tragedy, there was strength in unity, solace in shared memories.

Beside me, the others stood in somber solidarity. No words were spoken as we watched the pyres, our thoughts and emotions mingling in the stillness of the night. Time seemed to stretch, each moment etched with the weight of our loss, the presence of those we would never see again.

As the flames continued to dance, the crowd began to slowly empty as they paid their respects and left, each person carrying their own burden of grief and reflection.

Eventually, it was just the five of us left, our presence a testament to the connection that bound us together— a bond forged in the crucible of loss and resilience.

With a final glance at the pyres, we turned away, our steps heavy but resolute. The night air held a sense of quiet comfort, a reminder that life carried on even in the face of tragedy. As we walked away, our hearts were illuminated by the memory of the one we had lost, a memory that would guide us in the days and challenges that lay ahead.

❨ ☽

Kaelan's room exuded an air of warmth and comfort, the dim lighting casting soft shadows that danced across the walls. It was a sanctuary of sorts, a place where one could retreat from the outside world. The walls were lined with bookshelves, filled to the brim. The centerpiece was a majestic four-poster bed, its draperies cascading down like a sheltering canopy.

As I entered the room, I kicked off my heels and placed my earrings delicately on the polished surface of Kaelan's dresser. My movements were deliberate as if shedding the weight of the world with each action. Kaelan stood at the end of the bed, his gaze unwavering as he watched me, concern etched into his features.

"Are you alright?" He inquired softly, his voice laced with genuine worry. I turned to face him, my eyes meeting his with an honesty that transcended words. My response was as simple yet powerful "No," a raw admission of my emotional turmoil.

Without hesitation, I closed the distance between us. I pulled him into a kiss that was fueled by a myriad of emotions— grief, frustration, desire, and an unyielding need for solace. Our lips met with urgency and longing, the intensity of our connection evident in every press and pull of our mouths.

The kiss was wild, a tempest of emotions unleashed— a raw, untamed yearning that sought to find respite in the touch of another. In that moment, the boundaries that often separated us were shattered, my body seeking comfort and connection beyond the confines of words.

Kaelan pulled away, his breath ragged as he sought to comprehend the whirlwind of emotions that had enveloped me. "What are you doing?" He asked, his voice astonished but concerned. I met his gaze, my eyes filled with vulnerability and resolve.

"I don't want to feel like this anymore," I confessed, my voice low and laden with the weight of my sorrow. "Even if it's just for a little while, help me feel something else, Kaelan."

My words hung in the air, a desperate plea for a reprieve from the overwhelming grief that had consumed me. As I stepped back, slowly beginning to remove my dress, Kaelan's eyes darkened with a potent mixture of desire and understanding— a silent promise to offer me the solace I sought, even if just for a few fleeting moments.

With deft movements, Kaelan undid the buttons of his dress shirt, his gaze never leaving mine. As his shirt fell to the floor, I moved closer, my hands roaming across the hard planes of his chest.

His skin was warm beneath my fingers, the muscles underneath taut with a sensual energy that beckoned me to explore further. I leaned in, kissing his neck softly, my tongue tracing along the line of his jaw. His hands found my hips, pushing me roughly against the bedpost as he ground against me.

The sensation of his body pressed against mine sent a shiver through me, and I let out a moan. His hands found the clasp of the bra I had worn for the occasion, undoing it and tossing it to the floor. I felt his fingers brush across my nipples, teasing the sensitive buds until I ached for more attention.

My breath caught in my throat as his lips met mine once again, his tongue sliding into my mouth, seeking out mine. I melted against him, giving in to the moment.

I could feel his arousal pressing against my leg, and I longed to feel him inside me, filling me, driving away the restless ghost of my grief. But he seemed determined to take his time, savoring me as his hands and lips explored my body. He leaned down and I gasped as his teeth grazed my nipple, his tongue flicking out to soothe the spot. He was relentless, teasing me until I was writhing in his arms. His hand slid down my stomach, fingers ghosting over my hip before coming to rest between my thighs.

I bit back a moan as his finger brushed against my clit, and I arched up into his touch. I could hear his breathing quicken and knew he was just as aroused as I was. I wanted to cry out, to beg him to take me right there, but his fingers were doing things to me that rendered me incapable of coherent speech. He seemed to know exactly what I needed, and when he finally slid my panties aside and pushed a finger inside me, I nearly lost control.

He withdrew quickly, only to slide two fingers inside me instead. I couldn't help myself; I cried out, arching my back and grinding against his hand. "Oh, gods," I whispered.

"Please," I begged him. He didn't answer, instead moving his thumb to circle my clit. I groaned, my head falling back as I surrendered to the pleasure he was giving me.

It wasn't long before I was shuddering in his arms, a rush of release crashing through me. But it wasn't enough. I wanted more, needed more. As if reading my mind, Kaelan slid his hands under my thighs and lifted me. I wrapped my legs around his waist and clung to him as he carried me to the bed.

He laid me down gently, his gaze drinking in the sight of me, my skin flushed, my nipples erect, and my aching core slick with desire. I lay back watching him as he undressed. His eyes were dark, his lips swollen from our kisses. He looked like an angel come to earth, and I knew I would never look at another man the same way. He was gorgeous, and I was desperate for him.

He positioned himself above me, the tip of his cock brushing against my entrance. I moaned, arching my hips up to meet him. And then, with a single, powerful thrust, he was inside me. I cried out, overwhelmed by the feeling of him filling me so completely. I wrapped my legs around him, pulling him closer, needing him deeper.

He kissed me, his tongue searching out mine as he began to move slowly within me. He rocked his hips, pushing deep and then withdrawing almost all the way out. I whimpered, my nails digging into his shoulders.

"More," I gasped. "Please, I need more."

He groaned, his lips finding mine again as he thrust harder and faster. Our bodies moved in sync, each thrust bringing me closer to the edge. I clung to him, my cries echoing off the walls.

His breath was hot against my skin. His hands gripped my hips as he drove into me, his cock hitting all the right places.

I was lost in the feeling, in the exquisite sensation of being so full, so close to him. He was everything I wanted, everything I needed. He was my salvation, my escape from the pain and sorrow that had been consuming me.

As he buried himself inside me, the grief, the fear, the uncertainty—it all melted away, replaced by a blissful euphoria. In that moment, there was no sadness, no grief. There was only us, our bodies entwined, and the pleasure building between us.

He buried his face in my neck, his lips trailing hot kisses along my jawline. He thrust deep and hard, the friction sending waves of pleasure coursing through my body. "Don't stop," I breathed. My words were swallowed by a moan as he hit that spot deep inside me. I writhed beneath him, my nails digging into his back. He growled, his pace increasing as he drove me higher and higher.

My orgasm crashed over me like a tidal wave, and I screamed his name. He continued to move inside me, holding me tight as I rode out my climax.

When the waves subsided, he withdrew and flipped me around, pulling my ass against him. "Hold onto something, little witch," he said breathlessly. I grabbed the headboard of the bed, bracing myself as he entered me again.

He was relentless, pounding into me with a fierce passion. I pushed back against him, meeting him thrust for thrust. His hands gripped my hips, his fingers digging into my flesh. He reached a hand up and placed it around my neck, tilting my head back. I was his, and he was claiming me.

"Come for me," he demanded. "I want to feel you come on my cock." I couldn't resist, his words pushing me over the edge once again.

My body clenched around him, and I cried out as another orgasm tore through me. He kept moving, chasing his own release, his grip on my neck tightening slightly. With a guttural cry, he came, filling me.

We collapsed together, spent and sated. He held me close, stroking my hair as we both caught our breath. For a moment, the weight of my grief lifted, and I allowed myself to enjoy the feeling of his arms around me, his breath against my neck.

We stayed like that for a while, basking in the afterglow of our lovemaking. But eventually, reality set in, and the pain of my loss came crashing back. I sat up, the tears coming before I could stop them.

Kaelan wrapped me in his arms and pulled me close. "I'm sorry," I sobbed.

"There's nothing to be sorry for," he whispered. He held me as I wept, his heart breaking along with mine.

Later that night, as I lay curled in his arms, I knew that no matter how much time passed, part of me would always grieve the loss of my friend. But Kaelan had given me a gift tonight— a precious reprieve from the anguish, an outlet for the overwhelming emotions that threatened to drown me.

And for that, I was eternally grateful.

Chapter Twenty-Nine

I picked my dress up from where I had tossed it on the floor, my fingers trailing over the fabric as I put it back on. Kaelan's eyes held a questioning light, his concern evident as he asked, "Are you sure you don't want to stay?"

I shook my head softly, a faint smile touching my lips. "I think I'm going to spend some time with Wren," I answered, my voice gentle but resolute. "After everything that's happened, we both need some time to just be there for each other."

Kaelan nodded his understanding, his expression one of support. He walked over to me, drawing me into a tender kiss that carried a sense of warmth and reassurance. When he finally pulled away, his voice was soft, tinged with a touch of sentiment. "I'm here whenever you need me."

I returned his affection with a gentle kiss on his cheek, my gratitude shining in my eyes. "Thank you for everything," I murmured, feeling guilty over what I was about to do.

Leaving his bedroom, I closed the door behind me, my steps quiet as I moved through the hallway. However, my destination wasn't the werewolf camp as I told Kaelan, not yet. Instead, I quietly padded into the library.

I entered the library with a soft exhale, feeling the familiar embrace of the quiet surroundings. My gaze shifted around the room, scanning the shelves for the book containing the spell for spirit merging. I saw it and began to approach the shelf when I finally noticed Harker.

She sat among a fortress of books, her attention engrossed in her reading. My heart sank for a moment as I realized my plan might have been thwarted. I forced a smile and walked closer, trying to mask my surprise. Harker greeted me warmly, her eyes lifting from the pages to meet mine. "Hey, how are you?"

"I'm fine," I replied, my voice steady. "Just thought I'd grab an interesting book on blood magic to take home and read."

Harker nodded, returning to her reading. I felt relief as I continued to the shelf, my movements casual as I retrieved the book I needed. I held it carefully, ensuring that Harker couldn't see the cover if she glanced my way. But my task wasn't complete yet; I needed supplies from the drawers.

Casting a quick glance at Harker, who remained absorbed in her reading, I silently made my way to the supply drawers. The subtle clinks of vials and the soft rustle of papers filled the air as I swiftly gathered what I needed, stuffing them into a bag with practiced efficiency. Harker remained oblivious, lost in her world of words.

With the bag secured, I approached the exit, ready to make my escape when a familiar presence materialized before me. Elara stood there, her ethereal form regarding me with curiosity. My steps faltered, and I came to a stop, my heart racing.

Elara's gaze held mine, and I felt a shiver run down my spine. I was faced with a choice: to be truthful or to weave another layer of deception.

My heart raced as she glared down at me, and for a moment, I was certain she had seen through my ruse. My mind raced, trying to come up with a plausible explanation. Elara's voice cut through the tension, her tone calm but tinged with irritation. "What do you think you're doing, taking a book out of the library?"

I swallowed hard, forcing a casual tone. "Relax, Elara. It's just one book. I'll bring it back."

Elara regarded me for another moment before finally replying, "See that you do or there will be hell to pay," she promised before she turned away, her form gliding back to the shelves where she resumed moving books around.

A quiet sigh of relief escaped me, and I quickly left the library, the weight of the book and supplies in my bag a constant reminder of my risky endeavor. As I stepped into the open air, I cast a quick glance around, confirming that no one else was around. I called upon Nyxen and he swiftly appeared at my side.

"Shift me to the apartment," I whispered to him, and the world around me blurred as Nyxen's magic enveloped me. In an instant, I was transported to my apartment, standing in the dimly lit room. I exhaled, grateful that my secret mission had gone unnoticed.

I moved to the kitchen, grabbed a small pot, and emptied my bag on the counter. The ritual required a potion, something I had never done before. But with the careful instructions from the book I had taken, it shouldn't prove too difficult, hopefully.

I filled the pot with water and set it to boil, waiting anxiously. I began adding the ingredients pilfered from the library in the order the book called for. As it simmered and bubbled in the pot a strange smell wafted through the apartment, mixing with the still lingering scent of stale smoke.

My heart hammered as the last ingredient was added and a thick black liquid was left. My stomach turned at the sight, and I had to swallow back the urge to gag. But as much as I didn't like the look of it, it had to be the final product.

Taking a deep breath, I poured the contents into a vial and tucked it into my pocket.

A sense of anticipation ran through me. This was it. My plan was finally coming to fruition.

I glanced out the window and noticed the sun setting over the horizon.

The night was upon me, and it was time for the second part of the ritual. I put the rest of my supplies back in the bag and I ascended the stairs to the rooftop, the cool night air brushing against my skin. The stars glimmered overhead, offering a sense of serenity among the chaos that had recently consumed my life. I found a secluded spot, and settled down, my thoughts turning inward as I contemplated the weight of my decision and the path that lay ahead.

With a steady hand and a focused mind, I set up my makeshift altar on the rooftop. I placed silver and white candles down, along with moonstone and selenite, their energy mingling with the magic I was about to perform. I carefully placed the vial of binding potion alongside them, my heart pounding with apprehension.

Gently, I opened the book before me, its pages illuminated by the moonlight. It was a guide, a map to navigate the intricate ritual of merging spirits. My fingers traced over the words, committing the incantation to memory, though I kept the book open as a reference, not wanting to make any mistakes.

Taking a deep breath, I struck a match and lit the candles, their flames dancing to life. The air was filled with the soft, sweet smell of herbs that I burned in the silver chalice I had brought. Ague, butcher's broom, and monkshood mingled together, creating an otherworldly aroma that seemed to carry its own kind of magic.

I began the chant, my voice steady but infused with the weight of my purpose. "*Sub luna plena, fata nostraconiunguntur,*" I intoned, the ancient words rolling off my tongue with a natural ease. As I continued, I felt a connection forming, an invisible thread weaving through the fabric of reality.

"*Duae animas confluere, nexus divinus,*" I continued, my focus unbroken. With each word, I could sense the energy building around me, a hum of power that mingled with the elements I had invoked. This ritual required both spirit magic and blood magic. The first of its kind I had encountered.

"*Sanguine et nebula, stamus uniti,*" I continued, my voice taking on an eerie quality in the night. The bond I sought felt tangible, a bridge between realms that pulsed with a life of its own.

With a practiced gesture, I drew a silver dagger across both of my arms, cutting the skin just enough to let my blood flow into the chalice. The pain was secondary to the purpose, and I watched as the scarlet drops mingled with the potion and herbs, the mixture shimmering with an otherworldly light.

"*Saltus cosmicus, manu in manu,*" I proclaimed, my voice determined. The energy in the air seemed to respond, swirling and pulsating around me as though acknowledging the power of the moment.

As I reached the final lines of the chant, I felt a surge of energy, a connection forming between me and the First Witch. "*Misce essence mostrum, spiritus ignis,*" I declared. The threads of destiny and magic intertwined.

"*Sun aspectu lunae, destini volant liberi*," I concluded, my voice echoing through the night as I completed the incantation. The candles flickered and danced, their flames burning with an otherworldly intensity.

With the chant concluded, I took a deep breath, the weight of the moment settling on me. The ritual was set, and the consequences, whatever they may be, were now in motion. I took the vial off of the table and quickly drank its contents, retching at the taste. My body immediately began to vibrate with energy.

As I focused on my thoughts and intentions, I visualized a silver thread of light extending from my heart, reaching out across the ethereal divide to the First Witch. With each breath, I felt the connection strengthening, an intangible bridge between our spirits forming.

Carefully, I poured the content of the chalice onto a silver plate, the mixture reacting with the moonlight in a mesmerizing dance. A mist rose from the plate, swirling and shimmering as if infused with the very essence of magic. Amid this enchanting display, the form of the First Witch began to emerge, her presence captivating.

Hovering before me, the First Witch extended her hand, her palm upturned and inviting. With anticipation and apprehension, I placed my hand upon hers, palm to palm. The instant our skin made contact, an electric surge coursed through me, the energy around us intensifying to a level that overwhelmed my senses.

I fought to stay upright, to maintain the connection as the energy swirled around us. The air crackled, and in the distant, cloudless sky, a bolt of lightning illuminated the horizon. It was as though the very elements were acknowledging the potency of the moment.

Among the tempest of energy, the First Witch's voice echoed within me, her words carried on the currents of power. "Be steadfast, daughter, this is the most perilous part of the spell." Suddenly, pain shot through my very core. Pain that radiated through every fiber of my being like white-hot fire, threatening to consume me entirely.

I gritted my teeth and clenched my fist, determined to endure the agony. With each passing moment, the pain grew in intensity, testing my resolve and pushing me to my limits. I fought to maintain my focus, to keep my palm centered on hers despite the torment that sought to break me.

With each pulse of agony, I could feel a piece of myself being stripped away, leaving only an emptiness in its wake. It was a terrifying feeling, as though my soul were being devoured. The instinctual impulse to recoil was almost impossible to resist, but I steeled my nerves and stood my ground.

The air around me grew thick and heavy and the energy splintered through me. As my body trembled and my strength wavered, the First Witch's voice cut through the chaos. "Fight through the pain, Vale," she urged, her tone firm yet oddly comforting. "Your spirit must withstand the trial, or your soul will be consumed in the crucible of this connection."

With her words echoing in my mind, I summoned every ounce of my willpower. My body shook, sweat beading on my forehead as I grappled with the searing pain. Through sheer determination I pushed back against the torment, forcing myself to stand firm even as my vision blurred and my senses teetered on the edge of oblivion.

The waves of agony continued to crash over me, threatening to consume me entirely. The First Witch's desperate cry pierced through the chaos, a lifeline of encouragement through the torment. "Almost there, Vale. Keep fighting!" I clung to her words, summoning every ounce of my strength to push back against the pain that seared through my body. It felt as if I were being torn apart, my soul unraveling in the trial of the ritual.

With a final unyielding surge of magic that felt like it would rip me apart, the spell completed itself and the pain ebbed away. Gasping for air, I stood there, my body trembling as the energy settled around me. The spirit of the First Witch still stood before me, a small smile etched on her face.

"I knew you could do it, daughter," she said, her words carrying a sense of pride and admiration. Exhausted, but relieved, I managed a weak smile in return.

"Is it over? Is it done?" I asked her, my voice barely a whisper. The First Witch nodded, confirming that the process was indeed finished. I tried to steady my breathing. "What comes next?"

"Now, I shall be with you always, to guide and to teach you." Her response came directly into my mind, the connection between us already established.

The weight of her words settled in, uncertainty coursing through me. With a final smile, the First Witch's form dissipated, leaving me standing alone in the moonlit space. As the silence settled around me, the gravity of what I had just done hit me. I had bound myself to the First Witch, merging our spirits together. The thought was daunting, and yet, strangely comforting.

I stood there for a long moment, contemplating the consequences of my actions. There would be no turning back now. With a quiet exhale, I gathered the supplies I had used, not wanting to leave behind any evidence. Descending the stairs, I couldn't help but wonder if I had made the right choice. The uncertainty gnawed at me, a nagging doubt that lingered even as I prepared to face the unknown path that lay ahead.

Chapter Thirty

My body ached as if I had been hit by a bus. I groaned softly as I tried to find a comfortable position on the cot I had slept on in Wren's tent. The events of the previous night came rushing back to me— the pain, the merging, the connection with the First Witch. Then coming back here to relive old memories of Juniper with Wren, drowning our sorrows in weed and alcohol.

Wren's voice filtered through the haze as he worked in his makeshift kitchen. "Coffee?" He offered, glancing in my direction.

I managed a weak smile, my dry lips parting to respond, "Yes, in an I.V. drip straight into my bloodstream, please."

He chuckled, a warm sound amid my discomfort. The aroma of brewing coffee slowly filled the tent, mingling with the scent of the camp beyond the tent's walls.

Wren turned to face me and sighed. "Vale, this whole situation...how did we end up here?"

I let out a rueful laugh at his abrupt subject change, the sound tinged with exhaustion. "Not too long ago, we were chasing bounties and running a bookshop together," I mused. "And now look at us."

He shook his head, a small smile playing on his lips. "I never thought our lives would take such a turn and definitely not so quickly," he admitted, his gaze distant.

I nodded in agreement. It had been a whirlwind journey, one that neither of us could have predicted.

As I shifted to a sitting position, my sore muscles protested at the movement. Wren handed me a cup of coffee and I gratefully took a sip, the warmth spreading through me in the chilly morning air. The two of us sat in companionable silence for a moment, both lost in our own thoughts. Little did Wren know about the significant step I had taken the night before, a secret I carried within me, a choice that would undoubtedly shape our future in ways we couldn't yet comprehend.

I fidgeted with the fraying hem of my shirt, conflicted emotions swirling within me. I needed to tell Wren about what had happened but the words stuck in my throat.

"Wren, there's something—" I began hesitantly, but just then the tent flap was thrust open and Venna strode in.

"Oh, hello Vale," she said, clearly not expecting me to still be here.

I offered her a small nod in greeting. Despite the interruption, I couldn't help but feel a sense of warmth toward Venna. There was an air of capability and honesty about her that I could appreciate.

"Wren, there's a dispute between some of the wolves that requires your intervention," Venna stated matter-of-factly.

Wren sighed, his expression briefly reflecting the ever-present burden of leadership before smoothing into calm resolve. "Duty calls, it seems," he said rising to his feet.

I tried to keep my voice light. "Don't worry about me, go take care of things."

As Wren turned to leave, his gaze lingered on me a moment longer, his eyes narrowing slightly. "Is it just me, or is there something different about you?"

My heart raced. Could he already sense the change? I scrambled for nonchalance. "Different? Not that I can think of." I forced a casual shrug, waving my hand, hoping he couldn't see right through me.

"Wait," he began, narrowing his eyes. "What the hell happened to your hand?"

I had forgotten that Wren had yet to notice my darkened fingertips. I quickly stuffed my hands in my pockets.

Venna looked over at me, curiosity flashing in her eyes.

Avoiding eye contact, I kept my expression neutral. I knew I should probably come clean, but the truth was too much to bear at the moment, and I wasn't ready to have that conversation. Instead, I took a deep breath and tried to steady my racing pulse.

Wren continued to scrutinize me. "What's going on, Vale?"

"It's nothing," I said dismissively. "Just a side effect from magic gone wrong."

Wren raised an eyebrow. "A side effect? Are you sure that's all it is?"

I gave a small nod.

"Vale..." Wren trailed off.

"It's fine, Wren. Really," I insisted. "I've got it under control."

"I hope so," he replied, his tone skeptical. "I'll see you soon, okay?" With that, he ducked through the tent flap, leaving me alone with my churning thoughts once more. I let out a shaky breath, the secret still balanced precariously on my tongue. I would tell him, but perhaps not just yet. The time didn't feel right and maybe I was a little bit of a coward.

Alone, I closed my eyes and reached out tentatively with my mind. "First Witch?" I called softly, still unsure of the newfound connection.

Her voice echoed within me, at once intimate yet strangely distant. *"Yes, child? What is it you seek?"*

I could feel her presence surrounding me as if she stood there in the tent. It was strangely comforting, like a cool breeze on a hot day. "Will others be able to tell that our spirits have merged?" I asked in my mind. "Will they sense the change in me?"

The First Witch was thoughtful.

"This ritual has marked your soul and altered you on a fundamental, cosmic level. Those who know you well may perceive subtleties in your manner, your speech, and maybe even your scent. The very fabric of your spirit now carries glimmers of ancient magic."

I bit my lip, considering her words. Wren had noticed a difference already, it was only a matter of time before the truth came to light.

Sensing my concern, the First Witch continued gently.

"Do not fear, child. The blending of spirits is not inherently light or dark magic. Focus instead on nurturing our bond, on gaining the knowledge I can impart."

I nodded, resolve steeling within me. She was right— this gift could help protect those I cared for. I would embrace it fully. There was no turning back.

The First Witch's presence retreated from my mind like a fading dream as I stood. Before facing Wren again, I needed time to process all that had transpired. "Nyxen," I called softly, summoning my familiar from the shadows. In moments, his sly fox-like form materialized before me, eyes gleaming with silent attentiveness.

"I need you to shift me home," I told him, my voice steady despite my inner turmoil.

I felt an unfamiliar echo of something brush across my mind, thinking it was the First Witch again. But as I looked at Nyxen, I realized it was him. I gaped at my familiar and waited for more, but that fleeting brush was all that happened. Stunned, I wondered what else the bond would unlock between us. Seconds later, the inky void embraced me, blurring my surroundings until I found myself standing in the familiar confines of my apartment.

The old cat padded over to me, meowing loudly and winding between my legs. I fed him and scratched him on the head as he purred, happily satisfied.

With a deep breath, I moved to shower and change, seeking a few precious moments to myself, moments that got rarer and rarer as the days passed.

❨ ☽

The musty air of the library enveloped me as I poured over ancient texts on blood magic, searching for the key to unlocking my full potential. Elara's ghostly form had appeared earlier, scolding me for improperly shelving the book I had taken the night before, before flitting off to rearrange the shelves once more.

With the grumpy ghost appeased for now, I refocused my efforts, secretly conversing with the First Witch in my mind. "I'm trying to tap into my blood magic without spilling blood, but it feels like I'm constantly straining for it," I confessed.

The First Witch's voice echoed through me, patient but firm.

"You mustn't force it, child. Your magic flows steadily in your veins and with my help, it will be easier now. Open yourself and it shall come."

Taking a deep, centering breath, I allowed my body to relax and cleared my mind. I released the tension of effort, trusting in the magic that was as much a part of me as I was of it. As the weight lifted from my shoulders, I felt the subtle hum of power within and allowed it to rise to the surface, flowing through me in a soothing wave.

Immediately, I was aware of a change. Where before my magic was like a river, rushing and turbulent, now it was like an ocean, vast and deep, a limitless expanse of potential. With the connection of the First Witch established my blood magic roared through me easily.

The First Witch spoke again, her words carrying a touch of awe.

"Well done, daughter."

The power that surged through me felt different, almost alien. Yet it was somehow also intimately familiar, like a long-forgotten memory. The sensation was both exhilarating and terrifying.

I pushed aside the feeling of unease and focused on channeling my energy, eager to test the limits of the newfound connection. As I extended a finger, a tiny spark danced across my skin, a manifestation of the power coursing through me.

With a thought, I willed the spark to grow and it obeyed, blossoming into a crackling flame. I grinned, amazed at the ease with which the magic flowed. With a flick of my wrist, the flame morphed into a swirling ball of fire, casting a warm glow around the dim library.

I could feel the First Witch marveling at the sight, and a surge of pride swelled within me. This was only the beginning, I could sense it. With her guidance, there was no limit to what I could achieve.

"Yes!" I exclaimed, before immediately clamping a hand over my mouth. Across the room, Harker startled violently at the sudden noise, nearly toppling out of her chair. She shot me a reproachful glare while I smiled apologetically.

"Sorry about that," I offered lamely before turning my focus inward once more. I had done it— accessed my power without pain or sacrifice. The First Witch's connection had unlocked the door between magic and body, forever changing my tide of abilities. But this was just the beginning. It was time to put my newfound power to the test.

It had been two days since my revelation in the library, and I was determined to make the most of my time. I had made incredible progress with the help of the First Witch, who told me her name was Rowena, discovering new abilities that my mind couldn't even begin to fathom. My body had never felt so strong and agile and my blood magic had become more and more effortless to summon.

Outside Kaelan's house, I focused on honing my powers. The air crackled around me as I conjured balls of fire, propelling them towards a target I had set up. With a surge of energy, I released a particularly potent fireball that struck the target dead-on, reducing it to smoldering ashes. A victorious smirk tugged at my lips as I reveled in the power coursing through me.

However, my concentration was disrupted by Kaelan's voice behind me. "Remind me not to ever get on your bad side, little witch." His words brought a genuine laugh from me and I leaned in to plant a quick kiss on his cheek. As he asked about my activities, I shrugged, telling him I was just practicing and enjoying the progress I was making.

"Well about about a quick break for lunch?" he asked, smiling at me.

Kaelan's proposal of a lunch break was enticing and we headed to the kitchen together. I couldn't shake off the sense of guilt that had been gnawing at me. Kaelan's presence was comforting, but the weight of the secret I was carrying pressed heavily on my conscience.

"Seems like you're progressing finally," he said as he prepared food for the two of us. His mention of my swift advancement only intensified my guilt. He set a sandwich before me at the table.

I picked at my food, trying to ease my troubled thoughts. Kaelan's concern was genuine, and my heart ached to tell him the truth. But the fear of his reaction, the potential danger that my connection with Rowena presented, held me back.

I mustered a weak smile, hoping to deflect any growing suspicions. "Just putting in some extra effort, I guess," I said, my voice unsteady. Kaelan gave me a warm look, but I couldn't help but feel a chasm growing between us, widening with the weight of my secret.

I pushed my food aside, suddenly not hungry. Kaelan noticed and gave me a quizzical look. "What's wrong?"

"Nothing," I replied, not wanting to worry him. "I'm just not as hungry as I thought I was."

"Vale," he started. "What's really going on? You've been distant lately. Is it because of Juniper?"

I looked at him, not knowing how to respond. His question brought the guilt surging forward, threatening to overwhelm me. "I don't want to talk about it," I mumbled, getting up and leaving the room. But Kaelan followed close on my heels.

"If something is wrong, please tell me." He insisted, grabbing my waist and spinning me around. His eyes searched my face, his expression worried. "What's wrong, Vale? Talk to me."

The sight of him was almost enough to break me. I longed to tell him everything, to share the burden with someone else. But the image of him running away, of him leaving me, was too much. I shook my head, not meeting his gaze.

"Vale…" he said softly, his hand coming up to cup my chin. He tilted my head up until I was looking into his eyes. "Please," he whispered, his thumb gently stroking my jaw.

The tenderness in his touch was my undoing. I felt my resolve crumbling as my carefully constructed wall of secrecy came crashing down. I closed my eyes and took a deep shuddering breath.

"I made my decision about the First Witch," I admitted, my voice barely a whisper. "I made up my mind days ago, the day of Juniper's funeral. I performed the ritual that night."

There was a moment of silence, and I was afraid to open my eyes, afraid to his the disappointment and hurt on Kaelan'sface. When I finally did, the devastation there was like a slap in the face.

"Why didn't you tell me?" he asked, his voice tight with barely controlled emotion.

"Because I knew you would try to stop me and I was afraid of what would happen if you did."

There was another long silence, Kaelan's eyes boring into me. When he finally spoke, his voice was thick with anger. "Afraid what would happen? Afraid that I would try and save your soul? You knew I didn't want this for you and yet you chose it anyway. You chose to go behind my back and make the choice for both of us."

"You wouldn't have understood," I said, my voice cracking.

"And you wouldn't have listened," he shot back, his anger rising.

"How could I have listened when I knew you wouldn't support me?" I cried. His eyes were dark and stormy, his mouth set in a hard line.

"Because I love you, Vale! And I know you better than you think. You're too quick to make a decision, to do something drastic. It's going to get you killed."

His words hit me like a ton of bricks, stealing the breath from my lungs. The anger in his eyes was replaced by a raw vulnerability that shook me to my core.

"You love me?" I breathed, hardly daring to believe it.

"Of course I do," he said, his voice rough with emotion. "I've loved you since I first saw you in Erebus. But now...I don't know if I can trust you."

I swallowed hard, the pain of his words cutting deep. "You can trust me Kaelan," I said, my voice hoarse with the effort of holding back tears. He shook his head, his expression torn.

"I don't know if I can, Vale. You're playing with powers you don't understand. You're meddling with forces that are beyond you. You're in way over your head, and I don't know if I can pull you back out."

With that, he turned and walked away, leaving me standing alone, my heart breaking. As he retreated, the dam holding back my tears finally broke and a sob escaped my throat. My shoulders slumped as the weight of his words and my decisions crashed down on me. Tears streamed down my face as I stood in the empty room, the only sound the echo of Kaelan's footsteps as he walked away.

Chapter Thirty-One

The next few days passed in a blur. Kaelan and I barely spoke, our relationship strained by my decision. The guilt and shame of my actions hung heavy on my heart. My magic training was not going well. I couldn't focus and my spells were half-hearted and weak. Every attempt seemed futile and I was plagued with doubts about my decisions.

The First Witch, Rowena, sensed my turmoil. She had been more and more present since Kaelan's confrontation and she did not mince words.

"Your heart is not in your training."

"No, it's not," I admitted. "I'm sorry, but I can't stop thinking about Kaelan. About what he said."

"And what was that?"

"That he loved me," I said softly, the words bringing a flutter to my heart. "But also that he didn't know if he could trust me anymore."

"And what did you say?"

"I didn't say anything. I just let him walk away," I paused, my heart aching at the memory. "I'm afraid Rowena," I whispered. "I'm afraid that I've lost him. That I've lost myself."

"You have not lost yourself. But you are at a crossroads. Your journey is only just beginning, and you must choose the path you will take."

"I'm not sure I know how to make that choice," I admitted, my voice barely above a whisper.

"Yes, you do."

Her words rang with a certainty that took me by surprise.

"You are stronger than you know, Vale. Your strength is not in your magic but in your heart. Trust your instincts and you will find a way."

Her words echoed through me, filling me with a sense of hope. As her presence faded from my mind, I was left alone with my thoughts. Her advice had been cryptic but the meaning was clear—I needed to follow my heart.

I had been so caught up in trying to control everything that I had lost sight of what was most important. I needed to make things right with Kaelan. Even if he couldn't forgive me, even if he walked away for good, I needed him to know the truth.

I knew what I had to do; it was time to find Kaelan. But as I made my way through the house, my steps sure and determined, he was nowhere to be found. After searching everywhere, my heart sank. He wasn't here.

Defeated, I made my way back to the library. The space was quiet and comforting, the shelves filled with the knowledge I had come to appreciate. I took a seat in one of the chairs, my thoughts racing.

As I sat there, a realization struck me. The study I had unlocked when first accessing my spirit magic, I hadn't checked there. With newfound energy, I hurried to the door. It was locked as usual, so I quickly unlocked it with a spell.

I stepped inside, the cool air welcoming me. As my eyes adjusted, I saw the room was full of artifacts and books, a wealth of knowledge. However, none of that interested me. There was something far more important here.

I found him, sitting in the corner, his gaze downcast. "Kaelan," I breathed a sigh of relief.

He looked up, his eyes wide. "Vale," he whispered disbelief in his voice.

"I'm sorry," I said, taking a step towards him. "I'm sorry for every-thing. For lying to you, for going behind your back, for choosing the path I did. But most of all, I'm sorry for not listening to you, for not trusting your judgment. You were right, I was being reckless. I was blinded by my grief over Juniper, blinded by my desire to protect everyone. But in doing so, I put myself in danger, and I lost sight of what's important to me."

"And what's that?" he asked, his voice gentle.

"You." I breathed. "You're what's important to me. Your friend-ship, your support, your love. I love you, Kaelan. And I'm sorry it's taken me so long to realize it. But I know now. I know what I want, and that's you. If you'll still have me."

I had laid my heart bare and now I stood there, waiting. I waited for his answer, praying he would give me another chance.

Kaelan rose to his feet and crossed the distance between us. He reached out and cupped my face, his touch gentle and sure.

"You'll always have me," he whispered.

His lips met mine and the room faded away. Nothing else mattered, the only thing that existed was us. We were together.

As we pulled away, he pressed his forehead to mine and my heart swelled with joy. "I love you," I whispered, the words sending a thrill through me.

"I've loved you before I even met you, and I'll love you until my dying breath. You are the most important thing to me now. Just you," he replied, his voice filled with a deep tenderness.

"Thank you," I breathed, "for not giving up on me."

"Never," he said. "I'm with you, now and always."

I closed my eyes and let his words wash over me. It was a promise I knew he would keep. He kissed me again, a tender and claiming kiss. His arms wrapped around me, pulling me close. I gave in, leaning into his touch. His shadows pressed around us and I felt the world shift. When the shadows receded we were in his bedroom.

"This is not like the other times we were here," he murmured.

"Oh really? Then what is it?"

He leaned in, his breath hot on my neck. "It's a new beginning."

His words sent a shiver of anticipation through me. This was new territory for us, and I couldn't wait to explore it. His lips brushed against mine, shooting sparks of passion through me. My hands roamed his body, savoring the feel of him. Our bodies pressed together, heat rising between us.

Our kisses deepened, our passion building. We were both hungry for each other, and our clothes came off easily, revealing our eager bodies. As we sank onto the bed, I knew this was right. We were meant to be together, and nothing could tear us apart.

I took his hand and placed it on my breast, feeling his fingers gently squeeze it. He kissed me again and I felt him slowly moving down my neck, kissing every inch of skin he touched. My hands slid down his muscled back, pulling him closer. His kisses moved lower and I moaned as his tongue swirled around my nipple.

His touch was driving me crazy, and I arched my back, desperate for more. "There is one more thing," he said, biting down on my peaked nipple.

"What is it?" I gasped, his sharp teeth making me shudder.

"Where I'm from, when two decide to become one, blood is shared between them," he said, looking me in the eye.

"What do you mean, blood is shared?"

He took his time before responding, kissing my breasts again. His touch was driving me crazy.

"I want you to bite me, and I want to bite you." He said, his words sent an unexpected thrill through me. I didn't understand, but I was willing to try anything at this point.

He brought his hand to my breast, squeezing it roughly. I moaned, feeling his other hand move lower. "I'll mark you here," he said, his fingers sliding between my legs, causing me to gasp softly. "I want to share blood with you, Vale. I want to claim you as mine."

"Yes," I whispered, wanting to please him. He smiled, a predatory grin, and then his mouth was on mine. He kissed me roughly, his tongue exploring every inch of my mouth, laying claim to it.

I shuddered, my body responding to his touch. I was completely under his spell and I didn't want to escape. His fingers continued their exploration, this thumb brushing against my clit. I moaned, my hips jerking against his hand, wanting more.

"I'm going to make you cum, and then I'm going to sink my teeth into you," he growled, his voice filled with desire.

He slipped two fingers inside me and I gasped, the sensation sending soft waves of pleasure through my body. I rocked against his hand, his thumb rubbing my clit. I was already so close to the edge, my body electrified by his touch.

"Kaelan," I gasped, feeling the orgasm building inside me. He slid a third finger in, and I moaned loudly as he pushed them deeper into me. My head fell back as I arched against him and he leaned over me, kissing my neck.

His fingers moved faster, his thumb rubbing over me in a delicious rhythm. I held onto him, my fingers digging into his back.

"Come for me," he whispered, his teeth scraping against my sensitive skin. His words sent me over the edge and I cried out as the orgasm crashed through me. My body trembled as pleasure pulsed through me, hot and fierce.

He pulled his fingers from inside of me and I whimpered softly as he licked them clean. I stared up at him, breathing heavily. He smiled down at me, fangs flashing in the dim light.

"Now it's my turn," he growled, his voice thick with desire. He slowly trailed kisses down my body, over my breasts, across the plane of my stomach. His head dipped down as he kissed the inside of my thigh.

I moaned, my fingers tangling in his hair. I was aching for him, craving him. He looked up at me, his eyes filled with lust.

"Are you ready, little witch?" he asked.

"Yes," I breathed, my heart pounding in my chest.

"I'm going to taste you now," he whispered, his fingers gripping my thighs. He pushed my legs apart, his eyes never leaving mine.

I watched as his head dipped down, his mouth hovering above my clit. He inhaled deeply, and a low groan escaped his lips. "You smell divine, like pure sunshine," he said, his tongue darting out to flick against my swollen clit. I moaned, my hands gripping the sheets beneath me.

He licked me again, his tongue circling my clit before moving lower. He pushed his tongue inside me and I cried out, my hips bucking against his face.

"Kaelan," I moaned, feeling the pleasure build inside of me again.

"Tell me you want it. Tell me you want me to bite you." He growled, his tongue sliding back up to my clit.

"Yes, please, Kaelan." I gasped. "Bite me."

He growled again and without any more warning his teeth sank into the soft flesh of my inner thigh.

I screamed as the orgasm tore through me, my body shuddering with pleasure. The sensation was like nothing I had ever experienced before. He drank deeply of me and groaned, closing his eyes. I felt the pressure building inside me and, before I could even process it, power exploded out of me.

I cried out, the energy rushing through me. I felt the connection between us grow stronger, an almost tangible thread connecting me to him.

His mouth left my thigh and he looked up at me, his eyes flashing.

The power inside me was intoxicating and I knew he felt it too.

We stared at each other and I felt the bond between us tighten. We were connected now, in a way that went beyond the physical. We were bonded.

My hands reached up and I ran my fingers along his sharp jaw.

He kissed my palm and nipped at my thumb, his teeth pricking the skin. I shivered and he licked the tiny wound.

He leaned forward and kissed me, his tongue parting my lips. I could taste the sweetness of my blood on his tongue and it sent a wave of heat through my body.

"You taste like wildfire, little witch, it's absolutely intoxicating," he said trailing kisses along my neck. I shuddered, my body still humming with pleasure and energy.

"It's your turn," I whispered.

He grinned, his eyes darkening. "And what are you going to do to me?"

"I'm going to bite you," I said, sitting up and pushing him down on the bed. He smirked, his eyes full of hunger.

I straddled him, his cock pressing against my pussy. I ground my hips down onto him and he groaned. "Fuck, Vale. You're driving me crazy."

I grinned, feeling powerful and sexy. "Good." I leaned down and kissed him, our tongues dancing together. He moaned, his hands gripping my hips.

"Ride me, Vale," he growled.

I reached between us and guided his cock to my entrance. He watched me with intense eyes as I slowly sank down onto him, taking his entire length. The feeling of him stretching me was ecstasy. We both groaned as I began to move over him, rocking my hips against his.

"Fuck," he growled, his fingers digging into my skin. The feeling of his cock was incredible and the friction of our bodies moving together was overwhelming.

"Gods, Kaelan. You feel so good," I moaned, bouncing up and down on him. He was rock-hard and I could tell he was close.

"Bite me, Vale," he said, his voice husky. I leaned down without hesitation and sank my teeth into the flesh of his neck, my small fangs easily piercing the skin. His blood coated my tongue, sweet and spicy, sending shivers throughout my body. I moaned against his neck as indescribable heat flooded through me.

He groaned, his hips thrusting up into me. "Fuck, yes," he said breathlessly. He gripped my hips tightly and flipped me onto my back, his cock still buried inside me. He began to fuck me hard, his hips slamming against mine.

"Fuck, Kaelan. Don't stop," I cried, writhing with pleasure.

He growled, his hips moving faster, his cock driving deeper into me.

I was teetering on the edge and I knew I was close. The feeling of him inside me, the taste of his blood, and the connection between us was all too much. I cried out as the orgasm crashed through me, wave after wave of pleasure.

Kaelan groaned, his hips jerking violently and I knew he was close too. He buried his face in my neck, his fangs scraping against the sensitive skin.

"Fuck, Vale. I'm going to come," he moaned. He thrust into me a few more times before his body tensed, his cock pulsing inside me as he found his release.

We lay there for a few moments, breathing heavily. His body covered mine, and his shadows wrapped around us, pulling us close.

I could feel his heartbeat against mine and it was the most intimate moment of my life.

He leaned down and kissed me softly and I melted into him.

We stayed like that for a while, tangled together, the bond between us solidifying.

Finally, he broke the silence.

"I've wanted this for so long," he said, his voice gentle. "To claim you, to make you mine. I never thought it would actually happen."

"I'm sorry it took me so long," I replied, running my fingers through his hair.

"It doesn't matter," he said. "We're here now. And that's all that matters."

I smiled, leaning up and kissing him softly.

"I love you, Kaelan," I whispered.

"I love you, too, little witch."

I closed my eyes, starting to drift off to sleep before the brush of Kaelan's lips against mine had me opening my eyes to look up at him.

"You are mine," Kaelan whispered, the words sending a thrill through me.

"And you are mine," I replied, the words feeling right. We were joined, bound by love and blood, and nothing would ever tear us apart.

Chapter Thirty-Two

Entering the bookshop for the first time since Juniper's death was like stepping into a world frozen in time. The dusty scent of books mixing with the faint aroma of herbs from the back created a bittersweet concoction that hung in the air. I was alone, facing the counter.

My initial purpose had been to locate some books for customer orders. But as I rummaged through the shelves and drawers, I stumbled upon a collection of old receipts. They bore Juniper's distinctive handwriting, her distinctive loops and swirls etched onto the paper and the realization hit me like a tidal wave.

Tears welled up in my eyes as I traced the delicate curves of her letters, lost in memories of her vibrant presence in the bookshop. She had been the heart and soul of this place, dusting bookshelves with a smile on her face or nurturing herbs in the backroom. Always happy, always with that infectious smile that could brighten even the gloomiest day.

With great reluctance, I forced myself to put away the receipts, tucking them back where they belonged. It was difficult to let go of these physical reminders, but I needed to focus on my tasks, to continue the work we had started together.

The bookshop, despite the temporary closure of its usual day-to-day operations, still held a responsibility to fulfill the back orders that our loyal customers had placed. It was a way to honor Juniper's memory, to keep her spirit alive within these walls. With a heavy heart, I began searching for the requested books, my every step echoing in the silence.

As I meticulously pulled books from their designated spots on the shelves, my focus narrowed on my task, seeking solace in the familiarity of the bookshop's quiet. The soft rustling of pages and the occasional creak of the floorboards beneath my feet created a tranquil atmosphere, a stark contrast to the turmoil that had engulfed my world.

Then, with an unwelcome jolt, the door chime tinkled melodiously, tearing me from my reverie. I turned to face the unexpected intrusion, ready to inform the visitor that we were closed for the day. However, my words faltered, freezing in my throat as I took in the sight before me.

Two towering fae males stood framed by the entrance, their presence commanding attention as their sharp and deadly features caught the dim light filtering through the windows. They exuded an air of power and danger, their beauty and menace an intoxicating blend.

The first fae male had silver hair that curled around his pointed ears. His sharp, angular features were accentuated by a pair of piercing almond-shaped violet eyes. He was strong and muscular, though his build leaned towards the leaner side, giving him an agile and lithe appearance. Every movement he made exuded grace and precision as if he were a predator silently stalking its prey.

In contrast, the second fae male was slightly taller, with close-cropped dark brown hair. His physique was more robust and muscular than his companion's, hinting at the raw power concealed beneath his casual demeanor. His eyes were a mesmerizing shade of grey.

With my heart racing, I managed to stammer out, "Sorry, but we're closed." It was a feeble attempt to dismiss them, one I knew it wouldn't be enough to send them on their way.

The fae with silver hair took a deliberate step toward me. His captivating eyes bore into mine and his voice, laced with a dangerous allure, filled the space between us. "We're here to take you home, princess."

My instincts screamed at me to retreat, to put as much distance as possible between myself and these intruders. A surge of anxiety coursed through me, but I stood my ground. My voice quivered only slightly as I responded, "Sorry, not interested."

The other fae male scoffed, his lips twisting into a condescending sneer. He gestured toward me, as he started to speak to his companion. But the silver-haired one silenced him with a warning glance before addressing me. His tone was gentler, but no less firm. "Please, come with us, princess. We don't want to harm you." The unspoken implication was there that they would though, if they had to.

I had heard enough. My mind raced, trying to figure out a way to escape the situation. The door behind the fae was still open and if I could reach it, maybe I could lose them in the crowd outside.

Before I could act, however, the dark-haired fae lunged at me, moving with a speed and grace that was unnaturally predatory.

I shrieked in terror, the sound reverberating through the room as I scrambled backward. In an instant, the fae was upon me, his hands gripping my arms, and a sickening dread swept through me. He was too strong, and I had no hope of fighting him off.

The silver-haired fae's eyes narrowed, and he snarled at his companion. "Aerion, you fool, what are you doing? You're frightening the poor girl!"

The dark-haired fae, Aerion, ignored his companion's scolding and tightened his grip on my arms. "The sooner you accept your fate, the easier it will be for you," he sneered, his eyes glittering with malice.

I struggled futilely against his hold, my mind reeling with confusion and fear. Who were these fae and what did they want with me?

I had to find a way to escape, or I feared the worst would happen.

Suddenly, the silver-haired fae was beside me, his expression grim but determined. He laid a hand on my shoulder, his touch surprisingly gentle, and spoke softly. "Princess, we mean you no harm. Please come with us peacefully and all will be explained."

Despite the fae's assurances, I was wary. There was no telling what they might do if I refused. But the silver-haired fae's touch seemed to calm my racing heart and I found myself reluctantly nodding.

He smiled and I was struck by his beauty, his sharp, angular features softened by the kindness in his eyes. He extended his hand and I took it, allowing him to lead me toward the door.

"Daughter! Clear the magic ensnaring your mind!"

Rownea's voice echoed in my head, pulling me from my trance as I realized that the fae had used magic on me to make me cooperate. Anger surged through me and I wrenched my hand away from the silver-haired fae, putting distance between us.

He stared at me in surprise, his brows furrowed.

"You can't force me to go with you," I said, my voice shaking. "I won't let you use your magic on me again."

The fae exchanged glances, their expressions inscrutable. Then the silver-haired one turned to me, his tone carefully measured. "Princess, we're just trying to protect you. There are those who would do you harm if they knew who you were. That's why we need to get you out of here before it's too late."

Aerion's patience was clearly wearing thin. He rolled his eyes and muttered, "Let's just take her and go."

But the silver-haired fae remained steadfast, his gaze locked on mine. "Give us a chance, princess. Let us explain."

I hesitated, torn between the desire to escape and the strange pull I felt toward the fae. Their magic was compelling and I knew it would be easy to succumb to it. But I was determined to stay in control of my own mind and I shook my head.

"I'm not going anywhere with you," I said, trying to sound more confident than I felt.

The silver-haired fae nodded and his tone was calm and respectful as he replied. "We understand your trepidation. But we're not going to leave you here, princess. It's not safe."

Before I could protest, before I could call up my magic, the silver-haired fae lifted his palm. A glowing orb appeared and he launched it toward me. I gasped as it collided with my body, enveloping me in a warm, golden light. The fae's magic filled me and I was overwhelmed by its power and beauty.

I felt a tug on my consciousness and then the world faded away in a blinding light.

When the light subsided, we were no longer in the bookshop. I sat on the ground, propped upright by a large tree. I looked around, confused, and saw that we were in the middle of a dense forest. I didn't recognize any of the trees or plants around me, and panic began to set in. The fae watched me from a few steps back with concern.

"Where are we?" I demanded.

"We're in the fae realm," the silver-haired fae said gently.

My eyes widened in disbelief. "You brought me to Elysian?"

"We didn't have a choice, princess. It was the only way to keep you safe."

My heart pounded and I felt dizzy. The fae realm was a dangerous place and I was in danger of being swept up in its magic. I stood up on shaky legs.

"Take me back," I said. "Now."

The silver-haired fae sighed, his expression grim. "We can't do that, princess. We have a duty to protect you."

My fear morphed into anger.

"You can't just kidnap me and expect me to go along with it! I have a life back home, a life I need to get back to."

The dark-haired fae laughed cruelly.

"Your human life is over, princess. You belong here, in the fae realm, with your own kind."

My hands curled into fists and my magic burned beneath my skin.

"I am not your princess. Now take me back, or I'll make you regret ever coming near me."

The silver-haired fae held out his hands, his expression pleading. "Please, princess, try to understand. There are others who will be coming for you. To use you as they please, and they won't be as gentle as us."

Aerion snorted and shook his head. "She's too much of a spoiled brat to understand, Thalion. Let's just tie her up and leave her here, so she can learn her lesson."

My fear and anger exploded and I lashed out at the dark-haired fae. He was too slow to react and my magic slammed into him, sending him flying backward. He crashed into a tree and I felt a grim satisfaction.

"Don't touch me," I growled, glaring at the other fae. "And don't you dare leave me here."

The silver-haired fae, Thalion the dark-haired one had called him, studied me, his expression thoughtful. "You're full of surprises, princess. Perhaps there's hope for you after all."

My glare intensified. "Hope for what? Do you think you can just drag me here and expect me to fall in line? I'm not some pet you can train."

Thalion smiled and my breath caught in my throat. "Perhaps not. But you're certainly an intriguing challenge."

He stepped toward me and my heart raced. "Stay away from me," I warned, taking a step back.

"I have no intention of harming you, princess," he said, his voice low and soothing.

"My own intentions are not that harmless, fae bastard," I said with a snarl.

He chuckled. "Spirited too. You'll be a welcome addition to our court."

"What do you mean by that?"

He shook his head. "It's not for me to say. You'll have to meet the others first."

The others? A sense of dread settled over me. "There are more of you?"

"There are seven fae princes in all, princess, and not all of them are as nice as we are," Aerion said, crossing his arms.

"I don't need anyone keeping me safe, I can take care of myself."

"That's yet to be seen, princess. Now, come along. Our court is waiting not too far from here."

Aerion glowered at me. "If she can't even handle two of us, how is she supposed to deal with the rest?"

The silver-haired fae shot him a scathing look. "We'll take things slowly, won't we, princess?"

I nodded, trying to appear calm and composed, but inside, my heart was racing. The thought of being surrounded by a full court of fae was terrifying. If that happened, I doubted if I would ever get away. I had to try now.

With a sudden burst of energy, I launched myself at Thalion. He was surprised but easily sidestepped my attack, leaving me stumbling forward. I quickly regained my balance and turned to face him, magic swirling around my hands.

He smirked. "I see you're a fighter. But you'll never beat us, princess."

I bared my teeth. "Don't underestimate me, fae. I can take you both on."

"As amusing as it would be to watch you try, we don't have time for this," Aerion sneered. "Just knock her out and let's go."

I braced myself for another attack, but it never came. Instead, Thalion reached out and stroked my cheek. His touch was gentle and a strange sense of calm washed over me.

"Don't fight us, princess. We only want what's best for you."

His words echoed in my head and the fight drained out of me. He was right. I had no chance against them and they were only trying to keep me safe.

"Vale, fight the magic. Do not let his compulsion overpower you."

I felt the coercion of his words, the magic he was using to convince me to surrender. My resolve hardened and I shook my head.

"No," I said, my voice firm. I stepped back and launched a fireball directly at his chest. He dodged, but his surprise was evident. "I'm not going to surrender to you, or anyone," I said.

Thalion looked impressed. "So be it, princess. We'll have to do this the hard way."

He launched a counterattack, his magic crashing into me like a tidal wave. I barely had time to throw up the shield I had briefly practiced with the First Witch before his power engulfed me, threatening to overwhelm my senses. My legs buckled under the onslaught and I fell to my knees. But I clung to my resolve, pushing back against his magic with everything I had.

Our powers clashed, the air crackling with energy. I dug deep, drawing on every ounce of strength I had, refusing to give in.

Thalion's smile faded, his expression hardening. "You're stronger than I expected, princess," he said. I didn't respond, focusing on keeping my shield up. "But you're no match for me. You may as well give up now."

I gritted my teeth and pushed harder, refusing to back down.

Aerion watched, an amused smirk on his lips. "She's not going to give up, you know. She's too stubborn."

"Yes, I'm beginning to realize that," Thalion replied, his gaze never leaving mine. "But we can't stay here forever. We need to get her to the palace, and quickly."

"Then just knock her out already," Aerion scoffed. "This is getting tiresome."

I knew they were right. I couldn't hold out against them forever. But I wasn't going down without a fight. I gathered every bit of power I had and threw it into my shield. Thalion staggered, taken aback by the force of my attack. He hesitated to throw his magic back at me and I used that hesitation to my advantage. "Nyxen!" I cried, and my familiar appeared beside me.

Aerion snarled, his eyes flashing. "That's cheating," he spat.

I shrugged, a grin spreading across my face. "Shift us now!" The shadows enveloped us and the last thing I saw was Thalion's face going wide with shock.

In a heartbeat, we were transported to another part of the forest.

"Where are we?"

"You are still in the fae realm, you must find a portal."

We couldn't be that far. I heard crashing sounds in the distance and knew the fae were tracking my scent.

I had no choice. "Nyxen, I need you to shift me as close to a portal as you can."

My familiar didn't hesitate and a heartbeat later, the shadows carried us across the realm. When the darkness receded, I found myself standing in front of a massive tree.

My breath caught. The doorway to the mortal realm. It was beautiful, a towering oak tree covered in vibrant green leaves.

"Hurry, they're almost here." Rowena's voice was urgent.

I sprinted forward, reaching for the portal. But before I could make contact, something slammed into me, sending me sprawling to the ground.

Aerion stood over me, his face contorted with rage. "You're not going anywhere, princess." He must have been able to shift in some way too.

He raised his hand and I knew he was about to unleash his magic on me.

Rowena's voice rang in my head. *"Vale, you must fight him!"*

I didn't know if I had the strength, but I had to try. I pushed myself to my feet and faced the dark-haired fae.

He threw his power at me and I threw up a shield, deflecting his attack. He snarled and threw another spell at me. "Give it up, princess. You can't win."

"Fucking try me," I said, deflecting his attack again.

We continued to trade spells and each time I managed to hold my own. I could see Aerion getting angrier and angrier, his attacks growing more vicious.

Finally, he unleashed a barrage of attacks, his magic battering my shield. I staggered under the onslaught, struggling to keep my shield up. He lunged at me, his hands curled into claws. But I was ready for him and I dodged out of the way, letting him fall face-first onto the ground.

"Nyxen, help me!"

The familiar responded immediately, appearing by my side.

"Keep him off me!"

The shadowkin obeyed, throwing itself at the dark-haired fae, distracting him long enough for me to jump through the portal to the other side. The last thing I saw was the fury in the fae's eyes before the world vanished around me.

Chapter Thirty-Three

I emerged in the forest surrounding the town. I knew it well and could make it back home without any problem. But I was wary, knowing that the fae might follow me.

"You did well, child. But they will keep coming for you."

"Let them, I won't be so easily captured next time." I snarled

"Be careful, Vale. You don't know what these fae are capable of."

I needed to leave before they came out of the portal and pulled me back to the fae realm. I called Nyxen to my side and asked him to shift me to Kaelan's house. The wards there would ensure they couldn't find me. But for now, I couldn't go back to the bookshop, not when they knew to look for me there.

Once Nyxen had shifted me, I made my way toward the front door but before I could even reach for the handle, the door swung open.

Kaelan stood before me, his expression stormy. "Vale, are you all right?"

"No, but I will be."

"What happened?"

"Fae. They kidnapped me and brought me back to their realm."

Kaelan's eyes widened and he grabbed my arm, pulling me into the house. "What did they want with you?"

"I'm not sure but they said they were going to keep me safe," I said pulling him into a hug.

"Safe? Around fae?" Kaelan scoffed.

"They said something about a court and their princes. Apparently, there are seven of them. Just like with the demon lords."

Kaelan's expression darkened. "They were fae princes?" I nodded my head, and he cursed under his breath.

"What does that mean?" I asked, a knot forming in my stomach.

"It means they're not going to give up, and they'll be back."

"Then I'll just have to be ready for them."

Kaelan studied me, his gaze searching. "Are you sure you're okay?"

"No, I'm not okay, but I'm not going to let them scare me either. How did you know I was missing?"

"The First Witch came to me in my dreams and warned me you were in danger. I went to the bookshop in search of you and I smelt the others that had been there. I just didn't know where to find you. I can back here to regroup."

I could only imagine what had gone through his head. "What did the First Witch say about the fae?"

"Just that she didn't know who had taken you but they were not to be trusted."

"Well, she's not wrong."

"I'm going to make you some tea and you can tell me everything." I followed him into the kitchen, and he set about preparing a pot of tea. While he busied himself, I told him everything that had happened. He listened intently, his expression growing darker by the minute.

"Fae princes, that is a problem and one that needs to be addressed."

Suddenly, my phone started buzzing. I pulled it out and checked the caller I.D. It was Wren. I picked it up, placing the phone to my ear. "Wren, I—"

But my words were cut off by Venna. "Vale, there's been an attack on the camp, you need to get here, now." I looked to Kaelan, horrified.

"We're on our way," I said and hung up.

"I didn't catch all of that. What is it?" Kaelan asked.

"An attack, on the camp. They need us there, now." I tried to push down the growing panic in my stomach. He nodded, pulling me into his arms and shifted us to the camp.

We arrived to a scene of chaos. The camp was in disarray, several tents were on fire and supplies were strewn about. People were running around, trying to help the injured. Venna was directing the efforts, her expression grim. When she saw us, she hurried over.

"Vale, thank goodness you're here."

"What happened?" I asked, wondering where Wren was.

"There was an attack, by demons. They came out of nowhere and attacked us before we even knew what was happening."

"Demons, here?" Kaelan asked.

"It gets worse," Venna said.

"How can it get any worse?" I asked, a horrible feeling in my gut.

"They took Wren."

"No," I gasped, feeling like I'd been punched in the stomach. My vision started turning black and I felt like I was going to be sick.

"They took Wren," Kaelan repeated as his anger surged.

"Yes. But they wanted Vale." She said, cutting her eyes at me.

"How do you know?" I asked, the blackness closing in on me.

"They demanded you be handed over or they would kill him. But Wren refused and then they took him."

"Oh gods," I gasped and Kaelan grabbed my hand, trying to ground me.

"I have the others looking for him, but we haven't had any luck yet."

"I can track them," Kaelan said.

"We have to leave now!" I cried, full-on panic evident in my voice.

"Vale, calm down and use your head. We can't just run into this blindly, we need to prepare. You can't be reckless," Kaelan said, grabbing me by the arms so that I was looking into his eyes.

"But they could be hurting him. They could be killing him!" I sobbed. I knew I wouldn't recover if something happened to him. I needed to get him out. Now.

"We will get him back, Vale. I promise. But we have to do this the right way."

I took a deep breath, trying to calm my racing heart. "You're right. What's the plan?"

"We will gather our resources and go after him. We cannot afford to lose you as well."

"And you think that will be enough? They already got him once." I asked, still on the verge of panic.

"That was a surprise attack. We will not let it happen again." He said, his grip on my arms tightening.

I looked at Kaelan, taking a few more deep breaths. I needed to keep a level head. "What about the fae? Shouldn't we be worried about them as well?"

"They are not the biggest threat at the moment," Kaelan said.

I nodded, knowing he was right. "Okay. Let's do this. Kaelan and I will work on finding Wren. You need to take care of the people here and try and make the camp more secure." I said, turning to Venna.

She shook her head incredulously. "No way am I staying here while my alpha is out there in danger."

"You have to. You're the only one we can trust with this, Venna. They took him because they wanted me, so I need to be the one to bring him back."

Venna shook her head once again. "Absolutely not, end of discussion. I'm coming too."

I took a deep breath, knowing we didn't have time to argue. "Fine, then let's get moving."

Venna called out to another werewolf and ordered him to take care of the pack, her voice commanding but shaken.

Kaelan shifted Venna back to the house while I shifted with Nyxen. We converged in the library. Harker gave us a curious look as we came in and I caught her up to speed quickly.

"Can you track Wren?" I asked Kaelan.

"Not exactly, but I can track the demons and that's a good place to start."

"Then what are we waiting for?" Venna asked, her tone impatient.

"We're going to have to be smart about this. If we're not careful, they could use Wren as leverage." Kaelan told her and my heart clenched at the thought.

"What's the plan then?" I asked, wanting to get moving.

"I'll track them first and find out what we're up against. Once I know, I can come up with a better plan. We don't want to go in there unprepared."

"Agreed," I said.

Kaelan's expression grew serious. "Once we find him, we'll need to be quick and careful. They're not going to let him go without a fight."

"And we'll be more than capable of handling them," Venna said.

"Don't underestimate them," Kaelan growled. "They're cunning and they're strong. We can't take any chances."

"I won't," Venna said. "But nothing's going to stop me from getting my alpha back."

"Stay safe," I told him, and he looked at me, hesitating before nodding.

Kaelan shifted away to begin tracking the demons and we stayed back, with nothing else to do but wait.

❨ ☽

Kaelan had been gone for what seemed like hours and I was pacing a hole in the carpet. Venna was restless too and had shifted between her forms a few times, but that hadn't helped calm her nerves.

"Do you think he's all right?" she asked, and I could hear the worry in her voice.

"I'm sure he's fine. He knows how to take care of himself." But despite my words, I was worried too.

Just then, Kaelan shifted back into the room and my heart skipped a beat.

"What did you find?" I asked him immediately.

"It's not good. The demons are Zephyrian's and they took him back to his keep. I can't shift in or out of it, so I didn't see where they took him," Kaelan said, looking at me with concern.

"Fuck." I cursed.

"We'll have to be careful," Kaelan said. "I could barely get a glimpse of him without being spotted."

"But you saw him?" Venna asked and Kaelan nodded.

"Yes, and he's alive, but he doesn't look good."

I took a deep breath, trying not to imagine what they might be doing to him. "Did you see how many there were?"

"About a dozen," Kaelan said.

"That's more than we've fought before," Venna pointed out.

"We can handle it," Kaelan said, determination in his voice.

"If they've taken him to Zephyrian's keep, that must mean the lord is planning a trap for me. He's not stupid, I doubt he would do anything rash." I said and the others nodded.

"We'll have to be smart about this," Kaelan agreed. "We can't go in blind, we need a plan."

"Nyxen," I said, remembering what Elara had told me about familiars being spies. "If I can get Nyxen in there, he could show us where Wren is being kept."

"That might work," Kaelan said.

"What are you talking about?" Venna asked.

"Nyxen is a shadowkin, he can move through the shadows undetected. I can send Nyxen in and then we can come up with a strategy based on what he finds."

"Do you think the demons would be able to sense him?" Venna asked.

"As far as I know, they can't," I said.

"Then it's worth a try," Kaelan said.

We wasted no time putting the plan into action. I called Nyxen and explained what he needed to do. The shadowkin looked up at me with knowing eyes. I felt his consciousness brush up against my mind with a feeling of understanding.

With that, my familiar turned and disappeared into the shadows. We waited with bated breath for his return, hoping he wouldn't be caught. After what felt like an eternity, Nyxen returned, his eyes filled with sadness.

"What did you find?" I asked him, uncertainly gnawing at my stomach.

My familiar looked up at me and suddenly a picture of Wren was in my mind. He was chained, his body beaten and bloody. I felt a surge of rage and my vision began to darken.

"No," I said, trying to stay in control.

"What is it, Vale?" Kaelan said, his hand on my arm.

"I saw him, he's...he's hurt," I said, my voice cracking with emotion.

"We'll get him out of there, I promise," Kaelan replied, his voice filled with anger.

"How are we going to do that?" Harker asked, speaking up for the first time. My heart ached in my chest knowing she wanted to come with us. We'd need the numbers.

"There are too many of them. We won't be able to fight our way through," Venna said.

"But there has to be a way," I said, desperation in my voice.

"I think I may have a solution," Harker said.

All of our heads snapped up in her direction. "What is it?" I asked her, surprised.

"We need a diversion. Something that will draw their attention away from Wren." Harker said, grinning savagely.

"And how do you plan on doing that?" Venna asked.

"I'm very good with explosives," She explained, her grin widening.

We all stared at her in shock for a few moments. "Where in the world did you learn how to handle explosives?" I asked her, stunned.

"I can have hobbies too, you know. I've been around for a long time, you'd be surprised what I've picked up."

"Where would we even get them?" I asked incredulously.

"I know a guy," Harker said casually. "And we're going to need a big distraction if we want to get Wren out of there."

"What if it doesn't work?" I asked, my stomach twisting at the thought.

"It has to," Kaelan said. "Otherwise, we're going to have to come up with something else, and we don't have time."

Harker nodded. "Leave it to me, I'll have everything we need within the hour."

I looked around at my friends and felt a surge of hope. We were going to get Wren back, and the demons would pay for what they'd done.

Chapter Thirty-Four

"You're sure about this?" I asked Harker for probably the tenth time.

"Yes," she said, a bit exasperated. "This will work. I promise."

"Okay, I believe you," I said, though I didn't feel as confident as I sounded.

We were crouched behind a pile of rubble, overlooking the entrance to Zephyrian's keep, Venna and Kaelan were close by. The keep, a colossal edifice of pure malevolence, reached toward the heavens with jagged spires that clawed at the sky. Its walls, constructed from a black, obsidian-like stone, exuded an aura that seemed to drink in the very light itself. Gargoyles, twisted into grotesque visages of demonic beings, perched upon the battlements, their malevolent expressions leering down at any who dared approach.

"I'll create a chain reaction that will start small, but it will grow. I'll place the explosives at the key points along the walls. When they detonate, the whole thing will go up like a bonfire. They'll never see it coming."

I could only hope she was right.

"Are you ready?" Harker asked.

"Yes, just give us the signal when it's time," I told her.

"Good luck," Harker said, and then she was off, creeping through the shadows to set up the explosives.

"What do you think will happen to the keep if this works?" Venna asked, a hint of worry in her voice.

"It doesn't matter," Kaelan replied. "The only thing that matters is getting Wren out safely."

With each passing moment, tension coiled within us, like a bowstring drawn taut. We waited in silence, each heartbeat pounding in our ears, until Harker's signal would ignite the spark that could either free Wren or seal our fates within the shadowy abyss of the keep.

"We need to make sure we get Wren out quickly. Once the fires start, the demons will be disoriented. But that won't last long." Kaelan said quietly.

I could feel the anxiety mounting in the pit of my stomach. We were so close to getting Wren back but it still felt like we were so far away.

Suddenly, a sound like thunder echoed across the night, followed by an explosion that shook the ground beneath us.

"That's the signal!" Kaelan yelled and we were on the move.

We raced toward the keep, the sounds of chaos growing louder with each step. The walls were already engulfed in flames, the gargoyles reduced to piles of rubble.

"We need to get in there," Kaelan said, his voice urgent.

"Nyxen!" I cried and my familiar appeared before me, his eyes glowing. "Show us the way in."

With a flick of his shadowy tail, Nyxen led the way toward a hidden entrance, a concealed door hidden behind a huge twisted tree that had remained untouched by the initial explosion.

The air was thick with smoke and ash, burning the inside of my nose as I breathed. My eyes felt as if they were on fire. The ash was thick in my mouth, gritty like sand, but instead of washing it away, I wondered what it would be like as the last thing I tasted.

We followed Nyxen down the labyrinthine corridors, our footsteps echoing off the walls. Nyxen knew where he was going, guiding us through the winding pathways and darkened chambers as if they were an open book.

I could hear the sound of demonic snarls growing louder around us and my stomach twisted in fear. Nyxen turned a corner and we rushed after him, only to find ourselves face-to-face with a small group of demons. We all stared at each other in shock for a moment before they charged towards us with incredible speed and ferocity, their claws outstretched and their teeth bared menacingly. Kaelan and Venna unleashed a flurry of attacks that kept them at bay, while I focused on infusing my own energy into my weapon to create an even more powerful force of destruction.

My powers surged through me as I brandished my weapon, allowing me to unleash torrents of fire that incinerated the demons before they could get close. It was like nothing I had ever experienced before; each swing of my axe burned away the darkness as if it were never there in the first place. After what felt like an eternity we had finally cleared out all the demons in our path, leaving only smoldering embers and bits of ash behind us.

We pressed on, driven by the unwavering desire to find Wren and free him from this nightmarish prison.

As we fought our way through the corridors, the air grew hotter, the stench of sulfur more pronounced. The sound of distant explosions and the roar of flames echoed through the halls and I could feel the heat radiating from the inferno above.

"We're running out of time," Kaelan shouted. "We need to find him, now!"

My familiar continued to guide us, the shadows clinging to him as he darted through the corridors.

Finally, Nyxen stopped in front of a large iron door. He looked up at us with his glowing yellow eyes and nodded. We had arrived at the entrance to the dungeons. The door was locked, but it didn't matter. With a surge of power, I blasted it off its hinges, the metal buckling under the force of my magic.

The air felt heavy and oppressive within the dungeons; it seemed almost like a living, breathing thing. The darkness clung to our skin as we made our way down to the cells below. Torches flickered on the walls, casting an eerie orange light throughout the corridors as our feet echoed with each step we took. The screams of the damned echoed through the corridors and the walls were lined with the torture implements of the demented creatures that lurked within its depths.

"Vale, watch out!" Kaelan shouted. I whirled around just in time to see a monstrous demon, twice the size of a man, bearing down on me.

I reacted instinctively, summoning a wave of flame that engulfed the creature. It shrieked in agony, its flesh bubbling and sizzling in the inferno. But it was not enough.

The beast lashed out with its massive claws, tearing through my defenses. Pain lanced through me as the razor-sharp talons ripped into my flesh. I staggered backward, my blood spraying in the air.

Kaelan leaped forward, his blade slicing through the creature's neck in a single, fluid motion. The beast's head tumbled to the ground, the light fading from its eyes.

"Vale, are you okay?" Kaelan asked, his eyes filled with concern.

"I'll be fine," I said, the wound already beginning to heal. "Let's keep moving."

As we moved through the dungeons, the sound of the inferno raging above us grew louder and the temperature increased even more.

"We're running out of time," Kaelan shouted.

"Nyxen, can you find Wren?" I asked, fear for my best friend clawing at me.

My familiar sped around another corner and suddenly I caught the scent of Wren. Finally, a door appeared.

"He's in there!" I said as we rushed toward it. I made quick work of this door as well.

As we stepped into the chamber, the sight before us was a vision from a nightmare. Wren was chained and suspended in the air by his arms, his body covered in gashes and blood. His clothes were in tatters and his face was a mask of agony.

"Wren!" I cried, racing to his side.

"Vale?" he whispered, his voice barely audible.

"Yes, it's me. I'm here."

I released the shackles binding him and he fell to the ground, crumpling to the stone floor.

"We need to get out of here, now," Kaelan shouted.

"Come on, Wren, you have to get up," I pleaded, hauling him to his feet.

His eyes fluttered open and he looked at me weakly.

"You shouldn't have come for me," he whispered and my heart clenched.

"I would never leave you behind." I slung his arm over my shoulder while Kaelan grabbed his other one and we stumbled from the chamber.

The roar of the fire above us was deafening and the smoke was starting to fill the room.

Wren leaned heavily on us as we hurriedly made our way out of the chamber. The thick smoke was making it difficult to breathe and the flames raged ever closer. Venna stayed close behind, covering our retreat as we made our way back up the stairs.

Suddenly, a deafening crash echoed through the dungeon and a huge chunk of the ceiling crashed down, narrowly missing us. The impact sent us flying and we crashed into the ground, Wren crying out in pain.

We lay there, stunned for a moment, the flames closing in on us. Wren's head lay against the cold, hard stone. I knew we were running out of time, that any second we would be consumed by the flames. A low growl rose in his throat as he slowly got to his feet, the pain evident on his face. He swayed unsteadily, but his eyes were filled with determination.

"I will not be defeated," he snarled, his voice hoarse and raspy. "I will not die here."

"We're not dying here," I said, my own voice strained from the smoke.

"Wren, are you okay?" Kaelan asked, supporting his weight once again.

"I'm fine," he said, though I could see the pain written all over his face.

"Come on, we need to get out of here," Venna urged.

Together, we managed to stagger our way out of the dungeon, the heat and smoke becoming too much to bear.

Each step was a battle against time. The inferno had consumed much of the keep, and it was a miracle the structure had not collapsed entirely. The very walls seemed to groan with the weight of impending destruction.

We stumbled and staggered through the suffocating heat and acrid smoke. Wren's injuries were severe and he could barely stand on his own. I channeled healing magic into him as best as I could while still keeping us moving, though it sapped at my strength, weighing down my steps.

Finally, we reached the entrance Nyxen had guided us to and I could see the faint glimmer of moonlight beyond. It was our only way out.

As we burst out into the courtyard of the burning keep, hope briefly flared within us. The moonlight illuminated the chaos around us, the fiery destruction contrasting sharply with the serene night sky. However, our relief was short-lived.

Before us stood a demon who I could only guess was Zephyrian, a towering and ominous figure, flanked by fifteen of his demonic minions. His eyes glowed with an unnatural crimson light and his wicked smile sent a shiver down my spine. His molted black and grey skin was covered in intricate tattoos that seemed to writhe and twist in the flickering light. "There's no way we can escape this," Kaelan muttered under his breath.

"Ah, the brave intruders have made it. How delightful." Zephyrian's voice echoed through the courtyard, a chilling and resonant sound that seemed to reverberate within our very souls.

Wren, though battered and weak, managed to stand beside me, his determination unwavering. Venna tightened her grip on her weapon, her expression resolute, readying to shift into her wolven form. We were outnumbered and cornered, but we would not go down without a fight.

Zephyrian raised a hand and his demonic horde surged forward with a guttural battle cry, a nightmarish wave of clawed and fanged creatures.

Kaelan stepped forward to meet them, his sword gleaming in the moonlight, and the battle began in earnest.

I unleashed a torrent of flames, incinerating the demons closest to us, but more kept coming.

Kaelan and Venna fought with valiant ferocity, his weapons and her fangs flashing in the moon's pale glow. They cut down demon after demon, but there were simply too many.

I could feel myself weakening, my reserves of energy dwindling.

Zephyrian watched the battle with cruel amusement, his crimson eyes glittering in the darkness. He seemed content to let his minions do the fighting, and his malicious presence loomed over us like a malignant shadow.

I glanced at Wren and my heart clenched. His wounds were deep and he was struggling to remain conscious. If we didn't get out of here soon, we would all die.

I poured every last ounce of energy into my magic, a desperate bid to save us from the inevitable.

A wave of pure, white-hot flame erupted from my hands, burning away the demons closest to me. Kaelan and Venna took advantage of the distraction, cutting a path through the horde. We ran, a final sprint toward freedom.

But Zephyrian would not let us escape so easily. He stepped forward, blocking our path, his twisted smile sending a chill down my spine.

"This isn't over," he said, his voice cold and calculating.

I looked at Wren, his face pale and streaked with blood, and my resolve hardened.

I stepped forward, my weapons drawn, ready to fight for our lives.

Zephyrian laughed, a cold and hollow sound, and the demons surged forward once more.

The battle was fierce and the odds were stacked against us. But we fought with everything we had. We knew this could be our last stand, our last chance at salvation. We would not give up.

The night sky was ablaze with the flames of battle. I looked over at my companions, their faces grim, determined. We were outnumbered, but we would not be broken. The demons came at us in waves, their claws and fangs gleaming in the moonlight. Kaelan and I fought back-to-back, our weapons flashing in the night.

A demon surged forward and grabbed me, wrapping his grotesque arms around me and squeezing until I was sure my bones would crack. I screamed out in pain, struggling against the powerful creature.

It was then I noticed Venna had been similarly captured as well and Kaelan was currently surrounded by a circle of demons.

Zephyrian stood before us, a cruel smile on his lips, savoring the moment. "Enough," he said

The demon holding me released its grip and I fell to the ground, my limbs aching. I looked up at the demon lord and the anger within me swelled.

"You will not take us," I spat. "I will not let you."

Zephyrian laughed, a chilling sound. "Oh, my dear. You have no say in the matter."

He gestured and the demons surrounding Kaelan closed in. Kaelan lashed out, his sword cutting through one of the demons, but it was no use. They overwhelmed him, pinning him to the ground.

I looked around desperately, my eyes falling on the burning keep.

"The flames…" I whispered a desperate idea forming in my mind.

"What are you talking about?" Zephyrian asked casually and the flames suddenly died out, the keep still standing. I gasped.

Zephyrian smiled. "My little trickster," he mused. "You think you can destroy me with fire? The fires of the keep are my own. They do my bidding, not yours."

"You'll pay for what you've done," I snarled, rage burning inside me.

Zephyrian's expression hardened, his eyes flashing with menace. "I think not," he said, "and you and I, Vale, we have so much to talk about."

Before I could react, Zephyrian raised his hand, and a wave of dark magic washed over me, dragging me into unconsciousness.

Chapter Thirty-Five

I stirred weakly, my head throbbing and aching. The darkness seemed to press in around me as I groggily opened my eyes. I was in an oppressive throne room that seemed to stretch endlessly in all directions. The walls were adorned with grotesque tapestries illustrating terrifying scenes of anguish and torment and the air was thick with a suffocating malevolence.

My head pulsed with pain as I groggily took in my surroundings. The others lay nearby, still unconscious, their forms sprawled out like discarded toys.

As I tried to sit up, I realized I couldn't move. An invisible force held me in place, pinning me to the cold, stone floor. Panic surged within me as I struggled against the unseen bonds.

Zephyrian observed my efforts with an unsettling amusement, his eyes gleaming. He reclined casually on a twisted throne, crafted from the bones of his fallen enemies, his features a mask of cruel mockery.

"Welcome back," he purred, his voice sending shivers down my spine.

I continued to strain against my invisible restraints, desperate to free myself. Zephyrian chuckled softly, his amusement growing as I fought against his magic.

"I've waited a long time to meet you, Vale," he said with a sinister grin, his crimson eyes locked onto mine. "Over twenty-three years to be exact."

"Why am I here?" I spat, my voice echoing in the vast chamber.

Zephyrian laughed, the sound dripping with cruelty. "I think you know the answer to that," he replied, his gaze piercing through me.

"What do you want with me?" I demanded, my anger and fear mingling into a potent mix.

"Isn't it obvious?" Zephyrian taunted, his voice dripping with poison. "I want to use you. I want to harness your powers and make them my own."

His words sent a chill down my spine and my stomach churned with unease. The thought of my magic, my very essence, being used for such dark purposes was horrifying.

"I will never serve you," I snarled, my resolve unwavering even in the face of this powerful demon lord.

Zephyrian sneered, his expression hardening with determination. "We will see about that," he said, rising to his feet with an eerie poise that made my heart race.

Zephyrian approached me with an unsettling grace that belied his rancorous presence. Each step he took echoed in the vast chamber, a haunting symphony of power and dominance. The air seemed to thicken with dread as he drew nearer, his dark silhouette commanding the space around him.

He crouched before me, his deep crimson eyes like pools of blood that threatened to drown my resolve. The flickering torches on the chamber's walls cast eerie shadows across his chiseled features, emphasizing the cruel contours of his smile.

"You are strong," he mused, his voice a soft hiss that sent shivers down my spine. "But you are no match for me."

My heart raced, my defiance battling with my fear as I stared into those unrelenting red eyes.

"I will never submit," I seethed, my voice filled with anger and resolve.

"We shall see," Zephyrian repeated, his gaze intensifying, his suffocating aura closing in around me like a vice.

I screamed as a searing agony pierced my skull. It was as if a thousand needles had been driven into my mind. My cries echoed through the chamber as Zephyrian's dark presence invaded my thoughts, his power overwhelming my pitiful defenses.

The pain was excruciating and I writhed against my bonds, desperate to escape. But it was futile. The demon lord was too strong, his influence too pervasive. As I struggled against his control, I could feel my mind being torn apart. Zephyrianlaughed, a chilling and mocking sound, as he tore through my psyche.

He was merciless, his assault relentless. With each passing moment, his power grew, and mine diminished. I was no match for him. "No," I cried out through gritted teeth, tears leaking down my cheeks as my mind became a battleground between my will and his dark dominion. I could feel him sifting through my memories, his touch leaving a trail of agony and violation in its wake.

"You've hidden yourself well," Zephyrian murmured, his voice dripping with ominous intent. His words hung heavy in the air, like a dark prophecy of things to come. The torchlight danced in his crimson eyes as he leaned closer, his predatory gaze dissecting every inch of me.

My jaw clenched and I ground my teeth together as I fought against his invasive power. The very core of my being rebelled against the intrusion, my entire body trembling with the effort to resist.

"I will not be used," I growled, my words emerging as a defiant whisper, choked with the strain of my resistance. Every fiber of my being was aflame.

Zephyrian's power surged and the pain intensified, coursing through my mind like molten iron. My vision blurred as I struggled against the torment, my breath coming in short, ragged gasps.

The demon lord leaned closer, his face inches from mine. I could smell the fetid stench of his breath, a rancid odor that reeked of death and decay. *"Don't fight it,"* Zephyrian's voice echoed in my mind, a sinister whisper that slithered through the corners of my consciousness. "You belong to me now, Vale. But you always have been mine, my precious daughter."

The pain momentarily receded, granting me a fleeting respite. Confusion and disbelief pierced through the anguish. "What... What did you call me?" I stammered, my voice quivering with fear and disbelief.

Zephyrian's smile widened, revealing a row of pointed perfectly white teeth, each one gleaming like a predatory trap. His crimson eyes glowed with perverse satisfaction.

"My daughter," he declared, the words laced with an unsettling pride. "My heir, my most beloved creation. You have finally returned to me. And soon, the realms will tremble at the mere mention of your name, Valerian Blight."

Daughter.

The word echoed through my mind like a bell, its significance reverberating through the very depths of my soul. My heart hammered against my chest, and I could feel the blood draining from my face.

Daughter.

The truth struck me like a blow, knocking the air from my lungs.

Daughter.

My father.

A cold, numb horror spread through me, a sensation so chilling that it was almost unbearable. My head throbbed with a relentless intensity, each pulse echoing in the cavernous chamber. My heartbeat was a cacophonous drumbeat of fear and desperation. Gasping for air, I felt like I was drowning in a sea of terror.

"What are you talking about?" My words escaped my trembling lips in a strangled gasp, my throat constricting with a vice-like grip of apprehension. The world around me blurred as I tried to make sense of the nightmarish revelation unfolding before me.

Zephyrian loomed over me, that sinister aura emanating from his very being. His expression twisted into one of contempt.

"Your mother, she was a fool," he hissed, his voice dripping with disdain. His words slithered into the air, a venomous revelation. "She tried to hide you from me, but I found you. You were born of my seed, Vale, and now you will serve me."

The chamber seemed to grow darker, the shadows dancing on the walls as if animated by the demon lord's words. His very presence was oppressive, a physical weight bearing down on me.

"You lie," I declared, my voice quivering with rage and terror. My vow was a desperate cry of defiance, a beacon of resistance against the encroaching darkness.

Zephyrian's sneer deepened, his gaze boring into me like a blade. It was a gaze that promised suffering, cruelty, and an unyielding determination to break me.

His laugh echoed through the chamber, a harsh and grating sound that sent shivers down my spine. "Deny it all you want," he taunted. "It doesn't change the truth."

"I will not submit," I declared, my resolve strengthened by the fury that surged through me. "You may have corrupted my mother, but you will not corrupt me."

"We'll see," he retorted, his words laden with a frigid cruelty that sent a shiver down my spine.

He resumed his assault on my mind, his psychic power like a relentless tempest, tearing through my mental defenses. His mental claws raked through my memories, a grotesque violation that left behind an agonizing trail of desolation and torment.

I screamed, my voice a raw, anguished cry that echoed through the very depths of my soul. My body convulsed with torment but my spirit fought valiantly against the inexorable invasion, determined not to be consumed by the darkness that threatened to crush me.

The air grew thick as Zephyrian's words slithered from his lips, a venomous serenade to my torment. His voice echoed through the chamber, each syllable carving a deeper trench of despair into my psyche.

"It's pointless to resist," he taunted, his voice laced with a cruel satisfaction. The dark aura that enveloped him seemed to coalesce, forming an impenetrable shroud around my very existence. "You're mine now and soon you will understand your destiny. You were made to serve me, to help me rule this world and the next."

His fingers, cold and skeletal, closed around my arm in a vice-like grip. Panic surged within me as I realized his intent, but it was too late. With a swift, violent motion, he yanked my arm toward his gaping maw. The world seemed to blur in a nightmarish haze as he sank his teeth into my flesh, the searing pain of his bite eclipsing all rational thought.

I screamed a guttural cry that tore through the very fabric of my being, but my cries fell upon deaf ears. Powerless and immobilized, I could only watch in abject horror as he drank deeply of my blood. Each swallow was a grotesque communion with darkness, an unholy sacrament that bound me further to my tormentor.

"You're a monster," I gasped, the words choked by my anguish. My tears flowed unchecked, mingling with the rivulets of blood that coursed down my arm.

Zephyrian's laughter, cold and cruel, filled the chamber, blood dripping from his lips like a macabre testament to his evil.

"And you are a child of monsters," he sneered, his words echoing through the abyss of my despair.

With a final, contemptuous release, he let go of me, and I tumbled to the unforgiving stone floor, my body wracked with an agony that transcended the physical. Fear clung to me like a suffocating shroud, and I could do nothing but lie there, broken and defeated, as the demon lord loomed over me.

The venomous atmosphere in the chamber hung like an ominous cloud, our confrontation a cruel dance of defiance and dominance. My voice, barely more than a breath, quivered with the remnants of my shattered spirit.

"I will never be like you," I hissed, my words a feeble but unyielding declaration.

Zephyrian's smile, devoid of empathy, twisted into a cruel and knowing smirk. His eyes bore into mine, relishing the torment he inflicted.

"Time will tell," he purred, his voice dripping with dark amusement. "In the meantime, I think I'll keep you and your friends here, as my guests. After all, we have so much to catch up on. Or if you want to continue to resist, I could always make an example out of one of them. Maybe I could start with that demon of yours."

Dread pooled in the pit of my stomach like molten lead. The mere suggestion of harm befalling Kaelan sent a bone-chilling wave of terror through me.

"No," I whispered, my voice trembling with an icy chill.

"Then accept your fate," Zephyrian declared, his tone cold and unwavering. "You'll never leave this place."

His words bore down on me, the hopelessness of our situation suffocating. But within the depths of my despair, a flicker of determination remained.

"You're wrong," I said, the words gaining strength as they left my lips. "And you can go fuck yourself."

I clung to the ember of resistance, the spark of defiance that refused to be extinguished. Despite the overwhelming odds, I refused to submit to the darkness that threatened to consume us all.

Zephyrian's sinister laughter reverberated through the vast chamber once more, each echoing note a cruel reminder of our dire predicament. His voice, dripping with venom, painted an unsettling portrait of the evil that lurked within him.

"Oh, I'd expect nothing less from my daughter," he said, his words laden with a twisted pride that sent shivers down my spine. With a dismissive wave of his outstretched hand, he signaled to the group of my friends who still lay there unconscious.

My heart sank as I watched in helpless horror, the creeping dread threatening to overwhelm me.

"Please, don't," I begged, my voice quivering with desperation, the weight of impending tragedy bearing down upon me.

"This is only the beginning," Zephyrian taunted, his words laced with venomous delight. He approached my friends with slow, deliberate steps, his eyes dancing with cruel amusement.

My defiance surged within me, a flicker of fiery determination in the face of impending doom.

"I'll kill you," I hissed, my voice a vehement oath.

Zephyrian's grin widened, his fangs glinting ominously in the dim light.

"You can try," he said with chilling nonchalance, his attention now fully turned away from me as he advanced toward my vulnerable friends. It had all come to this, and none of the preparations, none of the training had been able to stop it.

Chapter Thirty-Six

The dimly lit throne room seemed to close in around me as I lay there, my heart pounding with fear and anger. My friends lay unconscious on the cold stone floor. I had endured the torment of his dark magic, but I could not bear to see them hurt because of me.

Zephyrian's cruel laughter echoed through the chamber as he advanced toward Kaelan, who remained immobilized by the demon lord's control. My voice trembled as I screamed for Zephyrian to stop, pleading for Kaelan's safety.

But my plea fell on deaf ears. Zephyrian, with a sadistic grin, grabbed Kaelan by his raven hair, hauling him up off the ground as if he were a ragdoll. Kaelan's eyes were clouded, his body unresponsive to the distress etched across his features as he woke up.

"Get your hands off of him," I hissed venom in my voice.

Zephyrian's laughter grew more menacing, filling the chamber with a chilling echo. His crimson eyes burned with malice, the very image of the devil incarnate.

"He belongs to me," the demon lord sneered, tightening his grip on Kaelan's hair. "You see, he's been working for me for over two hundred years. Isn't that right, little princeling?" He tossed Kaelan back down to the floor, releasing the magical bonds holding him as he struggled to stand.

Kaelan, his breathing labored, looked up at me with an expression of horror. My mind reeled. This couldn't be. My heart stopped at Zephyrian's words. I stared in disbelief at Kaelan, willing him to deny it, praying that he would somehow prove Zephyrian's lies false. Confusion gnawed at my resolve as I struggled to comprehend his words. Kaelan had been by my side, fighting against Zephyrian's forces. How could he have been working with the demon lord all this time?

I shook my head in disbelief, refusing to accept the words that were tearing through my heart. Kaelan would never betray us. I had seen the depth of his love and commitment and witnessed his unwavering loyalty in the face of countless dangers. Zephyrian's words were nothing but poison, meant to sow doubt and despair. "You're lying," I hissed, my fists clenched with anger. "Kaelan would never betray me."

Zephyrian's smile remained unchanged, chilling and cruel. "You're wrong about that, daughter," he sneered, each word a venomous blade. "He's been feeding me information about you from the beginning, in hopes I would unbind his powers."

"Shut your mouth, Zephyrian," Kaelan said through gritted teeth.

I shook my head, a profound sense of disbelief and betrayal coursing through me. The world seemed to spin, and my heart was gripped by an icy claw. Kaelan, the man I loved and trusted, had deceived us all. The pain was unbearable, and tears stung in my eyes as I struggled to process this nightmarish revelation.

"You bastard," I hissed, my voice choked with emotion, the words directed at Zephyrian but echoing with the bitter taste of betrayal.

Zephyrian's sinister grin only widened in response to my anguish. He reveled in our suffering, finding perverse pleasure in the chaos he had sown.

"Your beloved princeling sold you out," Zephyrian taunted, his voice dripping with venom, his crimson eyes locked onto mine.

Desperate for some sign of innocence in Kaelan's eyes, I turned my gaze toward him, searching for any flicker of denial, any trace of the man I thought I knew. But all I found was guilt and anguish etched into his features. My heart splintered at the sight, and a deep, agonizing pain settled in my chest.

"Vale, please let me explain," Kaelan began, his voice a plea, but Zephyrian swiftly silenced him with a chilling command.

"No, you will stay silent," the demon lord ordered.

"Vale, I would never—"

Zephyrian's eyes narrowed, and he lifted his hand with a cold, calculated precision, pointing it directly at Kaelan.

"Enough," he hissed, his voice echoing throughout the chamber like a harbinger of doom.

A bolt of malevolent black energy erupted from his outstretched fingertips, striking Kaelan square in the chest. My heart stopped as Kaelan's body convulsed in excruciating torment. He crumpled to the floor, writhing in pain, his anguished cries cutting through the air.

I watched in heart-wrenching helplessness as Zephyrian's dark power mercilessly tormented Kaelan, my own body paralyzed by the shock of it all. Zephyrian's eyes met mine, and a sinister smirk twisted his lips."Although I guess his end of the deal is done, he did end up bringing you right to me. It's only fair I unbind his powers. Let's see what happens when we let the demon out to play, shall we?" Zephyrian turned back to Kaelan, waving his hand.

Kaelan's agonized screams seemed to rip through the very fabric of the room, a symphony of torment that mirrored the devastating transformation unfolding before my eyes. His body contorted, muscles rippling and bulging as his skin darkened to an inky black around the edges, a grotesque metamorphosis under the malevolent influence of Zephyrian'sdark powers.

Horns erupted from Kaelan's skull, great black twisted things that reached upwards. His eyes, once a warm and comforting shade, now blazed with a hellish light that sent shivers down my spine. I couldn't tear my gaze away from the horrifying spectacle. Two immense black wings, tainted by the same dark energy, burst forth from his back, unfurling like a nightmare.

Before me lay a creature utterly foreign and nightmarish, a perversion of the man I had loved. Kaelan was no more, replaced by this monstrous abomination, a pawn in Zephyrian's twisted game.

The demon lord's laughter, a mockery of humanity, reverberated throughout the chamber, a relentless reminder of the cruelty that now defined this place. Kaelan, his body transformed and his spirit shattered, lay on the cold stone floor, his breathing ragged and labored. My heart ached for him, broken in pieces as I watched the man I had once cherished reduced to this wretched state.

Zephyrian's dark magic had accomplished its cruel purpose, stripping Kaelan of his identity and changing him into something unrecognizable. The pain of betrayal coursed through me like a relentless storm, a tempest of anguish that threatened to drown me.

He had deceived me. He had manipulated me. And I, blinded by love and trust, had fallen for his treacherous ruse, accepting him with open arms into my heart.

A storm of emotions raged within me, the conflicting currents of anger, sorrow, and confusion. I wanted to hate him, to unleash the torrent of my rage upon him, to scream and cry and curse him for the agony he had inflicted. But in that moment, all I felt was an overwhelming sorrow that threatened to consume me.

"Kaelan," I whispered, my voice trembling and cracked, tears now streaming down my face.

My voice seemed to cut through the haze, reaching him, a painful reminder of the depth of our connection, now forever tainted by his betrayal. Kaelan turned his head toward me, his tears mingling with the inky darkness that marred his once-pure features. He began to speak, to explain, to beg for understanding, but his voice was silenced by the harsh command of Zephyrian.

"Silence," the demon lord barked, his voice an unyielding decree that kept Kaelan's protests and pleas buried beneath the weight of his dark magic, leaving us all ensnared in this nightmare of betrayal and despair. "That's not all you did though, is it princeling? You've forged a blood bond with her."

I could feel the tension in the air as his words seemed to hang heavy between us. A look of shock and horror crossed Kaelan's face as his dark eyes locked with mine. I felt like the wind had been knocked out of me, the realization of the enormity of his deception weighing down on me like an anchor. I had given myself to him fully, sharing everything I had to offer, even my blood.

But it was all a lie.

My heart was broken. The tears rolled down my cheeks as the anguish threatened to consume me. Zephyran's cruel laughter echoed through the chamber, an icy dagger to the soul.

I wished, more than anything, that I could believe Kaelan, that there was still a part of the man I had loved hidden within him. I longed for the truth to be different, for his feelings for me to have been genuine. But the bitter reality hung heavy around me — I had been deceived, my trust had been exploited, and my heart lay in shattered pieces.

My desire to retaliate against the one who had orchestrated this torment surged within me, but I knew it was futile. Zephyrian's power was absolute, his control over Kaelan unbreakable. Leaving me impotent and incapable of doing anything but bearing witness to the excruciating culmination of his treachery.

As Zephyrian reveled in his triumph, his cruel smile and malicious glee twisted my pain into something far darker. He turned his gaze toward me, relishing the anguish he had wrought.

The demon lord's voice slithered like venom as he addressed me, taunting me with the threat of what was to come. "Now, daughter, it's time to finish what I started."

Hatred coursed through me, a burning inferno that threatened to consume me from within. "Go to hell," I spat, my defiance a feeble but unyielding response.

Zephyrian's laughter, devoid of empathy, echoed chillingly off the chamber's stone walls. "Oh, my dear, we're already there. Now, how shall I break your heart next? Perhaps your dear werewolf over here?"

My throat went dry as Zephyrian began to approach Wren, who remained unconscious and vulnerable on the unforgiving floor. My anguish transformed into an indomitable scream, a primal and piercing cry. "Don't touch him, you son of a bitch!"

He halted, his twisted grin growing wider. "So predictable, daughter."

I was prepared to unleash another agonized scream, my desperation reaching a fever pitch, when a bolt of dark energy pierced the air, striking Zephyrian squarely in the chest. Shock and pain contorted his features as he stumbled backward. The bonds that held me captive crumbled, freeing me from its grip.

Zephyrian shifted his attention to Kaelan, his confusion and anger intertwining into a deadly dance on his countenance. "What are you doing, slave?" he snarled.

Kaelan's eyes blazed with incandescent fury, his fists clenched with unwavering resolve. "I am no one's slave," he hissed, his voice steady and unyielding, a stark contrast to the trembling uncertainty that had defined him just moments ago.

Zephyrian's malevolent laughter reverberated through the chamber, his eyes narrowing as they locked onto Kaelan. The atmosphere grew thick with tension, and the very air seemed to hold its breath as they assessed each other like predators preparing for a battle of dominance.

The circle of confrontation tightened, and my gaze remained fixed on the impending clash. The urgency to intervene clawed at my insides, yet I remained paralyzed by the sheer intensity of the standoff.

Zephyrian made the first move with calculated grace, unleashing another torrent of dark energy toward Kaelan. However, Kaelan proved prepared, evading the oncoming attack with a fluidity that spoke of his determination. In retaliation, he launched a counterattack, a potent surge of energy that surged like a roaring tempest, directly at Zephyrian.

The demon lord was unable to avoid the brunt of the strike, and the impact threw him violently backward, his body crashing against the hard stone wall.

I could barely breathe, my heart hammering in my chest as I watched the unfolding drama. A part of me couldn't believe the turn of events, a glimmer of hope blossoming in the darkness that had consumed me.

Zephyrian staggered to his feet, a vicious snarl contorting his features, his crimson eyes burning with rage. He lunged toward Kaelan, closing the gap between them with a supernatural speed that was barely discernible.

His attack connected, striking Kaelan squarely in the chest, and sending him sprawling across the ground. However, Kaelan wasted no time, springing to his feet and readying himself for the next assault.

Their magical exchanges painted the chamber with bursts of brilliant and maleficent light. The room seemed to shake under the power of their conflict, its foundations threatened by the unrelenting force of their unleashed magic.

The battle raged on, both warriors proving equally matched in terms of power and skill. Frozen no more, I found my resolve, my own magical essence welling up inside me, my very blood singing with its potent energy. I refused to stand idly by in the face of our potential demise, determined to go down fighting, whatever the cost.

The room crackled with electricity, the dark souls within it locked in a cataclysmic struggle. My body surged with the fierce might of my unleashed magic.

"Enough!" Zephyrian's command boomed through the chamber, his voice an echoing force that seemed to emanate from the very walls themselves.

With an outstretched hand, a bolt of black lightning shot forth, striking Kaelan with a brutal force. My heart twisted as he was propelled backward, colliding violently with the unforgiving stone wall before crumpling to the floor, his motionless form a stark testament to the devastation he had endured.

Without hesitation, I ran toward Zephyrian, my own pain a distant concern. With fierce determination, I unleashed my fire, searing it toward the demon lord, its intensity striking him directly in the chest.

The demon lord staggered backward, his agonized hiss filling the chamber. "You'll pay for that," he snarled, his crimson eyes blazing with unbridled fury.

"No, I don't think I will," I countered.

Zephyrian's relentless assault continued, but this time, I was ready. Drawing on the depths of my power, I summoned a shield, a swirling vortex of magic that absorbed the full brunt of his assault. The impact sent shockwaves rippling through the chamber, the very air humming with our struggle.

Our battle was a fierce contest of wills, each of us vying for supremacy in this torrential clash of magic.

With every passing moment, my own power surged within me, a fiery torrent that coursed through my veins. I launched counterattacks, seeking to find a chink in Zephyrian's formidable defenses. But he remained resolute, his dark magic an impenetrable barrier that thwarted my every attempt.

In a bold and desperate maneuver, I charged toward Zephyrian, closing the gap between us. His eyes widened with surprise as I closed in, a brief flicker of vulnerability before I unleashed the full force of my magic directly at him.

My blow struck home, slamming him backward with an explosion of energy. Zephyrian was thrown off his feet, the impact shattering the stone floor beneath him.

For a brief moment, I allowed myself a flicker of hope, a fleeting respite from the endless tide of fear and despair.

However, my relief was short-lived, the momentary lull in our battle shattered by Zephyrian's chilling laugh. He rose to his feet, a dark smile twisting his lips.

"I will end you," Zephyrian sneered, his crimson eyes aflame with a hatred that seemed to scorch the very air around him.

But I was far from ready to concede defeat. My determination blazed brighter than ever as I pushed forward, refusing to succumb to the pain and exhaustion that gnawed at the edges of my consciousness. Every fiber of my being was devoted to my magic, and every ounce of my strength focused on breaking free from Zephyrian's hold.

The oppressive force of Zephyrian's power bore down on me like an unyielding weight, and despite my fervent efforts, it was increasingly clear that his strength surpassed my own.

"Give in, daughter," he taunted, his voice dripping with malevolence. "You cannot win. You are too weak."

Every fiber of my being strained against his dominion, but it was a futile struggle. The despair of my helplessness threatened to engulf me, yet I wouldn't surrender.

"I will never give up," I declared through gritted teeth. "Not while I have breath in my body."

Zephyrian's laughter, like the cackling of a malevolent specter, echoed in the chamber, sending a cold shiver down my spine.

"Then breathe no more," he hissed, a sadistic grin distorting his features.

His dark magic surged, an insidious force that coursed through my very core. I gasped, my lungs rebelling as the air was forcibly expelled from them. My vision wavered, and I felt my consciousness slipping away like a fading ember. On my knees, I clutched at my constricting throat, the searing pain in my chest intensifying with each passing moment. The world blurred into a haze, and I teetered on the precipice of oblivion.

The cacophony of battle faded into a distant echo as Rowena's voice resounded in the recesses of my mind, a lifeline in the abyss of despair.

"Vale, you can still stop this."

"How?" My mental plea was tinged with desperation.

"Take my strength, child. Use my power. Unleash your dark magic."

I closed my eyes, shutting out the chaos and despair that surrounded me. With profound determination, I reached out within the ethereal plane, my mind grasping for the pulsating energy that resonated within Rowena. The connection was instant, a fusion of spirits that transcended the physical realm. Her power surged into me, a torrent of strength that filled the void of my desperation.

With newfound vigor, I rose to my feet, the very essence of Rowena's magic coursing through my veins, intertwining with my own. A wellspring of blood magic surged within me, dark and potent. Zephyrian's eyes widened, momentarily betraying his cool facade as I unleashed a torrent of dark fire toward him. The spell struck him with unrelenting force, throwing him off balance. I stared in awe at the black and blue flames writhing around my hands, the inky black on my fingertips expanding.

"Hellfire," Rowena whispered in astonishment.

I pressed the advantage, my focus unwavering. Another incantation flowed from me, and then another, the magic rippling in relentless waves. Rowena's power surged through me like a torrent, pushing me beyond my mortal limits. It consumed me, blurring the line between myself and the ancient spirit that had offered her essence.

With each spell, Zephyrian weakened, his defenses slowly crumbling under the relentless onslaught. But his own resolve was unbroken, and with a feral growl, he countered my attacks with his own.

Our spells collided, the dark energies erupting in an explosion of magical chaos. The very foundations of the chamber quaked, the ancient stones threatening to collapse. We stood locked in a stalemate, neither willing to relent.

A glint of victory gleamed in his eyes, his cruel smile a twisted promise of triumph.

My blood pounded in my ears, and the world seemed to slow, every detail crystallizing in stark clarity. My gaze swept the chamber, taking in the scene before me. Wren, Venna, and Harker remained motionless, their lifeless forms a grim reminder of the stakes. Kaelan, too, lay unmoving, his body a battered testament to the violence he had endured.

Anguish threatened to overwhelm me, but I fought against the tide, refusing to let despair break my will.

Rowena's voice was a soothing presence in my mind, a steady beacon amid the storm of turmoil and anguish.

"Fight, Vale. Don't let him win."

Her words echoed within me, a resounding conviction. I drew on the last dregs of my strength, channeling Rowena's power into one final spell. With a feral scream, I unleashed the full force of our combined magic, the hellfire raging like a ferocious tempest. The very air seemed to shudder, the ground quaking under the sheer power of the spell.

Zephyrian's eyes widened in surprise, and then a look of anguish contorted his features. A guttural cry tore from his throat as the spell struck him, his body withering under the intense onslaught.

Zephyrian, once indomitable, now fell to his knees, his face twisted in pain and disbelief. The darkness that had reigned within the throne room waned, replaced by a surge of newfound hope and determination.

His gasp, a fragile whisper of disbelief, hung in the air like a death knell. His once-imposing figure now knelt, broken and defeated. His crimson eyes, once ablaze with dominance, flickered with fear.

"This can't be," he croaked, his voice strained. "You're nothing. You can't defeat me."

Step by deliberate step, I approached him, the dark magic within me seething and crackling like a tempestuous storm. Each footfall resonated with the weight of centuries of suffering, each heartbeat echoing with defiance.

"You were wrong about me," I declared, the words resonating with the force of a hurricane. "I'm not your daughter. I'm your reckoning."

The very essence of the dark fire surged through me, a potent manifestation of my resolve. It was a torrent, an unyielding deluge, a cataclysmic force of nature that surged forth. A relentless barrage of hellfire erupted, the malevolent energy consuming Zephyrian.

His anguished scream filled the chamber, a cacophonous crescendo of torment that reverberated off the cold, unforgiving stone walls. It was a sound that encapsulated the suffering he had wrought upon countless souls, a reflection of the agony that had stained the realms.

As the fires of my magic consumed him, a blinding light emanated from Zephyrian, casting stark shadows that danced across the chamber. The very air seemed to tremble as he disintegrated into a swirling cloud of ash, his final cry of despair echoing in the fading reverberations.

The explosive release of energy sent me hurtling backward, my body colliding with the unforgiving stone wall. Pain shot through me, and I gasped, my vision swimming. The darkness that surrounded me in the aftermath of the cataclysm closed in, like a shroud claiming its victory. Consciousness slipped away, and I succumbed to the welcoming embrace of oblivion.

Chapter Thirty-Seven

My return to consciousness was a gradual ascent from the depths of oblivion. A persistent heaviness weighed upon my eyelids, a reminder of the intensity of the battle. It was as if my very being resisted the notion of waking, seeking refuge from the harsh reality.

In my dimly lit bedroom, Wren sat in a worn chair by the window, his gaze drawn to the world outside. He was bandaged, his arm wrapped in a sling and his forehead marred by a jagged gash. His eyes, which had witnessed so much, now carried a subtle glimmer of relief.

"You're awake," he said, and a gentle smile curved upon his lips.

His words broke the fragile cocoon that had enveloped me, and the full weight of reality descended upon me, the gravity of it all pressing down upon my weary soul.

Kaelan had been lost. Worse, he had betrayed us, his mind and body twisted into a tool of Zephyrian's design. And yet, a glimmer of hope burned brightly, a flicker of possibility among the darkness. Kaelan had overcome Zephyrian's hold and with the last vestiges of his free will, he had aided us in defeating the demon lord. I wasn't sure if it made a difference to me, though.

The events flashed before my mind's eye, an unbidden parade of torment and anguish. The images were a haunting testament to the sacrifices that had been made.

And yet, there was a strange comfort in the knowledge that, at least for now, we had succeeded.

I swallowed, the dryness of my throat a painful reminder of the physical and emotional toll of the battle.

Wren stood up and offered me a cup. "Here, drink this."

The liquid was lukewarm, but the water was a welcome relief. It slid down my parched throat and I felt a hint of renewed vigor.

Wren sat back down in his chair, his gaze never leaving me. "How are you feeling?"

"I'm alive," I replied, my voice a hoarse whisper.

He nodded, his eyes conveying the depth of his understanding.

"How long was I out?" I asked, attempting to mask the tremor of unease in my tone.

"It's been four days since the battle."

"Four days," I murmured. The revelation sent a shiver of disquiet down my spine. It felt like a lifetime had passed since I'd faced off against Zephyrian. "Where's Kaelan?"

Wren's eyes flitted back towards the window, a haunted shadow passing over his features. "He left," he replied softly, his voice carrying the weight of uncertainty.

A lump formed in my throat, a mix of emotions rising within me. My feelings for him were a tangled web of confusion, and I wasn't sure if I was ready to deal with them.

Wren's gaze was fixed on me, his concern a tangible presence in the room. "Are you going to be alright, Vale?"

I forced a smile, a hollow gesture meant to conceal the anguish I felt. "I'll be fine."

The lie hung in the air, a fragile pretense that could never truly mask the truth.

Wren's eyes held an unspoken understanding, yet he nodded.

I closed my eyes and tried to shut out the pain, to ignore the reality of my loss. But the ache remained, a persistent reminder of the sacrifices I had made.

We fell into silence, and I listened to the sound of the wind, a quiet whisper that filled the empty space between us.

With determination, I sat up in bed, wary of the wounds I still possessed.

"Vale," Wren began, his voice tinged with concern. "What happened in that throne room? When we regained consciousness, you were unconscious, and Kaelan..."

A shiver coursed through me as I recalled the haunting transformation Kaelan had undergone in Zephyrian's grip.

"He was a monster," I whispered, the words tasting like bitterness and betrayal. "He had been working with Zephyrian all along, feeding him information about me. He knew about the attack on the factory that night, he's responsible for Juniper's death."

The admission poured out of me, an overwhelming rush of grief and guilt. The tears that had threatened before now spilled freely, tracing down my cheeks.

"How could I have been so blind?" I said, my voice quivering with anguish and self-recrimination. "I should have seen through his lies, I should have known."

Wren's voice was gentle and filled with empathy as he responded, his fingers enveloping mine in a reassuring grip. "You can't blame yourself for this, Vale. You couldn't have known."

I couldn't help but shake my head, the weight of my own guilt pressing down on me like a vice. "But that's just it, Wren. I should have known. I should have seen through the deception. I let my feelings blind me to the truth."

His expression softened, sympathy shining in his eyes. "I'm so sorry, Vale. I wish there was something I could do to ease your pain."

I managed a small, wistful smile despite the turmoil within. "There's nothing anyone can do, but at least Zephyrian is gone. At least I managed to do that."

The words were tinged with a touch of pride, and a grim satisfaction filled me. I had succeeded, despite the odds stacked against me.

I glanced at Wren, who still held my hand, his thumb brushing lightly across my knuckles. He smiled, his eyes bright with admiration.

"That's not true, Vale," he said. "You did so much more than that. You saved us all. And without you, the whole world would be lost."

I took a deep breath, his words a comforting presence. "Thank you, Wren. I needed to hear that."

Wren grinned, his gaze warm and understanding. "Anytime, Vale."

I reached up and pushed my hair from my face and stopped, stunned, looking at my blackened hands. The inky blackness that had started at my fingertips crept down the fingers on each hand and grazed my palms. The result of my use of dark magic in defeating Zephyrain. I let out a shuddering exhale. Everything about me had changed due to my magic, and now the effects could be seen on the outside as well.

"Yeah, I had noticed that," Wren said staring at my hands. "What happened there?"

I realized I had never explained to Wren the consequences of dark magic, for fear he'd learn what I had done to Rafe. I let out another shaky breath and put my darkened hands in my lap.

"It's what happens to a witch when they use dark magic," I explained. "It started when I used dark magic to help you take out Rafe. I guess it grew worse when I used hellfire to defeat Zephyrian."

He stared at me for a long moment, processing my words. "That moment, before I killed him, he stumbled. He had looked confused. That was you?"

I nodded my head, not trusting myself to say anything else. His eyes widened and the corner of his mouth twitched up in a half smile. Then he laughed, the sound filling the room with light. I blinked, uncertain of his reaction. He stopped, his eyes crinkling with mirth.

"Vale," he said, still grinning. "You are incredible."

A slow smile spread across my face, and for the first time since the battle, I felt a spark of hope. Maybe things would turn out alright, after all. The laughter continued and I knew we were going to be ok.

"Okay, but enough about me," I changed the subject, pushing the thought of my hands out of my mind. "What about you, Wren? Are you okay?"

He shrugged, a rueful smile tugging at his lips. "As well as can be expected, I suppose. My injuries aren't that bad, thankfully. But I still feel the effects of the battle."

I nodded, the memory of the grueling conflict etched into my mind. "I'm glad you're okay, Wren."

He chuckled softly, his voice tinged with wry humor. "Yeah, me too. Now, come on. We've both been through a lot. Let's get you some food."

I allowed him to help me out of bed and lead me into the dining area.

My stomach growled, a reminder of my physical needs. I realized how hungry I was as the delicious aroma of fresh food reached my nose.

I sat down at the table, the familiar surroundings offering a sense of comfort. Wren placed a bowl of steaming stew in front of me, and I tucked in ravenously.

Curiosity tugged at me, pulling my thoughts back to the ordeal we had escaped. "How did we get out of the demon realm once Zephyrian was taken care of?" I asked, seeking to fill in the gaps.

Wren's eyes grew distant as he recounted the events. "Kaelan helped. He transformed back into his regular form and then shifted us all back to the portal. Once we made it back here, he said he needed to leave before you woke up."

My heart dipped at the thought of Kaelan's departure, mingling feelings of betrayal and loss. "I see," I replied, the words escaping me with a heaviness I couldn't shake.

I forced myself to focus on the positive, on the fact that we had somehow made it through the ordeal and that the world was safe for the time being.

The familiar sights and sounds of my home washed over me and for the first time since the battle, a sense of normalcy returned. I finished the rest of the meal, enjoying the simple pleasure of eating good food. The cat jumped up on the table and regarded me with curious eyes while I scratched him under the chin.

As the last morsels were savored, I leaned back in my chair and looked at Wren. "So," he began, his tone light. "What's the plan?"

The question was a welcome diversion and I pondered it for a moment. My resolve strengthened as I spoke, my voice laced with unwavering determination. "Now we move on. We take down the rest of Zephyrain's followers, we fix the camp. We make sure no one can ever threaten us again."

Yet, beneath my facade of confidence, I harbored doubts about the future. I had no clear vision of what lay ahead, only a steadfast belief that, with Wren by my side, I could face anything.

"Do you think he'll come back?" Wren's question took me by surprise, turning my thoughts back to Kaelan.

I met Wren's gaze and the weight of uncertainty settled upon me. "Kaelan?" I said, my voice tinged with doubt. I shook my head, acknowledging my own uncertainty. "I don't know. And honestly, I don't know if I want him to."

Wren's sympathetic smile was a gentle reassurance in the face of my tumultuous emotions. His grip on my hand offered solace, a silent promise of unwavering support.

"Maybe it's better this way," he suggested his words like a soothing balm for my wounded heart.

"Maybe," I replied softly, though the weight of uncertainty pressed upon me. The truth was, I didn't know if anything would ever truly be better again. The wounds ran deep and the scars of betrayal were etched into my very soul.

"What do we tell the camp?" Wren's practical question broke through the tumult of my thoughts, grounding me in the present.

"We tell them the truth," I responded with unwavering determination. "We tell them that Zephyrian is dead. And we tell them that we will never let anything like this happen again."

A fire kindled within me, a fierce resolve that burned bright amid the darkness. I would not let the sacrifices of those we had lost be in vain. I would rebuild the camp, and I would ensure that the threat of Zephyrian and his followers was forever eliminated.

And, despite the uncertainty and the pain, I would find a way to move on.

◖ ◗

I had spent most of the afternoon catching up with the rest of the camp. Wren had given everyone a quick update on the details, but there was much to discuss. The battle had shaken everyone, and the need to debrief was a discernible need.

Their evening meal was a joyous occasion, filled with the camaraderie of our little community. It was a welcome reprieve from the darkness, a reminder that, despite everything, life would go on.

I made my way back to Wren's tent, the exhaustion of the day taking its toll. The sky was streaked with hues of crimson and gold as the sun set on the horizon. A sense of peace washed over me, a momentary respite from the chaotic events that had plagued me.

I paused for a moment, breathing in the crisp air, the smell of pine trees and wildflowers a pleasant reminder of the beauty of the world.

The flaps of the tent rustled as Wren emerged, a grin on his face.

"Come on," he said, gesturing for me to follow him. "I've got a surprise for you."

Curious, I trailed after him, weaving through the tents until we came to a clearing on the edge of the camp.

A large bonfire was lit, casting a warm glow across the gathering of people.

I spotted several familiar faces and a warmth spread through me at the sight of our Otherworlder friends.

"Welcome back," Venna said, pulling me into a hug. Her eyes were alight with joy, and I was overcome with a sense of gratitude for her presence.

"We're so glad you're okay," Harker chimed in, her face shining with relief.

The rest of the group chimed in with greetings and I felt a deep appreciation for the community we had created.

The atmosphere was festive, the air filled with the crackling of the fire and the sounds of laughter. The warmth of the flames was a stark contrast to the icy chill of the demon realm and I basked in the comforting presence.

The evening passed by in a blur of companionship and shared memories. As the hours wore on, the exhaustion of the day caught up to me and the lure of sleep became too strong to resist.

I bid my farewells to the group and made my way back to Wren's tent. As I approached, a movement from the corner of my eye caught my attention.

A figure stood at the edge of the forest, his dark hair reflecting the moonlight. My heart skipped a beat as I realized who it was.

"Kaelan," I breathed, unable to keep the disbelief from my voice.

"Hey," he replied, his tone casual, as if he had just seen me the day before.

Anger rose within me, fueled by the betrayal that had torn me apart. "What are you doing here?" I asked, my voice sharp.

He shrugged, his expression unreadable. "I came to see you."

I shook my head, trying to make sense of his words. "Why? You left, remember?"

He sighed, his shoulders slumping as he ran a hand through his hair. "I needed to get away. I needed to clear my head. And I thought maybe it would be easier for you if I wasn't around."

His admission caught me off guard, and a surge of mixed emotions welled up within me. "I had hoped you were gone for good."

He frowned, his eyes filled with sadness. "I'm so sorry, Vale. I didn't mean to hurt you. When Zephyrian ordered me to get close to you, I did everything I could to feed him lies, to steer him off your path."

His apology was sincere and I found myself wanting to believe him. Yet, the memory of his treachery lingered, a shadow that could not be so easily dismissed.

"It was hard," he continued, his voice soft. "Pretending to be someone I wasn't. But I did it for you, Vale. Because I knew that if I could convince Zephyrian that I was on his side, I could use that as a way to protect you. And that's all I ever wanted."

"And what about this blood bond Zephyrian talked about?" I asked angrily.

Kaelan's expression was pained, the weight of remorse evident in his tone. "It's a connection formed through sharing a witch's blood, it formed the day you healed me in the library. It wasn't locked into place though until you took my blood. We're connected through the bond, and it strengthens over time. It's a lot like the bond you have with your familiar."

My head spun with the revelation.

He paused, a shadow of sorrow clouding his eyes. He spoke the next words slowly as if he was afraid to reveal too much. "When you were... taken. The First Witch didn't tell me. I felt it. I was overwhelmed by it. And I couldn't ignore the pull, no matter how much I wanted to. The need to find you, the need to protect you was overwhelming. It's a powerful force."

"Why didn't you tell me?"

"Because I was afraid. Afraid that if you knew the truth, you would run. Afraid that the connection would overwhelm you."

I swallowed, my heart pounding in my chest. So much had been kept from me, so much had been revealed.

"I don't want it," I said, my voice full of emotion.

"You can't change it," Kaelan said softly. "You can't change what happened."

"I can't forgive it either," I said.

He took a step towards me, his hand outstretched. "I don't want to hurt you, Vale. I never did."

The ache in my heart grew, the turmoil within me intensifying. "How can I trust you?" I whispered, my voice quivering with emotion.

He hesitated, his eyes searching mine. "You can't."

The answer was raw and honest and it struck me like a blow.

"But I'm asking you to try," he continued, his tone earnest. "Please, Vale. Give me a chance. I'll prove myself to you, I swear it."

His plea tugged at my heartstrings. Despite the pain, a part of me still cared for him. The connection between us was undeniable, but now I knew it must be the blood bond.

"I can't," I said finally, shaking my head. "I'm sorry, Kaelan. But I can't."

The ache within me grew, a sense of loss permeating every fiber of my being.

His eyes were filled with sadness. "I understand."

He took a step back, his eyes lingering on mine for a moment before he turned and disappeared into the forest, leaving me alone with my thoughts.

I stood there, the night air enveloping me like a cloak. The moon hung high in the sky, the stars twinkling like diamonds. The scene should have been serene, but inside, I felt as though a piece of me had been ripped away.

I turned and headed back towards Wren's tent, the sound of his voice calling my name a welcome distraction.

"Vale, is that you?"

"Yes, it's me."

He emerged from the shadows, a look of concern on his face. "Is everything okay?"

"Yeah, everything's fine," I replied, trying to mask the turmoil within me.

"Are you sure?"

I nodded, trying to force a smile. "Yes, I'm sure."

He regarded me for a moment, his eyes filled with uncertainty. Then, without a word, he pulled me into his arms, holding me close.

The gesture was simple, yet it was exactly what I needed. The warmth of his embrace was a soothing balm for the anguish within me.

"Thank you," I whispered, the words conveying the depths of my gratitude.

He held me tighter, the rhythmic beat of his heart a calming presence. "Anytime, Vale."

And, despite the confusion and uncertainty, I knew one thing for certain. Wren was by my side and I was not alone.

As the night embraced us and the stars sparkled above, I whispered softly, "Together, we'll find our way forward, Wren, and we'll chase away the darkness."

ABOUT THE AUTHOR

Ember East (she/they) lives in Murfreesboro, TN, but was raised in Western KY. She spends her days reading, writing, crocheting, and taking care of her three feral children and her over-affectionate dog. She is AuDHD, and wants all of her neurodivergent readers to know that following your dreams is possible with hard work and lots of coffee. She's dreamed of seeing her name on the spines of the books that line her shelves since she was nine years old, and now she isn't even using her real name, what a schmuck. She plans to write many more books for as long as possible.